ALISTAIR MacLEAN's reputation as an outstanding writer of suspense was established with the success of his first novel, *H.M.S. Ulysses*. That story grew out of his background in the Royal Navy, where he spent five years as a torpedo man during World War II.

Several of his highly successful and critically acclaimed works have been made into motion pictures, including *The Guns of Navarone, Ice Station Zebra*, and *Where Eagle*   *Satan Bug* ha   screen.

Fawcett Crest and Gold Medal Books
by Alistair MacLean:

H.M.S. ULYSSES
THE GUNS OF NAVARONE
SOUTH BY JAVA HEAD
THE SECRET WAYS
NIGHT WITHOUT END
FEAR IS THE KEY
THE BLACK SHRIKE
THE GOLDEN RENDEZVOUS
THE SATAN BUG
ICE STATION ZEBRA
WHEN EIGHT BELLS TOLL
WHERE EAGLES DARE
FORCE 10 FROM NAVARONE
PUPPET ON A CHAIN
CARAVAN TO VACCARES
BEAR ISLAND
THE WAY TO DUSTY DEATH
BREAKHEART PASS
CIRCUS
THE GOLDEN GATE
SEAWITCH

The SATAN BUG

by Alistair MacLean

*[This book was originally published
under the pseudonym of Ian Stuart.]*

FAWCETT GOLD MEDAL • NEW YORK

To BILL CAMPBELL

CHAPTER 1

There was no mail for me that morning, but that was no surprise. There had been no mail for me in the three weeks I'd been renting that tiny second-floor suite of offices near Oxford Street. I closed the door of the outer eight-by-ten office, skirted the table and chair that might one day house a receptionist if the time ever came that Cavell Investigations could run to such glamorous extras, and pushed open the door marked PRIVATE.

Behind that door lay the office of the head of Cavell Investigations, Pierre Cavell. Me. And not only the head but the entire staff. It was a bigger room than the reception office—I knew that because I'd measured it, but only a trained surveyor could have told it with the naked eye.

I'm no sybarite, but I had to admit that it was a pretty bleak sort of place. The distempered walls were of that delicate tint of off-gray pastel, shading from off-white at floor level to off-black just below the ceiling, that only London fog and the neglect of years can achieve. In one wall, overlooking a narrow grimy courtyard, was a tall narrow window, washed on the inside, with a monthly calendar close by. On the linoleum-covered floor a square desk, not new, a swivel chair for me, a padded leather armchair for the client, a strip of threadbare carpet to keep the client's feet from getting cold, a hat rack, and a couple of green metal filing cabinets, both empty. Nothing more. There was no room for anything more.

I was just lowering myself into the swivel chair when I heard the deep double chime of the bell in the reception room and the sound of hinges creaking. "Ring and Enter" the legend on the corridor door read, and someone was doing just that. Ringing and entering. I opened the top left-hand drawer of my desk, pulled out some papers and envelopes, scattered them before me, pulled a switch by my knee, and had just risen to my feet when the knock came at my inner door.

The man who entered was tall, thin, and a close student of the *Tailor and Cutter*. A narrow-lapelled coat hung over an immaculately cut charcoal suit in the latest Italian line, and in his suede-gloved left hand he carried his other glove, black bowler, brief case, and a few inches up his wrist, a tightly rolled, horn-handled black umbrella. He had a long pale narrow face, thin black hair parted in the middle and brushed almost straight back, rimless glasses, an aquiline nose, and on the upper lip a thin black line that, on closer inspection, still looked like a thin black line—a miniaturization of the moustache brought to an almost impossible state of perfection. He must have carried a micrometer about with him. He looked for all the world like a top-flight city accountant; I couldn't see him as anything else.

"Excuse my walking straight in like this." He smiled briefly, three gold caps in the upper teeth, and half glanced over his shoulder. "But it seems your secretary—"

"That's all right. Please come in." He even talked like an accountant, controlled, positive, slightly overprecise in the articulation. He offered me his hand, and the handshake, too, was in character: quick, neat, giving nothing away.

"Martin," he introduced himself. "Henry Martin. Mr. Pierre Cavell?"

"Yes. Won't you sit down, Mr. Martin?"

"Thank you." He waited till I was moving round the corner of my desk, gave the seat of the leather chair an unostentatious flick with his glove, the kind of flick that was meant to be as much imagined as seen, sat down gingerly, very straight, feet together, brief case balanced with scrupulous care across his touching knees, and looked around him slowly, missing nothing, a faint smile not showing his teeth. "Business not—ah—so very brisk these days, Mr. Cavell?"

Maybe he wasn't an accountant after all. Accountants, as a rule, are polite, well-mannered and slow to give unnecessary offense. But then, maybe he wasn't feeling quite himself. People who come to see private detectives are seldom in a normal frame of mind.

"I keep it this way to fool the Inspector of Taxes," I explained. "How can I help you, Mr. Martin?"

"By giving me some information about yourself." He was no longer smiling and his eyes were no longer wandering.

"About myself?" My voice was sharp, not razor-edged, just the voice of a man who hasn't had a client in all the three weeks he's been in business. "Please come to the point, Mr. Martin. I have things to do." So I had. Lighting my pipe, reading the morning paper, things like that.

"I'm sorry. But about yourself. I have you in mind for a

very delicate and difficult mission. I must be sure you are the man I want. That is reasonable, I think?"

"Mission?" I looked speculatively at Henry Martin and thought I could get to disliking him without too much trouble. "I don't carry out missions, Mr. Martin. I carry out investigations."

"Of course. When there are investigations to carry out." The tone was too neutral to take specific offense. "Perhaps *I* should supply the information. Please bear with my unusual method of approach for a few minutes, Mr. Cavell. I think I can promise that you will not be sorry." He opened his brief case, brought out a buff folder, abstracted a stiff sheet of paper and began to read, paraphrasing as he went along.

"Pierre Cavell. Born Lisieux, Calvados, of Anglo-French parents. Father, civil engineer, John Cavell of Kingsclere, Hampshire; mother, Anne-Marie Lechamps of Lisieux. Mother of Franco-Belgian descent. One sister, Liselle. Both parents and sister killed in air attack on Rouen. Escaped fishing-boat, Deauville-Newhaven. While still in late teens parachuted six times into northern France, each time brought back information of great value. Parachuted into Normandy D-Day minus two. At end of war recommended for no fewer than six decorations—three British, two French, and one Belgian."

Henry Martin looked up and smiled thinly.

"The first discordant note. Decorations refused. Some quotation to the effect that the war had aged you fast and that you were too old to play with toys. Joined regular British Army. Rose to Major in Intelligence Corps, understood to have co-operated closely with M.I.6., counter-espionage, I believe. Then joined police. Why did you leave the Army, Mr. Cavell?"

I'd throw him out later. Right now I was too intrigued. How much more did he know—and how? I said: "Poor prospects."

"You were cashiered." Again the brief smile. "When a junior officer elects to strike a senior officer, policy dictates that he should choose a man below field rank. You had the poor judgment to select a major-general." He glanced at the paper again. "Joined Metropolitan Police. Rapid rise through the ranks—one must admit that you do appear to be rather gifted in your own line—to position of Inspector. In last two years seconded for special duties, nature unspecified. But we can guess. And then you resigned. Correct?"

"Correct."

9

"On a record card, 'Resigned' looks much better than 'Dismissed.' Which is what you would have been, had you remained another twenty-four hours. You do appear to have what amounts to a genius for insubordination. Something to do with an assistant commissioner, I understand. But you still had friends, quite powerful friends. Within a week of your resignation you had been appointed as head of security in Mordon."

I stopped what I was doing, which was squaring off the papers on my desk, and said quietly: "Details of my record are readily available, if you know where to look. But you have no right to possess that last item of information." The Mordon Microbiological Research Establishment in Wiltshire had a security rating that would have made access to the Kremlin seem simple.

"I am perfectly aware of that, Mr. Cavell. I possess a great number of items of information that I shouldn't. Like the additional item that I know that, in keeping with your record, you were also dismissed from this post. Like yet another item—the real reason why I am here today: I know *why* you were dismissed."

The accuracy of my first deduction in the detecting business, that my client was an accountant, spoke ill for my prospects: Henry Martin wouldn't have recognized a balance sheet if it had been handed to him on a silver salver. I wondered what his line of business might really be, but I couldn't even begin to guess.

"You were dismissed from Mordon," Martin went on precisely, "primarily because you couldn't keep a still tongue in your head. Oh, nothing to do with security, we know that." He removed his rimless glasses and polished them thoughtfully. "After fifteen years in your line you probably don't even tell yourself half of what you know. But you talked to top scientists, directors, in Mordon, and you made no secret of your opinion of the nature of the work in which they were engaged. You are not the first person to comment bitterly on the fact that this establishment, referred to in Parliamentary estimates as the Mordon Health Center, is controlled exclusively by the War Office. You knew, of course, that Mordon is concerned mainly with the invention and production of microbiological organisms for use in war—but you are one of the few who know just how ghastly and terrifying are the weapons that have been perfected there, that armed with those weapons a few planes could utterly destroy *all* life in *any* country in the space of a few hours.

You had very strong opinions about the indiscriminate use of such a weapon against an unsuspecting and innocent civilian population. And you made your opinion known in many places and to many people inside Mordon. Too many places, too many people. So today you are a private detective."

"Life's unjust," I agreed. I rose to my feet, crossed to the door, turned the key in the lock and pocketed it. "You must realize, Mr. Martin, that you have already said too much. The sources of your information about my activities at Mordon. You're not leaving here till you tell me."

Martin sighed and replaced his spectacles.

"Melodramatic, understandable, but totally unnecessary. Do you take me for a fool, Cavell? Do I *look* a fool? What I told you I had to tell you to gain your co-operation. I will put my cards on the table? Quite literally." He drew out a wallet, found a rectangle of ivory cardboard and placed it on the table. "Mean anything to you?"

It meant a great deal. Across the middle of the card ran the legend, "Council for World Peace." At the bottom right-hand corner: "Henry Martin, London Secretary."

Martin pulled his chair close and leaned forward, his forearms on my desk. His face was intent, serious.

"Of course you know about it, Mr. Cavell. I don't think I exaggerate when I say that it is by far the greatest force for good in the world today. Unlike most of the other organizations which flaunt the word 'peace' on their banners, we have no communist affiliations. Neither are we anti-communists. All we want is peace, a sane workable peace. Our council cuts across race, religion, and politics. You will have heard that our Prime Minister and most members of the Cabinet belong. I do not wish to comment on that. But I can state that most of the church dignitaries in Britain, whether Protestant, Catholic or Jewish, are members. Our list of titled members reads like *Debrett's*, of other distinguished members, like *Who's Who*. The Foreign Office, who really *know* what's going on and are more afraid than any, are solidly on our side. We have the support of all the best, the wisest, the most far-seeing men in the country today. I have very powerful men behind me, Mr. Cavell. The council is equally strong in America, France, Germany and indeed throughout Western Europe—even the neutralist Swedes and Swiss are strong supporters." He smiled faintly. "We even have influential members in Mordon."

All he said I knew to be true—except that bit about Mordon, and maybe that had to be true, to account for his knowledge. I wasn't a member of the council myself, not being the right type for inclusion either in *Debrett's* or *Who's Who*, but I knew that the Council for World Peace, a society semi-secret in its nature inasmuch as it recognized that diplomatic negotiations were best not conducted through newspaper headlines, was of only the most recent origin but already regarded throughout the Western World as one of the last best hopes for mankind.

Martin took the card from me and slipped it back in his wallet. "All I am trying to say is that I am a respectable man working for a pre-eminently respectable body."

"I believe that," I said.

"Thank you." He dipped into his brief case again and brought out a steel container about the size and shape of a hip-flask. "There is, Mr. Cavell, a militarist clique in this country, of whom we are frankly terrified, who promise to wreck all our dreams and hopes. Madmen, who are talking, every day more loudly, of waging a preventive war against the Soviet Union. Germ warfare. It is highly unlikely that they will win their way. But it is against the most unlikely contingencies that we have to be most warily on our guard." He spoke like a man who had rehearsed his speech a hundred times.

"Against this bacteriological assault there could and would be no defense. A vaccine against this virus *has* been developed, after two years of the most intensive research, but the only supplies in the world are in Mordon." He paused, hesitated, then pushed the flask across the table to me. "A statement that is no longer quite accurate. This flask was removed from Mordon three days ago. The contents can be cultured to produce sufficient vaccine to immunize any nation on earth. We are our brothers' keepers, Mr. Cavell."

I stared at him. I said nothing.

"Please take this, at once, to this address in Warsaw." He pushed a slip of paper across the table. "You will be paid a hundred pounds now, all expenses, and a hundred pounds on your return. A delicate mission, I realize, perhaps even a dangerous one, although in your case I should not think so. We have investigated you very carefully, Mr. Cavell. You are reputed to know the byways of Europe as a taxi-driver knows the streets of London: I do not foresee that frontiers will present you with much difficulty."

"And my anti-war sympathies," I murmured.

"Of course, of course." The first trace of impatience. "We

had to check most carefully, you realize that. You had the best all-over qualifications. You were the *only* choice."

"Well, now," I murmured. "This is flattering. And interesting."

"I don't know what you mean," he said brusquely. "Will you do it, Mr. Cavell?"

"No."

"No?" His face became very still. "You say 'no'? This, then, is the extent of your precious concern about your fellow man? All this talk in Mordon—"

"You said yourself that my business wasn't very brisk," I interrupted. "I haven't had a client for three weeks. For all indications to the contrary, I won't have one for three months. And," I added, "you said yourself I was the *only* choice."

The thin mouth twisted in a sneer.

"You don't positively refuse to go, then?"

"I don't positively refuse."

"How much?"

"Two hundred and fifty pounds. Each way."

"Your last word?"

"That's it."

"Mind if I say something, Cavell?" The man was losing his manners.

"Yes, I mind. Keep your speeches and moralities for your council. This is a business deal."

He stared at me for a long moment, eyes hostile behind thick glasses, then reached again into his brief case and brought out five flat packets of treasury notes, laid them neatly on the table before him and glanced up at me. "Two hundred and fifty pounds. Exactly."

"Maybe the London branch of the council should get itself a new secretary," I suggested. "Was it myself or the council that was to be defrauded of the extra one-fifty pounds?"

"Neither." The tone came with the eyes, glacial both of them. He didn't like me. "We offered a fair price, but in a matter of such importance were prepared to meet extortion. Take your money."

"After you've taken off the rubber bands, stacked the notes together and counted them out, fifty fivers, in front of my eyes."

"My God!" The cool meticulous speech had gone and something almost savage came to take its place. "No wonder you were kicked out of so many jobs." He ripped off the bands, stacked the notes and counted them off separately. "There you are. Fifty. Satisfied?"

"Satisfied." I opened my right-hand drawer, picked up the notes, address and flask, dropped them in the drawer and closed it, just as Martin was finishing the securing of the straps on his brief case. Something in the atmosphere, maybe an extra stillness from my side of the table, caused him to look up sharply, and then he became as immobile as myself, except for his eyes, which continued to widen until they seemed to take up all the space behind his rimless glasses.

"It's a gun all right," I assured him. "A Japanese Hanyatti nine-shot automatic, safety catch off and indicator, I observe, registering full. Don't worry about the scotch tape over the mouth of the barrel, that's only to protect a highly delicate mechanism. The bullet behind will go through it, it'll go through you, and if you had a twin brother sitting behind you it would go through him also. Your forearms on the table, please."

He put his forearms on the table. He kept pretty still, which is the way people usually do when they're peering down into the barrel from a distance of three feet, but his eyes had gone back to normal quickly and he didn't seem all that worried that I could notice. This troubled me, for if any man had a right to be worried it was Henry Martin. Maybe this made Henry Martin a very dangerous man.

"You have an unusual way of conducting business, Cavell." No shake in the voice, just a dry contempt. "What is this, a hold-up?"

"Don't be silly—and don't you wish it were. I already have your money. You asked me earlier if I took you for a fool. The time and circumstances didn't seem right for an immediate answer, but I can give it to you now. You are a fool. You're a fool because you forgot that I worked in Mordon. I was security chief there. And the first job of any security chief is to know what goes on in his own bailiwick."

"I'm afraid I don't understand."

"You will. This vaccine here—it's designed to give immunity against which particular virus?"

"I'm only an agent for the Council for World Peace."

"It doesn't matter. What matters is that all the vaccines, up till now, have been made and stored exclusively in Horder Hall, Essex. The point is that if that flask came from Mordon in contains no vaccine. It probably contains one or other of the viruses.

"Secondly, I know that it is normally impossible for any

man, Council for World Peace sympathizer or not, to take top-secret viruses out of Mordon, no matter how clever or surreptitious he is. When the last man has left the laboratories, fourteen-hour time clocks come into operation and the opening combination overriding those is known to only two men. If anything has been taken, it has been taken by force and violence. That demands an immediate investigation.

"Thirdly, you said the Foreign Office was solidly on your side. If that's the case, why all this cloak-and-dagger approach to me to smuggle the vaccine through? The diplomatic bag to Warsaw is the obvious answer.

"Finally, and your biggest blunder, my friend, you forgot the fact that I have been engaged in one form or other of counter-espionage for quite some time. Every new body or organization that's set up in Britain automatically comes under the microscope. As did the Council for World Peace when it set up its headquarters here. I know one of the members, an elderly, stout, bald, and shortsighted character who is the complete antithesis to you in every way. His name is Henry Martin, and he's the secretary of the London branch of the council. The real one."

He looked at me steadily for a few moments, not scared, his forearms still resting on the table, then said quietly: "There doesn't seem to be much more left to say, does there?"

"Not much."

"What are you going to do?"

"Turn you over to the Special Branch. With you goes a tape of our conversation. Just as a routine precaution, I switched on a recorder before you came into this room. Not evidence, I know, but the address, flask, and your thumbprint on fifty fivers will be all the evidence they require."

"It does look as if I made a mistake about you," he admitted. "We can make a deal?"

"I can't be bought. Not, at least, for fifty miserable fivers."

A pause, then softly: "Five hundred?"

"No."

"A thousand? A thousand pounds, Cavell, inside the hour."

"Keep quiet." I reached over to the phone, laid the receiver on the table and began to dial with my left forefinger. I'd reached the third number when a sharp knock came to my office door.

I let the receiver lie and got to my feet, making no noise. The corridor door had been shut when Martin had come into my room. No one could open that corridor door without the bell chiming. I'd heard no chime; there had been no chime. But someone was in the outer office now, just outside my door.

Martin was smiling. It wasn't much of a smile, but it was there. I didn't like it. I moved my gun and said softly: "Face into that corner, Martin, hands clasped behind your neck."

"I don't think that's necessary," he said calmly. "That man outside the door is a mutual friend."

"Do it now," I said. He did. I crossed to the door, standing well to one side, and called out: "Who's there?"

"Police, Cavell. Open up, please."

"Police?" The words carried familiar overtones, but then there were a great number of people around who were able to imitate a great number of voices. I glanced at Martin, but he hadn't moved. I called out: "Your credentials. Under the door with them."

There was a movement on the other side of the door, then an oblong of cardboard slid into view on the floor. No badge, no credentials, nothing like that, just a calling card bearing the words "D. R. Hardanger," and a Whitehall telephone number. The number of people who knew that this was the only form of identification that Superintendent Hardanger used would be very few. And the card matched the voice. I unlocked and open the door.

Superintendent Hardanger it was, big, burly, red-faced, with the jowls of a bulldog, dressed in the same faded gray raglan and black bowler that he'd worn in all the years I'd worked with him. I caught a glimpse of a smaller man behind him, a khaki-clad arm and leg, no more. I'd no time to see more, for Hardanger had moved his sixteen stone of solid authority four feet into my office, forcing me to take a couple of backward steps.

"All right, Cavell." A flicker of a smile touched the abnormally light blue eyes. "You can put that gun away. You're quite safe now. The police are here."

I shook my head. "Sorry, Hardanger, but I'm no longer working for you. I have a license for this gun, and you're in my office without permission." I nodded towards the corner. "Search this character and then I'll put my gun away. Not till then."

Henry Martin, hands still behind his neck, turned slowly round. He grinned at Hardanger, who smiled back and said: "Shall I search you, John?"

"Rather not, sir," Martin said briskly. "You know how ticklish I am."

I stared at them, from Hardanger to Martin, then back again. I lowered my gun and said wearily: "All right, what gives?"

"I'm genuinely sorry about this, Cavell," Hardanger said in his rough, gravelly voice. "But necessary. How necessary, I'll explain. This man's name really is Martin—John Martin. Of the Special Branch. Inspector. Recently returned from Toronto. Want to see his credentials, or will my word do?"

I crossed to my desk, put the gun away and brought out the flask, money, and slip of paper with the Warsaw address. I could feel the tightness in my face, but I kept my voice quiet.

"Take your damned props, Martin, and get out. You too, Hardanger. I don't know what this stupid charade, this farrago of rubbish was for, and I'll be damned if you can make me care. Out! I don't like smart alecks making a fool of me and I won't play mouse to any man's cat, not even the Special Branch's."

"Easy up now, Cavell," Hardanger protested. "I told you it was necessary and —"

"Let me talk to him," the man in khaki interrupted. He came round Hardanger and I could see him clearly for the first time. Army officer, and no subaltern either, slight, spare, authoritative, the type I'm allergic to. "My name is Cliveden, Cavell. Major-General Cliveden. I must—"

"I was cashiered from the Army for taking a swing at a major-general," I interrupted. "Think I'd hesitate to do it again, now I'm a civilian? You, too. Out. Now."

"I told you what he was like," Hardanger muttered to no one in particular. He shrugged his shoulders heavily, thrust his hand into the pocket of his raglan coat and brought out a wrist watch. "We'll go. But first I thought you might like to have this. A keepsake. He had it in London for repair and it was delivered to the General's office yesterday."

"What are you talking about?" I said harshly.

"I'm talking about Neil Clandon. Your successor as security chief in Mordon. I believe he was one of your best friends."

I made no move to take the watch from the outstretched hand.

"'Was,' you said? Clandon?"

"Clandon. Dead. Murdered, if you like. When someone broke into the central laboratories in Mordon late last night—early this morning."

I looked at the three of them, then turned away to stare

17

out through the grimy window at the gray fog swirling along Gloucester Place. After a time I said: "You'd better come in."

Neil Clandon had been found by a patrolling security guard shortly after two o'clock that morning, in the corridor beside the heavy steel door leading to number one lab in E block. That he was dead was beyond dispute. What he had died of was not yet known, for in an establishment staffed almost entirely by doctors, no one had been allowed to approach the dead man. The strictness of the rule was absolute. When the alarm bells rang, it was a job for the Special Branch and the Special Branch alone.

The senior guard had been summoned and had approached within six feet of the body. He had reported that Clandon had been violently ill before dying, and that he had obviously died in convulsions and great agony. The symptoms had all the hallmarks of prussic acid poisoning. Had the guard been able to get the typical bitter almond smell, this of course would have put the tentative diagnosis beyond reasonable doubt. But that, of course, had been impossible. All guards on internal patrol had to make their rounds in gas-tight suits with a closed-circuit breathing apparatus.

The senior guard had noticed something else. The time-clock setting on the steel door had been altered. Normally it was set to run from six p.m. till eight a.m. Now it was set to run from midnight. Which meant that access to number one lab would be impossible before two p.m., except to those who knew the combination that overrode the time lock.

It was the soldier, not Hardanger, who supplied this information. I listened to him and said: "Why you? What's your interest in all this?"

"Major-General Cliveden is the second-in-command of the Royal Army Medical Corps," Hardanger explained. "Which automatically makes him the director of the Mordon Microbiological Research Establishment."

"He wasn't when I was there."

"My predecessor has retired," Cliveden said curtly, but the underlying worry was clear to see. "Ill health. First reports naturally came to me. I was in London. I notified the Superintendent immediately. And on my own initiative, I ordered an oxyacetylene team from Aldershot to rush there; they will open the door under Special Branch supervision."

"An oxyacetylene team?" I stared at him. "Are you quite mad?"

"I don't understand."

"Cancel it, man. Cancel it at once. What in God's name made you do that? Don't you know anything about that door? Apart from the fact that no acetylene equipment in existence could get through the special steel of that door inside hours, don't you know that the door itself is lethal? That it's filled with a near-lethal gas? That there's a central insulator-mounted plate inside the door that damn well *is* lethal—charged with two thousand volts?"

"I didn't know that, Cavell." His voice was low. "I've only just taken over."

"And even if they did get inside? Have you thought of what would happen then? You're scared, aren't you, Major-General Cliveden, you're terrified at the thought that someone has already been inside. Maybe that someone was careless. Maybe that someone was very careless, maybe he knocked over a container or cracked a sealed culture tank. A tank or container, for instance, with botulinus toxin—which is one of the viruses both made and stored in number one lab. It takes a minimum of twelve hours' exposure to air to oxidize the toxin and render it harmless. If anyone comes into contact with it before oxidization, they're dead men. Before midday, that is. And Clandon, had you thought of him? How do you know the botulinus didn't get him? The symptoms are exactly the same as those of prussic acid poisoning. How do you know the two guards weren't affected? The senior guard who spoke to you—if he had been affected the botulinus would have got him as soon as he'd taken off his mask to speak to you. He'd have died in agonies a minute later. Have you checked that he's still alive?"

Cliveden reached for the phone. His hand was shaking. While he was dialing, I said to Hardanger: "Right, Superintendent, the explanation?"

"Martin here?"

I nodded.

"Two good reasons. The first was that you were our number one suspect."

"Say that again."

"You'd been sacked," he said bluntly. "Left under a cloud. Your opinion of Mordon's place in the scheme of things was well known. You have a reputation for taking the law into your own hands." He smiled without humor. "I've had plenty experience of that from you."

"You're loony. Would I murder my best friend?" I said savagely.

"You were the only outsider who knew the whole security set-up in Mordon. The only one, Cavell. If anyone could get into and out of that place, it was you." He paused for a significant moment. "And you are now the only man alive who knows the combinations for the various laboratory doors. The combinations, as you know, can only be altered in the factory where the doors are made. After your departure, the precaution of changing them was not thought necessary."

"Dr. Baxter, the civilian director, knows the combinations."

"Dr. Baxter is missing. We can't trace him anywhere."

I said nothing. I walked over to the window and stared down into the fog, vaguely aware of Cliveden's voice on the phone. I reached for my tobacco pouch and had started filling my pipe, as much tobacco going on the floor as in the bowl, when Hardanger spoke again, the low rumble quiet in my ear.

"We had to find out fast how the land lay. This was the best way. The only way. Immediately after you left home, this morning, we checked with your wife. She said—"

"You've been round at my house?" I stared at him. "Bothering Mary? Questioning her? I rather think—"

"Don't trouble," Hardanger said dryly. "You'd get no satisfaction from breaking in false teeth. I wasn't there, sent a junior officer. Silly of me, I admit, asking a bride of two months to turn in her husband. Of course she said you hadn't left the house all night."

I looked at him without speaking. His eyes were exactly on a level with mine. He said: "Are you wondering whether to haul off at me for even suggesting that Mary may be a liar, or why she didn't phone to tip you off?"

"Both."

"She's no liar. You forget how well I know her. And she didn't tip you off because we disconnected your phone, both at home and here. We also bugged this phone before you arrived this morning—I heard every word you said to Martin on the phone in your outer office." He smiled. "You had me worried for a few minutes there."

"How did you get in? I didn't hear you. The bell didn't go off."

"The fuse box is in the outer corridor. All very illegal, I'm afraid."

I nodded. "I'll have to change that."

"So you're in the clear, Cavell. An Oscar for Inspector Martin, I should say. Twelve minutes flat to find out what we wanted to know. But we *had* to know."

"Why? Why that way? A few hours' leg-work by your men, checking taxis, restaurants, theaters, and you'd have known I couldn't possibly have been in Mordon last night."

"I couldn't wait." He cleared his throat with unnecessary force. "Which brings me to my second reason. If you're not the killer, then you're the man I want to find the killer. Now that Clandon is dead, you are the only man who knows the entire security set-up at Mordon. No one else does. Damned awkward, but there it is. If anyone can find anything, you can."

"Not to mention the fact that I'm the only man who can open that door, now that Clandon is dead and Baxter missing."

"There's that, too," he admitted.

"There's that, too," I mimicked. "That's all you really want. And when the door is open, I can run along and be a good boy."

"Not unless you want to."

"You mean that? First Derry, now Clandon. I'd like to do something."

"I know. I'll give you a free hand."

"The General won't like it." No one ever called Hardanger's ultimate superior by his name: very few even knew it.

"I've already fixed it with the General. You're right, he doesn't like it. I suspect he doesn't like you." Hardanger grinned sourly. "Often the way with relatives."

"You did that in advance? Well, thanks for the compliment."

"You were the number one suspect. But I never suspected you. All the same, I had to be sure. So many of our best men have gone over the wall in the past few years."

"When do we leave?" I said. "Now?" Cliveden had just replaced the receiver on its rest. His hand still wasn't very steady.

"If you're ready."

"I will be in a moment." Hardanger was a past master at keeping his expressions buttoned up, but there was a speculative curiosity in those eyes that he couldn't hide. The sort of look he'd give a man who'd just put a foot wrong. I said to Cliveden: "The guards at the plant? Any word?"

"They're all right. So it can't have been botulinus that got Clandon. The central laboratories are completely sealed up."

"And Dr. Baxter?"

"Still no sign of him. He——"

"Still no sign? That makes two of them, now. Coincidence, General. If that's the word I want."

"I don't know what you're talking about," he said irritably.

"Easton Derry. My predecessor in Mordon. He vanished a couple of months ago—just six days after he was the best man at my wedding—and *he* still hasn't turned up. Surely you knew?"

"How the hell should I?" A very testy little man indeed, I was glad he wasn't a civilian doctor and myself one of his patients. "I've only been able to get down there twice since my appointment . . . Anyway, Baxter. He left the laboratories all right, checking out slightly later than usual. He didn't return. He lives with a widowed sister in a bungalow near Alfringham, five miles away. He didn't come home at all last night, she says." He turned to Hardanger. "We must get down there immediately, Superintendent."

"Right away, sir. Cavell is going to come with us."

"Glad to hear it," Cliveden said. He didn't look it and I couldn't blame him. You don't make major-general without developing an army mind in the process, and the army mind sees the world as a neat, orderly and regimented place, with no place at all in it for private detectives. But he was trying to be courteous and make the best of a bad job, for he went on: "We'll need all the assistance we can get. Shall we go?"

"Just as soon as I've phoned my wife to let her know what's happening—if her phone's been reconnected." Hardanger nodded. I reached for the receiver, but Cliveden's hand was on it first, pressing it firmly down on its cradle.

"No phoning, Cavell. Sorry. Must have absolute security on this. It's imperative that no one—no one—knows that anything has happened at Mordon."

I lifted his wrist, the phone came up in his hand and I took it from him. I said: "Tell him, Superintendent."

Hardanger looked uncomfortable. As I dialed, he said apologetically: "I'm afraid Cavell is no longer in the Army, sir. Nor under the jurisdiction of the Special Branch. He is—um—allergic to authority."

"Under the Official Secrets Act we could demand——"

"Sorry, sir." Hardanger shook his head heavily. "Classified information voluntarily disclosed to a civilian outside a government department is no longer an official secret. No one made us tell Cavell anything, and he never asked us to. He's under no obligation. And we want his co-operation."

I made my call, told Mary that no, I wasn't under arrest, that I was going down to Mordon and would call her later in the day. After I hung up, I took off my jacket, strapped on a felt shoulder holster and stuck the Hanyatti into it. It was a big gun, but it was a big jacket with plenty of room in it; unlike Inspector Martin I didn't go in much for the Italian line. Hardanger watched me expressionlessly, Cliveden disapprovingly; twice he made to say something, twice he thought better of it. It was all very irregular indeed. But so was murder.

CHAPTER 2

The Army had a helicopter waiting for us, but the fog was too heavy. Instead we went down to Wiltshire in a big Jaguar saloon driven by a plain-clothes policeman who took far too much satisfaction in leaning with all his weight on both accelerator and siren button. But the fog lifted as we cleared Middlesex, the roads were fairly clear, and we made it intact to Mordon by just after midday.

Mordon is an architectural monstrosity, a guaranteed blot on any landscape. Had the designer—if it had a designer—based it on an early nineteenth-century prison, which it exactly resembles, he couldn't have achieved an uglier or more repulsive structure. But Mordon is only ten years old.

Grim, gray and gaunt under the darkly lowering October skies of that day, Mordon consisted of four parallel rows of squat, flat-topped concrete buildings, three stories high; each row, in its repellent forbidding lifelessness, for all the world like condemned and abandoned Victorian tenements in the worst slums of the great city. But a fitting enough façade for the work that went on behind the walls.

Each row of buildings was about a quarter of a mile in length, with about two hundred yards separating the rows. The space between the buildings and the boundary fence—five hundred yards at the nearest approach—was completely open, completely clear. No trees, no bushes, no shrubs, not even a clump of flowers. A man can hide behind a bush. He might even be able to hide behind a clump of flowers. But he can't hide behind a blade of grass two inches high—and nothing higher grew in the bleak desolation of the grounds of Mordon.

The term boundary fence—not a wall, people can hide

behind walls—was a misnomer. Any World War II concentration camp commandant would have sold his soul for Mordon; with fences like those a man could sleep soundly at night.

The outer barbed wire fence was fifteen feet high and sloped outward at so sharp an angle that the top was four feet out of line with the foot. A similar fence, only sloping the other way, paralleled the outer fence for its entire perimeter, at a distance of about twenty feet. The space between those fences was patrolled at night by Alsatians and Doberman pinschers, trained man-hunters—and, if need be, man-killers—answerable only to their own army handlers. Three feet inside the second fence and actually below its overhang was a two-strand trip-wire fence, of so fine a metal as to be normally almost invisible—and certainly would be invisible to anyone climbing down at nighttime from the top of that second fence. And then, another ten feet away, was the last fence, each of its five strands running through insulators mounted on concrete posts. The electric current passing through those wires was supposed to be less than lethal—if, that is, you were in good health.

To make sure that everyone got the general idea, the Army had put up notice boards at ten-yard intervals round the entire perimeter of the outer fence. There were five different types of notices. Four of them, black on white, read: DANGER KEEP OUT BY ORDERS; WARNING GUARD DOGS IN USE; PROHIBITED PLACE; and ELECTRIFIED FENCES; the fifth, a violent red on yellow, said simply: W. D. PROPERTY: TRESPASSERS WILL BE SHOT. Only a madman or a complete illiterate would have attempted to break his way into Mordon.

We came on the public ring road that completely surrounded the camp, bore right by the gorse-covered fields, and after a quarter of a mile turned into the main entrance. The police driver stopped just short of the lowered boom and wound down his window as a sergeant approached. The sergeant had a machine-pistol slung over his shoulder, and it wasn't pointing at the ground, either. The guards at Mordon were under strict and specific instructions, and one of those was that injured feelings and apprehension in visitors were a matter of no moment at all. Security was everything.

"Don't point that damned gun at me," the police driver snapped.

"Identification and nature of business, please." The gun didn't move.

"It's all right, Sergeant." Cliveden had wound down his rear window. "Let us through."

"Yes, sir." No salute, the gun still motionless. "Mr. Cavell, here, I know. The other three gentlemen please raise their hands."

"What the hell—" Hardanger began.

"At once, please." The sergeant moved his gun a trifle. "Look on the other side."

We looked. Two other soldiers, both with machine-pistols pointing at our windows. Three pairs of hands rose slowly to shoulder level.

"Right, Sergeant." Cliveden's voice was glacial. "You've overstepped your authority. You heard me tell—"

"Don't be silly." I kept my voice low. "You know nothing about the security set-up here. Sergeant Driscoll is acting as per instructions. How was he to know that you weren't being held hostage with a gun in your ribs to take the others through? But he knows now."

Cliveden subsided. Driscoll lowered his gun, gave a signal to a man we couldn't see. The boom rose, the car moved on and halted before heavy steel crash gates. We left the car, passed through a steel side door and made our way into a one-story block marked RECEPTION.

Three men waited for us there. Two I knew—Colonel Weybridge, deputy commandant of Mordon, and Dr. Gregori, Dr. Baxter's chief assistant in E block. Weybridge, though technically under Cliveden's command, was the real boss of Mordon: a tall, fresh-faced man with black hair and an incongruously iron-gray moustache, he was reputed to be an outstanding doctor. Mordon was his life; he was one of the few with his own living accommodations on the premises, and it was said that he never passed outside the gates twice a year. Gregori was a tall, heavy, swarthy, dark-eyed man, an Italian and ex-professor of medicine from Turin, and a brilliant microbiologist greatly respected by his fellow scientists. The third man was a bulky, shapeless character in a bulky, shapeless tweed suit. who looked so much like a farmer that he had to be what he turned out to be—a policeman in plain clothes. Inspector Wylie, of the Wiltshire Constabulary.

Cliveden and Weybridge made the introductions, then Hardanger took over. Generals and colonels or not, army establishment or not, there was no question as to who was in complete charge. Hardanger made it clear from the start.

He said bluntly: "Inspector Wylie, you shouldn't be here. No member of any county constabulary has any right to be inside those gates. But I doubt if you knew that, and I'm sure you're not responsible for your presence here. Who is?"

"I am." Colonel Weybridge's voice was steady, but he was on the defensive. "The circumstances are unusual, to say the least."

"Let me tell it," Inspector Wylie put in. "Our headquarters got a call late last night, about eleven-thirty, from the guardhouse here, saying that one of your car crew—I understand jeeps patrol the ring road all night—had given chase to some unidentified man who seemed to have been molesting or attacking a girl just outside your grounds. A civilian matter, outside army jurisdiction, so they called us. The duty sergeant and constable were here by shortly after midnight, but found nothing and no one. I came along this morning, and when I saw the fences had been cut—well, I assumed there was some connection between the two things."

"The fences cut?" I interrupted. "The boundary fences? It's not possible."

"I'm afraid it is, Cavell," Weybridge said gravely.

"The patrol cars," I protested. "The dogs, the trip-wires, the electric fences. How about them?"

"You'll see yourself. The fences are cut, and that's all that's to it." Weybridge wasn't as calm as he seemed on the surface, not by a long way. I would have taken long odds that he and Gregori were badly frightened men.

"Anyway," Inspector Wylie went on calmly, "I made inquiries at the gate. I met Colonel Weybridge there and he asked me to make inquiries—discreet inquiries—to try to trace Dr. Baxter."

"You did that?" Hardanger asked Weybridge. The voice was speculative, the tone neutral. "Don't you know your own standing orders? That all inquiries are to be handled by your own security chief or my office in London?"

"Clandon was dead —"

"Oh, God!" Hardanger's voice was a lash. "So now Inspector Wylie knows that Clandon is dead. Or did you know before, Inspector?"

"No, sir."

"But you do now. How many other people have you told, Colonel Weybridge?"

"No one else." His voice was stiff, his face pale.

"Thank heaven for that. Don't think I'm carrying security to ridiculous lengths, Colonel, for it doesn't matter what you think or what I think. All that matters is what one or two people in Whitehall think. They give the orders, we carry them out. The instructions for an emergency such as this are quite clear. We take over—completely. You wash your hands of it—completely. I want your co-operation, of course, but it must be co-operation on *my* terms."

"What the Superintendent means," Cliveden said testily, "is that amateur detecting is not discouraged, it's forbidden. I suppose that includes me, too, Hardanger?"

"Don't make my job more difficult than it is already, sir."

"I won't. But as Commandant, I must ask for the right to be kept informed of all progress, and the right to be present when number one lab in E block is opened up."

"That's fair," Hardanger agreed.

"When?" Cliveden asked. "The lab, I mean."

Hardanger looked at me. "Well? The twelve hours you spoke of are up."

"I'm not sure." I looked at Dr. Gregori. "Has the ventilation system been started up in number one?"

"No. Of course not. Nobody's been near the place. We left everything strictly alone."

"If anything had been, say, knocked over," I went on carefully, "would oxidization be complete?"

"I doubt it. Air's too static."

I turned to Hardanger. "All those labs are specially ventilated by filtered air later cleaned in a closed-circuit special compartment. I would like this switched on. Then maybe in an hour."

Hardanger nodded. Gregori, dark eyes worried behind his thick lenses, phoned instructions, then left with Cliveden and Weybridge. Hardanger turned to Inspector Wylie.

"Well, Inspector, it seems you're in possession of information you shouldn't have. No need to issue the usual dreadful warnings to you, I suppose."

"I like my job," Wylie smiled. "Don't be too hard on old Weybridge, sir. Those medical men just aren't security-minded. He meant well."

"The paths of the just—that's me—are made thorny and difficult by those who mean well," Hardanger said heavily. "What's this about Baxter?"

"Seems he left here about six-thirty last night, sir. Bit later than usual, I gather, so he missed the special bus to Alfringham."

"He checked out, of course?" I asked. Every scientist leaving Mordon had to sign the Out register and hand in his security tag.

"No doubt about that. He had to wait for the ordinary

27

service bus that passed the road end at six-forty-eight. Conductor and two passengers confirm that someone answering to our description—no names, of course—got on at the road end, but the conductor is quite positive that no one of that description got off at Alfringham Farm, where Dr. Baxter lives. He must have gone all the way to Alfringham, or Hardcaster, the terminus."

"He just vanished." Hardanger nodded. He looked consideringly at the burly, quiet-eyed man. "Like to work with us on this, Wylie?"

"It would make a change from checking up on the old foot-and-mouth," Wylie admitted. "But our Super and the Chief Constable might have something to say about that."

"They could be persuaded, I think. Your office is at Alfringham, isn't it? I'll call you there."

Wylie left. As he passed through the doorway we caught sight of an army lieutenant, hand raised to knock on the door. Hardanger cocked an eye and said: "Come in."

"Morning, sir. Morning, Mr. Cavell." The sandy-haired young lieutenant looked tired, but his voice was brisk and alert in spite of that. "Wilkinson, sir. Officer in charge of the guard patrols last night. Colonel said you might want to see me."

"Considerate of the colonel. I do. Hardanger, Superintendent Hardanger. Glad to meet you, Wilkinson. You the man who found Clandon last night?"

"Perkins—a corporal of the guard—found him. He called me, and I had a look at him. Just a look. Then I sealed E block, called the colonel and he confirmed."

"Good man," Hardanger approved. "But we'll come to that later. You were notified of the wire-cutting, of course?"

"Naturally, sir. With—with Mr. Clandon gone, I was in charge. We couldn't find him, not anywhere. He must have been dead even then."

"Quite. You investigated the wire-cutting, of course?"

"No, sir."

"No? Why not? Your job, surely?"

"No, sir. It's a job for an expert." A half-smile touched the pale, tired face. "We carry automatic machine guns, Superintendent, not microscopes. It was pitch black. Besides, by the time a few pairs of regulation army boots had churned the place up, there wouldn't have been much left to investigate. I set a four-man guard, sir, each man ten yards from the break, two inside and two out, with orders that no one should be allowed to approach."

"Never looked to find such intelligence in the Army," Hardanger said warmly. "That was first-class, young man." A faint blush of color touched Wilkinson's pale face as he tried hard not to show his pleasure. "Anything else you did?"

"Nothing that would help you, sir. I sent another jeep—there's normally three on patrol at a time—round the entire perimeter of the fence to make a spotlight search for another break. But this was the only one. Then I questioned the crew of the jeep who'd made this wild-goose chase after the man who was supposed to have attacked the girl, and warned them that the next time their—ah—chivalrous instincts got the better of them they would be sent back to their regiments. They're not supposed to leave their jeeps, no matter what the provocation."

"You think this episode of the distressed young lady was just a blind? To let someone nip in smartly and unobserved with a pair of wire-cutters?"

"What else, sir?"

"What else, indeed," Hardanger sighed. "How many men usually employed in E block, Lieutenant?"

"Fifty-five, sixty, sir."

"Doctors?"

"A mixed bunch. Doctors, microbiologists, chemists, technicians, army and civilian. I don't know too much about them, sir. We're not encouraged to ask questions."

"Where are they now? I mean, E block is sealed off."

"In the refectory lounge. Some of them wanted to go home when they found E block shut up, but the colonel—Colonel Weybridge—wouldn't let them."

"That's convenient. Lieutenant, I'd be grateful if you'd lay on two orderlies, or messengers, or whatever. One for me; one for Inspector Martin, here. Inspector Martin would like to talk to those E block men, individually. Please make arrangements. If there are any difficulties, you are free to say that you have the full authority of General Cliveden behind you. But first I'd like you to come along with and identify us to your guards at this gap in the fence. Then tell all the guards, the men who man the jeeps and the dog-handlers to be at the reception office in twenty minutes. The ones who were on duty before midnight, I mean."

Five minutes later, Hardanger and I were alone at the break in the fences. The guards had withdrawn out of earshot and Wilkinson had left us.

The barbed wire on the outer fence was strung between curving reinforced concrete posts like junior editions of modern city lighting standards. There were about thirty strands on the fence, with roughly six inches between each pair. The fourth and fifth strands from the bottom had been cut, then re-joined with heavy gray twine tied round the barbs nearest the cuts. It had taken a pretty sharp pair of eyes to discover the break.

There had been no rain for three days, and there was no trace of footmarks. The ground was damp, but that was still from the heavy dew of the previous night. Whoever had cut those wires had left long before the dew had begun to settle.

"Your eyes are younger than mine," Hardanger said. "Sawn or cut?"

"Snipped. Cutters or pliers. And have a look at the angle of the cut. Slight, but it's there."

Hardanger took one end of the wire in his hand and peered at it.

"From left at the front to right at the back," he murmured. "The way a left-handed man would naturally hold cutters or pliers to obtain maximum leverage."

"A left-handed man," I agreed. "Or a right-handed man who wanted to confuse us. So a man who's either left-handed, or clever, or both."

Hardanger looked at me in disgust and made his way slowly to the inner fence. No footprints, no marks between the fences. The inner fence had been cut in three places; whoever had wielded those cutters would have felt more secure from observation from the ring road. The point we had yet to establish was why he had felt so secure from the attention of the police dogs patrolling the area between the two fences.

The trip-wires under the overhang of the second fence were intact. Whoever had cut that fence had been lucky, indeed, in not stumbling over them. Or he'd known their exact location. Our friend with the pliers didn't strike me as a man who would depend very much on luck.

And the method he'd adopted to get through the electric fence proved it. Unlike most such fences, where only the top wire carried the current all the way, the others being made live by a vertical joining wire cable at each set of insulators, this fence was live in every wire throughout. The alarm bell would be rung by the shorting of any of those wires to earth, as when someone touched them, or by the cutting of any of the wires. This hadn't fazed our friend with the pliers—insulated pliers, quite obviously. The two strands of TRS cable lying on the ground between two posts showed this clearly enough. He'd bent one end of one strand onto the lowest insulator of one post, trailed it across the ground and done the same with the lowest insulator on the next post, so providing an alternate pathway for the current. He'd done the same with the pair of insulators above these, then simply cut away both lowermost wires and crawled through under the third wire.

"An ingenious beggar," Hardanger commented. "Almost argues inside information, doesn't it?"

"Or somebody just outside the outer fence with a powerful telescope or binoculars. The ring road is open to public traffic, remember? Wouldn't be hard to sit in a car and see what type of electric fence it was, and I daresay if the conditions were right he could have seen the trip-wires on the inner fence glistening in the sun."

"I daresay," Hardanger said heavily. "Well, it's no damn good us staying here and staring at this fence. Let's get back and start asking questions."

All the men Hardanger had asked to see were assembled in the reception hall. They were sitting on benches around the wall, fidgeting and restless. Some of them looked sleepy, all of them looked scared. I knew it would take Hardanger about half of one second to sum up their mental condition and act accordingly. He did. He took his seat behind a table and looked up under his shaggy brows, the pale blue eyes cold and penetrating and hostile. As an actor, he wasn't all that far behind Inspector Martin.

"All right," he said brusquely. "The jeep crew. The ones who made the wild-goose chase last night. Let's have you."

Three men—a corporal and two privates—rose slowly to their feet. Hardanger gave his attention to the corporal.

"Your name, please?"

"Muirfield, sir."

"You in charge of the crew last night?"

"Yes, sir."

"Tell me what happened."

"Yes, sir. We'd completed a circuit of the ring road, stopped to report everything O.K. at the main gate, and then left again. It would be about eleven-fifteen, sir, give or take a minute or two. About then, sir."

Hardanger frowned. "Don't you make regular time circuits, so many an hour, so long to a circuit?"

"No, sir. We're under orders not to have any set times. People could take advantage of it, like burglars studying a policeman's beat." His glance shifted momentarily to me. "It was Mr. Cavell here who first gave those instructions. They haven't been changed since he—er—left."

"I see. Go on," Hardanger said impatiently.

"About two hundred and fifty yards past the gates, we saw this girl running into the headlights. She looked wild, disheveled-like, her hair all over the place. She was half-screaming, half-crying, a funny noise. I was driving. I stopped the jeep, jumped out, and the others came after me. I should have told them to stay where they—"

"Never mind about what you should have done. The story, man!"

"Well, we came up to her, sir. She'd mud on her face and her coat was torn. I said—"

"Ever seen her before?"

"No, sir."

"Would you recognize her again.?"

He hesitated. "I doubt it, sir. Her face was in a fair old mess."

"She spoke to you?"

"Yes, sir. She said—"

"Recognize her voice? Any of you recognize her voice? Can you be quite sure of that?"

Three solemn shakes of their heads. They hadn't recognized her voice.

"All right," Hardanger said wearily. "She pitched the tale of damsel in distress. At the psychological moment someone conveniently betrayed his presence and started running. You all took off after him. Catch a glimpse of him?"

"A glimpse only, sir. Just a blur in the darkness. Could have been anyone."

"He took off in a car, I understand. Just another blur, I take it?"

"Yes, sir. Not a car, sir. A truck. A closed van type, sir. A Bedford."

"I see." Hardanger stopped and stared at him. "A Bedford! How the devil do you know? It was dark, you said."

"It was a Bedford," Muirfield insisted. "I'd know the engine anywhere. And I'm a garage mechanic in civvy street."

"He's right, Superintendent," I put in. "A Bedford does have a very distinctive engine note."

"I'll be back." Hardanger was on his feet and it didn't need any clairvoyance to see him heading for the nearest telephone. He glanced at me, nodded at the seated soldiers and left.

I said, pleasantly enough: "Who was the dog-handler in number one last night?" The circuit between the two barbed-wire fences was divided into four sections by wooden hurdles; number one was the section in which the break-in occurred. "You, Ferguson?"

A dark, stocky private in his middle twenties had risen to his feet. Ferguson was regular Army, a born old soldier, tough, aggressive, and not very bright.

"Me," he said. There was truculence in his voice, not very much, but more waiting there if I wanted it.

"Where were you at eleven-fifteen last night?"

"In number one. With Rollo. That's my Alsatian."

"You saw the incident that Corporal Muirfield here has described?"

"Course I saw it."

"Lie number one, Ferguson. Lie number two, and you'll be returned to your regiment before the day is out."

"I'm not lying." His face was suddenly ugly. "And you can't talk to me like that, *Mister* Cavell. You can't threaten *me* any more. Don't think we don't all know you were sacked from here!"

I turned to the orderly. "Ask Colonel Weybridge to come here. At once, please."

The orderly turned to go, but a big sergeant rose to his feet and stopped him.

"It's not necessary, sir. Ferguson's a fool. It's bound to come out. He was at the switchboard having a smoke and a cup of cocoa with the gatehouse communications number. I was in charge. Never saw him there, but I knew about it and didn't worry about it. Ferguson always left Rollo in number one—and that dog's a killer, sir. It was safe enough."

"It wasn't, but thanks. You've been in the habit of doing this for some time, haven't you, Ferguson?"

"I haven't." He was scowling, sullen. "Last night was the first—"

"If there was a rank lower than private," I interrupted wearily, "you'd stay in it till the end of your days. Use what little sense you have. Do you think whoever arranged this decoy move and was standing by with his pliers ready to break in would have done it *unless* he knew for certain you wouldn't be on patrol at that particular time? Probably after Mr. Clandon finished his eleven p.m. rounds visit to the main gate every night, you went straight into the gatehouse for your smoke and cocoa. Isn't that it?"

He stood staring down at the floor in stubborn silence until the sergeant said sharply: "For God's sake, Fergie, use your loaf. Everybody else here can see it. So can you."

Again silence, but this time a sullen nod of defeat.

"We're getting someplace. When you came here you left your dog—Rollo—behind?"

"Yes, sir." Ferguson's days of truculent defiance were over.

"What's he like?"

"He'd tear the throat out of any man alive, from the general downwards," Ferguson said with satisfaction. "Except me, of course."

"He didn't tear out any throats last night," I pointed out. "I wonder why?"

"He must have been got at," Ferguson said defensively.

"What do you mean, 'got at'? Did you have a look at him before you turned him into his compound last night?"

"Look at him? Course not. Why should I? When we saw the cut outer fence, we thought whoever done it must have caught sight of Rollo and run for his life. That's what I would have bloody well done. If—"

"Fetch the dog here," I said "But, for God's sake, muzzle him first." He left and while he was away Hardanger returned. I told him what I'd learned, and that I'd sent for the dog.

Hardanger asked: "What do you expect to find? Nothing, I think. A chloroform pad or something like that would leave no mark. Same if some sort of dart or sharply tipped weapon with one of those funny poisons had been chucked at him. Just a pin-prick that's all there would be."

"From what I hear of our canine pal," I said, "I wouldn't try to hold a chloroform pad against his head if you gave me the crown jewels. As for those funny poisons, as you call them, I don't suppose one person in a hundred thousand would lay hands on one of them or know how to use them even if he did. Besides, throwing or firing any sharp-tipped weapon against a fast-moving, thick-coated target in the dark would be a very dicey proposition indeed. Our friend of last night doesn't go in for dicey propositions, only for certainties."

Ferguson was back in ten minutes, fighting to restrain a wolf-like animal that lunged out madly at anyone who came near him. Rollo had a muzzle on, but even that didn't make me feel too confident. I didn't need any persuasion to accept the sergeant's word that the dog was a killer.

"Does this hound *always* act like this?" I demanded.

"Not usually." Ferguson was puzzled. "In fact, never. Usually perfectly behaved until I let him off the leash—then he'll go for the nearest person, no matter who he is. But he even had a go at me this afternoon—half-hearted, like, but nasty."

It didn't take long to discover the source of Rollo's irritation. Rollo was suffering from what must have been a very severe headache indeed. The skin on the forehead, just above eye-level, had a swollen, pulpy feeling to it, and it took four men all their time to hold the dog down when I touched this area with the tips of my forefingers. We turned him over, and I parted the thick fur on the throat till I found what I was looking for—two triangular jagged tears, deep and very unpleasant-looking, about three inches apart.

"You'd better give your pal here a couple of days off," I said to Ferguson, "and some disinfectant for those gashes on his neck. I wish you luck when you're putting it on. You can take him away."

"No chloroform, no fancy poisons," Hardanger admitted when we were alone. "Those gashes—barbed wire, hey?"

"What else? Just the right distance apart. Somebody pads his forearm, sticks it between a couple of strands of barbed wire, and Rollo grabs it. He wouldn't bark—those dogs are trained never to bark. As soon as he grabs, he's pulled through and down on to the barbed wire and can't pull himself free unless he tears his throat out. And then someone clouts him at his leisure with something heavy and hard. Simple, old-fashioned, direct, and very, very effective. Whoever the character we're after, he's no fool."

"He's smarter than Rollo, anyway," Hardanger conceded heavily.

CHAPTER 3

When we went up to E block, accompanied by two of Hardanger's assistants newly arrived from London, we found Cliveden, Weybridge, Gregori and Wilkinson waiting for us. Wilkinson produced the key to the heavy wooden door.

"No one been inside since you locked the place after seeing Clandon?" Hardanger asked.

"I can guarantee that, sir. Guards posted all the time."

"But Cavell here asked for the ventilation system to be

switched on. How could that be done without someone going inside?"

"Duplicate switches on the roof, sir. All fuse boxes, junctions and electrical terminals are also housed on the roof. Means that the repair and maintenance electricians don't even have to enter the main building."

"You people don't miss much," Hardanger admitted. "Open up, please."

The door swung back; we all filed through and turned down the long corridor to our left. Number one lab was right at the far end of the corridor, at least two hundred yards away, but that was the way we had to go; there was only the one entrance to the entire block. Security was all. On the way we had to pass through half a dozen doors, some opened by photoelectric cells, others by handles fifteen inches long. Elbow handles. Considering the nature of the burdens that some of the Mordon scientists carried from time to time, it was advisable to have both hands free all the time.

We came to number one lab—and Clandon. Clandon was lying just outside the massive steel door of the laboratory, but he wasn't any more the Neil Clandon I used to know—the big, tough, kindly, humorous Irishman who'd been my friend over too many years. He looked curiously small now, small and huddled and defenseless, another man altogether. Not Neil Clandon any more. Even his face was the face of another man: eyes abnormally wide and staring, as one who had passed far beyond the realms of sanity into a total and terror-induced madness, the lips strained cruelly back over clenched teeth in the appalling rictus of his dying agony. And no man who looked at that face, at the convulsively contorted limbs, could doubt that Neil Clandon had died as terribly as man ever could.

They were all watching me, that I was vaguely aware of, but I was pretty good at telling my face what to do. I went forward and stooped low over him, sniffing, and found myself apologizing to the dead man for the involuntary wrinkling distaste of my nose and mouth. No fault of Neil's. I glanced at Colonel Weybridge, and he came forward and bent beside me for a moment before straightening. He looked at Wilkinson and said: "You were right, my boy. Cyanide."

I pulled a pair of cotton gloves from my pocket. One of Hardanger's assistants lifted his flash camera, but I pushed his arm down and said: "No pictures. Neil Clandon's not going into anyone's morgue gallery. Too late for pictures, anyway. If you feel all that like work, why don't you start on that steel door there? Fingerprints. It'll be loaded with them—and not one of them will do you the slightest damn bit of good."

The two men glanced at Hardanger. He hesitated, shrugged, nodded. I went through Neil Clandon's pockets. There wasn't much that could be of any use to me—wallet, cigarette case, a couple of books of matches, and in the left-hand jacket pocket, a handful of transparent papers that had been wrapped round butterscotch sweets.

I said: "This is how he died. The very latest in confectionery—cyanide butterscotch. You can see the sweet he was eating on the floor there, beside his head. Have you such a thing as an analytical chemist on the premises, Colonel?"

"Of course."

"He'll find that sweet, and possibly one of those butterscotch papers, covered with cyanide. I hope your chemist isn't the type who licks his fingers after touching sticky stuff. Whoever doctored this sweet knew of Clandon's weakness for butterscotch. He also knew Clandon. Put it another way, Clandon knew him. He knew him well. He knew him so well and was so little surprised to find him here that he didn't hesitate to accept a butterscotch from him. Whoever killed Clandon is not only employed in Mordon—he's employed in this particular section of E block. If he weren't, Clandon would have been too damn busy suspecting him of everything under the sun to even consider accepting anything from him. Narrows the field of inquiry pretty drastically. The killer's first mistake—and a big one."

"Maybe," Hardanger rumbled. "And maybe you're oversimplifying and taking too much for granted. Assumptions. How do you know Clandon was killed here? You've said yourself we're up against a clever man, a man who would be more likely than not to obscure things, to cause confusion, to cast suspicions in the wrong place by killing Clandon elsewhere and then dragging him here. And it's asking too much to believe that he just happened to have a cyanide sweet in his pocket that he just happened to hand to Clandon when Clandon just happened to find him doing what he was doing."

"About the second part I don't know," I said. "I should have thought myself that Clandon would have been highly suspicious of *anyone* he found here late at night, no matter who he was. But Clandon died right here, that's for sure." I looked at Cliveden and Weybridge. "How long for cyanide poisoning to take effect?"

"Practically instantaneous," Cliveden said.

"And he was violently ill, here," I said. "So he died here. And look at those two faint scratches on the plaster of the wall. A lab check on his fingernails is almost superfluous; that's where he clawed for support as he fell to the floor. Some 'friend' gave Clandon that sweet, and that's why I'd like the wallet, cigarette case and books of matches printed. There's just a chance in a thousand that the friend may have been offered a cigarette or a match, or that he went through Clandon's wallet after he was dead. But I don't think there's even that chance in a thousand. But I think the prints on that door should be interesting. And informative. I'll take a hundred-to-one in anything you like that the prints on that door will be exclusively of those entitled to pass through that door. What I really want to find out is whether there's been any sign of deliberate smearing, as with a handkerchief or gloves, in the vicinity of the combination, time-lock, or circular handle."

"There will be," Hardanger nodded. "If your assumption that this is strictly an inside job is correct, there will be. To bring in the possibility of outsiders."

"There's still Clandon," I said.

Hardanger nodded again and turned away to watch his two men working on the door. Just then a soldier came up with a large fiber case and a small covered cage, placed it on the floor, saluted nobody in particular and left. I caught the inquiring lift of Cliveden's eyebrow.

"When I go into that lab," I said, "I go in alone. In that case is a gas-tight suit and closed-circuit breathing apparatus. I'll be wearing that. I lock the steel door behind me, open the inner door and take the hamster in this cage in with me. If he's still alive after a few minutes—well, it's clear inside."

"A hamster?" Hardanger turned his attention from the door, moved across to the cage and lifted the cover. "Poor little beggar. Where did you acquire a hamster so conveniently?"

"Mordon is the easiest place in Britain to acquire a hamster conveniently. There must be a couple hundred of them within a stone's throw from here. Not to mention a few thousand guinea pigs, rabbits, monkeys, parrots, mice and fowls. They're bred and reared on Alfringham Farm—where Dr. Baxter has his cottage. Poor little beggar, as you say. They've a pretty short life and a far from sweet one. The R. S. P. C. A. and the National Anti-Vivisection Society would sell their souls to get inside here. The Official Secrets Act sees to it that they don't. Mordon is their waking nightmare and I don't blame them. Do you know that over a hundred thousand animals died inside those walls last year—many of them in agony. They're a sweet bunch in Mordon."

"Everyone is entitled to his opinions," General Cliveden said coldly. "I don't say I entirely disagree with you." He smiled without humor. "The right place for airing such sentiments, Cavell, but the wrong time."

I nodded, acknowledgment or apology, he could take it how he liked, and opened the fiber case. I straightened, gas suit in hand, and felt my arm gripped. Dr. Gregori. The dark eyes were intense behind the thick glasses, the swarthy face tight with worry.

"Don't go in there, Mr. Cavell." His voice was low, urgent, almost desperate. "I beg of you, don't go in there."

I said nothing, just looked at him. I liked Gregori, as did all his colleagues without exception. But Gregori wasn't in Mordon because he was a likable man. He was there because he was reputed to be one of the most brilliant microbiologists in Europe. An Italian professor of medicine, he'd been in Mordon just over eight months. The biggest catch Mordon had ever made, and it had been touch and go at that; it had taken cabinet conferences at the highest levels before the Italian government had agreed to release him for an unspecified period. And if a man like Dr. Gregori was worried, maybe it was time I was getting worried too.

"Why shouldn't he go in there?" Hardanger demanded. "I take it you must have very powerful reasons, Dr. Gregori?"

"He has indeed," Cliveden said. His face was as grave as his voice. "No man knows more about number one lab than Dr. Gregori. We were speaking of this a short time ago. Dr. Gregori admits candidly that he's terrified, and I'd be lying if I didn't say that he's got me pretty badly frightened, too. If Dr. Gregori had his way he'd cut through the block on either side of number one lab, build a five-foot-thick concrete wall and roof round it and seal it off forever. That's how frightened Dr. Gregori is. At the very least, he wants this lab kept closed for a month."

Hardanger gave Cliveden his usual dead-pan look, transferred it to Gregori then turned to his two assistants. "Down the corridor till you're out of earshot, please. For your own sakes, the less you know of this, the better. You, too, Lieutenant. Sorry." He waited until Wilkinson and the two men had gone, looked quizzically at Gregori, and said: "So you don't want number one lab opened, Dr. Gregori? Makes you number one on our suspect list, you know."

"Please. I do not feel like smiling. And I do not feel like

talking here." He glanced quickly at Clandon, looked as quickly away. "I am not a policeman—or a soldier. If you would—"

"Of course." Hardanger pointed to a door a few yards down the passage. "What's in there?"

"Just a storeroom. I am sorry to be so squeamish—"

"Come on." Hardanger led the way and we went inside. Just a storeroom as Gregori had said, windowless, concrete floor, wooden shelves lined with carboys, retorts, tubes, bottles and all the paraphernalia of chemical research. Oblivious of the 'No smoking' signs, Gregori had lit a cigarette and was smoking it in rapid, nervous puffs.

"I must not waste your time," he said. "I will be as brief as I can. But I *must* convince you." He paused, then went on slowly, "This is the nuclear age. This is the age when tens of millions go about their homes and their work in daily fear and dread of the thermonuclear holocaust which, they are all sure, may come any day, and must come soon. Millions cannot sleep at night for they dream too much—of our green and lovely world, and their children lying dead in it."

He drew deeply on his cigarette, stubbed it out, at once lit another. He said through the drifting smoke: "I have no such fears of a nuclear Armageddon and I sleep well at nights. Such war will never come. I listen to the Russians rattling their rockets, and I smile. I listen to the Americans rattling theirs, and I smile again. For I know that all the time the two giant powers are shaking their sabers in their scabbards, while they're threatening each other with so many hundreds of megaton-carrying missiles, they are not really thinking of their missiles at all. They are thinking, gentlemen, of Mordon, for we—the British, I should say—have made it their business to ensure that the great nations understand exactly what is going on behind the fences of Mordon." He tapped the brickwork beside him. "Behind this very wall here. The ultimate weapon. The world's one certain guarantee of peace. The term 'ultimate weapon' has been used too freely, has come almost to lose its meaning. But the term, in this case, is precise and exact. If by 'ultimate,' one means total annihilation."

He smiled, a little self-consciously.

"I'm being melodramatic, a little? Perhaps. My Latin blood, shall we say? But listen carefully, gentlemen, and try to understand the full significance of what I'm going to say. Not the General and Colonel, of course, they already know; but you, Superintendent, and you, Mr. Cavell.

"We have developed in Mordon here over forty different types of plague germs. I will confine myself to two. One of them is a derivative of the botulinus toxin—which we had developed in World War II. As a point of interest, a quarter of a million troops in England were inoculated against this toxin just before D-day and I doubt whether any of them know to this day what they were inoculated against.

"We have refined this toxin into a fantastic and shocking weapon, compared to which even the mightiest hydrogen bomb is a child's toy. Six ounces of this toxin, gentlemen, distributed fairly evenly throughout the world, would destroy every man, woman and child alive on this planet today. No flight of fancy." His voice was weighted with heavy emphasis, his face still and somber. "This is simple fact. Give me an airplane and let me fly over London on a windless summer afternoon with no more than a gram of botulinus toxin to scatter, and by evening seven million Londoners would be dead. A thimbleful in its water reservoirs, and London would become one vast charnel house. If God does not strike me down for using the term 'ideal' in this connection, then this is the ideal form of germ warfare. The botulinus toxin oxidizes after twelve hours' exposure to the atmosphere and becomes harmless. Twelve hours after country A releases a few grams of botulinus over country B, it can send its soldiers in without any fear of attack by either the toxin or the defending soldiers. For the defending soldiers would be dead. And the civilians, the men, the women, the children. They would all be dead. All dead."

Gregori fumbled in his pocket for another cigarette. His hands were shaking and he made no attempt to conceal the fact. He was probably unaware of it.

I said: "But you used the term 'ultimate weapon,' as if we alone possessed it. Surely the Russians and Americans—"

"They have it, too. We know where Russia's laboratories in the Urals are. We know where the Canadians manufacture it—the Canadians were leaders in the field until recently—and it's no secret that there are four thousand scientists working on a crash program in Fort Detrick in America to produce even deadlier poisons, so hurried a crash program that we know that scientists have died and eight hundred of them fallen ill over the past few years. They have all failed to produce this deadlier poison. Britain has succeeded, which is why the eyes of the world are on Mordon."

"Is it possible?" Hardanger's tone was dry, but his face was set. "A deadlier poison than this damn botulinus? Seems kind of superfluous to me."

"Botulinus has its drawbacks," Gregori said quietly. "From a military viewpoint, that is. Botulinus you must breathe or swallow to become infected. It is not contagious. Also, we suspect that a few countries *may* have produced a form of vaccine against even the refined type of drug we have developed here. But there is no vaccine on earth to counteract the newest virus we have produced—and it's as contagious as a brush fire.

"This other virus is a derivative of the polio virus—infantile paralysis, if you will—but a virus the potency of which has been increased a million times by—well, the methods don't matter and you wouldn't understand. What does matter is this: unlike botulinus, this new polio virus is indestructible—extremes of heat and cold, oxidization, and poisons have no effect upon it, and its life span appears to be indefinite, although we believe it impossible—we hope it impossible—that any virus could live for more than a month in an environment completely hostile to growth and development; unlike botulinus it is highly contagious, as well as being fatal if swallowed or breathed; and, most terrible of all, we have been unable to discover a vaccine for it. I myself am convinced that we can never discover a vaccine against it." He smiled without humor. "To this virus we have given a highly unscientific name, but one that describes it perfectly—the Satan Bug. It is the most terrible and terrifying weapon mankind has ever known, or ever will know."

"No vaccine?" Hardanger said. His tone wasn't dry this time, but his lips were. "No vaccine at all?"

"We have given up hope. Only a few days ago, as you will recall, Colonel Weybridge, Dr. Baxter thought we had found it—but we were completely wrong. There is no hope, none in the world. Now all our efforts are concentrated on evolving an attenuated strain with a limited life span. In its present form, we obviously cannot use it. But when we do get a form with a limited life span—and its death *must* be caused by oxidization—then we have the ultimate weapon. When that day comes, all the nations of the world may as well destroy their nuclear weapons. From a nuclear attack, no matter how intense, there will always be survivors. The Americans have calculated that even a full-scale Soviet nuclear attack on their country, with *all* the resources at Russia's disposal, would cause no more than seventy million deaths—no more, I say!—with possibly several million others as a result of radiation. But half the nation would survive, and in a generation or two that nation would rise again. But a nation attacked by the Satan Bug would never rise again, for there would be no survivors."

I hadn't been wrong about Hardanger's lips being dry, he was licking them to make speaking easier. Someone should see this, I thought. Hardanger scared. Hardanger truly and genuinely frightened. The penitentiaries of Britain were full of people who would never have believed it.

"And until then," Hardanger said quietly, "Until you have evolved this limited life-strain?"

"Until then?" Gregori stared down at the concrete floor. "Until then? Let me put it this way. In its present form the Satan Bug is an extremely refined powder. I take a saltspoon of this powder, go outside into the grounds of Mordon and turn the saltspoon upside down. What happens? Every person in Mordon would be dead within the hour, the whole of Wiltshire would be an open tomb by dawn. In a week, ten days, all life would have ceased to exist in Britain. I mean all life. The Plague, the Black Death—as nothing compared with this. Long before the last man died in agony, ships or planes or birds or just the waters of the North Sea would have carried the Satan Bug to Europe. We can conceive of no obstacle that can stop its eventual world-wide spread. Two months, I would say, two months at the very most.

"Think of it, Superintendent, think of it. If you can, that is, for it is something really beyond our conception, beyond human imagination. The Lapp trapping in the far north of Sweden. The Chinese peasant tilling his rice fields in the Yangtze valley. The cattle rancher on his station in the Australian outback, the shopper on Fifth Avenue, the primitive in Tierra del Fuego. Dead. All dead. Because I turned a saltspoon upside down. Nothing, nothing, *nothing* can stop the Satan Bug. Eventually all forms of life will perish. Who, what will be the last to go? I cannot say. Perhaps the great albatross forever winging its way round the bottom of the world. Perhaps a handful of Eskimos deep in the Arctic basin. But the seas travel the world over, and so also do the winds; one day, one day soon, they too would die."

By this time I felt like lighting a cigarette myself, and I did. If any enterprising company had got around to running a passenger rocket service to the moon by the time the Satan Bug got loose, they wouldn't have to spend all that much on advertising. Hardanger said in a strained voice: "I don't believe it, I can't believe it. I just *can't*."

"Not 'don't' or 'can't,' Superintendent," Cliveden said gravely. " 'Won't' is the word you want. And God only knows, I don't blame you. Just an old defense mechanism of nature's. When the thought is too shattering for absorption, the mind refuses to accept it. But Dr. Gregori is completely right; I would give anything in the world if he were completely wrong."

"What I'm afraid of, you see," Gregori went on quietly, "is what we may find behind that door. I have not the mind of a detective, but I can see things when they lie plainly before me. Whoever broke his way into Mordon was a desperate man playing for desperate stakes. The end justified by any means—and the only ends to justify such terrible means would be some of the stocks in the virus cupboard."

"Cupboard?" Hardanger drew down his bushy brows. "Don't you lock those damn germs away somewhere safe?"

"They are safe," I said. "The lab walls are of reinforced concrete and paneled with heavy-gauge milled steel. No windows, of course. This door is the only way in. Why shouldn't it be safe in a cupboard'?"

"I didn't know." Hardanger turned back to Gregori. "Please go on."

"That's all." Gregori shrugged. "A desperate man. A man in a great hurry. The key to the locker—just wood and glass—I have in my hand here. See? He would have to break in. In his haste and with the use of force, who knows what damage he may not have done, what virus containers he might not have knocked over or broken. If one of those had been a Satan Bug container, and there are but three in existence ... Maybe it's only a very remote chance. But I say to you, in all sincerity and earnestness, if there was only one chance in a hundred million of a Satan Bug container having been broken, there is still more than ample justification for never opening that door again. For if one is broken and one cubic centimeter of tainted air escapes—" He broke off and lifted his hands helplessly. "Have we the right to take upon ourselves the responsibility of being the executioners of mankind?"

"General Cliveden?" Hardanger said.

"I'm afraid I agree. Seal it up."

"Colonel Weybridge?"

"I don't know, I don't know." Weybridge took off his cap, ran his hands through the short, dark hair. "Yes, I do know. Seal the damn place up."

"Well. You're the three men who should really know what

44

they are talking about." Hardanger pursed his lips for a moment, then glanced at me. "In the face of expert unanimity, it should be interesting to hear what Cavell thinks."

"Cavell thinks they're a pack of old women," I said. "I think your minds are so gummed up with the idea of the Satan Bug on the loose that you're incapable of thinking at all, far less thinking straight. Let's look at the central fact—central supposition, rather. Dr. Gregori bases all his fears on the assumption that someone has broken in and stolen the viruses. He thinks there's one chance in a thousand that one of the containers may have been broken, so if that door is opened there's one chance in a thousand of menace to mankind. But if he has actually stolen the Satan Bug, then the menace to mankind becomes not one in a thousand—but a thousand-to-one. For heaven's sake, take the blinkers off for a moment and *try* to see that a man on the loose with the viruses presents infinitely greater danger than the remote chance of his having broken a container inside those doors. Simple logic says that we must guard against the greater danger. So we *must* get inside that room—how else can we begin to get any trace of the thief and killer, to try to guard against the infinitely greater danger? We must, I say.

"Or I must. I'm dressing up and taking that hamster in there. If the hamster survives, good and well. If he doesn't, I don't come out. Fair enough?"

"Of all the damned arrogance," Cliveden said coldly. "For a private detective, Cavell, you have an awful lot of gall. You might bear in mind that *I'm* the Commandant in Mordon and *I* make all the decisions."

"You did, General. But not any more. The Special Branch has taken over—completely. You know that."

Hardanger ignored us both. Grasping at straws, he said to Gregori: "You mentioned that a special air-filtration unit was working inside there. Won't that have cleared the air?"

"With any other virus, yes. Not with the Satan Bug. It's virtually indestructible, I tell you. And it's a closed-circuit filtration unit. The same air, washed and cleaned, is fed back in again. But you can't wash away the Satan Bug."

There was a long pause, then I said to Gregori: "If the Satan Bug or botulinus is loose in this lab, how long would it take to affect the hamster?"

"Fifteen seconds," he said precisely. "In thirty seconds it will be in convulsions. In a minute, dead. There will be reflex muscle twitchings, but it will be dead. That's for the Satan Bug. For botulinus, only slightly longer."

45

"Don't stop me from going in," I said to Cliveden. "I'll see what happens to the hamster. If he's O.K., then I'll wait another ten minutes. Then I'll come out."

"If you come out." He was weakening. Cliveden was nobody's fool. He was too clever not to have gone over what I had said and at least some of it must have made sense to him.

"If anything—any virus—has been stolen," I said, "then whoever stole it is a madman. The Kennet, a tributary of the Thames, passes by only a few miles from here. How do you know that madman isn't bent over the Kennet this instant, pouring those damned bugs into the water?"

"How do I know you won't come out if that hamster does die?" Cliveden said desperately. "Good God, Cavell, you're only human. If that hamster does die, do you expect me to believe that you're going to remain in there till you die of starvation? Asphyxiation, rather, when the oxygen gives out? Of course you're going to come out."

"All right, General, suppose I come out. Would I still be wearing the gas suit and breathing apparatus?"

"Obviously." His voice was curt. "If you weren't and that room was contaminated—well, you couldn't come out. You'd be dead."

"All right, again. This way." I led the way out to the corridor, indicated the last corridor door we'd passed through. "That door is gas-tight. I know that. So are those outside double windows. You stand at that corridor door—have it open a crack. The door of number one lab opens on it—I'll see me as soon as I begin to come out. Agreed?"

"What are you talking about?"

"This." I reached inside my jacket, pulled out the Hanyatti automatic, knocked the safety catch off. "You have this in your hand. If, when the lab door opens, I'm still wearing the suit and breathing apparatus, you can shoot me down. At fifteen feet and with nine shots, you can hardly fail to. Then you shut the corridor door. Then the virus is still sealed inside E block."

He took the gun from me, slowly, reluctantly, uncertainly. But there was nothing uncertain about his eyes and voice when finally he spoke.

"You know I shall use this, if I have to?"

"Of course I know it." I smiled, but I didn't feel much like it. "From what I've heard I'd rather die from a bullet than the Satan Bug."

"I'm sorry I blew my top a minute ago," he said quietly. "You're a brave man, Cavell."

46

"Don't fail to mention the fact in my obituary in the *Times*. How about asking your men to finish off printing and photographing that door, Superintendent?"

Twenty minutes later the men were finished, and I was all ready to go. The others looked at me with that peculiar hesitancy and indecision of people who think they should be making farewell speeches but find the appropriate words too hard to come by. A couple of nods, a half wave of a hand, and they'd left me. They all passed down the corridor and through the door, except General Cliveden, who remained in the open doorway. From some obscure feeling of decency, he held my Hanyatti behind his body where I couldn't see it.

The gas suit was tight and constricting, the closed-circuit breathing apparatus cut into the back of my neck, and the high concentration of oxygen made my mouth dry. Or maybe my mouth was dry anyway. Three cigarettes in the past twenty minutes—a normal day's quota for me, I preferred to take my slow poisoning in the form of a pipe—wouldn't have helped any, either. I tried to think of one compelling reason why I shouldn't go through that door, but that didn't help either: there were so many compelling reasons that I couldn't pick and choose between them, so I didn't even bother trying. I made a last careful check of suit, mask, and oxygen cylinders, but I was only kidding myself: this was about my fifth last careful check. Besides, they were all watching me. I had my pride. I started spelling out the combination on the heavy steel door.

A fairly complicated and delicate operation at any time, the operation of opening that door was made doubly difficult by reinforced-rubber-covered fingers and poor vision afforded by slanted goggles. But exactly a minute after I'd begun, I heard the heavy thud as the last spin of the dial energized the powerful electromagnets that withdrew the heavy central bolt; three complete turns of the big circular handle and the half-ton door eased slowly open under the full weight of my shoulder.

I picked up the hamster's cage, eased in quickly through the opening door, checked its swing and closed it as swiftly as possible. Three turns of the inner circular handle and the vault door was locked again. The chances were that in so doing I had wiped off a fair number of prints, but I wouldn't have wiped off any prints that mattered.

The rubber-sealed, frosted-glass door leading into the laboratory proper was at the other end of the tiny vestibule.

47

Further delay would achieve nothing—nothing apart from prolonging my life, that was. I leaned on the fifteen-inch elbow handle, pressed open the door, passed inside and closed the door behind me.

No need to switch on any lights—the laboratory was already brilliantly illuminated by shadowless neon lighting. Whoever had broken into the lab had either figured that the government was a big enough firm to stand the waste of electricity, or he'd left in such a tearing hurry that he'd had no time to think of lights.

I'd no time to think of lights either. Nor had I the inclination. My sole and overriding concern was with the immediate welfare of the tiny hamster inside the cage I was carrying.

I placed the cage on the nearest bench, whipped off the cover, and stared at the little animal. No bound man seated on a powder keg ever watched the last few minutes of sputtering fuse with half the mesmerized fascination, the totally exclusive concentration with which I stared at that hamster. The starving cat with upraised paw by the mouse hole, the mongoose waiting for the king cobra to strike, the ruined gambler watching the last roll of the dice—compared with me, they were asleep on the job. If ever the human eye had the power of transfixion, that hamster should have been skewered alive.

Fifteen seconds, Gregori had said. Fifteen seconds only and if the deadly Satan Bug virus was present in the atmosphere of that lab, the hamster would react. I counted off the seconds, each second a bell tolling toward eternity, and at exactly fifteen seconds the hamster twitched violently. Violently, but nothing compared to the way my heart behaved, a double somersault that seemed to take up all the space inside the chest wall before settling down to an abnormally slow heavy thudding that seemed to shake my body with its every beat. Inside the rubber gloves the palms of my hands turned wet, ice-cold. My mouth was dry as last year's ashes.

Thirty seconds passed. By this time, if the virus was loose, the hamster should have been in convulsions. But he wasn't, not unless convulsions in a hamster took the form of sitting up on its hind legs and rubbing its nose vigorously with a couple of tiny and irritated paws.

Forty-five seconds. A minute. Maybe Dr. Gregori had over-estimated the virulence of the virus. Maybe this was a hamster with an abnormally tough and resistant physique? But Gregori didn't strike me as the sort of scientist who would make any mistakes, and this looked like a pretty puny hamster to me. For the first time since entering the room, I started to use the breathing apparatus.

I swung the top of the cage back on its hinges and started to lift out the hamster. He was still in pretty good shape as far as I could tell, for he wriggled from my hand, jumped down onto the rubber-tiled floor and scurried away up a long passage between a table and a wall-bench, stopping at the far end to get on with scratching his nose again. I came to the conclusion that if a hamster could take it, I could too; after all I outweighed him by about five hundred to one. I unbuckled the straps behind my neck and pulled off the closed-circuit breathing apparatus. I took a long, deep lungful of air.

That was a mistake. I admit you can hardly heave a vast sigh of relief at the prospect of keeping on living yet awhile just by sniffing cautiously at the atmosphere, but that is what I ought to have done. I could understand now why the hamster had spent his time in rubbing his nose with such disgusted intensity. I felt my nostrils try to wrinkle shut in nauseated repugnance as the vile smell hit them. Sulphurated hydrogen had nothing on it.

Holding my nose, I started moving around the benches and table. Within thirty seconds, in a passage at the top of the laboratory, I found what I was looking for, and what I didn't want to find. The midnight visitor hadn't forgotten to switch out the lights, he'd just left in such a tearing hurry that the thought of light switches would never even have crossed his mind. His one ambition in life would have been to get out of that room and close both doors tightly behind him just as quickly as was humanly possible.

Hardanger could call off his search for Dr. Baxter. Dr. Baxter was here, still clad in his white, knee-length overall, lying on the rubber floor. Like Clandon, he'd obviously died in contorted agony. Unlike Clandon, whatever had killed him hadn't been cyanide. I know of no type of death associated with this strange blueness of the face, with the outpouring of so much fluid from eyes, ears and nose, and above all, with so dreadful a smell.

Even to look was revolting enough. The idea of making a closer approach was more repugnant still, but I forced myself to do it anyway.

I didn't touch him. I didn't know the cause of death, but I had a pretty fair idea, so I didn't touch him. Instead, I stooped low over the dead man and examined him as carefully as was possible in the circumstances. There was a small contused area behind the right ear, with a little blood where the skin had been broken, but no noticeable swelling. Death had supervened before a true bruise had had time to form.

A few feet beyond him, lying on the floor at the base of the wall furthest from the door, were fragments of dark-blue curved glass, and a red plastic top—the shattered remnants, obviously, of some container or other; there were no signs at all of what the container had once held.

A few feet away in this wall was an inset, rubber-sealed glass door; behind this, I knew, lay what the scientists and technicians called the menagerie—one of four in Mordon. I pushed open the door and went inside.

It was a huge windowless room, as large, almost, as the laboratory itself. All the wall spaces and three room-length benches were taken up by literally hundreds of cages of all types—some of a sealed-glass construction with their own private air-conditioning and filtration units, but most of the standard open-mesh type. Hundreds of pairs of eyes, mostly small, red and beady, turned to stare at me as I entered. There must have been between fifteen hundred and two thousand animals in that room altogether—mostly mice, ninety percent of them mice, I should have guessed, but also about a hundred rabbits and the same of guinea pigs. From what I could see, they all seemed in fair enough health; anyway, all of them had clearly been affected in no way at all by what had happened next door. I made my way back to the lab, closing the communicating door behind me.

Almost ten minutes I'd been inside now, and nothing had happened to me yet. And the chances were remote that anything would happen now. I cornered the hamster, returned him to his cage, and left the lab to open the heavy steel outer door. Just in time I remembered that General Cliveden would be waiting not far from that door, ready to fill me full of holes if I emerged still wearing the gas suit—Cliveden would be understandably trigger-happy and could easily miss the fact that I'd removed the breathing apparatus. I climbed out of the gas suit and opened the door.

General Cliveden had the automatic at eye level, at the full stretch of his arm, pointing toward the widening crack of the doorway and myself. I don't say he was happy at the prospect of shooting me, but he was ready enough for it all the same. And it was a bit late now to tell him that the Hanyatti had a hair trigger. I said quickly: "It's all right. The air is clear inside."

He lowered his arm and smiled in relief. Not a very happy smile, but still a smile. Maybe the thought had come to him too late in the day that he himself should have volunteered to go inside instead of me.

"Are you perfectly sure, Cavell?" he asked.

"I'm alive, aren't I?" I said irritably. "You'd better come inside." I went back into the lab and waited for them.

Hardanger was the first through the door. His nose wrinkled in involuntary disgust and he said: "What in hell's name is causing that vile smell?"

"Botulinus!" It was Colonel Weybridge who supplied the answer, and in the shadowless neon lighting his face seemed suddenly gray. He whispered again, "Botulinus."

"How do you know?" I demanded.

"How do I—" He stared down at the floor, then looked up to meet my eyes. "We had an accident a fortnight ago. A technician."

"An accident," I repeated, then nodded. "You would know the smell."

"But what the devil—" Hardanger began.

"A dead man," I explained. "Killed by botulinus. At the top of the room. It's Dr. Baxter."

No one spoke. They looked at me, then at each other, then followed me silently up the lab to where Baxter lay.

Hardanger stared down at the dead man. "So this is Baxter." His voice held no expression at all. "You are quite sure? Remember, he checked out of here about half past six last night."

"Maybe Dr. Baxter owned a pair of wire-cutters," I suggested. "It's Baxter, all right. Someone coshed him, then stood at the lab door and flung a botulinus container against this wall, closing the lab door behind him immediately afterwards."

"The fiend," Cliveden said hoarsely. "The unspeakable fiend."

"Or fiends," I agreed. I moved across to Dr. Gregori, who had sat down on a high stool. He had his elbows on a bench and his face was sunk in his hands. The straining fingertips made pale splotches against the swarthy cheeks, and his hands were shaking. I touched him on the shoulder and said: "I'm sorry, Dr. Gregori. As you said, I know you're neither soldier nor policeman. You shouldn't have to meet with these things. But you must help us."

"Yes, of course," he said dully. He looked up at me, and the dark eyes were smudged and with tears in them. "He was—he was more than just a colleague. How can I help, Mr. Cavell?"

"The virus cupboard. Check it, please."

"Of course, of course. The virus cupboard. What on earth could I have been thinking of?" He stared down at Baxter in fascinated horror, and it was quite obvious what he was thinking of. "At once, at once."

He crossed to a wooden cupboard with a glazed front, and tried to open it. A couple of determined tugs, and then he shook his head.

"It's locked. The door's locked."

"Well." I was impatient. "You have the key, haven't you?"

"The only key. Nobody could have got in without this key. Not without force. It—it hasn't been touched."

"Don't be so damned silly. What do you think Baxter died of—influenza? Open that cupboard."

He turned the key with unsteady fingers. No one was looking at Baxter now—we'd eyes only for Dr. Gregori. He opened both doors, reached up and brought down a small rectangular box. He opened the lid and stared inside. After a moment his shoulders sagged and he seemed different altogether, curiously deflated, head bowed very low.

"They're gone," he whispered. "All of them. All nine of them have been taken. Six of them were botulinus—he must have used one on Baxter!"

"And the others," I said harshly to the bowed back. "The other three?"

"The Satan Bug," he said fearfully. "The Satan Bug. It's gone."

CHAPTER 4

The management refectory canteen at Mordon had something of a reputation among the more gourmet-minded of the staff, and the chef that had prepared our lunch was right on form; maybe the presence at our table of Dr. MacDonald, a colleague of Gregori's in number one lab and president of the mess, had something to do with it. However it was, it seemed that I was the only person with any appetite at all that day. Hardanger only picked at his food, and neither Cliveden nor

Weybridge made hardly any better a showing. Gregori ate nothing at all, just sat staring at his plate; he excused himself abruptly in the middle of the meal, and when he came back in five minutes he looked white and shaken. Probably, I thought, he'd been sick. Violent death wouldn't be much in the line of a professor specializing in the cloistered work of chemical research.

The two fingerprint experts weren't there. They were still hungry. Aided by three other detectives recruited locally through Inspector Wylie, they'd spent over an hour and a half fingerprinting the entire inside of the laboratory and were now collating and tabulating their results. The handle of the heavy steel door and the areas adjoining the combination lock had been heavily smeared with a cotton or linen material—probably a handkerchief. So the possibility of an outsider having been at work couldn't be entirely excluded.

Inspector Martin came in towards the end of the meal. He'd spent all his time until then taking statements from the temporarily jobless scientists and technicians barred from E block, and he wasn't finished yet by a long way. Every statement made by those interviewed about their activities the previous evening would have to be rigorously checked. He didn't say how he was getting on, and Hardanger, predictably, didn't ask him.

After lunch I accompanied Hardanger to the main gate. From the sergeant on duty there we learned who had been in charge of the checking-out clock the previous evening. After a few minutes, a tall blond fresh-faced corporal appeared and saluted crisply.

"Corporal Norris, sir. You sent for me."

"Yes," Hardanger said. "Take a seat, please. I've sent for you, Norris, to ask you some questions about the murder of Dr. Harold Baxter."

The shock tactics worked better than any amount of carefully delicate probing could have done. Norris, already in the process of lowering himself gingerly into his chair, sat down heavily, as if suddenly grateful to take the weight off his feet, and stared at Hardanger. The eyes widening in a gaze of shocked incredulity, the opened mouth would have been within the compass of any moderately competent actor. But the perceptible draining of color from the cheeks was something else again.

"The murder of Dr. Baxter," he repeated stupidly. "Dr. Baxter—he's *dead?*"

"Murdered," Hardanger said harshly. "He was murdered in his laboratory last night. We know for a fact, never mind how, that Dr. Baxter never left Mordon last night. But you checked him out. You *say* you checked him out. But you didn't. You couldn't have. Who gave you his security tag and told you to forge his signature? Or maybe that someone did it himself. How much did they pay you, Norris?"

The corporal had been staring at Hardanger in numbed bewilderment. Then the numbness passed, and his native Yorkshire toughness reasserted itself. He rose slowly to his feet, his face darkening.

"Look, sir," he said softly. "I don't know who you are. Someone pretty important, I suppose, a police inspector, or one of those M.I.6. chaps. But I can tell you this. Say that to me just once again, and I'll knock your bloody head clean off."

"I believe you would, too." Hardanger was suddenly smiling. He turned to me. "Not guilty, eh?"

"He could hardly be that good," I agreed.

"I hardly think so. Forgive me, Norris. I had to find out something, and I had to find out fast. I'm investigating a murder. Murder isn't a nice business, and sometimes I've got to use tactics that aren't very nice either. Understand?"

"Yes, sir," Norris said uncertainly. He was slightly mollified, but only slightly. "Dr. Baxter. How—I mean, who—"

"Never mind that just now," Hardanger said briskly. "You checked him out. In this book here. Eighteen hundred and thirty-two hours, it says. That right?"

"If the book says so, sir. That time stamp's automatic."

"You took his security tag from him—this one?" He held it up.

"Yes, sir."

"Didn't happen to speak to him, did you?"

"As a matter of fact, sir, yes."

"About what?"

"Just the weather and the like, sir. He was always very friendly to us chaps. And his cold. About his cold. He'd a pretty bad one. Coughing and blowing his nose all the time."

"You saw him clearly?"

"Course I did. I've been guard here for eighteen months, and I know Dr. Baxter as well as my own mother. Dressed in his usual—checkered ulster, trilby and those heavy horn glasses of his."

"You'd swear to it in court? That it was Dr. Baxter, I mean?"

He hesitated, then said: "I'd swear to it. And both my mates on duty saw him also. You can check with them."

We checked, then left to return to the administrative block. I said: "Did you really think Baxter stayed behind last night?"

"No," Hardanger admitted. "He left all right—and came back with his pliers. Either alone or with someone else. Which on the face of it, would appear to make Baxter a bad 'un. But it seems that an even badder 'un disposed of him. When thieves fall out, perhaps."

"You thought the signature genuine?"

"As genuine as any signature can ever be. No one ever signs his signature the same way twice. I think I'll get on to the General in London straight away. An all-out check on Baxter might turn up something very interesting. Especially past contacts."

"You'll be wasting your time. From the point of view of security, Baxter was sitting in the hottest seat in Europe—boss of number one lab in Mordon. Every step he's taken from the day he learned to walk, every word he's said since, every person he's met—they would have checked and rechecked a hundred times. Baxter's clean. He's just too big a fish to get through the security mesh."

"So were a number of other characters who are now either in jail or Moscow," Hardanger said grimly. "I'm phoning London now. Then checking with Wylie to see if they've turned up anything on that Bedford that was used as a getaway car. Then I'm going to see how Martin and the fingerprint boys are getting on. Coming?"

"No. I'd like to check with the internal guards who were on duty last night, and mooch around on my own a little."

He shrugged. "I've no jurisdiction over you, Cavell. But if anything turns up—you'll let me know?" he added suspiciously.

"Think I'm crazy? With a guy walking around with the Satan Bug in his vest pocket, do you think I'm going to start a one-man war?"

He nodded, still a little suspiciously, and left me. I spent the next hour checking with the six internal guards who had been on duty before midnight the previous night, and learned what I had expected to learn—nothing. All of them were well-known to me, which was probably the real reason why Hardanger had wanted me down in Mordon, and all of them had been on duty in Mordon for at least three years. All of their stories tallied and none of it helped at all. With two guards I made a minute check of all windows and the entire roof area of E block, and I was just wasting my time.

No one had seen Clandon from the time he left Lieutenant Wilkinson at the gatehouse, just after eleven p.m., till his body had been found. Normally, no one would have expected to see him, for after making his rounds, Clandon retired for the night to the little concrete cottage he had to himself less than a hundred yards from E block. This cottage faced onto the long glass corridor of the block, and as a security precaution the lights burned night and day. It was no great trick to guess that Clandon had seen something suspicious in E block and gone to investigate. No other reason could have accounted for his presence outside number one laboratory.

I made my way to the gatehouse and asked for the register book showing the names and nature of business of all those who had checked in and out of Mordon the previous day. There were several hundred of those altogether, but all but a very few of them were staff regularly employed there. Groups of special visitors to Mordon were not infrequent: visiting scientists from the Commonwealth and Nato countries, or an occasional small group of M.P.'s who were given to asking awkward questions in the Commons and were brought down to Mordon to see for themselves the sterling work being carried out there on the health front against anthrax, polio, Asian flu, and other diseases; such groups were shown exactly what the Mordon authorities wanted them to be shown, and usually came away no wiser than they had arrived. But on that previous day, there had been no such groups of visitors; there had been fourteen callers altogether, all of them concerned with the delivery of various supplies. I copied down their names and the reasons for their visits, and left.

I phoned the local car-hire firm, asked for the indefinite hire of one of their cars and that it should be brought and left at the gates of Mordon. The clerk who took my call was pretty sticky about it; his firm had had a couple of similar phone calls from unknowns in the past year and neither car had ever been seen again, but I gave him Inspector Wylie as a reference and finally got it fixed up. Another call to Alfringham, this time to the Waggoner's Rest, and I was lucky enough to get a room. The last call was to London, to Mary. I told her to pack a suitcase for me and one for herself and bring them both down to the Waggoner's Rest. There was a train from Paddington that would get her down by half-past six.

I left the gatehouse and went for a walk through the grounds. The air was cold and a chill October wind blowing, but I didn't walk briskly. I paced slowly up and down beside the inner fence, head bowed, gazing down at my feet most of the time. Cavell lost in thought, or so I hoped any onlooker would think. I spent the better part of an hour there, paralleling the same quarter-mile of fence all the time, and at last I found what I was looking for. Or so I thought. Next circuit round I stopped to tie my shoelace, and then there was no more doubt in my mind.

Hardanger was still in the administrative block when I found him. He and Inspector Martin were poring over freshly developed batches of photographic prints. Hardanger looked up and grunted: "How's it going?"

"It's not. Any progress with you?"

"No prints on Clandon's wallet, cigarette case, or books of matches—except his own, of course. Nothing of any interest on the doors. We've found the Bedford van—rather, Inspector Wylie's men have found a Bedford van. Reported missing this afternoon by a chap called Hendry, an Alfringham carrier with three of those vans. Found less than an hour ago, by a motorcycle cop in the Hailem Woods. Sent my men across there to try it for prints."

"It's as good a way of wasting time as any."

"Maybe. Do you know the Hailem Woods?"

I nodded. "Halfway between here and Alfringham, there's a 'B' road that forks off to the north. About a mile and a half along that road. There may have been woods there once, but they've gone now. You wouldn't find a couple of dozen trees in the entire area now—outside gardens, that is. Residential— what's called a good neighborhood. This fellow Hendry—a check been made?"

"Yes. Nothing there. One of those solid citizens, not only the backbone of England but a personal friend of Inspector Wylie's. They play darts for the same pub team. That," Hardanger said heavily, "puts him beyond the range of all suspicion."

"You're getting bitter." I nodded at the prints. "From number one lab, I take it. A first-class job. I wonder which of the prints belongs to the man who lives nearest to the spot where the Bedford was found."

He gave me an up-from-under glance. "As obvious as that, is it?"

"Isn't it? It would seem to leave him pretty well out.

57

Dumping the evidence on your own doorstep is as good a way as any of putting the noose round your own neck."

"Unless that's the way we're intended to think. Fellow called Chessingham. Know him?"

"Research chemist. I know him."

"Would you vouch for him?"

"In this business, I wouldn't vouch for St. Peter. But I'd wager a month's pay he's clear."

"I wouldn't. We're checking his story, and we'll see."

"We'll see. How many of the prints have you identified?"

"Fifteen sets altogether, as far as we can make out, but we've been able to trace only thirteen."

I thought for a minute, then nodded. "That would be about right. Dr. Baxter, Dr. Gregori, Dr. MacDonald, Dr. Hartnell. Chessingham. Then the four technicians in that lab—Verity, Heath, Robinson and Marsh. Nine. Clandon. One of the night guards. And, of course, Cliveden and Weybridge. Running a check on them?"

"What do you think?" Hardanger said testily.

"Including Cliveden and Weybridge?"

"Cliveden and Weybridge!" Hardanger stared at me, and Martin backed him up with another stare. "Are you serious, Cavell?"

"With someone running around with the Satan Bug in his pants pockets I don't think it's time for being facetious, Hardanger. Nobody—*nobody*—is in the clear." He gave me a long hard look, but I ignored it and went on, "About those two sets of unidentified prints—"

"We'll print every man in Mordon till we get them," Hardanger said grimly.

"You don't have to. Almost certainly they belong to a couple of men called Bryson and Chipperfield. I know them both."

"Explain yourself."

"They're the two men in charge of running Alfringham Farm—the place that supplies all the animals for the experiments carried out here. They're usually up here with a fresh supply of animals every week or so—the turnover in livestock is pretty heavy. They were here yesterday. I checked on the register book. Making a delivery to the animal room in number one laboratory."

"You say you know them. What are they like?"

"Young. Steady, hard-working, very reliable. Live in adjacent cottages on the farm. Married to a couple of very nice girls. They have a kid apiece, a boy and a girl, each about six

58

years old. Not the type, any of them, to get mixed up in anything wrong."

"You guarantee them?"

"You heard what I said about St. Peter. I guarantee nothing and nobody. They'll have to be checked. I'll go, if you like. After all, I have the advantage of knowing them."

"You will?" Hardanger let me have his close look again. "Like to take Inspector Martin with you?"

"All one to me," I assured him. It wasn't, but I'd manners.

"Then in that case, it's not necessary," Hardanger said. There were times, I thought, when Hardanger could be downright unpleasant. "Report back anything you find. I'll lay on a car for you."

"I already have one. Car-hire firm."

He frowned. "That was unnecessary. Plenty of police and army cars available. You know that."

"I'm a private citizen now. I prefer private transport."

I found the car at the gate. Like so many rental machines, it was a great deal older than its actual age. But at least it rolled and took the weight off my feet. I was glad to take the weight off my feet. My left leg hurt, quite badly, as it always did when I had to walk around for any length of time. Two eminent London surgeons had more than once pointed out to me the advantage of having my left foot removed, and sworn that they could replace it with an artificial one not only indistinguishable from the genuine article but guaranteed pain-free. They had been quite enthusiastic about it, but it wasn't their foot and I preferred to hang on to it as long as possible.

I drove to Alfringham, spent five minutes there talking to the manager of the local dance-hall, and reached Alfringham Farm just as dusk was falling. I turned in through the gates, stopped the car outside the first of the two cottages, got out and rang the bell. After the third attempt, I gave it up and drove to the second cottage. I'd get an answer there. Lights were burning behind the windows. I leaned on the bell, and after some seconds the door opened. I blinked in the sudden wash of light, then recognized the man before me.

"Bryson," I said. "How are you? Sorry to burst in like this, but I'm afraid I've a very good reason."

"Mr. Cavell!" Unmistakable surprise in his voice, all the more pronounced in the sudden conversational hush from the room behind him. "Didn't expect to see you again so soon. Thought you'd left these parts, I did. How are you, sir?"

"I'd like a few words with you. And with Chipperfield. But he's not at home."

"He's here. With his missus. Turn about in each other's house for our Saturday-night get-together." He hesitated, exactly as I would have done if I'd settled down with some friends for a quiet drink and a stranger had broken in. "Delighted to have you join us, sir."

"I'll only keep you a few minutes." I followed Bryson into the brightly lit living-room beyond. A log fire burnt cheerfully in the fireplace, and around it were a couple of small settees and a high chair or two. In the center was a low table with a bottle and some glasses. A comfortable, homely scene.

A man and two women rose as Bryson closed the door behind me. I knew all three—Chipperfield, a tall blond man, the outward antithesis in every way of the short stocky Bryson, and the two men's wives, blonde and dark to match their husbands, but otherwise with a strong similarity—small, neat and pretty, with identical hazel eyes. The similarity was hardly surprising—Mrs. Bryson and Mrs. Chipperfield were sisters.

After a couple of minutes, during which civilities had been exchanged and I'd been offered a drink—and accepted for my sore leg's sake—Bryson said: "How can we help you, Mr. Cavell?"

"We're trying to clear up a mystery about Dr. Baxter," I said quietly. "You might be able to help. I don't know."

"Dr. Baxter? In number one lab?" Bryson glanced at his brother-in-law. "Ted and me—we saw him only yesterday. Quite a chat with him, we had. Nothing wrong with him, sir, I hope?"

"He was murdered last night," I said.

Mrs. Bryson clapped her hands to her mouth and choked off a scream. Her sister made some sort of unidentifiable noise and said: "No, oh no!" But I wasn't watching them; I was watching Bryson and Chipperfield, and I didn't have to be a detective to see that the news came as a complete shock and surprise to both of them.

I went on: "He was killed last night, before midnight. In his lab. Someone threw a deadly virus poison over him and he must have died in minutes. And in great agony. Then that someone found Mr. Clandon waiting outside the lab and disposed of him also—by cyanide poisoning."

Mrs. Bryson rose to her feet, her face paper-white, her sister's arms around her, blindly threw her cigarette into the fireplace and left the room. I could hear the sound of someone being sick in the bathroom.

"Dr. Baxter and Mr. Clandon dead? Murdered?" Bryson's

face was almost as pale as his wife's had been. "I don't believe it, I don't believe it." I looked at his face again. He believed it all right. He listened to the sounds coming from the bathroom, and then said with as much angry reproach as his shaken state would allow: "You might have told us private-like, Mr. Cavell. Without the girls being here, I mean."

"I'm sorry." I tried to look sorry. "I'm not myself. Clandon was my best friend."

"You did it on purpose," Chipperfield said tightly. He was normally a likable and affable young man, but there was nothing affable about him right then. He said shrewdly: "You wanted to see how we all took it. You wanted to know if *we* had anything to do with it. Isn't that it, Mr. Cavell?"

"Between eleven o'clock and midnight last night," I said precisely, "you and your brother-in-law, here, were up for exactly five dances at the Friday-night hop in Alfringham. You've been going there practically every Friday night for years. I could even tell you the names of the dances, but I won't bother. The point is that neither of you—nor your wives—left the hall for an instant during that hour. Afterwards, you went straight into your Land Rover and arrived back here shortly after twelve-twenty. We have established beyond all doubt that both murders took place between eleven-fifteen and eleven-forty-five. So let's have no more of your silly accusations, Chipperfield. There can be no shadow of suspicion about you two. If there was, you'd be in a police cell, not seeing me sitting here drinking your whisky. Speaking of whisky—"

"Sorry, Mr. Cavell. Damned silly of me. Saying what I did, I mean." Chipperfield's relief showed in his face as he rose to his feet and poured more whisky into my glass. Some of it spilled onto the carpet, but he didn't seem to notice. "But if you know we've nothing to do with it, what can we do to help?"

"You can tell me everything that happened when you were in E block yesterday, I said. "Everything. What you did, what you saw, what Dr. Baxter said to you and you to him. Don't miss out a thing, the tiniest detail."

So they told me, taking it in turns, and I sat there looking at them with unwavering attention and not bothering to listen to a word they said. As they talked, the two women came in, Mrs. Bryson giving me a pale, shamefaced half-smile, but I didn't notice it; I was too busy doing my close listening act. As soon as the first decent opportunity came, I finished my whisky, rose and made to leave. Mrs. Bryson said something apologetic about her silliness, I said something suitably apologetic in return, and Bryson said: "Sorry we haven't been able to be of any real help, Mr. Cavell."

"You have helped," I said. "Police work is largely confined to the confirming and eliminating of possibilities. You've eliminated more than you would think. I'm sorry I caused such an upset, I realize this must be quite a shock to both you families, being so closely associated with Mordon. Speaking of families, where are the kids tonight?"

"Not here, thank goodness," Mr. Chipperfield said. "With their grandmother in Kent—the October holidays, you know, and they always go there then."

"Best place for them, right now," I agreed. I made my apologies again, cut the leave-taking short and left.

It was quite dark outside now. I made my way back down to the hired car, climbed in, drove out through the farm gates and turned left for the town of Alfringham. Four hundred yards beyond the gates, I pulled into a convenient lay-by, switched off engine and lights.

My leg was aching badly now, and it took me almost fifteen minutes to get back to Bryson's cottage. The living-room curtains were drawn, but carelessly. I could see all I wanted to, without trouble. Mrs. Bryson was sitting on a settee, sobbing bitterly, with her husband's free arm round her. The other held a tumbler of whisky and the tumbler was more than half full. Chipperfield, a similar glass in his hand, was staring into the fire, his face dark and somber. Mrs. Chipperfield, on the settee, was facing me. I couldn't see her face, only the fair hair shining in the lamplight as she bent over something held in her hand. I couldn't see what it was, but I didn't have to. I could guess with the certainty of complete knowledge. I walked quietly away and took my time in making my way back to the car. I still had twenty-five minutes before the London train was due in Alfringham. The train—and Mary.

Mary Cavell was all my life. Two months, only, I'd been married to her, but I knew it would be that way till the end of my days. All my life. An easy thing for any man to say, easy and trite and meaningless, and perhaps a little cheap. Until you saw her, that was. Then you would believe anything. I knew around a dozen men—there were probably far, far more—who loved Mary Cavell and would continue to do so while they lived. I don't think any of them really grudged her to me, and I can't think of any of them who would have hesitated to kill me, had I brought her to harm. To arouse feelings like that in people, you have to be something very special. That was Mary Cavell. Something very, very rare indeed. The best-loved person I'd ever known.

She was small and blonde and beautiful, with amazing green eyes. But it wasn't that that made her special; you could reach out your arms in the streets of London in the evening rush hour and pick up half a dozen girls without really trying, all of them small and blonde and beautiful. Nor was it just the infectious happiness that left no one untouched, her irrepressible gaiety, her obvious delight in a life that she lived with the intensity of a tropical humming-bird. There was something else. There was a shining quality about her, in her face, in her eyes, in her voice, in everything she said and did, that made her the only person I'd ever known who'd never had an enemy, male or female. There is only one word to describe this quality—the old-fashioned and much-maligned term "goodness." She hated do-gooders, those she called the goody-goodies, but her own goodness surrounded her like a tangible, a visible magnetic field. A magnetic field that automatically drew to her more waifs and strays, more people broken in mind and body than a normal person would encounter in a dozen lifetimes. An old man dozing away his last days in the thin autumn sunshine on a park bench, a bird with a broken wing—they all came alike to Mary. Broken wings were her specialty, and I was only now beginning to realize that for every wing we saw her mend, there was another the world knew nothing about. And, to make her perfect, she had the one drawback which kept her from being inhumanly perfect—she had an explosive temper that could erupt in a most spectacular fashion and to the accompaniment of the most shockingly appropriate language, but only when she saw the bird with the broken wing—or the person responsible for breaking it.

She was my wife, and I still wondered why she married me. She could have chosen almost any man she'd ever known, but she'd chosen me. I think it was because I had a broken wing. The German tank-track that had crushed my leg in the mud at Caen, the gas shell that had scarred one whole side of my face—Adonis would never have claimed it for his own, anyway—beyond hope of plastic surgery and left me with a left eye that could just barely tell the difference between night and day, that made me a bird with a broken wing.

The train came in, and I saw her jumping down lightly from a compartment about twenty yards away, followed by a burly, middle-aged character with a bowler hat and umbrella, carrying her suitcase—the dead image of the big city tycoon who spends his business hours grinding in the faces of the poor and evicting widows and orphans. I'd never seen him before, and I was certain that neither had Mary. She just had that effect on people; the most unlikely citizens fought each other for the privilege of helping her, and the tycoon looked quite a fighter.

She came running down the platform to meet me and I braced myself for the shock of impact. There was nothing inhibited about Mary's greetings, and although I still wasn't reconciled to the raised eyebrows of astonished fellow travelers, I was getting accustomed to them. I'd last seen her only this morning, but I might have been a long-lost loved one coming home for the first time after a generation in the Australian outback. I was setting her down on terra firma as the tycoon came up, dumped the cases, beamed at Mary, tipped his bowler, turned away, still beaming at her, and tripped over a railway barrow. When he'd got up and dusted himself, he was still beaming. He tipped his bowler again and disappeared.

"You want to be careful how you smile at your boy friends," I said severely. "Want me to spend the rest of my life working to pay off claims for damages against you? That oppressor of the working class that just passed by—he'd have me wearing the same suit for the rest of my life."

"He was a very nice man indeed." She looked up at me, suddenly not smiling. "Pierre Cavell, you're tired, worried stiff, and your leg is hurting."

"Cavell's face is a mask," I said. "Impossible to tell his feelings and thoughts—inscrutable, they call it. Ask anyone."

"*And* you've been drinking whisky."

"It was the long separation that drove me to it." I led the way to the car. "We're staying at the Waggoner's Rest."

"It sounds wonderful. Thatched roofs, oak beams, the inglenooks by the blazing fire." She shivered. "It *is* cold. I can't get there fast enough."

We got there in three minutes. I parked the car outside a modernistic confection in gleaming glass and chrome. Mary looked at it, then at me and said: "This is the Waggoner's Rest?"

"You can see what the neon sign says. Outdoor sanitation

and boll weevils in the bedposts have gone out of fashion. And they'll have central heating."

The manager, at the moment doubling as receptionist, would have felt more at home in an eighteenth-century 'Waggoner's Rest.' Red-faced, shirt-sleeved and smelling powerfully of the breweries, he scowled at me, smiled at Mary and summoned a ten-year-old boy, presumably his son, who showed us to our room. It was clean enough and spacious enough and overlooked a back courtyard decked out in a poor imitation of a continental beer garden. More important, one of the windows overlooked the porchway leading into the court.

The door closed behind the boy and Mary came up to me. "How is that stupid leg of yours, Pierre? Honestly?"

"It's not so good." I'd given up trying to tell lies about myself to Mary, as far as I was concerned she was a human lie-detector. "It'll ease up. It always does."

"That armchair," she ordered. "And the stool, too. You're not using that leg again tonight."

"I'm afraid I'll have to. Quite a bit. Damn nuisance, but it can't be helped."

"It can be helped," she insisted. "You don't have to do everything yourself. There are plenty of men—"

"Not this time, I'm afraid. I have to go out. Twice. I want you to come with me the first time, that's why I wanted you here."

She didn't ask any questions. She picked up the phone, ordered whisky for me, sherry for herself. Old shirt-sleeves brought it up, huffing a bit after climbing the stairs. Mary smiled at him and said: "Could we have dinner in our room, please?"

"Dinner?" Shirt-sleeves stiffened in outrage, his face going an impossible shade redder. "In your room? Dinner! That's a good 'un! Where do you think you've landed—Claridge's?" He brought his gaze down from the ceiling, where he'd been imploring heaven, and looked at Mary again. He opened his mouth to speak, closed it, kept looking at her, and I knew he was a lost man. "Claridge's," he repeated mechanically. "I—well, I'll see what can be done. Against the house rules, mind you—but—it'll be a pleasure, ma'am."

He left. I said: "There should be a law against you. Pour me some whisky. And pass that phone."

I made three calls. The first was to London, the second to Inspector Wylie and the third to Hardanger. He was still at

Mordon. He sounded tired and irritated, and I didn't wonder. He'd had a long and probably frustrating day.

"Cavell?" His voice was almost a bark. "How did you get on with those two men you saw? At the farm, I mean."

"Bryson and Chipperfield? Nothing there. There are two hundred witnesses who will swear that neither of them were within five miles of Mordon between eleven and midnight last night."

"What are you talking about? Two hundred—"

"They were at a dance. Anything turned up in the statements made by our other suspects in number one lab?"

"Did you expect anything to turn up?" he said sourly. "Do you think the killer would have been so dumb as to leave himself without an alibi? They've all got alibis—and damn good ones. I'm still not convinced there wasn't an outsider at work."

"Chessingham and Dr. Hartnell. How strong are their stories?"

"Why those two?" His voice was a suspicious crackle.

"I'm interested in them. I'm going to see them tonight and I wondered what their stories were."

"You're not going to see anyone without my say-so, Cavell." His voice was pretty close to a shout. "I don't want people blundering in—"

"I won't blunder. I'm going, Hardanger. The General said I was to have a free hand, didn't he? Blocking my way—which you can do—is not my idea of giving a free hand. The General wouldn't like it, Hardanger."

A silence. Hardanger was bringing himself under control. At last he said, in a quieter tone: "You gave me to believe that you didn't suspect Chessingham."

"I want to see him. He's not only acute and observant, he's more than usually friendly with Dr. Hartnell. It's Hartnell I'm really interested in. He's an outstanding research man, young and financially irresponsible. He thinks because he's clever with bugs, he can be the same on the stock market. Three months ago Hartnell put all his cash into a fly-by-night company that had splurged its adverts in all the national dailies. He lost the lot. Then he mortgaged his house a few weeks before I left Mordon. I believe he lost most of that too, trying to recoup."

"Why in hell didn't you tell me that before?" Hardanger demanded.

"It just suddenly came to me this evening."

"It just suddenly came—" Hardanger's voice cut off as if

he had been strangled. Then he said thoughtfully: "Isn't that too easy? Jumping on Hartnell? Because he's heading for the bankruptcy court?"

"I don't know. As I say, he's not clever at everything. I've got to find out. Both have alibis, of course?"

"Both were at home. Their families vouch for them. I want to see you later." He'd given up. "I'll be at the County in Alfringham."

"I'm at the Waggoner's Rest. A couple of minutes away. Could you come round to see us? About ten?"

"Us?"

"Mary came down this afternoon."

"Mary?" There was surprise in his voice, suspicion that he didn't get round to elaborating, but above all, pleasure. One good reason Hardanger had for not liking me too much was that I'd made off with the best secretary he'd ever had; she'd been with him three years, and if any person could ever be said to be the apple of an eye—like a basilisk, it was Mary.

He said he would be around at ten.

CHAPTER 5

I drove out to Hailem Woods with Mary sitting strangely silent by my side. Over dinner I'd told her the whole story—the whole story. I'd never seen her scared before, but she was that now. Badly. Two frightened people in a car.

We reached Chessingham's house about a quarter to eight. It was an old-fashioned, flat-roofed, stone-built affair, with long narrow windows and a flight of stone steps leading up to the front door over a moat-like trench that ran right round the house and gave light to the basement. High trees, sighing in the cold night wind, surrounded the house on four sides, and it was beginning to rain heavily. It was a place and a night in keeping with our mood.

Chessingham had heard the car and met us at the top of the steps. He looked pale and strained, but there was nothing in that; everyone who was in any way connected with E block had every reason for looking pale and strained that day.

"Cavell," he said. He didn't offer his hand, but opened the door wide and stood sideways to let us in. "I heard you were in Mordon. Must say I didn't expect you out here, though. I thought they asked me enough questions today, as it was."

"This is a pretty unofficial visit," I assured him. "My wife, Chessingham. When I bring along my wife, I leave the handcuffs at home."

It wasn't funny. He shook hands reluctantly with Mary and led us into an old-fashioned sitting-room with heavy Edwardian furniture, velvet drapes from ceiling to floor, and a fire burning in a huge open fireplace. There were two people sitting in high-backed armchairs by the fire. One was a good-looking young girl of nineteen or twenty, slender, brown-haired and brown-eyed like Chessingham himself. His sister. The other, obviously, was his mother, but much older than I had expected his mother to be. A closer inspection showed that she wasn't really so old, she just looked old. Her hair was white, her eyes had that curious glaze you sometimes see on old people who are coming to the end of their road, and the hands resting on her lap were thin and wrinkled and criss-crossed with blue veins. Not an old woman—a sick woman, a very sick woman, prematurely aged. But she sat very erect and there was a welcoming smile on her thin, rather aristocratic features.

"Mr. and Mrs. Cavell," Chessingham said. "You've heard me speak of Mr. Cavell. My mother, my sister Stella."

"How do you do, both of you?" Mrs. Chessingham had that assured, direct, no-nonsense voice that would have gone well with a Victorian drawing-room and a houseful of servants. She peered at Mary. "My eyes aren't what they used to be, I'm afraid—but, my goodness, you are a beautiful girl. Come and sit beside me. How on earth did you manage it, Mr. Cavell?"

"I think she must have mistaken me for someone else," I said.

"These things happen," Mrs. Chessingham said precisely. For all their age, her eyes could still twinkle. She went on: "That was a dreadful thing that happened out at Mordon today, Mr. Cavell. Dreadful. I have been hearing all about it." A pause, again the half-smile. "I hope you haven't come to take Eric to jail already, Mr. Cavell. He hasn't even had dinner yet. All this excitement, you know."

"Your son's only connection with this affair, Mrs. Chessingham, is that he is unfortunate enough to work in number one laboratory. Our only interest in him is his complete and final elimination as a suspect. Every narrowing of the field is an advancement of a kind."

"He doesn't have to be eliminated," Mrs. Chessingham said

with some asperity. "Eric has nothing to do with it. The idea is ridiculous."

"Of course. You know that, I know that, but Superintendent Hardanger, who is in charge of investigations, doesn't know that. All statements *must* be checked, no matter how unnecessary the checking. I had a great deal of difficulty in persuading the Superintendent that I should come instead of one of his own officers." I saw Mary's eyes widen, but she recovered herself quickly.

"And why did you do that, Mr. Cavell?" I was beginning to feel sorry for young Chessingham, he must have felt foolish and ineffectual with his mother taking command in this fashion.

"Because I know your son. The police don't. Saves seventy-five percent of the questioning straight away. And Special Branch detectives can ask a great number of brutal and unnecessary questions in a case like this."

"I don't doubt it. Nor do I doubt that you could be as ruthless as any man I've ever known, if the occasion arose. But I know you won't on this occasion." She sighed and shifted her hands to the arms of her chair. "I hope you will excuse me. I am an old woman and not very well, and so I have some privileges—dinner in bed is one." She turned and smiled at Mary. "I'd like to talk to you, my child. I have so few callers—I make the most of them. Would you like to help me negotiate those dreadful stairs while Stella sees to the dinner?"

When we were alone Chessingham said: "Sorry about Mother. She does tend—"

"I think she's a wonderful woman. No need to apologize." His face lightened a little at that. "About your statement. You said you were at home all night. Mother and sister will of course vouch for that?"

"Of course." He smiled. "They'd vouch for it whether I was at home or not."

"I'd be surprised if they wouldn't, after seeing them," I nodded. "Your mother could say anything, and she would be believed. Not your sister. She's young and inexperienced, and any competent policeman could break her down inside five minutes. If you were in any way involved, you're too smart not to see that, so your story has to be true. Can they vouch for the entire night—up to eleven-fifteen, say?"

"No." He frowned. "Stella went to bed about ten-thirty. After that I spent a couple of hours on the roof."

"Chessingham's observatory? I've heard of it. No one can prove you were up there?"

"No." He frowned again, thinking, "Does it matter? I haven't even a bicycle, and there's no public transport at that time of night. If I was here after ten-thirty, I couldn't have made it to Mordon by eleven-fifteen, anyway. Four and a half miles, you know."

"Do you know how the crime was carried out?" I asked. "I mean, have you heard? By someone making a diversion to allow someone else to cut through the fences? The red herring got away in a Bedford van stolen from Alfringham."

"I'd heard something like that. The police weren't very communicative, but rumors get around."

"Did you know that the van was found abandoned only one hundred and fifty yards from your house?"

"A hundred and fifty yards!" He seemed genuinely startled, then stared moodily into the fire. "That's bad, isn't it?"

"Is it?"

He thought briefly, then grinned. "I'm not as smart as you think. It's not bad, it's good. If I were driving that van, I'd have had to go to Alfringham first for it—after leaving here at ten-thirty. Also, if I were the driver, then I obviously couldn't have gone to Mordon—I'd have been making my supposed getaway. Thirdly, I wouldn't have been so damned stupid as to park it at my front door. Fourthly, I can't drive."

"That's pretty conclusive," I admitted.

"I can make it even more conclusive," he said excitedly. "Lord, I'm just not thinking at all tonight. Come up to the observatory."

We went up the stairs. We passed a door on the first floor and I could hear the subdued murmur of voices. Mrs. Chessingham and Mary talking. A Slingsby ladder led us up into a square hut affair built in the center of the flat roof. One end of the hut was blanked off with plywood, an entrance covered by a hanging curtain. At the other end was a surprisingly large reflector telescope set in a perspex cupola.

"My only hobby," Chessingham said. The strain had left his face to be replaced by the eager excitement of the enthusiast. "I'm a member of the British Astronomical Association, Jupiter Section, and a regular correspondent for a couple of astronomical journals—some of them depend almost exclusively on the work of amateurs like myself—and I can tell you that there's nothing less amateurish than an amateur astronomer who's been well and truly bitten by the bug. I wasn't in bed till almost two o'clock this morning—I was making a series of photographs for *The Astronomical Monthly* of the Red Spot in Jupiter and the satellite Io occluding its own shadow." He was smiling broadly in his relief now. "Here's their letter commissioning me to do them—they've been pleased with some other stuff I've sent in."

I glanced at the letter. It had to be genuine, of course.

"Got a set of six photographs. Beauties, too, although I say it myself. Here, I'll let you see them." He disappeared behind the curtain, which I took to be the entrance of his darkroom, and reappeared with a batch of obviously new photographs. I took them. They looked terrible to me, just a bunch of grayish dots and streaks against a fuzzily dark background. "Not bad, eh?"

"Not bad." I paused and said suddenly: "Could anyone tell from those pictures when they were taken?"

"That's why I brought you up here. Take those to the Greenwich observatory, have them work out the precise latitude and longitude of this house, and they could tell you within thirty seconds when each of those photographs were taken. Go on, take them with you."

"No, thanks." I handed back the photographs and smiled at him. "I know when I've already wasted enough time—and I've wasted far too much. Send them to *The Astronomical Monthly* with my best wishes."

We found Mary and Stella talking by the fireside. A few civilities, a polite refusal of a drink and we were on our way. Once in the car I turned the heater switch up as far as it would go, but it didn't seem to make any difference. The switch probably wasn't attached to any heater. It was bitterly cold and raining heavily. I hoped the rain would ease.

I said to Mary: "What did you find out?"

"I hate this business," she said intensely. "I hate it. This sneaking, underhanded approach to people. The lies—the lies to a lovely old person like Mrs. Chessingham. And to that nice girl. To think I worked all those years for the Superintendent and never thought—"

"I know," I said. "But you have to fight fire with fire. Think of this double murderer. Think of this man with the Satan Bug in his pocket. Think of—"

"I'm sorry. I really am sorry. It's just that I'm afraid I was never cut out to be—well, never mind. I didn't find out much. They have a maid—that's why dinner was ready shortly after Stella rose. Stella lives at home—her brother insists on it, insists she spend all her time looking after her mother. Her mother is really pretty ill, I gathered from

Stella. May go at any time—though she's been told by her doctor that a transfer to a warm climate, like Greece or Spain, might add ten years to her life. Some dangerous combination of asthma and a heart condition. But her mother doesn't want to go, says she'd rather die in Wiltshire than vegetate in Alicante. Something like that. That was all, I'm afraid."

It was enough. It was more than enough. I sat without speaking, thinking maybe the surgeons who wanted to give me a new foot had the right of it, when Mary said abruptly: "And you? Learn anything?"

I told her what had happened. At the end she said: "I heard you telling the Superintendent that you really wanted to see Chessingham to find out what you could from him about Dr. Hartnell. What did you find out?"

"Nothing. Never asked him."

"You never—why on earth not?"

I told her why not.

Dr. Hartnell and his wife—they had no children—were at home. Both of them knew Mary—we'd met socially, once, during the brief time Mary had been staying with me when I lived in Mordon—but they clearly didn't regard our visit as a social call. Everyone I was meeting was nervous, very much on the defensive. I didn't blame them. I'd have been nervous, too, if I thought someone was trying to hang a couple of murders round my neck.

I went through the spiel about how my visit was only a formality and the unpleasant experience I was sparing them by coming myself instead of letting one of Hardanger's men do the questioning. Their activities in the earlier part of the evening were of no interest to me. I asked them about the later part and they told me. At nine-thirty, they said, they had sat down to watch television—specifically, "The Golden Cavaliers," a TV version of a successful stage play that had just finished a long run in London.

"Did you see that?" Mary broke in. "So did I. Pierre was out late last night with a business friend and I turned it on. I thought it was wonderful." For some minutes they discussed the play. I knew Mary had seen it and I knew she was finding out whether they also had really seen it, and there was no question but that they had. After some time I said: "When did it finish?"

"About eleven."

"And then?"

"A quick bite of supper and bed," Hartnell said.

"By, say, eleven-thirty?"

"By that, at the latest."

"Well, that's perfectly satisfactory." I heard Mary clear her throat and looked across casually. Her steepled fingers were resting lightly in her lap. I knew what that meant—Hartnell was lying. This I couldn't understand—but I'd faith in her judgment.

I glanced at the clock. I'd asked for a call at eight-thirty and now it was exactly that. Inspector Wylie was on time. The bell rang, Hartnell spoke into the phone, then handed it to me. "For you, Cavell. The police, I think."

I spoke, holding the earpiece frantically away from my head. Wylie had a naturally carrying voice, and I'd asked him to be good and loud. He was. He said: "Cavell? Ah, you told me you were going to be there, so I took a chance. This is urgent. Nasty spot of bother at Hailem Junction. Close tie-up with Mordon, if I'm not mistaken. Very unpleasant indeed. Can you get down there immediately?"

"As soon as I can. Where's Hailem Junction?"

"Not half a mile from where you are. The bottom of the lane, turn right and pass The Green Man. Just there."

I hung up, rose and hesitated. "That was Inspector Wylie. Some trouble at Hailem Junction. I wonder if I could leave Mary here for a few minutes? The Inspector said it was something unpleasant—"

"Of course." With his alibi accepted, Dr. Hartnell was almost jovial. "We'll look after her, old man."

I parked the car a couple of hundred yards down the lane, took my torch from the glove box and turned back towards Hartnell's house. A quick look through the lit window and I knew I had nothing to fear from that quarter. Hartnell was pouring drinks and all three seemed to be talking animatedly, the way people do when the strain is off. I knew I could rely on Mary to keep them talking there indefinitely. Mrs. Hartnell, I noticed, was still sitting in the chair she'd been occupying on our arrival, she hadn't even risen to greet us. Maybe her legs were troubling her—elastic stockings aren't as undetectable as some manufacturers would like to think.

The garage was locked by a heavy padlock, but the master locksmith who had been responsible for a tiny part of the training of myself and a score of others in the now distant past would have laughed at it. I didn't laugh at it, I was no master locksmith, but even so I had it open in less than two minutes. I hardly cut myself at all.

Somewhere along the line, Hartnell's ill-advised plunge into the stock market had compelled him to sell his car and now his sole means of transport was a Vespa scooter, although I knew he used a bus to and from Mordon. The scooter was in good condition and looked as if it had been cleaned recently, but I wasn't interested in the clean parts, only the dirty ones. I examined the machine closely and finally scraped off some of the dried mud under the front mudguard and put it in a polyethylene bag, which I sealed. I spent another two minutes looking around the garage, left and locked it.

Another quick check on the living-room showed the three of them sitting round the fire, drinking and talking. I made my way to the tool shed behind the garage. Another padlock. From where I was, I was now completely hidden from the house, so I took the chance of having a good long look at the padlock. Then I picked it and went inside.

The shed was no bigger than seven-by-five and it took me no longer than ten seconds to find what I was after. There had been no attempt to conceal anything. I used another couple of polyethylene bags, closed and locked the door behind me, and made my way back to the car. Soon afterwards I parked the car in Hartnell's driveway. Hartnell answered the doorbell.

"That didn't take you long, Cavell," he said cheerfully as he led me into his lounge. "What was—" His smile died away as he saw my face. "Was there—is there something wrong?"

"I'm afraid there is, " I said coldly. "Something very far wrong. You're in trouble, Dr. Hartnell. I'm afraid it looks to me like pretty bad trouble. Would you care to tell me about it?"

"Trouble?" His face tightened, but there was the shadow of fear in his eyes. "What the devil are you talking about, Cavell?"

"Come off it," I said. "I put some value on my time if you don't yours. And it's because I refuse to waste my time that I'm not going to hunt around for any fancy gentlemanly words to express myself. To be brief and blunt, Hartnell, you're a fluent liar."

"You've gone too far, damn you, Cavell!" His face was pale, his fists were clenched, and you could see that he was actively considering having a go at me, which, as a medical man forty pounds lighter than I was, he should have recognized as an unpromising course of action. "I won't take that line of talk from any man."

"You want to switch your TV channel, you've been

watching all the wrong plays. As for that line of talk, you'll have to take it from the prosecuting counsel in the Old Bailey, so you might as well have some practice in getting used to it. If you saw 'The Golden Cavaliers' last night, as you claimed, you must have had the TV set balanced on the handlebars of your scooter. The police constable who saw you passing through Hailem late last night made no mention of a TV set."

"I assure you, Cavell, I haven't the faintest idea—"

"You make me ill," I said disgustedly. "Lies I can forgive, but stupidity in a man of your caliber, no." I looked at Mary. "About this play, 'The Golden Cavaliers'?"

She lifted her shoulders, in discomfort and distress. "All TV broadcasts in southern England were badly affected by electrical disturbances last night. There were three breakdowns in the play and it didn't finish until twenty minutes to twelve."

"You must have a very special TV set indeed," I said to Hartnell. I crossed to a magazine stand and picked up a copy of the *Radio Times*, but before I could open it, Hartnell's wife spoke, a tremor in her voice.

"You needn't bother, Mr. Cavell. Last night's play was a repeat of Sunday afternoon's. We saw the play on Sunday." She turned to her husband. "Come on Tom, you'll only make it worse for yourself."

Hartnell stared miserably at her, turned away, slumped down in a chair and drained his glass in a couple of gulps. He didn't offer me any, but I didn't add lack of hospitality to his list of faults; maybe the time wasn't right. He said: "I was out last night. I left here just after ten-thirty. I had a phone call from a man asking me to meet him in Alfringham."

"Who was the man?"

"It doesn't matter. I didn't see him—he wasn't there when I arrived."

"It wouldn't have been our old pal, Ten-percent Tuffnell of Tuffnell and Hanbury, Consultants-at-Law?"

He stared at me. "Tuffnell—do you know Tuffnell?"

"The ancient legal firm of Tuffnell and Hanbury is known to the police of a dozen counties. They style themselves 'Consultants-at-Law.' Anybody can call themselves 'Consultants-at-Law.' There's no such thing, so the bona-fide legal eagles can't take any action against them. Tuffnell's only knowledge of law comes from the fairly frequent occasions on which he's been hauled before the Assize judges, usually on charges of bribery and corruption. They're one of the biggest money-lending firms in the country, and by all odds the most ruthless."

"But how—how did you guess—"

"No guess that it was Tuffnell. A certainty. Only a man with a powerful hold over you could have got you out at that time of night, and Tuffnell has that hold. He not only holds the mortgage on your house, but also your note of hand for another five hundred pounds."

"Who told you that?" Hartnell whispered.

"No one. I found out for myself. You don't think you're employed in the laboratory with the highest security rating in Britain without our knowing everything about you. We know more about your own past than you know yourself. That's the literal truth. Tuffnell it was, eh?"

Hartnell nodded. "He told me he wanted to see me at eleven sharp. I protested, naturally, but he said that unless I did what I was told he'd not only foreclose on the mortgage, but he'd have me in the bankruptcy court for that five hundred pounds."

I shook my head. "You scientists are all the same. Outside the four walls of your lab you ought to be locked up. A man who lends you money does so at his own risk and has no legal recourse. So he wasn't there?"

"No. I waited a quarter of an hour, then went to his house—a whacking great mansion with tennis courts, swimming pool, and what have you," Hartnell said bitterly. "I thought he might have made a mistake about the meeting place. He wasn't there. There was nobody there. I went back to the Alfringham office and waited a little longer, then came home. About midnight, it was."

"Anybody see you? You see anybody? Anybody who can vouch for your story?"

"Nobody. Nobody at all. It was late at night and the roads were deserted—it was bitterly cold." He paused, then brightened. "That policeman—he saw me." His voice seemed to falter on the last words.

"If he saw you in Hailem you could equally well have turned off for Mordon after leaving it." I sighed. "Besides, there was no policeman. You're not the only one who tells lies. So you see the spot you're in, Hartnell? A phone call for which we have only your word—no trace of the man alleged to have made it. Sixteen miles on your scooter, including a wait in a normally busy little town—and not a living soul saw you. Finally, you're deeply and desperately in debt—so desperate that you would be willing to do anything. Even break into Mordon, if the financial inducements were high enough."

He was silent for a moment, then pushed himself wearily to his feet. "I'm completely innocent, Cavell. But I see how it is—and I'm not all that a fool. So I'm going to be—what do you call it—detained in custody?"

I said: "What do you think, Mrs. Hartnell?"

She gave me a troubled half-smile and said hesitantly: "I don't think so. I—well, I don't know how a police officer talks to a man he's about to arrest for murder, but you don't talk the way I should imagine they do."

I said dryly: "Maybe you should be working in number one lab instead of your husband. As an alibi, Hartnell, your story is too ridiculously feeble for words. Nobody in their right minds would believe it for an instant, which means maybe that I'm not in my right mind. I believe it."

Hartnell exhaled a long sigh of relief, but his wife said with a strange mixture of hesitancy and shrewdness: "It could be a trap. You could think Tom guilty and be lulling him into—"

"Mrs. Hartnell," I said. "With respects, you are abysmally ignorant of the facts as they appertain to the wilds of Wiltshire. Your husband may think no one saw him, but I can assure you that the way between here and Alfringham is alive with people between ten-thirty and eleven p.m.—courting couples, gentlemen between pubs and homes upending their last bottles to prepare themselves for wifely wrath, old ladies and some not so old peering out between not-quite-closed curtains. With a squad of detectives, I could turn up a score of people by noon tomorrow—I'll wager a dozen Alfringham citizens saw Dr. Hartnell waiting outside Tuffnell's office last night. I'm not even going to bother finding out."

Mrs. Hartnell said softly: "He means it, Tom."

"I mean it. Somebody is trying to divert suspicion to you, Hartnell. I want you to remain at home for the next two days—I'll fix it at Mordon. You're to talk to no one—no one—during that time. Take to your bed if you have to, but talk to no one. Your absence from work, your indisposition will be thought peculiar in the circumstances and will make somebody think our suspicions are directed towards you. You understand?"

"Completely. I'm sorry I was such a fool, Cavell, but—"

"I wasn't very nice myself. Goodnight."

In the car, Mary said wonderingly: "What on earth is happening to the legendary Cavell toughness?"

"I don't know. Tell me."

"You didn't have to tell him that he wasn't under suspicion. After he'd told his story you could have just said nothing and let him carry on his work as usual. A man like that would be incapable of hiding the fact that he was worried to death, and that would have suited your purpose of making the real murderer think we're on to Hartnell just as well. But you couldn't do it, could you?"

"I wasn't like this before I got married. I'm a ruined man. Besides, if Hartnell really knew the evidence against him, he'd go off his rocker."

She was silent for some time. She was sitting on my left-hand side and I can't see people who are sitting to my left, but I knew she was staring up at me. Finally, she said: "I don't understand."

"I have three polyethylene bags in the rear seat. In one of them is a sample of dried red mud. Hartnell invariably takes the bus to work—but I found that mud, a peculiar reddish loam, under the front mudguard of his scooter, and the only place for miles around with that type of soil is a couple of fields near the main gates of Mordon. In the second bag is a hammer I found in his tool shed—it looks clean, but I'm betting that a couple of gray hairs sticking to the haft came from our canine pal, Rollo, who was so grievously clouted last night. The third bag contains a pair of heavily insulated pliers. They've been perfectly cleaned, but a comparison by electronic microscope of some scratches on them and the broken ends of the barbed wire in Mordon should give some very interesting results."

"You found all that?" she whispered.

"I found all that. Near-genius, I would say."

"You're worried to death, aren't you?" Mary asked. I made no reply, and she went on: "Even with all that, you still don't think he's guilty? I mean, that anyone should go to such lengths—"

"Hartnell's innocent. Of the killing, anyway. Someone picked the lock of his tool shed last night. Unmistakable scratches, if you know what to look for."

"Then why did you remove—"

"Two reasons. Because there are some policemen in this island who have been so rigidly indoctrinated with the belief that two and two must inevitably make four that they wouldn't think twice of bypassing the Old Bailey and dragging Hartnell to the nearest old oak tree. The red mud, hammer and pliers, together with Paul Revere's moonlight ride—it's pretty damning."

"But—but you said yourself that if he had been out last night there would have been witnesses—"

"Eyewash. I called Dr. Hartnell a fluent liar, but he isn't in my class. At night all cats are gray. During the dark any motorcyclist with heavy coat, crash helmet and goggles looks pretty much like any other motorcyclist with heavy coat, crash helmet and goggles. But I didn't see that there was anything to be gained by worrying Hartnell and his wife to death; if there was, I wouldn't have hesitated. Not with this madman running around with the Satan Bug. Besides, I want Hartnell *not* to be worried."

"What on earth do you mean?"

"I don't rightly know," I confessed. "Hartnell wouldn't kill a fly. But Hartnell is mixed up in something very fishy indeed."

"What makes you say that? You said he's clear. Why—"

"I told you I don't know," I said irritably. "Call it a hunch, call it something the subconscious mind cottoned onto and hasn't yet got around to transferring to some place where I'll recognize it. Anyway, my second reason for filching exhibits A, B, and C is that whoever planted the goods on Hartnell and started him on this wild-goose chase is going to be more than a little worried himself now. If the police either cleared Hartnell or clapped him in the hoosegow, our friend would know where he stood. But with Hartnell mysteriously and suspiciously remaining at home, and the police at the same time making no mention of having found exhibits A, B and C, the killer's going to be kept wondering just what the cops are up to. Indecision. Indecision hampers action, and hampering action buys time. We need all the time we can get."

"You have a low and devious mind, Pierre Cavell," Mary said at length, "but I think that if I were innocent of a crime and the evidence proved beyond any doubt that I was guilty, I'd rather have you investigating my case than anyone alive. By the same token, if I were guilty of a crime and there was no possibility of any evidence pointing to me, I'd rather have anyone else in the world except you investigating it. Or so my father says, and he should know. I know you'll find this man, Pierre."

I wished I could even begin to share her conviction. But I couldn't even begin. I was sure of nothing, nothing at all, except that Hartnell wasn't the blue-eyed innocent he appeared, nor his good wife, and that my leg was aching pretty fiercely. I wasn't looking forward very much to the remainder of that night.

We were back in the Waggoner's Rest just before ten o'clock. Hardanger was waiting for us in a deserted corner of the lounge, along with a dark-suited, unknown man who turned out to be a police stenographer. The Superintendent was studying some papers and scowling away into the middle distance from time to time, but the craggy face broke into a beam of pleasure when he looked up and saw us. Mary, rather. He was genuinely fond of her and found it difficult to understand why she had thrown herself away on me.

I let them talk for a minute or two, looking at Mary's face and listening to her voice and wishing vaguely for the hundredth time that I had tape and film to record the soft, lilting cadences of her voice and its fascinating shift and play of expression, in case the day should ever come when that would be all I would have left of her. Then I cleared my throat to remind them that I was still there. Hardanger looked at me, touched an internal switch, and the smile vanished.

"Turn up anything startling?" he asked.

"In a way. The hammer that laid out the Alsatian guard dog, the pliers that cut the wire, and apparent proof that Dr. Hartnell's scooter was in the vicinity of Mordon last night."

He didn't bat an eyelid. He said: "Let's go up to your room." We went, and once there Hardanger said to the man accompanying him: "Johnson, your notebook," and to me: "From the beginning, Cavell."

I told him everything that had happened that night exactly as it had been, omitting only what Mary had learned from Chessingham's mother and sister. At the end, Hardanger said: "You are convinced that it's a frame-up on Hartnell?"

"Looks like it, doesn't it?"

"Hadn't it occurred to you that there might be a double twist to this? That Hartnell planted it on himself?"

"Yes. But it's hardly possible. I know Hartnell. Outside his work he's blundering, nervous, unstable, and an ass—hardly the basic material for a ruthless, calculating criminal. And he'd hardly go the length of picking his own padlock. Anyway, it doesn't matter. I've told him to stay at home, meantime. Whoever stole the botulinus and the Satan Bug did so for a purpose. Inspector Wylie's pretty keen to get into the act. Let him have his men keep a round-the-clock watch on the house to see that Hartnell stays put. Hartnell, even if guilty, wouldn't be so mad as to keep the viruses in the house. If they're elsewhere and he can't get at them, that's one worry less. I also want a check made on his supposed scooter trip of last night."

"There'll be a watch kept and made," Hardanger promised. "Chessingham tip you off in any way about Hartnell?"

"Nothing useful. Just my own hunch. Hartnell was the only person I knew of in number one lab in a position to be blackmailed or coerced. The point is that someone else knows it, too. He also knew that Tuffnell was away from home. That other man is the man we want. How did *he* find out?"

"How did *you* find out?" Hardanger demanded.

"Tuffnell himself told me. I was here for a fortnight, some months ago, helping Derry check on a bunch of newly arrived scientists. I asked him to give me the names of all Mordon employees who were coming to him for financial assistance. Hartnell is only one of a dozen."

"Did you ask or demand?"

"Demanded."

"You know that's illegal," Hardanger said heavily. "On what grounds?"

"On the grounds that if he didn't, I'd enough information to put him behind bars for years to come."

"Had you that information?"

"No. But a shady character like Tuffnell has always a great deal to hide. He co-operated. Tuffnell may have talked about Hartnell. Or his partner, Hanbury."

"How about other members of his staff?"

"There are none. Not even a typist. In a business like that, you can't trust your own mother. Apart from them, Cliveden, Weybridge—possibly—Clandon, and myself knew. And Easton Derry, of course. No one else had access to the security files in Mordon. Derry and Clandon are gone. How about Cliveden?"

"That's ridiculous. He was at a War Office meeting till after midnight last night. In London."

"What's ridiculous about Cliveden having this information and passing it on to someone else?" Hardanger was silent, and I went on: "And Weybridge. What was *he* doing at zero hour last night?"

"Asleep."

"Who told you? Himself?" Hardanger nodded, and I went on: "Corroboration?"

Hardanger looked uncomfortable. "He lives alone in the officers' block. He's a widower with an orderly to look after him."

"That helps. How about the other check?"

"Seven others," Hardanger said. "One, as you said it would be, was a night guard. Been there only two days—and his transfer was a complete surprise to him. Sent from his regiment to take the place of a sick guard. Dr. Gregori was at home all night—he lives in a kind of high-class boarding-house outside Alfringham, and half a dozen people will swear he was there until at least midnight. That lets him out. Dr. MacDonald was at home with friends. Very respectable friends. Playing cards. Two of the technicians, Verity and Heath, were at the dance in Alfringham last night. They seem in the clear. The other two, Robinson and Marsh, were out on a double date with their girl friends. Cinema, café, then back to their homes."

"So you've turned up nothing at all?"

"Not a damn thing."

"But how about the two technicians and their girl friends?" Mary asked. "Robinson and Marsh—they provide each other's alibis. And there *was* a girl used as a decoy."

"Nothing there," I said. "Whoever is responsible for this lot is far too smart to fall into the elementary error of self-supporting alibis. If either of the two girls were strangers to these parts there might just possibly be something in it. But if Robinson and Marsh haven't changed their girl friends since the last time we checked on them, then they're just a couple of harmless local girls. The Superintendent here would have had the truth out of them in five minutes flat. Probably two."

"Two it was," Hardanger agreed. "Nothing there. We've sent all their footwear to the lab for a check—that fine red loam soil gets into the tiniest cracks and would be a dead giveaway—but it's purely routine. Nothing will come of it. You want a copy of all those statements and witnesses' reports?"

"Please. What's your next move?"

"What would yours be?" Hardanger countered.

"I'd have Tuffnell, Hanbury, Cliveden and Weybridge questioned, to see if they've ever spoken to anyone about Hartnell's financial difficulties. Then I'd have Gregori, MacDonald, Hartnell, Chessingham, Cliveden, Weybridge and the four technicians questioned—separately, of course—about the extent of their social life with the others. Whether they had ever been in one another's homes is a question that might be tossed in casually. And I'd have fingerprint squads move into all their houses at the same time to print as much of every house as possible. You'd have no trouble getting warrants for that little lot. If X maintains he's never been in Y's home, and you find prints proving him a liar—well, someone is going to have some interesting explaining to do."

"Including General Cliveden's and Colonel Weybridge's homes?" Hardanger asked grimly.

"I don't care whose feelings are wounded. This is no time to consider anyone's hurt pride."

"It's a long, long shot," Hardanger said. "Criminals with something to hide, particularly the connection between them, would never meet in each other's homes anyway."

"Can you afford to ignore even such a long shot?"

"Probably not," Hardanger said. "Probably not."

Twenty minutes after their departure with the polyethylene bags, I climbed out the window, clambered to the ground via the porch, picked up my car where I'd left it parked in a side street, and set off for London.

CHAPTER 6

It was exactly half-past two in the morning when I was shown into the library of the General's West End flat. The General welcomed me in a red quilted dressing gown and waved me to a seat. He hadn't been to bed—I could see that—the dressing gown meant nothing, he invariably wore it inside the house.

Six-feet-three and built to match, the General would never see seventy again, but his back was as straight, his complexion as fresh, and his eye as clear as of a man thirty years his junior. He had thick, iron-gray hair, an iron-gray, trimmed moustache, gray eyes, and the cleverest brain of any man I'd ever met. I could see he'd been doing some thinking with this brain and wasn't any too pleased with the conclusions he'd arrived at.

"Well, Cavell." His voice was clipped, incisive, vaguely military. "You've made a pretty mess of things."

"Yes, sir." He was the only man in the world who rated a 'sir' from me.

"One of my best operatives, Neil Clandon, is dead. Another as good, Easton Derry, is probably also dead, though only listed missing. Dr. Baxter, a great scientist and a great patriot—and how badly we need both—is dead. Whose fault, Cavell?"

"Mine." I looked at a convenient decanter. "I could do with a drink, sir."

"There rarely has been a time when you couldn't," he said acidly, and then, just one degree less acidic, "leg acting up?"

"A little. Sorry about this hour of the night, sir. It was essential. How do you want it—the story?"

"Straight, quick, and from the beginning."

"Hardanger turned up at nine a.m. Sent in an Inspector Martin, heavily disguised as God knows what, to test my loyalty first. I suppose you thought that one up, too. You might have warned me."

"I tried to," he said impatiently. "I was too late. The news of Clandon's death reached General Cliveden and Hardanger before it did me; I rang you up, but both your home and office phones were out of order."

"Hardanger did that," I nodded. "Anyway, I passed the test. Hardanger was satisfied and asked me to come to Mordon. Said he'd suggested it to you and you'd been reluctant. It must have taken quite a bit of doing to suggest something to Hardanger and leave him with the impression that he'd thought it up himself."

"It was. Never underestimate Hardanger. An outstanding policeman. He has no suspicions? You're sure?"

"That this was a put-up job? That it was you who engineered me out of the Special Branch and into Mordon, and then out of Mordon again? He has no suspicions. I guarantee."

"Right. The story."

I didn't waste words. That was one of the very first things an agent learned about the General—never to waste words with him. In ten minutes he'd all the relevant facts, and he'd never forget one of them.

"Almost word for word with Hardanger's reports that have already been filed with me through official channels," he commented. "Almost, I said. Good policemen concentrate only on relevancies. Your conclusions, Cavell?"

"What about the investigation I asked to be made down in Kent, sir?"

"Negative." I swallowed some more whisky. I needed it.

"Hardanger suspects Dr. Baxter to be a case of the biter bit," I said. "You know that already—he phoned asking for a security check on Baxter. He suspects that Dr. Baxter, probably accompanied by another man, broke into Mordon, and that thieves fell out, as a result of which Dr. Baxter met his death at the hands of his fellow breaker and enterer, an action that may have been either spur-of-the-moment or premeditated. What Hardanger doesn't know is that it was Dr. Baxter who first reported to Easton Derry, directly and privately, that minute amounts of rare and valuable viruses were disappearing from Mordon and asked for an investigation—or that it was Baxter who, as a result of our requests, had me removed from Mordon so that I could carry on investigations in London under cover of a private detective's business.

"Hardanger is wrong on both counts. Dr. Baxter didn't break into Mordon that night for the sufficient reason that he hadn't left it earlier that evening. The man behind this killing—a man working with a considerable organization, I should say—has kidnapped the children of Bryson and Chipperfield, the farm managers. The fact that the kids are not where their parents say they are, with their grandmother in Kent, is all the proof I want. Bryson and Chipperfield were given their choice—co-operation or two dead children. They co-operated. They carried crates of animals into number one lab on the afternoon of the killings. They were old regulars—the guards would never have thought of inspecting the crates. Inside two of those crates were two men fairly skillfully made up to resemble Dr. Baxter and someone we can call X.

"Eight crates were carried in that afternoon, and Bryson and Chipperfield followed their usual practice of not disturbing the lab work too much by bringing in all the crates first and leaving them in the corridor, just outside the lab, before carrying them all in. This, of course, is conclusive proof of highly detailed inside information. While the crates were there, one of the men inside—the one disguised as X—nipped smartly out into the adjoining cloakroom used by the scientists and technicians in number one. He probably hid in a locker. The other man—the one disguised as Baxter—was carried into the animal room. A dozen places where a man could hide there.

"Our inquiries show that the scientists and technicians drifted off singly that evening—they usually did. One of them —X—takes his chance of going into a momentarily empty cloakroom and changes over places with the impostor, to whom he hands his security tag. The fake X now leaves by the main gate, handing in his tag and forging the name. It was a pitch-dark night, and he'd only be one of hundreds crowding out. He was pretty safe.

"X goes back into the lab when the coast is clear and sticks a gun into Baxter. More likely this has already been done by the man dressed to impersonate Baxter. Anyway, it doesn't matter. Baxter was always the last to leave; he was responsible for setting the combination, and so they nailed him. By and by impostor B takes off and hands in Baxter's card at the gate.

"X, of course, can't just pocket the viruses, knock off Baxter and remove himself. As far as the gate guard is concerned, X has already checked out. He can't check out a second time. He knows it won't be safe to move until the last of the security rounds have been finished at eleven p.m. He waits till then, takes the viruses, belts Baxter over the head with his gun-butt and leaves, throwing a virus toxin at the unconscious man. He has to kill Baxter, because Baxter knew who he was. He didn't know, as we did, that Clandon was keeping a binocular watch every night on the corridor in E block, but it's highly likely that he suspected he might. He's not the man who would leave anything to chance. He must have known that this was the one possibility that might upset his plans. Hence the cyanide sweet. When Clandon came up after X had shut the door, X must have spun some yarn and got Clandon to accept the sweet. He obviously knew Clandon well, and Clandon knew him."

The General rubbed his moustache thoughtfully. "Ingenious, if nothing else. Basically, you must be right. But there's something wrong about that cyanide business. Far wrong. Clandon was looking for a man who had been stealing virus supplies, and he *must* have suspected that X was the man. I just don't see Clandon accepting this butterscotch. Besides, X was carrying a gun, probably silenced. Why not that? Why the cyanide?"

"I don't know, sir." I felt like adding that I hadn't been there.

"How did you get on to this in the first place?"

"The dog, sir. It had a couple of barbed-wire tears in its throat. It seemed likely that there might be blood on the wire itself. There was. It took me an hour to find it. On the inner wire. No one broke into Mordon that night: someone broke out."

"Why didn't Hardanger discover this?"

"He'd no reason to suspect what I did. I *knew* that Baxter hadn't broken in, and a check with the gate guard showed that Baxter had his face covered with a handkerchief and talked thickly through a cold when he left. That was enough.

Besides, Hardanger's men did get around to examining the wires. They concentrated on the outside one for an hour or so, and then moved to the inner fence."

"And found nothing?"

"There was nothing to find. I'd removed the blood."

"You're an unethical devil, Cavell."

"Yes, sir." That was good, coming from him. "Then a visit to Bryson and Chipperfield. A couple of steady, reliable characters—drinking like fish at five-thirty in the afternoon and spilling it when they poured. Mrs. Bryson smoking like a factory chimney—she's never smoked in her life. General air of quiet desperation, well concealed. But all very obvious."

"Suspects?"

"There's General Cliveden and Colonel Weybridge. Cliveden was in London at the time of the killing, but although he's only been in Mordon two or three times since taking over, he has two things against him. He has access to the security files and may have known of Hartnell's financial troubles—and it was strange that such a gallant soldier didn't volunteer to go into the lab instead of me. It was his place, not mine—he bosses Mordon."

"The two words 'gallant' and 'soldier' are not necessarily synonymous," the General said dryly. "Remember he's a doctor, not a fighting man."

"That's so. I also remember that two of the handful of double V.C.'s ever won were won by doctors. It doesn't matter. Same two arguments apply to Weybridge, with the additional two factors that he lives on the premises and has no alibi. Gregori, because he was too insistent, for what I regarded as insufficient reasons, to have the place sealed off for keeps. But the fact of the insistence itself, being so obvious, may remove suspicion, as does the fact that the virus locker door was opened by a key—and Gregori had what was thought to be the only key. What do we really know about Gregori, sir?"

"The lot. Every step he's taken from the cradle. The fact that he's not a British national made his screening twice as intensive as normal. That's from our side. Before he came here, he was doing highly secret work in Turin for the Italian government, and you can imagine the thorough going-over Gregori got from them. He's absolutely in the clear."

"Which should make me pretty reluctant to waste time on him. Only trouble is, judging from past records, everyone else seems in the clear also. Anyway, these are the first three suspects—and I think Hardanger is beginning to have ideas about one or more of these three."

"The ideas he got from you, eh?"

"I don't like it, sir. I don't like it because Hardanger is as straight as they come, and it goes against the grain to operate behind his back. I don't like saying or doing things which amount to deliberately misleading and deceiving him. And I don't like it because Hardanger is very smart indeed, and to keep him from tumbling to me I've got to devote almost as much time to keeping Hardanger reasonably satisfied as to investigating the case itself."

"Don't think I like it either," the General said heavily. "But it has to be. We're up against clever and determined men whose main weapons are secrecy, cunning and—"

"And violence."

"All right, then. Secrecy, cunning and violence. We must meet and destroy them on their chosen ground. I must employ the best weapon that comes to my hand. I know of no man who could, or would, presume to instruct you in any of those three. Secrecy. Cunning. Violence."

"I haven't been very cunning so far."

"You haven't," the General admitted. "On the other hand, when I said to you that you'd made a mess of things, I was being less than fair. The initiative invariably rests with the criminal. Anyway, what matters is that you are essentially a loner, a one-man band, while Hardanger is just as essentially an organization man. With an organization comes delegation of authority, dispersal of concentration, blunting of initiative, and lowered secrecy—and any and all of those mitigate against the chances of final success. Nevertheless, the organization is indispensable to you; it carries out all the groundwork and routine investigation that you couldn't possibly do yourself, and diverts attention and suspicion from yourself. As long as Hardanger, unwittingly or no, misleads the killer or killers as to the direction the inquiry is taking—well, that's all I want out of him."

"He's not going to like it when he finds out, sir."

"If he finds out, Cavell. And that's for me to worry about. Other suspects?"

"The four technicians. Barely possible. All of them were seen moving around during the evening at one time or another, and on the assumption that the killer was holed up in the lab between six and eleven o'clock, that lets them out. As far as the murders were concerned. Hardanger is carrying out a minute-by-minute check of their late-evening movements—one of them *might* have been the decoy. So might a thousand others—the decoy doesn't necessarily have anything to do with number one lab. Hartnell would appear to be in the clear—his alibi is so hopeless that it would seem to have to be genuine—but for all that, I have a feeling that there's something queer going on there and I'll be calling on him again.

"Then there's Chessingham—a very big question mark. As an assistant research chemist, his salary is no shakes—but it seems he can afford to run a big house, have a maid, and keep his sister at home to look after his mother. The maid's been there only two months. His mother, incidentally, is in a very bad way from a health viewpoint. Her doctor says that a shift to a warmer climate might add years to her life. She herself maintains that she doesn't want this shift, but that's probably only because she doesn't want to embarrass her son who she knows can't afford it. Maybe Chessingham would like the money to send her abroad. I'm sure, in fact. They're a pretty close family. I don't want Hardanger on this. Can you arrange to have Chessingham's bank account checked, a monitoring watch kept on all incoming and outgoing mail, a check made with local authorities to see whether a driving license has ever been issued in his name, a check made with the army unit in which he did his National Service to see if he ever drove a vehicle, and finally, a check on all the local money-lenders to see if Chessingham's on their books. He's certainly not with Tuffnell and Hanbury, the biggest sharks in the area, but there are a dozen others within twenty miles—and Chessingham never strays far from home. He may be borrowing money by mail from some London firm."

"Is that all you want?" The General was heavily ironic.

"I think it essential, sir."

"Is it? How about this excellent alibi he provided—the pictures of the transit of Jupiter or whatever it was—that could prove his presence at home down to a second, more or less. Don't you believe it?"

"I believe those pictures would show exactly when they were taken. I don't necessarily believe that Chessingham was there when they were taken. He's not only a fine scientist but an uncommonly clever lad with his hands. He built his own camera, radio, and TV set. He built his own reflector telescope, even hand-grinding the lenses. It would be no great trick for Chessingham to rig up a mechanism to take pictures automatically at pre-selected intervals. Or someone could have done it for him while he was elsewhere. Or the photographs themselves could have been taken elsewhere with a corresponding time allowance made for longitude differences, so as to give the same effect. And Chessingham's far too intelligent a bird not to have spotted right away that those photographs would have provided an alibi—yet he pretended that it only occurred to him while I was talking to him. He'd have thought it would have been too obvious and suspicious if it had all been cut and dried in advance."

"You wouldn't trust St. Peter himself, would you, Cavell?"

"I might. If there were sufficient independent witnesses to testify to any alibi he might have, that is. Giving anyone even the faintest shadow of the benefit of the doubt is the one luxury I can't afford. You know that, sir. And Chessingham isn't getting that shadow. Nor is Hartnell."

"Hmm." He peered at me from under the tufted gray of his eyebrows and said inconsequentially: "Easton Derry vanished because he played it too close to the cuff. I wonder how much *you* are holding back from me, Cavell?"

"What makes you say that, sir?"

"God knows, I'm a fool to ask you. As if you'd tell me, anyway." He poured a whisky for himself, but placed it on the mantelshelf without tasting it. "What's behind all this, my boy?"

"Blackmail. Of one kind or another. Our friend with the Satan Bug and botulinus virus in his pants pocket has the finest blackmail weapon in history. He's probably after money—very large sums of money. If the Government wants back the bugs, it'll cost them a fortune. Additional blackmail is that if the Government doesn't come across, he'll sell the bugs to a foreign power. At least, that's what I hope. What I'm afraid of is that we're dealing not with a criminal but a crackpot mind. Don't tell me that a crackpot couldn't have organized all this—some crackpots are brilliant. If it is a crackpot, it'll be one of the 'Mankind must abolish war or war will abolish mankind' brigade. In this case the threat would be on a smaller scale—you know, 'Britain must abolish Mordon or I'll abolish Britain.' That sort of thing. Probably a letter in the post right now to one of the big national dailies telling them he has the viruses and what he intends doing with them."

The General picked up his whisky glass and stared down into it with all the rapt attention of a soothsayer looking for an answer in his crystal ball. "What makes you think that? About the letter, I mean?"

"He'd have to, sir. Pressure is the essence of blackmail.

Our friend with the viruses must have the publicity. A terrified population—and how right they would be to be terrified—would bring such terrific pressure to bear that the Government would have to accede to any demands made upon them, or go out of office at once."

"Where were you between five minutes to ten and ten o'clock tonight?" he asked abruptly.

"Where was I—" I looked at him, long hard stare for long hard stare, then went on slowly: "In the Waggoner's Rest, in Alfringham. Speaking to Mary, Hardanger, and a plainclothes constable by the name of Johnston."

"I'm getting old, or senile, or both." The General shook his head irritably, then lifted a sheet of paper from the mantelshelf and handed it to me. "You'd better read this, Pierre." The 'Pierre' made it very bad indeed—and it was very, very bad indeed. It couldn't have been worse. A Reuter's dispatch-sheet, the message in typed capitals.

"Mankind must abolish war or war will abolish mankind," the typescript began. "It is now in my power to abolish the most dreadful form of war this world has ever known or ever will know—bacteriological warfare. I have in my possession eight ampoules of botulinus toxin which I took from the Mordon Research Establishment, near Alfringham, Wiltshire, twenty-four hours ago. I regret that two men were killed last night, but have no deep sorrow: what are two lives, when the lives of all mankind are at stake?

"The contents of any one of these ampoules, suitably dispersed, could destroy all life in Britain. I shall fight fire with fire, and destroy evil by the forces of evil.

"Mordon must cease to exist. That stronghold of the Antichrist must be utterly razed so that no stone be left standing. I order that all experiments in Mordon cease forthwith, and that the buildings in which this evil work is carried out be dynamited and bulldozed to rubble.

"You will broadcast acknowledgment and compliance on the B.B.C. news at 9 a.m. tomorrow morning.

"If I am disregarded, I shall be compelled to take steps the effects of which I dare not contemplate. But those steps I shall take. It is the wish of One who is greater than all that war upon earth shall cease forever, and I am His chosen instrument.

"Mankind must be saved from mankind."

I read through it again and laid the sheet down. This was the real McCoy—no one outside Mordon knew that eight ampoules had been stolen. The General said: "Well? Well?"

"A nut," I said. "Completely off his trolley. Mind you, he has a rather nifty line in prose."

"Good God, Cavell!" The General's face was set in hard lines, the cold, gray eyes angry. "A communication like that, and all you can do is—is to make feeble—"

"What do you want me to do, sir? Get out the sackcloth and ashes? Sure, it's terrible—but we were expecting it—or something like it. If ever there was a time to use our heads and not our hearts—well, this is the time."

"You're right." The voice was a sigh. "Of course you're right. And damnably accurate in your forecast!"

"This came by phone call from Alfringham? Between five to ten and ten o'clock tonight?"

"Sorry about that, too. I'm even ready to suspect myself. The message came to Reuter's in London. Dictated at slow speed. Reuter's thought it a hoax, but telephoned Alfringham just in case. The news of the theft and murders hasn't been officially released yet—typical army stupidity, for half of Wiltshire knew about the murders hours ago and so does Fleet Street. All Reuter's got was a denial, but the reaction to their questions convinced them that they were onto something very hot indeed. For two hours, believe it or not, they argued back and forth as to whether or not this item should be released to the press. The decision not to communicate came from the very top. They notified Scotland Yard, who notified me. By that time it was well after midnight. This is the original copy. A crackpot, you think?"

"A screw or two loose, but all the rest of his mental machinery is working just fine. He knows he has to have publicity to generate sufficient terror to bring pressure to bear, and to generate even more terror he gives the impression that he doesn't know that three of the eight ampoules in his possession contain the Satan Bug. If the public really thought he had the Satan Bug and might use it by mistake, they'd scream for him to be given anything on earth, just so long as he returned it."

"He may not *know* it is the Satan Bug." I'd never seen the General like this before, hesitant and uncertain under the grimly worried mask. "We can't assume he does."

"I can. He knows. Whoever it is, he knows. You're going to keep this out of the papers?"

"It'll buy us time. He must have publicity, as you say."

"How about the actual crime itself? The break-in, the murders?"

"It'll be in every paper in the country tomorrow—it's

already on the streets. Local Wiltshire correspondents got the tip-off early this evening. After that, there was nothing we could do about it."

"The reaction of the populace should be interesting." I finished my whisky and rose. "I'll be getting back, sir."

"What are you going to do?"

"I'll tell you, sir. I should start on Bryson and Chipperfield, but I'd be wasting my time. They won't speak; they'll be too terrified for their kids' lives, and besides, I'm convinced they wouldn't have seen either the man who gave the orders or the men they carried inside. I'm going to start over again with the number one lab people. A couple of phone calls to Cliveden and Weybridge. Hinting darkly, trying to provoke a reaction. Then a visit to Chessingham, Hartnell, MacDonald, Gregori, and the technicians. Nothing smart or sophisticated or clever. Put the wind up, suggesting I know more than I do. All I want is a basis for one tiny suspicion of any of them, and I'll take him into a deserted cellar and take him apart till I have all the truth."

"What if you're wrong about him?" The General seemed to be staring fixedly at a point just over my shoulder.

"I'll put him together again. If I can," I added indifferently.

"We have never operated in that way, Cavell."

"We've never had a lunatic with the power to wipe us all out, either."

"That's so, that's so." He shook his head. "Who's going to be the first object of your attentions?"

"Dr. MacDonald."

"MacDonald. Why MacDonald?"

"Doesn't it strike you as curious, sir, that of all the major dramatis personae, the *only* one without a shadow of suspicion against him is Dr. MacDonald? I find that very interesting. Maybe he forgot to frame himself when he was so busy framing everybody else, planting suspicion away from himself. This is an uncommonly dirty world, and I automatically suspect those as pure as the driven snow."

The General gazed at me in a long silence, then glanced at his watch. "You might just manage a couple of hours' sleep when you get back."

"I'll get all the sleep I want when I get the Satan Bug back."

"A man can go only so long without sleep, Cavell." The tone was very dry.

"It won't take me long, sir. My promise. I'll have the Satan Bug back in Mordon in thirty-six hours."

"Thirty-six hours!" A long, considering pause. "With any other man I'd laugh in his face. I've learned not to laugh in yours. But—thirty-six hours!" He shook his head: the General had been brought up in the old school, and he was too polite to tell me that I was a fool or a braggart or a liar, or all three. "The Satan Bug, you say. How about—how about the murderer?"

"Recovering the viruses is all that matters. Whether the killer is himself killed or handed over to the cops doesn't seem that important. Let him look out for himself."

"I'm more worried about you looking out for yourself. Be very careful, Cavell—a hard thought for you to take, but he may be a cleverer and more dangerous man than yourself." He reached out and touched me gently below the left shoulder. "I suppose you wear that Hanyatti in bed at night. You know you have no authority from me to use it?"

"I point it at people just to frighten them, sir."

"Giving people heart attacks doesn't come under the heading of frightening them. I won't detain you, boy. How's Mary?"

"Well, sir. She sent her love."

"From Alfringham, of course." He forgot for a moment that I was about his only subordinate who didn't curl up under his level stare, and let me have it with both barrels. "I'm not sure I like my daughter—my only child—being mixed up with something like this."

"I needed—I still need—someone I can trust. That's Mary. You know your own daughter as well as I do; she hates the business we're in, but the more she hates it the more impossible it is to keep her out of it. She thinks I shouldn't be allowed out alone. She'd have been down in Alfringham within twenty-four hours anyway."

The General looked at me for a moment, then nodded heavily and showed me to the door.

CHAPTER 7

Dr. MacDonald was a big, heavily built man in his late forties, with that well-weathered and spuriously tough look you quite often find among a certain section of the unemployed landed gentry who spend a great deal of time in the open air—much of it mounted on large horses in pursuit of small foxes. He had sandy hair, sandy eyebrows, a sandy moustache, and the smooth, full, tight, reddish-tanned face indicative of a devotion to the table, a well-stocked cellar, a fresh Gillette every morning, and an incipient heart condition. In his own rather arrogant and fleshy way, MacDonald was a pretty good-looking and impressive character, but at that moment he wasn't looking his best. Not that anyone would be when rubbing sleep from gummed eyelids and welcoming the unexpected caller at six-fifteen on a pitch-dark, raining and bitterly cold October pre-dawn.

Welcoming, perhaps, was not the right word.

"What the bloody hell do you mean by coming hammering on my door in the middle of the bloody night?" MacDonald demanded. He clutched a dressing gown more tightly about his shivering bulk and managed to prop an eye wide enough open to identify me in the faint wash of light coming from the porchway behind him. "Cavell! What the devil's the meaning of this?"

"I'm sorry, MacDonald." Civility. Turning the other cheek. "Terrible hour, I know. But I must talk to you. It's most urgent."

"Nothing's so damn urgent that you have to come hauling a man out of his bed at this time of night," he said furiously. "I've already told the police all I know. Anything you want, you can see me about in Mordon. Sorry, Cavell. Goodnight! Or good morning!" He took a long step back and swung the door in my face.

I'd no more cheeks to turn. The sole of my right foot caught the door before it engaged on the latch, and I kicked it open. Violently. The sudden transfer of weight to my bad leg didn't do my left foot any good at all, but it was nothing compared to what it did to MacDonald's right elbow which was where the flying door must have caught, for when I passed inside he was clutching his elbow with his left hand and doing a dervish dance, with language suitably geared to the occasion; he'd packed in the plummy *Debrett* accent in favor of broad Scots. For what he had to say, it was much more impressive. It was ten seconds before he was properly aware that I was standing there.

"Get out!" The voice was half-snarl, half-shout, the face twisted in malevolence. "Out of my house at once, you—" He got started in on my forebears, but I cut him short.

"Two men are dead, MacDonald. There's a madman on the loose with the power to turn that two into two million.

Two thousand million. Your convenience doesn't enter into it. I want answers to questions. I want them now."

"*You* want them? And who are *you* to want anything?" The heavy lips were curled into an expression that was half-sneer, half-grimace of pain, and the Oxford drawl was working again. "I know all about you, Cavell. Kicked out of Mordon because you couldn't keep your big mouth shut. You're only a so-called private detective, but I suppose you thought there might be better pickings going here than in the dirty little divorce cases you people specialize in. God knows how you managed to push your way into this, but as far as I am concerned you can push straight out again. You have no authority to ask me anything. You're not the police. Where are your credentials? Show me." To say that he was making no attempt to mask the sneer on his face or the contempt in his voice would have been understating the case.

I hadn't any credentials to show him, so I showed him the Hanyatti instead. It might be enough—bluster is usually a façade that conceals nothing. But it wasn't enough. Maybe there was more to Dr. MacDonald than I had thought.

"My God!" He laughed, not one of those laughs with a silvery tinkle of bells. An unpleasant laugh. "Guns! At six in the morning. Whatever next? Cheap melodramatic rubbish. I've got your number now, Cavell, by God, I have. A little ring to Superintendent Hardanger will soon fix you, mister cheap little private detective." Outside the demands of his job he was obviously no stickler for accuracy; cheap I may have been, but I was a good couple of inches taller than he was and at least as heavy.

The phone was on the table beside me. He took two steps towards it and I took one towards him. The muzzle of the Hanyatti caught him just under the breastbone and I stood aside as he jack-knifed and fell to the floor. It was brutal, high-handed, completely unjustifiable on the face of it and I didn't like it one little bit; but I liked even less the idea of a madman with the Satan Bug in his possession. I had to use every second I had. By and by, when it was all over, I'd apologize to MacDonald. But not now.

He rolled around for a bit, clutching his midriff with both hands and whooping in pain as he tried to drag air into his lungs. After a minute or so, he quietened down and struggled to his feet, still clutching his stomach, breathing very quickly, very shallowly, like someone who can't get oxygen enough quickly enough. His face was gray and puffy, and the bloodshot eyes held an expression that was pretty close to hatred. I didn't blame him any.

"This is the end of the road for you, Cavell." His voice came in hoarse gasps punctuated by half-sobbing inhalations. "You've gone too far this time. Unprovoked assault—"

He broke off, flinching; he saw the barrel of the Hanyatti arcing towards his face. Both hands were flung up in instinctive self-defense and he grunted in agony as my free hand caught him in the midriff again. He stayed down longer this time and when he finally dragged himself, trembling, to his feet, he was in pretty bad shape. His eyes were still burning mad, but there was something else in them now as well. Fear. I took two quick steps towards him, lifting the Hanyatti high. MacDonald took two corresponding steps back, then collapsed heavily on a settee as it caught him behind the knees. His face held rage and bewilderment, and fear, lest I hit him again; it also held hatred for both of us—for me because I was doing what I was doing, for himself because he knew he was going to do what I said. MacDonald wasn't ready to talk, but he was going to all the same and both of us knew it.

"Where were you on the night Baxter and Clandon were killed?" I asked. I remained on my feet, the Hanyatti ready.

"Hardanger has my statement," he said sullenly. "At home. I'd had three friends in for bridge. Until almost midnight."

"Friends?"

"A retired scientific colleague. The local doctor and vicar. Good enough for you, Cavell?" Maybe he was getting some of his courage back.

"Nobody more skilled at murder than doctors. And priests have been unfrocked before." I looked down at my feet, at the smooth gray sweep of wall-to-wall carpeting: if a man dropped his diamond tie-pin in that nap he'd have to call in a tracker dog. I said with no particular inflection: "Fancy line in floor coverings you have here, Doctor. Five hundred quid wouldn't have bought this little lot."

"Being clever, or just insolent, Cavell?" He *was* getting his courage back. I hoped he wasn't going to be so foolish as to get too much of it back.

"Heavy silk drapes," I went on. "Period furniture. Genuine crystal chandelier. A pretty big house, and I'd wager the whole house is furnished on the same scale. The same expensive scale. Where does the money come from, Doctor? You do the pools? Or just a bingo expert?"

For a moment he looked as if he were about to tell me to mind my own damn business, so I half lifted the Hanyatti again, not much, just enough to make him change his mind. He said stiffly: "I'm a bachelor with no dependents. I can afford to indulge my tastes."

"Lucky you. Where were you last night between nine and eleven p.m?"

He frowned and said: "At home."

"Are you sure?"

"Of course I'm sure." Apparently he'd decided that stiff indignation was his safest line.

"Witnesses?"

"I was alone."

"All night?"

"All night. My housekeeper arrives at eight each morning."

"That may be very unfortunate for you. No witnesses for last night, I mean."

"What the devil are you trying to tell me?" He seemed genuinely puzzled.

"You'll know soon enough. You don't run a car, do you, Doctor?"

"As it happens, I do."

"But you come to Mordon on an army bus."

"I prefer it that way. It's no concern of yours."

"True. What kind of car?"

"A sports car."

"What kind of sports car?"

"A Bentley Continental."

"A Continental. A sports car." I gave him a long look, but it was wasted. He was staring down at the carpet, maybe he *had* lost a diamond tie-pin there. "Your taste in cars is like your taste in rugs."

"It's an old car. Second-hand."

"When did you buy it?"

He looked up abruptly. "What does it matter? What are you trying to get at, Cavell?"

"When did you buy it?"

"Ten weeks ago." He was giving the carpet the once-over again. "Maybe three months ago."

"An old car, you say. How old?"

"Four years."

"Four years. They don't give away four-year old Continentals for box-tops. They give them away for about five thousand pounds. Where did you get five thousand pounds from three months ago?"

"I didn't. I paid one thousand pounds down. The rest over three years. It's the way most people buy their cars, you know."

"An extended credit scheme aimed at capital conservation. That's for people like you. For people like me, they call it hire-purchase. Let's see your hire-purchase agreement."

He brought it: a quick glance showed that he had been speaking the truth. I said: "What's your salary, Dr. MacDonald?"

"Just over two thousand pounds. The Government is not generous." He wasn't blustering or indignant any more. I wondered why.

"So that after taxation and living expenses, you couldn't possibly have as much as a thousand left at the end of the year. In three years, three thousand pounds. Yet, according to this agreement, you're going to pay off close to four thousand five hundred pounds—balance plus interest—in three years. How do you propose to accomplish this mathematical impossibility?"

"I have two insurance policies maturing inside the next year. I'll get them for you."

"Don't bother. Tell me, Doctor, why are you so worried, so nervous?"

"I'm not worried."

"Don't lie."

"All right, so I'm lying. I am worried. I am nervous. The questions you are asking would make anyone nervous."

Maybe he was right, at that. I said: "Why should they make you worried, Doctor?"

"Why? He asks me why." He glared up at me, then went back to looking for his diamond pin. "Because I don't like the trend of your questioning. I don't like what you're trying to prove. No man would."

"What *am* I trying to prove?"

"I don't know." He shook his head, not looking up. "You're trying to establish that I live beyond my means. I don't. I don't know what you're trying to prove."

I said: "You've got the old tartan eyes this morning, Doctor, and if you don't mind me saying so, you stink of stale whisky. You have all the signs of a man who had a heavy session with the bottle last night and is paying the price now—not, I suppose, that a couple of belts on the solar plexus improved matters. Funny thing is, you're listed on our books as a moderate social drinker. You're no alcoholic. But you were alone last night—and social drinkers don't drink alone. That's why they're social. But you were drinking alone, last night—drinking heavily, Doctor. I wonder why? Worried, perhaps? Worried even before Cavell and his worrisome questions ever came along?"

"I usually have a nightcap before retiring," he said defensively. He was still staring at the carpet, but his interest lay not in any tie-pin, but in not letting me see the expressions on his face. "*That* doesn't make me an alcoholic. What's a nightcap?"

"Or two," I agreed. "But when a nightcap turns out to be the better part of a bottle of whisky, it ceases to be a nightcap." I glanced round the room, then said: "Where's your kitchen?"

"What do you—"

"Damn it, don't waste my time!"

"Through there."

I left the room and found myself in one of those gleaming stainless steel montrosities that started out to be an operating theater and changed its mind at the last moment. More evidence of money. And on the gleaming sink, more evidence that Dr. MacDonald really had had an extended nightcap. A bottle of whisky, three-fifths empty, with the torn lead seal still lying beside it. An ashtray, full of mashed-up cigarettes. I turned as I heard a sound behind me. MacDonald was standing in the doorway.

"All right," he said wearily. "So I was drinking. I was at it for two or three hours. I'm not used to those things, Cavell. I'm not a policeman. Or a soldier. Two horrible, ghastly murders." He half shuddered; if it was acting, it was brilliant acting. "Baxter had been one of my best friends for years. And *why* was he killed? How do I know the killer hasn't another victim lined up? And I *know* what this Satan Bug can do. Good God, man, I'd reason to be worried. Worried stiff."

"So you had," I agreed. "So you still have—even although I *am* getting pretty close to him. And maybe he *is* after you next—the killer, I mean. It's a thought to bear in mind."

"You cold-hearted callous devil," he ground out. "In God's name, get and leave me alone."

"I'm just going. Keep your doors locked, Doctor."

"You're going to hear more of this, Cavell." Now that I'd announced my intention of leaving and had stuck the Hanyatti out of sight, he was recovering courage. "We'll see if you're so damned tough when you're up in court on an assault charge."

"Don't talk rubbish," I said shortly. "I never laid a finger on you. There's no mark on you. It's only your word against mine. Me, I'd take mine first any time."

I left the house. I saw the dark bulk of the garage where the Bentley was presumably housed, but I didn't give it a second glance or thought. When people want a nice, inconspicuous, unobtrusive car for a stealthy and unobtrusive mission, they don't go around borrowing Bentley Continentals.

I stopped at a phone box, and on the pretext of wanting Gregori's address, made two unnecessary calls—to Weybridge first, who couldn't, as I knew he couldn't, help me, and to Cliveden, who could and did. They were both pretty shirty about being disturbed at the crack of dawn, but quietened down when I told them that I had to have the information immediately because my investigations had now reached such a critical stage that I might have the case tied up before the day was out. Both of them tried to question me on the progress I was making, but I gave nothing away. That didn't take much finesse, for I'd nothing to give away in any event.

At seven-fifteen a.m. I was leaning on the doorbell of Dr. Gregori's house, more precisely the house in which he lived, a good-class boardinghouse run by a widow and her two daughters. Parked outside in front was a navy-blue Fiat 2100. Gregori's car. It was still pitch-dark, still cold and wet. I felt very tired, and my leg ached badly so that I had difficulty in concentrating on what had to be done.

The door opened and a plump woman, gray-haired and fiftyish, peered out into the darkness. This would be the landlady herself, Mrs. Whithorn, reputedly a cheerful and happy-go-lucky soul, of devastating untidiness and unpunctuality whose boardinghouse was the most sought-after in the area; her reputation as a cook was enviable.

"Who on earth is it at this time of morning?" Her voice held a good-natured exasperation. "Not the police again, I hope?

"I'm afraid so, Mrs. Whithorn. Cavell is my name. I'd like to see Dr. Gregori, please."

"Poor Dr. Gregori. He's already put up with enough from you people. But I suppose you'd better come in. I'll go and see if he's up yet."

"Just tell me where his room is and I'll find out for myself. If you please, Mrs. Whithorn."

She demurred a bit, then reluctantly told me where to find him. Five yards along the big hall, down a side passage, and I was outside his door—his name was on it. I knocked and waited.

I didn't have to wait long. Gregori must have been up, but only just. He wore a faded russet dressing gown over his pyjamas, and his swarthy face was swarthier than ever—he evidently hadn't yet got round to shaving.

"Cavell," he said. There was no particular warmth of welcome in his voice—people greeting the law at dawn are seldom in the most amiable frame of mind—but at least, unlike MacDonald, he was civil. "You'd better come in. And have a seat. You look worn out."

I felt worn out. I eased myself into the offered chair and looked around. Gregori didn't do himself as well as MacDonald in the way of furniture, but then it probably wasn't his furniture in the first place. The room I was in was furnished as a small study—his bedroom would be through the communication door in the far wall. A worn but still serviceable carpet, a couple of armchairs in the same category, one wall completely lined with bookcases, a heavy oak table with swivel chair, a typewriter and piled-up papers, and that was about it. In the stone hearth were the remains of last night's fire: smooth white ash, such as you get from burning beech. The room, though cold, was rather stuffy—Gregori had obviously not as yet succumbed to the English madness of flinging open windows under any and all conditions—and I seemed to smell some peculiar odor in the air, so faint as to be unidentifiable.

"If I can be of any help to you, Mr. Cavell?" Gregori prompted.

"Just routine inquiries, Dr. Gregori," I said easily. "Most uncivilized hour, I know, but we feel that time is not on our side."

"You have not been to bed?" he said shrewdly.

"Not yet. I've been busy—visiting. I'm afraid my choice of visiting hours doesn't make me very popular. I've just come from Dr. MacDonald, and I'm afraid he wasn't at all pleased to be dragged from his bed."

"No? Dr. MacDonald," Gregori said delicately, "is a somewhat impatient man."

"You get on well with him? On friendly terms?"

"A colleague, shall we say? I respect his work. Why, Mr. Cavell?"

"Incurable nosiness. Tell me, Doctor, have you an alibi for last night?"

"Of course." He looked puzzled. "I told it to Mr. Hardanger, in person. From eight until almost midnight I was at the birthday party for Mrs. Whithorn's daughter——"

"Sorry," I interrupted. "*Last* night—not the night before."

"Aha." He looked at me anxiously. "There have been—there have been no more killings?"

"No more," I reassured him. "Well, Doctor?"

"Last night?" He half smiled and shrugged. "An alibi? Had I known that an alibi would be required of me, I would not have failed to provide one. At what time, exactly, Mr. Cavell?"

"Let us say between nine-thirty and ten-thirty p.m."

"Alas, no. No alibi, I fear. I was in my room here, working all night on my book. Work therapy, you might call it, Mr. Cavell, after the dreadful experience of yesterday." He paused, then went on apologetically, "Well, not all night. From after dinner—about eight—till eleven. It was a good night for me in the circumstances—three whole pages." He smiled again, diffidently. "For the type of book I'm writing, Mr. Cavell, a page an hour represents excellent progress."

"And what type of book is that?"

"On inorganic chemistry." He shook his head and added wistfully: "It is unlikely that the citizens will be besieging the bookshops in order to buy it. The reading public for my speciality is limited indeed."

"That the book?" I nodded at the pile of papers on the desk.

"It is. One I began in Turin, more years ago than I care to remember. Examine it if you wish, Mr. Cavell. Not, I fear, that it would convey much to you. Apart from the rather abstruse nature of the subject-matter, it is in Italian—the language I prefer for writing."

I didn't tell him that I could read Italian almost as well as he spoke English. Instead I said: "You type directly onto paper?"

"But of course. My handwriting is that of the true scientist—almost completely indecipherable. But a moment!" He rubbed a thoughtful palm across a blue and bristly chin. "The typewriter. It may have been heard."

"That's why I asked. You think it likely?"

"I don't know. My rooms were specially chosen because of

my typing—must not disturb the other guests, you understand. There are no bedrooms either above or on either side of me. Wait now, yes, yes, I'm almost certain I heard a television program next door. At least," more doubtfully, "I think I did. Next door is what Mrs. Whithorn rather grandly calls her television lounge, but it is very poorly patronized, I fear—chiefly by Mrs. Whithorn herself and her daughters, and that not frequently. But I'm sure I heard something. Well, almost sure. Shall we ask?"

We asked. We went along to the kitchen where Mrs. Whithorn and one of her daughters were preparing breakfast. The aroma of sizzling bacon made my left leg feel weaker than ever.

One minute was enough. An hour-long vintage film had been shown on television the previous evening, and Mrs. Whithorn and two of her three daughters had watched the entire performance. The film had started precisely at ten, and as they passed Dr. Gregori's door into the lounge and after that had sat down, they could hear him typing on his machine. Not loud, not loud enough to be annoying, but perfectly distinct. Mrs. Whithorn had commented at the time that it was a shame Dr. Gregori should have so little time for leisure and relaxation, but she knew he would be eager to make up for the time lost at her daughter's party, his first night off for weeks.

Dr. Gregori made no attempt to hide his satisfaction.

"I'm very much indebted to this elderly film shown last night. And to you, Mrs. Whithorn." He smiled at me. "Your suspicions at rest, Mr. Cavell?"

"I never had any, Doctor. But that's how policemen must work—by the elimination of even the most remote possibilities."

Dr. Gregori saw me to the front door. It was still dark, still cold, still very wet indeed. The rain was bouncing high off the tarmac road. I was considering how best to introduce my now standard spiel about the remarkable progress I was making, when Gregori himself said suddenly: "I am not asking you to betray any professional confidences, Mr. Cavell, but well, do you think there is a chance that you'll get this fiend? Are you making any progress at all?"

"More than I would have thought possible twelve hours ago. Investigations have led me pretty far in what I believe to be the right direction. Very far, I might say, if it weren't for the fact that I'm up against a brick wall."

"Walls can be climbed, Mr. Cavell."

"So they can. And this one will be." I paused. "I don't know whether I should have said what I did. But I know you will keep it strictly to yourself."

He gave me his earnest reassurances on that point and we parted. Half a mile away I stopped at the first call-box and got through to London.

"Been to bed yet, Cavell?" the General greeted me.

"No, sir."

"Don't feel too badly about it. Neither have I. I've been very busy, indeed, making myself unpopular by dragging people out of their beds in the middle of the night."

"No more unpopular than I've made myself, sir."

"I daresay. With any results?"

"Nothing special. Yourself, sir?"

"Chessingham. No record of a civilian driving license having been issued to him at any time. This may not be definite— it may have been issued to him in some place other than his own country, although this would be unusual. As for his army record, it turns out, strangely enough, that he was in the R.A.S.C."

"The R.A.S.C.? Then the chances are that he did have a license. Did you find out, sir?"

"The only fact that I have been able to establish about Chessingham's army career," the General said dryly, "is that he actually was in the Army. The wheels of the War Office grind uncommonly slow at any time, but in the middle of the night they grind to a dead halt. We may have something by midday. What we do have now are some rather interesting figures supplied us less than half an hour ago by Chessingham's bank manager."

He gave me the figures and hung up. I climbed wearily into the car once more and headed for Chessingham's house. Fifteen minutes' drive and I was there. In the bleak half-light of dawn, the square-built house with its sunken basement looked more dreary and forbidding than ever. The way I was feeling didn't help matters any. I squelched my way up the flight of worn steps over the moat and pressed the bell.

Stella Chessingham appeared. She was neatly and attractively dressed in a flowered housecoat, and her hair was smoothly brushed, but her face was pale and the brown eyes were tired. She didn't look very happy when I told her I wanted to see her brother.

"I suppose you'd better come in," she said reluctantly. "Mother's still in bed. Eric's at breakfast."

He was. Bacon and eggs again. My leg felt weaker than

ever. Chessingham rose to his feet and said nervously: "Good morning, Mr. Cavell."

I didn't wish him a good morning back. I gave him my cold, impersonal stare—the kind only policemen and head waiters are allowed to use—and said: "I have to ask some more questions, Chessingham. I've been up all night and I'm in no mood for evasions. Straight answers to straight questions. Our investigations during the night have opened up some very interesting lines of inquiry and the main line leads straight here." I looked at his sister. "Miss Chessingham, I have no wish to distress you unnecessarily. It might be better if I interviewed your brother alone."

She looked at me with wide-open eyes, licked her lips nervously, nodded and turned to go. Chessingham said: "Stay here, Stella. I have nothing to hide from anybody. My sister knows everthing about me, Mr. Cavell."

"I wouldn't be so sure about that." The voice to match the stare. "If you wish to stay, Miss Chessingham, you may. Please remember afterwards that I asked you to go." Both were pale now, and very apprehensive indeed. On the basis of my ability to terrify people, I could have had a job with any Central European Secret Police at any time.

I said: "What were you doing last night, Chessingham? Round about ten o'clock, shall we say?"

"Last night?" He blinked. "Why do I have to account for my movements for last night?"

"The questions come from me. Please give an answer."

"I—well, I was at home. With Stella and Mother."

"All night?"

"Of course."

"There's no 'of course.' No visitors, no outsiders to testify to your presence here?"

"Just Stella and Mother."

"Just Miss Chessingham. At ten o'clock your mother would be in bed."

"Yes, in bed. I'd forgotten."

"I'm not surprised. Forgetting is your strong line. You forgot to tell me last night that you had been in the R.A.S.C."

"The R.A.S.C.?" He sat down at the table again, not to eat, and from the slight movements of his arms I could tell that one hand was gripping the other pretty strongly. "Yes, that's right. How did you know that?"

"A little bird told me. The same bird also told me that he had seen you driving an army vehicle." I was sticking my neck out, but I'd no option. Time was not on our side. "You said you couldn't drive."

"I can't." His eyes flickered to his sister, then back at me. "There's a mistake. Someone is making a mistake."

"That's you, Chessingham—if you keep denying it. What if I can produce four independent witnesses by nightfall who will swear to it that they have seen you driving."

"I may have tried once or twice. I'm—I'm not sure. I haven't a driving license."

"You make me sick," I said in disgust. "You're speaking and behaving like a moron. You're no moron, Chessingham. Stop beating about the bush and making a fool of yourself. You can drive. Admit it. Miss Chessingham, your brother can drive, can't he?"

"Leave Stella alone." Chessingham's voice was high, his face pale. "You're right, damn you, I can drive—after a fashion."

"I suppose you thought it very clever to abandon that Bedford van outside your house two nights ago? On the assumption that the police would never believe anyone capable of doing anything so obvious?"

"I was never near that van." His voice was almost a shout. "I swear it! I swear I was never near that van. I got frightened when you came round last night, and I said anything I could to—to strengthen my innocence."

"Innocence." I laughed my nasty policeman's laugh. "The photographs of Jupiter that you *said* you took. How did you take them? Or did someone else take them? Or did you rig up an apparatus to take the pictures automatically while you were away at Mordon?"

"What in the name of God are you talking about?" He was getting frantic. "Apparatus? What damned apparatus? Search the house from top to bottom and see if you can find—"

"Don't be so naïve," I interrupted. "Probably buried deep in the woods anywhere within fifty square miles of here."

"Mr. Cavell!" Stella Chessingham stood in front of me, her hands so tight that they were shaking, her face mad. "You're making a mistake, a terrible mistake. Eric has nothing to do with—with whatever it is. This murder. Nothing, I tell you! I *know*."

"Were *you* with him after half-past ten, the night before last? In his observatory? If you weren't, young lady, you don't know."

"I know Eric! I know he's completely incapable of—"

"Character testimonials are no good to me," I said

brusquely. "And if you know so much, perhaps you can explain to me how one thousand pounds comes to have been deposited in your brother's bank account in the past four months? Five hundred pounds on July third, the same on October third. Can you explain?"

They looked at each other, sick fear in their eyes and making no attempt to conceal it. When Chessingham managed to speak, on his second or third attempt, his voice was hoarse and shaking.

"It's a frame-up! Someone is trying to frame me."

"Shut up and talk sense," I said wearily. "Where did the money come from, Chessingham?"

He paused for a moment before replying, then said miserably: "From Uncle George." His voice had dropped almost to a whisper and he was glancing apprehensively ceilingwards.

"Decent of Uncle George," I said heavily. "Who's he?"

"Mother's brother." His tone was still low. "The black sheep of the family, or so it seems. He said he was completely innocent of the crimes with which he had been charged, but that the evidence against him had been so overwhelming that he'd fled the country."

I glared at him. Double talk at eight a.m. after a sleepless night wasn't much in my line. "What are you talking about? What crimes?"

"I don't know." Chessingham sounded desperate. "We've never seen him—he's phoned me twice at Mordon. Mother has never mentioned him—we didn't even know he existed until recently."

"You knew about this, too?" I asked Stella.

"Of course I did."

"Your mother?"

"Of course not," Chessingham said. "I told you, she never even mentioned his existence. Whatever he was accused of, it must have been something pretty bad. He said that if Mother knew where the money came from, she'd call it tainted and refuse it. We—Stella and I—want to send her abroad for her health and that money is going to help."

"It's going to help you up the steps of the Old Bailey," I said roughly. "Where was your mother born?"

"Alfringham." It was Stella who answered; Chessingham didn't seem capable of it.

"Maiden name?"

"Jane Barclay."

"Where's your phone? I'd like to use it."

She told me and I went out to the hall and put a call through to the General. Almost fifteen minutes elapsed before I returned to the breakfast room. Neither of the two appeared to have moved from the positions in which I left them.

"My God, you're a bright pair," I said wonderingly. "It would never have occurred to you, of course, to pay a visit to Somerset House. What would be the point? You knew you would be wasting your time. Uncle George never existed. Your mother never had a brother. Not that that will be news to you. Come on now, Chessingham, you've had time to think up a better explanation than that one. You couldn't possibly think up a worse one to account for the thousand pounds."

He couldn't think one up at all. He stared at me, his face grimly hopeless, then at his sister, then at the ground. I said encouragingly: "Well, there's no rush about it. You'll have a few weeks to think up a better story. Meantime, I want to see your mother."

"Leave my mother out of this, damn you." Chessingham had risen to his feet with such violence that his chair had gone over backwards. "My mother's a sick woman and an old one. Leave her alone, you hear, Cavell?"

I said to Stella: "Please go and tell your mother I'm coming up in a minute."

Chessingham started toward me, but his sister got in the way. "Don't, Eric. Please." She gave me a look that should have pinned me to the wall, and said bitterly: "Don't you see that Mr. Cavell is a man who always gets his own way?"

I got my own way. The interview with Mrs. Chessingham took no more than ten minutes. It wasn't just the most pleasant ten minutes of my life.

When I came downstairs, both Chessingham and his sister were waiting in the hall. Stella came up to me, big brown eyes swimming in a pale and frightened face, and said desperately: "You're making a fearful mistake, Mr. Cavell, a terrible mistake. Eric is my brother. I know him, I *know* him. I swear to you that he is completely innocent in everything."

"He'll have his chance to prove it." There were times when I didn't find any great difficulty in hating myself, and this was one of those times. "Chessingham, you would be wise to pack a case. Enough stuff to last you for a few days, at least."

"You're taking me with you?" He looked resigned, hopeless.

"I've neither the warrant nor the authority for that. Somebody will come, never fear. Don't be so silly as to try to run. A mouse couldn't get through the cordon round this house."

"A—a cordon?" He stared. "You mean there are policemen round—"

"Think we want you to take the first plane out of the country?" I asked. "Like dear old Uncle George?" It was a good enough exit line and I left it at that.

The Hartnells were to be my next—and last—call before breakfast that morning. Halfway there I pulled up at an A.A. box on a deserted wooded stretch of road, unlocked the booth and put a call through to the Waggoner's Rest. By and by Mary came on the phone, and after she'd asked me how I felt and I'd said fine and she'd more or less called me a liar, I told her I would be back in the hotel shortly after nine o'clock, to have breakfast ready for me, and to ask Hardanger to come round if he could.

I left the phone booth, and although my car was only a few yards away, I didn't dawdle any in reaching it—the cold gray rain was still sheeting down. For all my haste, though, I suddenly stopped with the door half-open and stared through the rain at a character coming down the road towards me. From a distance of less than a hundred yards he appeared to be a middle-aged, well-dressed citizen, wearing a raincoat and trilby, but there all resemblance to a normal human being ended. He was making his way down the rain-filled gutter by hopping around on his right foot, arms outstretched to balance himself, kicking a rusty tin can ahead of him. With every combined hop-and-kick, a gout of water went spraying up in the air.

I watched this performance for some time until I became conscious of the rain drumming heavily on my back and soaking through to my shoulders. Besides, even if he had escaped over a high wall, it was still rude to stare. Maybe if I were buried long enough in the wilds of Wiltshire, I, too, would take to playing hopscotch in the rain. Still with my eye on this apparition, I eased quickly into the driver's seat, pulling the door to behind me, and it was not until then that I discovered that the purpose of the hopscotch merchant was not to demonstrate the standard of loopiness in rural Wiltshire but to distract my attention from the back of my car where someone had been hiding crouched down on the floor.

I heard the slight noise behind me and started to twist, but

I was far too late; the blackjack must have been chopping down even as I heard the sound. My left foot was still on the wrong side of the steering column, and anyway, he was on my left or blind side. The blackjack made contact just below and behind my left ear with what must have been considerable force or accuracy, or both, for the agony and the oblivion were separated by only a hairsbreadth in time.

CHAPTER 8

It wouldn't be accurate to say that I woke up. The term "waking up" implies a fairly rapid and one-way transition from a state of unconsciousness to that of consciousness, and there was nothing either rapid or one-way about my progress through the twilit zone that separates those. One moment I was grayly aware that I was lying on something hard and wet, the next the awareness was gone. How long a time elapsed between the intervals of grayness I'd no means of knowing, and even if I had, my mind would have been too fuzzy to appreciate it. Gradually the spells of awareness became longer and longer, until eventually there was no more darkness, but I wasn't at all sure that this was in any way an improvement or a desirable state of affairs, for with returning comprehension come an all but paralyzing pain that seemed to hold my head, my neck and the right-hand side of my chest in an immense vise, a vise with some burly character inexorably tightening the handle. I felt the way a grain of wheat must feel after it has passed through a combined harvester.

Painfully I opened my good eye and swiveled it around until I located the source of the dim light. A grilled window high up on the one wall, just below the roof. I was in a cellar of some kind, of the semi-sunk basement type featured in Chessingham's house.

I'd made no mistake about the hardness of the floor. Or the wetness. Rough, unfinished concrete, with shallow pools of water on it, and whoever had left me there had thoughtfully dumped me right in the center of the largest puddle.

I was lying stretched out on the floor, partly on my back, partly on my right-hand side, with my arms behind my back in a ridiculously strained and uncomfortable position. I wondered vaguely why I chose to lie in this awkward position and found out when I tried to change it. Somebody had made a very efficient job of tying my hands behind my back, and from the numbness in my forearms it was a fair guess that he'd used considerable weight in the tying of the knots.

I made to gather my legs under me to jerk myself up to a sitting position, and discovered that they wouldn't gather. I just couldn't move them. I used their immobility to lever myself upwards to a sitting position, waited until the coruscating lights dancing before my eyes faded and vanished, then peered forward and down. My legs were not only tied at the ankles, they were secured to the metal upright in a wine bin, which took up practically the entire length of the wall beneath the window. And not only was I tied, but I was tied with PVC plastic flex. If I'd needed any confirmation that a professional had been at work, I didn't any more. Even a gorilla couldn't snap PVC, and nothing less than a pair of hefty pliers could possibly undo the knots—fingers were quite useless for the job.

Slowly, carefully—any rash movement and my head would have fallen off—I looked around the cellar. It was as featureless and just about as empty as any cellar could ever be: the window, the closed door, the wine bin and me. It could have been worse. No one pouring in water to drown me, no one flooding the confined space with a lethal gas, no snakes, no black widow spiders. Just the cellar and me. But bad enough.

I hitched myself forwards towards the wine bin and tried to snap the wire securing me to it by jerking my legs back as violently as I could, but all I did was add another pain to the overfull quota I had already. I struggled to free my hands, knowing before I began that I was only wasting my time, and gave up almost as soon as I had started. I wondered how long it would be before I died of starvation or thirst.

Take it easy, I said to myself. Think your way out of this, Cavell. So I thought, as best I could with my head hurting the way it did, but it didn't seem to do much good; all I could think of was how sore and uncomfortable I was.

It was then that I saw the Hanyatti. I blinked, shook my head and cautiously looked again. No doubt about it, the Hanyatti, the top of the butt just visible three or four inches below and to the side of the left-hand lapel of my coat. I stared at it and it still didn't go away. I wondered dimly how the man—men, certainly—who had dragged me there had missed it, and it slowly came to me that they had missed it because they hadn't looked for it in the first place. Policemen in Britain don't carry guns. I was—more or less—a policeman. Hence I didn't carry a gun.

I hunched up my left shoulder and reached my head as far down and to the left as possible, at the same time pushing the lapel away with the side of my face. On the third try I got my teeth to the butt, but they just slipped off the rounded surface when I tried to get a purchase and lift the gun from its holster. Four times I repeated this maneuver, and after the fourth attempt I gave up. Contorting my neck into that strained and unnatural position would have been uncomfortable enough in any event; added to the effects of the blackjack the only result of this contortion was to make the cellar swim dizzily around me. At the same time the maneuver brought a sharply piercing pain to my right chest, and I wondered drearily whether any of my ribs had been broken and were sticking into a lung. The way I felt, I was prepared to believe anything.

A brief rest, then I had twisted up until I was in a kneeling position. I bent sharply from the waist, my head coming close to the concrete floor to give gravity an assist in freeing the Hanyatti from the holster. Nothing happened. I tried again, overdid the violence of the forward jerk and fell flat on my face. When my head finally cleared, I repeated the process and this time the gun slid from the holster and clattered to the floor.

In the poor half-light of the cellar I knelt and peered anxiously at the gun. A character with a sadistic enough turn of mind might have considered it highly amusing to empty the gun and replace it in the holster. But I'd been spared the humorist. The loading indicator registered nine. The magazine was full.

I squirmed round on the floor, picked up the Hanyatti with my bound hands, slipped the safety catch, and dragged the gun around to my right side as far as the unnaturally twisted position of my left shoulder would allow. The folds of my jacket kept getting in the way of the automatic, but I strained and pushed until I could see about three inches of the barrel protruding beyond my side. I bent my knees and hitched myself forward until my feet were within fifteen inches of the muzzle.

For a brief moment I considered trying to shoot through the PVC that bound my ankles. But only for a brief moment. Buffalo Bill might have done it, but then Buffalo Bill had had binocular vision and I felt pretty certain he'd never performed any of his sharpshooting feats in dim half-light with numbed hands bound behind his back. The chances were a thousand-to-one that the net result achieved would be the anticipation of those two London surgeons who wanted to remove my left foot. I decided to concentrate instead on the eighteen-inch length of four twisted strands of PVC that attached my legs to the wine bin.

I sighted as best I could and squeezed the trigger. Three things happened, instantaneously and simultaneously. The recoil from the gun, together with the unnatural position in which I was holding it, made me feel as if my right thumb had broken; the reverberation of sound in that confined space had the same effect on my eardrums, and I felt a wind ruffle my hair as the ricocheting bullet, soundless in flight in that echoing intensity of sound, came within half an inch of ending my problems for good and all. And a fourth thing happened. I missed.

Two seconds later I fired again. No hesitation. If there was a watchdog upstairs taking his ease, he'd be charging down the cellar steps in a matter of moments to find out who was breaking up his happy home. Not only that, but I knew if I stopped to consider the chances of the ricochet being that half-inch lower this time, I never would get around to pulling that trigger.

Again the close thunder of the explosion, and this time I was sure that my right thumb had gone. But I hardly cared. The wire binding me to the wine bin was neatly severed in half. Buffalo Bill couldn't have done it any better.

I twisted, grabbed one of the wine bin supports with my all but useless hands, hoisted myself shakily to my feet, rested my left elbow on a convenient shelf and stood there waiting, staring at the door. Anyone coming to investigate would have to pass through that door, and as a target, a man at six feet was going to be a much simpler proposition altogether than a wire at eighteen inches.

For a whole minute I stood there, motionless apart from the trembling of my legs, straining to the utmost what little the gunshots had left me of my hearing. Nothing. I risked a couple of quick hops out to the center of the cellar and peered up through the high window in case my jailer was playing it careful and smart. Again nothing. Another couple of hops and I was by the door, testing the handle with my elbow. Locked.

I turned my back on the door, scrabbled around with the muzzle of the Hanyatti until I'd found the lock, and pulled the trigger. With the second shot, the door gave abruptly beneath my weight—it says much for my state of mind that I'd never even checked the positioning of the hinges to see whether the door opened inwards or outwards—and I fell heavily through the doorway onto the concrete passageway outside. If there was anyone waiting out there with the hopeful intention of clobbering me, he'd never have a better chance.

No one clobbered me because there was no one waiting there to clobber me. Dazed and sick, I pushed myself wearily to my feet, located a light switch and clicked it with my shoulder. The naked bulb, hanging at the end of a short flex above my head, remained dead. It could be a dud lamp, it could be a blown fuse, but my guess was that it meant no power at all: the air in that cellar had the musty lifelessness that bespoke long abandonment by whoever had once owned the house.

A flight of worn stone steps stretched up into the gloom. I hopped up the first two steps, teetered on the point of imbalance like a spinning top coming to rest, but managed to twist round quickly and sit down before I toppled. Once down, it seemed the safe and prudent thing to do to keep my center of gravity as low as possible by staying there, and I made it to the top of the stairs by jack-knifing upwards on the seat of my pants and the soles of my shoes.

The door at the head of the cellar stairs was also locked, but it wasn't my door and I still had five shots left in the Hanyatti. The lock gave at the first shot and I stumbled out into the hallway beyond.

The hallway, high, wide and narrow, featured what estate agents euphemistically call a wealth of exposed timbering—black, ugly, adze-cut oaken beams everywhere. Two doors on either side, both closed, a glass door at the far end, another beside me leading presumably to the rear of the house, a staircase above my head and an uneven parquet floor, thickly covered with a dust streaked by the confused tracks of footprints leading from the glass door to the spot where I was standing. The finest feature of the hall was the fact that it was completely deserted. I knew now I was alone. But for how long I didn't know. It seemed a poor idea to waste even a second.

I didn't want to smear the tracks in the hall, so I turned to the door beside me. For a change it was unlocked. I passed into another passage that gave on the domestic quarters—larder, pantry, kitchen, scullery. An old-fashioned house and a big one.

I went through those apartments, opening cupboards and

pulling drawers out onto the floor, but I was wasting my time. No signs here of hasty abandonment, the ex-owners had cleaned out the lot when they lit out. They hadn't left as much as a safety pin—not that a safety pin would have been of much value in cutting the PVC that bound hands and ankles.

The outside kitchen door was locked. I opened it and hopped out into the still heavily falling rain. I looked around me, but I could have been anywhere. An acre of overgrown garden completely run to seed, ten-foot-high hedges that hadn't felt a clipper in years, and dripping pines and cypresses, soughing under a dark and weeping sky. Wuthering Heights had nothing on it.

There were two wooden outbuildings not far away, one big enough to be a garage, the other less than half the size. I hopped my way toward the latter for the sound enough reason that it was the nearer of the two. The door hung crazily on twisted hinges that creaked dismally as I put my shoulder to the splintered wood.

It was a shed that had obviously been used as a workshop—to one side, below the filthy window, stood a massive workbench with a rusty vise still bolted in position. If it wasn't too rusted to turn, and if I could find some cutting tool to jam into it, that vise would be useful indeed. Only, as far as I could see, there were no cutting tools of any description, no tools of any kind; as in the house, so here—the departing owners had been nothing if not thorough when it had come to the removal of their goods and chattels. The walls were completely bare.

They had left only one thing, and that because it was quite useless—a square plywood box half-full of rubbish and woodshavings. With the aid of a piece of wood I managed to tilt the box and spill its contents on the floor. With the stick I stirred the jumble of odds and ends—pieces of wood, rusty screws, bent pieces of metal, twisted nails—and, at last, a very old and rusty hacksaw blade.

It took me ten minutes to jam the blade into the vise—my hands were now numbed to the point of almost paralytic uselessness—and another ten minutes to saw my way through the PVC binding my wrists. I could have done it in far less time, but as, with my hands behind my back, I couldn't see what I was doing, I had to go easy; I could have sawn through an artery or a tendon just as easily as through a wire and I wouldn't have been able to tell the difference. My hands were as lifeless as that.

They looked pretty lifeless too, when I'd severed the last PVC strand and brought them round to the front for examination, swollen to a size half as much again as normal, with smooth, bluish-purple distended skin, and the blood welling slowly from torn skin on the inside of both wrists and most of my fingers. I hoped that the dark flaking rust on the blade of the hacksaw that had caused those cuts wasn't going to give me blood poisoning.

I sat on the side of the box for five minutes, cursing savagely, as the mottled purple on my hands slowly began to vanish and the circulation came pounding back with the almost intolerably exquisite agony of a thousand barbed needles tearing at the flesh. When I could at last hold the hacksaw blade in my hands, I cut the PVC on my ankles and cursed some more, just as colorfully as before, till the blood supply in my feet came back to something like normal. I pulled up my shirt to have a look at the right-hand side of my chest, and just as quickly and roughly stuffed the shirt back under the waistband of my trousers. A prolonged inspection would only have made me feel twice as ill as I was already; in the few clear patches in the thick crust of blood that covered almost all of the side of my body, the grotesquely swelling bruises were already turning all the kaleidoscopic colors of the rainbow. I thought sourly that if the man who had used me for football practice had chosen the left instead of the right side of my chest, he'd have broken all his toes on the Hanyatti. It was as well that he hadn't.

I had the Hanyatti in my hand as I left the tool shed, but I didn't really expect to have to use it. I didn't go near the house—I knew I'd find nothing there except the footprints, and that was a matter for Hardanger's experts. From the front of the house a driveway curved away between dripping pines and I limped off down the weed-grown gravel. It would have to lead to a road of sorts.

A few paces, then I stopped and tried to think as best I could with my thinking equipment in the poor shape it was. Whoever had clobbered and tied me up might want it to be known that I had been temporarily removed from the scene; it was just as possible, for all I knew to the contrary, that he didn't. If he didn't, then he couldn't have been able to afford to leave my car where it had been and would have removed it. Where? What simpler and more logical than to hide Cavell's car where he had hidden Cavell? I headed back to the garage.

The car was there. I got in, slumped wearily back on the

cushions, sat there for two minutes, then climbed as wearily out again. If someone thought it would be to his advantage not to have people know I was out of commission, then it might equally well be to my advantage not to have that someone know that I was back in commission again. How this would be to my advantage I couldn't even begin to guess at the moment; my mind was so gummed up by weakness and exhaustion and the beating I had taken that coherent thought was beyond me. All I knew was that I was *dimly* aware that it *might* be to my advantage—and with the shape I was in, and considering the lack of progress I was making, I needed every advantage I could get. The car would be a dead giveaway. I started walking.

The driveway led to a road that was no more than a rutted track deep in water and viscous mud. I turned right, for the good enough reason that there was a long steep hill to the left, and after perhaps twenty minutes I came to a secondary road with a signpost reading, NETLY COMMON: 2 MILES. Netly Common, I knew, was on the main London-Alfringham road, about ten miles from Alfringham, which meant I'd been taken at least six miles from the A. A. box where I had been laid out. I wondered why; maybe that had been the only deserted house with a cellar within six miles.

It took me over an hour to cover the two miles to Netley, partly because of the shape I was in anyway, partly because I kept hopping into bushes and behind the cover of trees whenever a car or a cyclist came along. Netley Common itself I bypassed by taking to the fields—empty of all signs of life on that teeming and bitter October morning—and finally reached the main road where I sank down, half-kneeling, half-lying, in a ditch behind the screen of some bushes. I felt like a water-logged doll coming apart at the seams. I was so exhausted that even my chest didn't seem to be hurting any more. I was as bone-chilled as a mortuary slab and shaking like a marionette in the hands of a frenzied puppeteer; I was growing old.

Twenty minutes later I had grown a great deal older. Traffic in rural Wiltshire is never up to Piccadilly standards at the best of times, but even so it was having an off-day. In that time, only three cars and a bus had passed me, and as they were all full, or nearly so, none of them was of any use to me. What I wanted was a truck with only one man in it, or, failing that, a car with just the driver, although how any man alone in a car would react when he saw the wild, disheveled figure of a lifer on the lam or a refugee from a canvas jacket was anybody's guess.

The next car that came along had two men in it, but I didn't hesitate. I recognized the slow-moving, big, black Wolseley for what it was long before I could see the uniforms of the men inside. The car braked smoothly to a stop, and a big, burly sergeant, relief and concern in his face, was out and helping me to my feet as I stumbled up the bank. He had the arm and the build to carry weight and I let him take most of mine.

"Mr. Cavell?" He peered closely into my face. "It *is* Mr. Cavell?"

I felt I'd changed a lot in the past few hours but not all that much, so I admitted I was.

"Thank God for that. There's been half a dozen police cars and heaven only knows how many of the military out looking for you for the past two hours." He helped me solicitously into the back seat. "Now you just take it easy, sir."

"I'll do just that." I eased my squelching, sodden, mud-stained figure into a corner. "I'm afraid this seat will never be the same again, Sergeant."

"Don't you worry about that, sir—plenty more cars where this one came from," he said cheerfully. He climbed in beside the constable at the wheel and picked up the microphone as the car moved off. "Your wife is waiting at the police station with Inspector Wylie."

"Wait a minute," I said quickly. "No hullaballoo about Cavell returning from the dead, Sergeant. Keep it quiet. I don't want to be taken anywhere where I can be recognized. Know of any quiet spot where I could be put up and stay without being seen?"

He twisted and stared at me. He said slowly: "I don't understand."

I made to say that it didn't matter a damn whether he understood or not, but it wouldn't have been fair. Instead I said: "It is important, Sergeant. At least I think so. Any hideaway you know of?"

"Well." He hesitated. "It's difficult, Mr. Cavell—"

"There's my cottage, Sergeant," the driver volunteered. "You know Jean's away with her mother. Mr. Cavell could have that."

"Is it quiet, has it a phone, and is it near Alfringham?" I asked.

"All three of them, sir."

"Fine. Many thanks. Sergeant, please speak to your Inspector. Privately. Ask him to come to this cottage as soon as possible with my wife. With Superintendent Hardanger, if he's available. And have you—the Alfringham police, I mean—a doctor they can rely on? Who doesn't talk out of turn, I mean?"

"We do that." He peered at me. "A doctor?"

I nodded and pulled back my jacket. The rain of that morning had soaked me to the skin and the blood seeping through from the bruises, much diluted, had covered most of the shirt front in a particularly unpleasant shade of brownish red. The sergeant took a quick look, turned and said softly to the driver: "Come on, Rollie boy. You've always wanted to make like Moss and now's your chance. But keep your finger off that damned siren."

Then he reached for the microphone and started talking in a low and urgent voice.

"I'm not going into any damned hospital and that's final," I said irritably. With a couple of ham sandwiches and half a tumbler of whisky inside me, I was feeling much more my old nasty self again. "Sorry, Doc, but there it is."

"I'm sorry too." The doctor bending over me in the bed in that police bungalow was a neat, methodical and precise man with a neat, methodical and precise voice. "I can't make you go, more's the pity. I would if I could, for you're a pretty sick man in urgent need of radiological examination and hospital care. Two of your ribs seem cracked, and a third is definitely fractured. How badly and how dangerously I can't say. I don't have X-ray eyes."

"Not to worry," I said reassuringly. "With the way you've strapped me up I can't see any broken rib sticking into a lung, or out through my skin, for that matter."

"Unless you yield to an irresistible compulsion to indulge in violent gymnastics," the doctor said dryly, "we need not concern ourselves with the possibility of you stabbing yourself to death. What does concern me is the likelihood of pneumonia—broken bones plus the exhausting, unpleasant and very wet time you've been through provide an ideal breeding ground. Pneumonia together with broken ribs make for a very nasty condition. Cemeteries are full of people who could once have testified to that fact."

"Make me laugh some more," I said sourly.

"Mrs. Cavell." He ignored me and looked at Mary, sitting still and pale on the other side of the bed. "Check respiration, pulse, temperature, every hour. Any upward change in those—or difficulty in respiration—and please contact me at once. You have my number. Finally I must warn you and these gentlemen here"—he nodded at Hardanger and Wylie—"that if Mr. Cavell stirs from this bed inside the next seventy-two hours, I refuse to regard myself as in any way medically responsible for his well-being."

He picked up his tool-bag and took off. As the door closed behind him, I swung my legs off the bed and started to pull on a clean shirt. It hurt, but not as much as I expected it would. Neither Mary or Hardanger said anything, and Wylie, seeing that they had no intention of speaking, said: "You want to kill yourself, Cavell? You heard what Dr. Whitelaw said? Why don't you stop him, Superintendent?"

"He's off his rocker," Hardanger explained. "You'll observe, Inspector, that not even his wife tries to stop him? Some things in this life are a complete and utter waste of time, and making Cavell see sense is one of them." He glared at me. "So you've been coming all over clever and lone-wolfish again, haven't you? And you see what happens? Look at the bloody mess you're in now. Literally. Look at it. And nothing to show. When in God's name are you going to realize that our only hope lies in working together? The hell with your d'Artagnan methods, Cavell. System, method, routine, co-operation—that's the only way you ever get anywhere against big crime. And damn well you know it."

"I know it," I agreed. "Patient skilled men working hard under patient skilled supervision. Sure, I'm with you. But not here. No room for patience now. Patient men take time, and we have no time. You've made arrangements for an armed watch to be kept on that house I was in, and to have your sleuths examine the footprints?"

He nodded. "Your story. Let's not waste more time."

"You'll have it. Just as soon as you tell me why you haven't bawled me out for wasting valuable police time in searching for me, and why you haven't tried to use your authority to make me stay in bed. Are we worried, Superintendent?"

"The newspapers have the story," he said flatly. "About the break-in, the murders, the theft of the Satan Bug. We didn't expect that last thing. They're hysterical already. Screaming banner headlines in every national daily." He pointed to a pile of newspapers on the floor beside him. "Want to see them?"

"And waste more time? I can guess. That's not all that's worrying you."

"It isn't. The General was on the phone—he was looking for you—half an hour ago. Six Gestetner-duplicated letters delivered by special messengers this morning to the biggest concerns in Fleet Street. Character saying that his previous warning had been ignored; no acknowledgment of it on the nine A.M. B.B.C. news. The walls of Mordon still stood—some rubbish like that. Said that within the new few hours he would give a demonstration proving (a) he had those viruses and (b) he was willing to use them."

"Will the papers print it?"

"They'll print it. First of all they—the editors—got together and contacted the Special Branch at Scotland Yard. The Assistant Commissioner got in touch with the Home Secretary, and I gather there was some kind of emergency meeting. Anyway, a Cabinet order not to print. Fleet Street, I gather, told the Government to take a running jump at itself, told the Government that it is the servant of the people and not vice versa, and that if the nation stood in deadly peril—and that on the face of it, it certainly seemed to—the people had a right to know. They also reminded the Government that if they put one little foot wrong in this matter, they would be out on their ears overnight. The London evening papers will be on the streets about now. I'll bet the headlines are the biggest since VE day."

"The ball's up on the slates," I nodded. I watched Mary, her face expressionless and carefully not looking at me, button my shirt-cuffs—with both wrists bandaged and my fingers heavily scratched it was a bit much for me—and went on: "Well, it'll certainly provide the British public with a conversational change from the football pools, what so-and-so said on TV last night, and the latest rock-and-roll sensation." I went on to tell him of what had happened during the night, omitting my trip to London to see the General.

At the end, Hardanger said heavily: "Very, very interesting. Are you trying to tell me that you woke up in the middle of the night and—without telling Mary—started chasing and phoning around Wiltshire?"

"I'm telling you. The old secret police technique—and you can't beat it: get them at their sleepiest and most apprehensive, and you're already halfway there. And I didn't go to sleep in the first place. I went without telling you because I knew damned well it would go so much against all your training and instincts that you wouldn't hesitate to use force to stop me."

"If I had," he said coldly, "you might have a full set of ribs right now."

"If you had, we wouldn't have narrowed the list so much. Five of them. I let drop to all of them that we were getting pretty close to an answer, and one of them was scared enough to panic and try to stop me."

"You assume."

"It's a damned good assumption. Got a better? For a starter, I suggest we haul in Chessingham straight away. There's plenty on him and—"

"I forgot," Hardanger interrupted. "You phoned the General last night?"

"Yes." I didn't even bother to look shamefaced. "Wanted authority to hash about in my own way—knew you wouldn't grant it."

"Clever devil, aren't you?" If he guessed I was lying, there was no sign of it in his face. "You asked him to check on this fellow, Chessingham, his service career. Seems he was a driver in the R.A.S.C."

"That's it then. Going to pull him in?"

"Yes. His sister?"

"She wouldn't be guilty of anything other than covering up for her own flesh and blood. And the mother is in the clear. That's for sure."

"So. That leaves the four others you contacted this morning. You'd put them all in the clear?"

"I would not. Take Colonel Weybridge. The only certain facts we know about him are these: he has access to the security files and so would be in a position to blackmail Dr. Hartnell into co-operating—"

"You mentioned last night you thought Hartnell was in the clear."

"I said I'd reservations about him. Secondly, why didn't our gallant colonel, like his gallant commanding officer, volunteer to go into the lab instead of me? Was it because he *knew* the botulinus virus was loose in there? Thirdly, he is the only one without an alibi for the time of the murder."

"Good Lord, Cavell, you're not suggesting we pull in Colonel Weybridge? I can tell you we had a pretty nasty time from both Cliveden and Weybridge when we insisted on fingerprinting their quarters this morning. Cliveden actually phoned the Assistant Commissioner."

"And got his head in his hands?"

"In a gentlemanly sort of way. He hates our guts now."

"That helps. This fingerprinting of the suspects' houses. Anything turned up yet?"

"Give them a chance," Hardanger protested. "It's not one o'clock yet. Be a couple of hours before they finish tabulating their results. And I *can't* pull in Weybridge. The War Office would have my scalp in twenty-four hours."

"If this lad with the Satan Bug starts chucking it around," I said, "there won't be any War Office in twenty-four hours. People's feelings have ceased to be of any concern. Besides, you don't have to throw him in the cooler. Confine him to his quarters, open arrest, house arrest, whatever you call it. Anything turned up in the past few hours?"

"A thousand stones and nothing under any of them," Hardanger said grimly. "The hammer and pliers were definitely the ones used in the break-in. But we'd been sure of that anyway. Not a single useful print in the Bedford decoy van. The same for the telephone box which was used to make the call to Reuter's last night. We've put your money-lending friend, Tuffnell, and his partner through the mill, and had the Fraud Squad examine their books until we know as much about their business as they do themselves; we could have them both behind bars in a week, but I just can't be bothered. Anyway, Dr. Hartnell is definitely their only customer from number one lab. The London police are trying to trace the man who sent the letters to Fleet Street; if we're wasting our time down here, they might as well waste their time up there. Inspector Martin has spent the entire morning questioning everyone in number one lab about their social relations with each other, and the only thing he has turned up so far is that Dr. Hartnell and Chessingham were on visiting terms. We already knew that. We're having a check made on every known movement of every suspect in the past year, and we have teams of men checking with the occupants of every house within three miles of Mordon to see if they noticed anything strange or out of the way on the night of the murders. Something is bound to turn up sometime. If you spread the net wide enough and the meshes are small enough. It always does."

"Sure. In a couple of weeks. Or a couple of months. Our friend with the Satan Bug has promised to do his stuff in a few hours. Damn it, Superintendent, we can't just wait for something to turn up. Organization, no matter on how massive a scale, won't do it. Method number two, lighting a meerschaum making like Sherlock, isn't going to get us far, either. We have to provoke a reaction."

"You already provoked a reaction," Hardanger said sourly. "See where it got you? You want more reactions. How?"

"As a starter, investigate every financial transaction and every bank-book entry of everyone working in number one, every entry in the past year—and don't forget Weybridge and Cliveden. Let the suspects know. Then squads of policemen to every house. Search each house from top to bottom and have the searchers list every tiniest thing they find. This will not only worry the man we're after—it might actually turn up something."

"If we're going to go that far," Inspector Wylie put in, "we might as well throw the lot of them in the cooler. It's one sure way of taking our man out of circulation."

"Hopeless, Inspector. We may be dealing with a maniac, but he's a brilliant maniac. He'd have thought of that possibility months ago. He's got an organization—nobody in Mordon could possibly have delivered those letters in London this morning—and you can bet your pension that the first thing he'd have done after getting the viruses would be to get rid of them."

"We'll try stirring things up," Hardanger said reluctantly. "Though where I'm going to find all the men to—"

"Pull them off the house-to-house questioning. It's a waste of time."

He nodded, again reluctantly, and spoke at length on the phone while I finished dressing. When he put the phone down, he said to me: "I'm not going to waste my breath arguing. Go ahead and kill yourself. But you might think of Mary."

"I'm thinking of her all right. I'm thinking that if our unknown friend gets careless with the Satan Bug, there'll soon be no Mary. There'll be nothing."

This seemed to be a pretty effective conversation stopper, but after some time Wylie said thoughtfully: "If this unknown friend does give a demonstration, I wonder if the Government really would close down Mordon."

"Close it? Our pal wants it flattened to the ground. It's impossible to guess what they will do. Things are only at the badly scaring stage so far—no one's out-and-out terrified."

"Speak for yourself," Hardanger said sourly. "And just what are you thinking of doing now, Cavell? If you'll be kind enough to tell me," he added with heavy irony.

"I'll tell you. Don't laugh, but I'm going to disguise myself." I fingered the scars on my left cheek. "A little assistance from Mary and her war-paint, and these will be gone.

Horn-rim spectacles, and pencil moustache, gray suit, credentials identifying me as Inspector Gibson of the Metropolitan Police, and I'm a changed man."

"Who's going to supply the credentials?" Hardanger asked suspiciously. "Me?"

"Not necessary. I always carry them around with me, anyway, just in case." I ignored his stare and went on: "And then I'll call again on our friend, Dr. MacDonald. In his absence, if you understand. The good doctor, on a modest salary, manages to live like a minor Eastern potentate—everything except the harem—and maybe he discreetly keeps that somewhere else. Also drinking heavily because he's worried stiff, about the Satan Bug and his own personal safety. I don't believe him. So I'm calling on him."

"You're wasting your time," Hardanger said heavily. "MacDonald is above suspicion. Long, distinguished and spotless record. Spent twenty minutes this morning going over it."

"I've read it," I said. "Some of the star turns in the Old Bailey over the past few years have had immaculate records—until the law caught up with them."

"He's a highly respected character locally," Wylie put in. "Bit of a snob, associates only with the very best people, but everyone speaks very well of him."

"And there's more to your record than you've read, Cavell," Hardanger went on. "In the report there's only a brief mention of his wartime service in the Army, and it so happens I'm a personal friend of the colonel who commanded the regiment in the last two years of the war. I rang him up. Dr. MacDonald, it seems, has been strangely reticent about himself. Did you know that as a second lieutenant in Belgium in 1940, he won the D.S.O. and the bar, that he finished up as a lieut-colonel in a tank regiment with a string of medals as long as your arm?"

"I didn't, and I don't get it," I admitted. "He struck me as a phony-tough type who, if ever he'd done any valorous deeds, wouldn't have been backward about admitting them. He *wanted* me to think he was afraid: he didn't want me to think he was brave. Why? Because he knew he had to justify his heavy drinking, so he put it down to personal fear. But, in view of his record, it almost certainly wasn't that. Queer item number one. Queer item number two—why wasn't all this listed in his security report? Easton Derry compiled most of those dossiers—and Derry would be unlikely to overlook so large a gap in a man's history."

126

"I don't know about that," Hardanger admitted. "But this much is certain—if the report I had on MacDonald is correct, then on the face of it, it seems highly unlikely that a man so brave, selfless and patriotic could possibly be mixed up in anything like this."

"This colonel of MacDonald's regiment who told you about him—could you get him down here immediately?"

Hardanger let me have his cool, speculative look. "Thinking he's a phony in *every* sense? That this man's been substituted for the real MacDonald?"

"I don't know what to think. We must have another squint at his record card and check that Derry really did compile it."

"We can soon fix that," Hardanger nodded. This time he was on the phone for almost ten minutes, and when he'd finished with that, so had Mary with my face and I was all ready to go. Hardanger said: "You look bloody awful but I wouldn't recognize you if I saw you in the street. The file's in a safe in my hotel. Shall we go there?"

I turned to leave the room. Hardanger took a look at the palms and fingers of my hands, still slowly welling blood from the hacksaw scratches. He said irritably: "Why didn't you have the doctor bandage your fingers as well? Want to get blood poisoning?"

"Have you ever tried to use a gun with your fingers bandaged together?" I asked sourly.

"Well, man, a pair of gloves then. That's ridiculous."

"Just as bad. Couldn't get a finger through the trigger guard."

"Rubber gloves," he said impatiently. "Plastic."

"It's a point," I agreed. "Certainly it would hide those damn scratches." I stared at him without seeing him, then sat down heavily on the bed. "Hell's bells!" I said softly.

I sat very still for a few seconds. Nobody spoke. I went on, speaking more to myself than anyone else: "Rubber gloves. To cover the scratches. Then why not elastic stockings? Why not?" I looked up vaguely and saw Hardanger glancing at Wylie, maybe thinking that they had let the doctor go too soon, but Mary came to my rescue.

She touched my arm and I turned to look at her. Her face was set, her big green eyes wide with apprehension and the birth of an unpleasant certainty.

"Mordon," she whispered. "The fields round it. Gorse, they're covered with gorse. And she *was* wearing elastic stockings, Pierre."

"What in heaven's name—" Hardanger began harshly.

"Inspector Wylie," I interrupted. "How long would it take you to get an arrest warrant? Murder. Accessory."

"No time at all," he said grimly. He patted his breast pocket. "I have three of them here, already signed. Like you said yourself, there are times when we can't wait for the law. We fill 'em in. Murder, eh?"

"Accessory."

"And the name?" Hardanger demanded. He still wasn't sure that he shouldn't be calling the doctor.

"Dr. Roger Hartnell," I said.

CHAPTER 9

"What in the name of God are you talking about?" Dr. Roger Hartnell, a young man with a face suddenly old and tired and strained, stared at us, then at his wife who was standing rigidly beside him, then back at us again. "Accessory after murder. What *are* you talking about, man?"

"It's our belief that you know well enough what we are talking about," Wylie said calmly. It was the Inspector's bailiwick, and it was he who had just read out the charge and was making the formal arrest. He went on: "I have to warn you that what you say now may be used in evidence against you. It would help us if you made a full confession now, I admit, but arrested men have their rights. You may wish to take legal advice before you speak." Like hell he was going to take legal advice: he was going to talk before he left that house, and Hardanger, Wylie and I all knew it.

"Will someone please explain what this—this nonsense is about?" Mrs. Hartnell said coldly. The slightly supercilious incomprehension, the well-bred distaste were done to a turn, but the hostile rigidity of the figure overdone, the gripping hands so tightly clasped that the tremor showed. And she was still wearing the elastic stockings.

"Gladly," Wylie said. "Yesterday, Dr. Hartnell, you made a statement to Mr. Cavell here to—"

"Cavell?" Hartnell did some more staring. "That's not Cavell."

"I didn't like my old face," I said. "Do you blame me? Inspector Wylie is talking, Hartnell."

"To the effect," Wylie went on, "that you made a late trip, night before last, to see a Mr. Tuffnell. Intensive investigation has turned up several people who were in a position to have seen you, had you traveled in the direction you said you did at the time you said you did. Not one of those people saw you. That's point number one." And quite a good point it was, too, even if the purest fiction; the check had been made all right, but not a single witness found to confirm or deny Hartnell's story, which had been just as expected.

"Point number two," Wylie went on. "Mud was found last night under the front mudguard of your motor-scooter, a mud which seems to be identical with a red loam found locally only outside Mordon. We suspect you went there early in the evening to reconnoiter. Your machine is at present being moved to police laboratories for tests. Point number—"

"My scooter!" Hartnell looked as if a bridge had fallen on him. "Mordon! I swear to—"

"Number three. Later that night you took your scooter—and wife—to a spot near Chessingham's house. You almost gave yourself away to Mr. Cavell—you said that the policeman alleged to have seen you on your scooter could back up your story about the trip to Alfringham, and then you remembered, almost too late, that if he had seen you he would also have seen your wife on the pillion seat. We found the imprint of your scooter's wheels among bushes not twenty yards from where the Bedford had been abandoned. Careless, Doctor, very careless. I note you're not protesting that one." He couldn't. We'd found the imprints less than twenty minutes previously.

"Points four and five. Hammer used to stun the guard dog. Pliers used to cut the Mordon fence. Both found last night in your tool shed. Again by Mr. Cavell."

"Why, you filthy, sneaking, thieving—" His face twisted, the hair-trigger control suddenly snapped and he flung himself at me, clawed hands outstretched. He didn't get three feet; Hardanger and Wylie just moved in massively from either side and pinned him helplessly between their bulks. Hartnell struggled madly, uselessly, his insane fury increasing. "I took you in here, you—you swine! I entertained your wife. I did—" His voice weakened and faded, and when it came again it was another man talking. "The hammer used to stun the dog? The pliers? Here? In my house? They were found here? How could they have been found here?" He couldn't have been more bewildered if he'd heard the late Senator McCarthy declaring himself to be a lifelong Communist. "They *couldn't* have been found here. What are they

129

talking about, Jane?" He'd turned to his wife and his face was desperate.

"We're talking of murder," Wylie said flatly. "I didn't expect your co-operation, Hartnell. Please come along, both of you."

"There's some terrible mistake. I—I don't understand. A terrible mistake." Hartnell stared at us, his face hunted. "I can clear it up, I'm sure I can clear it up. If you have to take anyone with you, take me. But don't drag my wife along. Please."

"Why not?" I said. "You didn't hesitate to drag her along a couple of nights ago."

"I don't know what you're talking about," he said wearily.

"Would you say the same thing, Mrs. Hartnell?" I asked. "In view of the statement made by your doctor, who saw you less than three weeks ago, that you are in perfect health?"

"What do you mean?" she demanded. She was under better control that her husband. "What are you getting at?"

"The fact that you went to a chemist's in Alfringham yesterday and bought a pair of elastic stockings. The gorse outside Mordon is pretty vicious stuff, Mrs. Hartnell, and it was very dark when you ran off after decoying the soldiers from their truck. You were pretty badly scratched, weren't you? And you had to cover those scratches, didn't you? Policemen are just naturally suspicious—especially in a murder case."

"This is entirely ridiculous." Her voice was flat, mechanical. "How dare you insinuate—"

"You are wasting our time, Madam!" Hardanger spoke for the first time, his voice sharp and authoritative. "We have a policewoman outside. Must I bring her in?" Silence. "Very well, then, I suggest we leave for the police station."

"Could I have a few words with Dr. Hartnell, first?" I asked. "Alone, that is?"

Hardanger and Wylie exchanged glances. I'd already had their permission, but I had to have it again to make things right—for them—if the need arose at the trial.

"Why?" Hardanger demanded.

"Dr. Hartnell and I used to know each other fairly well," I said. "We were on fairly friendly terms. Time is desperately short. He might be willing to talk to me."

"Talk to you?" It's no easy feat to sneer and shout at the same moment, but Hartnell achieved it. "By God, never!"

"Time is indeed short," Hardanger agreed somberly. "Ten minutes, Cavell." He nodded to Mrs. Hartnell. She hesitated, looked at her husband, then walked out, followed by Hardanger and Wylie. Hartnell made to follow but I swung across and blocked his way.

"Let me past." His voice was low and ugly. "I've nothing to say to people like you." He gave a short description of what he thought people like me were like, and when I showed no signs of stepping aside he swung back his right fist for a clumsy round-house swing that a blind octogenarian could have parried or avoided. I showed him my gun and he changed his mind.

"Have you a cellar in your house?" I asked.

"A cellar? Yes, we—" He broke off and his face was ugly again. "If you think you're going to take me—"

I swung my left fist in imitation of his own cumbersome effort, and when he lifted his right arm in defense I tapped him with the barrel of the Hanyatti—just enough to take the fight out of him—caught his left arm up behind his left shoulder and marched him towards the rear of the house where a flight of steps led down to a cellar. I closed the door behind us and shoved him roughly onto a wooden bench. He sat there for some seconds, rubbing his head, then looked up at me.

"This is a put-up job," he said hoarsely. "Hardanger and Wylie—they knew you were going to do this."

"Hardanger and Wylie are hampered," I said coldly. "They're hampered by regulations concerning interrogation of suspects. They're hampered by the thought of careers and pensions. I have no such thoughts. I'm a private individual."

"And you think you'll get away with this?" he said incredulously. "Do you seriously think I won't talk about it?"

"By the time I have finished," I said impersonally, "I doubt whether you will be able to talk. I'll have the truth in fifteen minutes—and I won't leave a mark. I'm an expert on torture, Hartnell—a group of Belgian quislings gave me a course of instruction over a period of three weeks. I was the subject. Try hard to believe I don't care much if you are badly hurt."

He looked at me. He was trying hard not to believe me, but he wasn't sure. There was nothing tough about Hartnell.

"Let's try it the easy way first, though," I said. "Let's try it by reminding you that there's a madman on the loose with the Satan Bug, threatening to wipe out God knows how much of England if his conditions aren't met—and his first demonstration is due any hour."

"What are you talking about?" he demanded hoarsely.

I told him what Hardanger had told me and then went on: "If this madman wipes out any part of the country, the nation will demand revenge. They'll demand a scapegoat, and public pressure will be so terrific that they'll get their scapegoat. Surely you're not so stupid as not to see that? Surely you're not so stupid that you can't visualize your wife Jane with the hangman's knot under her chin as the executioner opens the trap-door. The fall, the jolt, the snapping of the vertebrae, the momentary reflex kicking of the feet—can you see your wife, Hartnell? Can you see what you are going to do to her? She is young to die. And death by hanging is a terrible death—and it's still the prescribed penalty for a guilty accessory to murder for gain."

He looked up at me, dull hate and misery in the sick eyes. In the half-light of the cellar his face was gray, and there was the sheen of sweat on his forehead.

I went on: "You realize that you can retract any statement you make to me here. Without witnesses, a statement is valueless." I paused and dropped my voice. "You're deep in this, aren't you?"

He nodded. He was staring at the floor.

"Who's the killer? Who's behind all this?"

"I don't know. As God is my judge, I don't know. A man rang me up and offered me money if I'd cause this diversion. Jane and myself. I thought he was crazy, and if he wasn't something stank about it ... I refused. Next morning two hundred pounds arrived by post with a note saying there would be three hundred pounds more if I did what I was told. A—a fortnight went by, and then he came on the phone again."

"His voice. Did you recognize his voice?"

"It was deep and muffled. I've no idea who it was. I think he was talking with something over the mouthpiece."

"What did he say?"

"The same as his note. There would be this other three hundred pounds if I did as he asked."

"And?"

"I said I would." He was still looking downwards. "I—I had already spent part of the money."

"Received the extra three hundred pounds?"

"Not yet."

"How much have you spent of the two hundred pounds you received?"

"About forty."

"Show me the rest of it."

"It's not here. Not in the house. I went out last night after you had been here and buried the remainder in the woods."

"What was the money in? Denominations, I mean?"

"Fivers. Bank of England fivers."

"I see. All very interesting, Doctor." I crossed to the bench where he was sitting, screwed my hand into his hair, jerked his head savagely upwards, jammed the barrel of the Hanyatti into his solar plexus and, as he gasped in pain, brought up the barrel and thrust it between his teeth. For ten seconds I stood like that, motionless, while he stared up at me with eyes crazy with fear. I felt slightly sick.

"One chance is all you get from me, Hartnell," I said in a low voice. "You've had that chance. Now the treatment. You rotten, contemptible liar. Expect me to believe a crazy story like that? Do you think the brilliant mind behind this would have phoned asking you to make a diversion knowing very well that the chances were high that you would at once go to the police, put them and the Army at Mordon on their guard and so ruin all his plans? Do you think this man, in an area where automatic exchanges are not yet installed, would have spoken to you when any operator with time on her hands could have listened in to every word he said? Are you so naïve as to imagine that I would be so naïve as to believe that? Do you believe that this man, with a genius for organization, would leave everything, the success of all his plans, dependent on the last-minute factor of the strength of your greed? Do you believe he'd pay in fivers, which can as often as not be traced and which could also have, if not his prints, then those of the cashier issuing them? Do you expect me to believe that he would offer five hundred pounds for the job when he could get a couple of experts from London to do it for a tenth of that? And finally, do you think I'd believe your yarn about burying the money in the woods at night—so that come the dawn if you were told to dig them up by the police you would be unable to find them again?" I stood back, taking the gun from his face. "Or shall we go and look for that money now?"

"Oh, God, it's useless." He was completely crushed, his voice a moan. "I'm finished, Cavell, I'm finished. I've been borrowing all over the place and now I'm over two thousand in debt."

"Cut the sob story," I said harshly. "It doesn't interest me."

"Tuffnell—the moneylender—was pressing me hard," he went on dully. He wasn't looking anywhere near me. "I'm mess secretary at Mordon. I've embezzled over six hundred pounds. Someone—God knows who or how—found out and sent me a note saying that if I didn't co-operate he'd lay the facts before the police. I co-operated."

I put the gun away. The ring of truth is far from having the bell-like clarity some innocents would believe, but I knew Hartnell was too beaten to prevaricate further. I said: "You have no clue at all as to the identity of the man sending the note?"

"No. And I swear I don't know anything about the hammer or the pliers or the red mud on the scooter."

I grunted noncommittally and said: "What part did Chessingham play in all this?"

"Chessingham? Chessingham?" He was so bogged down by the weight of his own private sorrow that he didn't clearly appreciate what I was saying. "What the hell has Chessingham to do with all this?"

"Forget it," I said. "Come on. Let's go down to the police station."

On the way out of the house we met half-a-dozen burly men in plain clothes. They would be one of the house-searching squads, the men who would be listing the contents of suspects' houses down to the last safety pin. Six men about to waste two or three hours of their valuable time. But I didn't tell them so.

My leg was now hurting so badly that they'd given me a police car and police driver, but even so I didn't enjoy the trip across to Dr. MacDonald's house. Time was running out and all I could see was a brick wall. That evening there would appear in all the papers a carefully worded account of how two Mordon scientists had been arrested and charged with murder and that the final solution of the theft of the Satan Bug was only hours away, and while it might, we hoped, lull the suspicions of the real killers, it wasn't advancing our cause very much. Blind men in a fog at midnight. And no leads, just no leads at all. Hardanger was going to open an intensive investigation in Mordon to find out who might have had access to the mess accounts: probably, I thought bitterly, only a couple of hundred people or so.

I was met at the door of Dr. MacDonald's house by his housekeeper. She was in her middle thirties, more than passably good-looking, and gave her name as Mrs. Turpin. Her face was like thunder, the face of the faithful retainer powerless to defend her master's property against ravage and assault. When I showed my false credentials and asked to be allowed in, she said bitterly that another prying nosey-parker more or less couldn't do any harm now.

The house appeared to be alive with plain-clothes policemen. I identified myself to the man in charge, a detective-sergeant by the name of Carlisle.

"Found anything interesting yet, Sergeant?"

"Hard to say. Been here over an hour, starting from the top, and we've found nothing that strikes me as suspicious in itself. Dr. MacDonald does seem to do himself pretty well, I must say. And one of my men, Campbell, who's dead keen on all this art rubbish, says that a lot of the pictures, pottery and other junk about the place is worth a fair bit of anyone's money. And you ought to see the darkroom he has in the attic; there's a thousand quid's worth of photographic equipment there if there's a penny's worth."

"Darkroom? That might be interesting. Never heard that Dr. MacDonald was interested in photography."

"Lord bless my soul, yes. He's one of the best amateur photographers in the country. He's the president of our photographic club in Alfringham. There's a cabinet through in his study there that's fair loaded with trophies. He makes no secret of that, I can assure you, sir."

I left him and his men to their search—if they couldn't find anything, neither could I—and went upstairs to the darkroom. Carlisle hadn't exaggerated any: Dr. MacDonald did himself as well in the way of cameras as he did in the other material things of life. But I didn't spend much time there; I didn't see how cameras came into the business at all. I made a mental note to bring an expert police photographer down from London to check the equipment in the one-in-a-thousand chance that something might turn up, and then went downstairs to see Mrs. Turpin.

"I'm really most sorry about all this upset, Mrs. Turpin," I said pleasantly. "Just pure routine, you know. Must be a pleasure for you to look after a beautiful place like this."

"If you've got any questions to ask, ask them," she snapped, "and none of your smart-alecky beating about the bush."

That didn't leave much room for finesse. I said: "How many years have you been with Dr. MacDonald?"

"Four. Ever since he came here. A finer gentleman you wouldn't find anywhere. Why do you ask?"

"He has a great deal of valuable stuff here." I listed about a dozen items, ranging from the magnificent carpeting to the paintings. "How long has he had those?"

"I don't have to answer any questions, Mr. Inspector." The helpful type.

"No," I admitted. "You don't. Especially if you wish to make things unpleasant for your employer."

She glared at me, hesitated, then answered my questions. At least half the stuff MacDonald had brought with him four years ago. The rest had been bought at fairly regular intervals since. Mrs. Turpin was one of those formidable women with a photographic memory for all the more monumental irrelevancies of life, and she could more or less quote the date, hour and the weather conditions at the time of the delivery of each item. I knew I'd be wasting my time even trying to confirm her statements. If Mrs. Turpin said such-and-such was so-and-so, then it was and that was all there was to it.

This certainly helped to set MacDonald in the clear. No sudden suspicious influx of wealth in the recent weeks or months, he'd been buying on this lavish scale over a period of years. Where he got the wherewithal to buy on this lavish scale I couldn't guess, but it hardly seemed important now. As he'd said himself, as an independent bachelor without relatives, he could afford to live it up.

I moved back into the sitting-room and saw Carlisle coming towards me with a couple of large files in his hands.

"We're giving Dr. MacDonald's study a thorough going-over now, sir. Listing everything, of course, but I thought these might interest you. Seems to be some sort of official correspondence."

It did interest me, but not in the way I expected. The more I turned up about MacDonald, the more innocuous he seemed. The file contained carbon copies of his letters to and replies from fellow scientists and various scientific organizations throughout Europe, mainly the World Health Organization. There was no doubt from those letters that MacDonald was a highly gifted and highly respected chemist and microbiologist, one of the top men in his own field. Almost half of his letters were addressed to certain affiliations of the WHO, particularly in Paris, Stockholm, Bonn and Rome. Nothing sinister or unpatriotic about that; this would be unclassified stuff and the frequent co-signature of Dr. Baxter on the carbon was guarantee enough for that. Besides, although it was supposed to be a secret, all the scientists in Mordon knew that their mail was under constant censorship.

I glanced through the file again and put it aside as the phone rang.

It was Hardanger, and he sounded fairly grim. What he had to say made me feel grim, too. A phone call to Alfringham had stated that if police investigations weren't suspended for twenty-four hours, something very unpleasant was going to happen to Pierre Cavell, who, as they would be aware, had disappeared. Proof that the caller knew where Cavell was would be forthcoming if police investigations were not halted by six o'clock that evening.

It wasn't this first part of it that made me feel grim. I said: "Well, we were expecting something like it. With all the threats I was dropping at the crack of dawn today they must have thought that I was making too much progress for their comfort."

"You flatter yourself, my friend," Hardanger said in his gravelly voice. "You're only a pawn. The call wasn't made to the police but to your wife at the Waggoner's Rest, telling her that if the General—he gave his full name, rank and address—didn't pull in his horns then she, Mary, would receive a pair of ears in the mail tomorrow. The caller said that he was sure that though she had been married only a couple of months she would still be able to recognize her husband's ears when she saw them."

I felt the hairs prickle on the back of my neck, and that had nothing to do with any imagined sensation of ear-cropping. I said carefully: "There are three things, Hardanger. The number of people in these parts who know we have been married only two months must be pretty few. The number of people who know that Mary is the general's daughter must be even fewer. But the number of people who know the General's true identity, apart from yourself and myself, can be counted on one hand. How in God's name could any criminal in the land know the General's true identity?"

"You tell me," Hardanger said heavily. "This is the nastiest development of the lot. This man not only knows who the General is but knows that Mary is his only child and the apple of his eye, the one person in the world who *might* be able to bring pressure to bear on him. And she'd bring the pressure, all right; the abstract ideals of justice don't matter a damn to women when their men's lives are in danger. The whole thing stinks, Cavell."

"To high heaven," I agreed slowly. "Of treason—and treason in high places."

"I don't think we'd better talk about it over the phone," Hardanger said quickly.

"No. Tried tracing the call?"

"Not yet. But I might as well waste time that way as any other."

He hung up and I stood there staring at the silent telephone. The General was a personal appointee of the Prime Minister and the Home Secretary. His identity was also known to the chiefs of espionage and counter-espionage—it had to be. An Assistant Commissioner, Hardanger himself, the Commandant and security chief at Mordon—and that ended the list of those to whom the General's identity was known. It was an ugly thought. I wondered vaguely how General Cliveden was going to enjoy the next couple of hours—I didn't require any powers of telepathy to know where Hardanger would be heading as soon as he had put down that phone. Of all our suspects, only Cliveden knew the General's identity. Maybe I should have been paying more attention to General Cliveden.

A shadow darkened the hall doorway. I glanced up to see three khaki-clad figures standing at the head of the outside steps. The man in the center, a sergeant, had his hand raised to the bell-push but lowered it when he caught sight of me.

"I'm looking for an Inspector Gibson," he said. "Is he here?"

"Gibson?" I suddenly remembered that was me. "I'm Inspector Gibson, Sergeant."

"I've something here for you, sir." He indicated the file under his arm. "I've been ordered to ask for your credentials first of all."

I showed them and he handed over the file. He said apologetically: "I'm under orders not to let that out of my sight, sir. Superintendent Hardanger said it came from Mr. Clandon's records offices, and I understand it's highly confidential."

"Of course." Followed by the sergeant who was flanked by a couple of hefty privates, I walked into the living-room, ignoring the outraged glare of Mrs. Turpin who had belatedly appeared on the scene. I asked her to leave and she did, glowering savagely.

I broke the seal and opened the file. It contained a spare seal for resealing the cover, and a copy of Dr. MacDonald's security report. I'd seen the report before, of course, when I'd taken over as head of security from the vanished Easton

Derry, but had paid no particular attention to it. I'd had no especial reason to. But I had now.

There were seven pages of foolscap. I went through it three times. I didn't miss a thing the first time, and if possible even less the next two. I was looking for even the tiniest off-beat jarring note that might give me even the most insubstantial lead, but I found not the slightest trace of anything that might have been helpful. The only odd thing, as Hardanger had pointed out, was the extremely scanty information about MacDonald's army career, information to which Easton Derry—who had indeed compiled the report—must have had access. But nothing, except for a remark at the foot of a page that MacDonald, entering the Army as a private in the Territorials in 1938, had finished his army career in Italy as a lieutenant-colonel in a tank division in 1945. The top of the following page held a reference to his appointment as a government chemist in northeast England early in 1946. This could have been just the way Easton Derry had compiled the report—or not.

With the blade of my penknife, and ignoring the sergeant's scandalized look, I pried open the buckram corner holding the top left-hand corners of the pages together. Under this was a thin wire staple, the kind of staple that comes with practically every kind of commercial stapler. I bent the ends back at right angles, slid the sheets off, and examined them separately. No sheet had more than one pair—the original pair—of holes made by the stapler. If anyone had opened that staple to remove a sheet, he'd replaced it with exceptional care. On the face of it, it looked as if that file hadn't been tampered with.

I became aware that Carlisle, the plain-clothes detective-sergeant, was standing beside me, holding a bundle of papers and folders. He said: "This might interest you, sir. I don't know."

"Just a moment." I clipped the sheets together again, pushed them into the file-holder, resealed it and handed it back to the army sergeant who took himself off along with his two companions. I said to Carlisle: "What are those?"

"Photographs, sir."

"Photographs? What makes you think I'll be interested in photographs, Sergeant?"

"The fact that they were inside a locked steel box, sir. And the box was in the bottom drawer—also locked—of a knee-hole desk. And here's a bundle found in the same place—personal correspondence, I would say."

"Much trouble in opening the steel box?"

"Not with the size of hacksaw I use, sir. We've just about tied it all up now, Inspector. Everything listed. If I might venture an opinion, you'll find little of interest on the list."

"Searched the whole house? Any basement?"

"Just about the filthiest coal-cellar you ever clapped eyes on." Carlisle smiled. "From what I've seen of Dr. MacDonald's personal tastes, he doesn't strike me as the type of man who would keep even coal in a coal-cellar if he could find a cleaner and more luxurious place for it."

He left me to his finds. There were four albums. Three of them were of the innocuous, squinting-into-the-sun type of family albums you can find in a million British homes. Most of the photographs were faded and yellow, taken in the days of MacDonald's youth in the twenties and thirties. The fourth album, of much more recent origin, was a presentation given to MacDonald by colleagues in the World Health Organization in recognition of his outstanding services to the WHO over many years—an illuminated address pasted to the inside front-board said so. It contained over fifty pictures of MacDonald and his colleagues taken in at least a dozen different European cities. Most of the photographs had been taken in France, Scandinavia and Italy, with a sprinkling from a few other countries. They had been mounted in chronological fashion, each picture with date and location caption, the last having been taken in Helsinki less than six months previously.

The photographs in the album didn't interest me; what did interest me was the one photograph that was missing. From its place in the album it had almost certainly been taken about eighteen months previously. Its caption had been all but obliterated by horizontal strokes made in the same white ink used for all captions. I switched on a light and peered closely at the obliteration. No question but that the place name had once started with a T. After that it was hard to say. The next letter could have been either an O or a D. O, I felt sure—there was no city in Europe beginning with TD. The remainder of the word was completely obliterated. TO . . . About six letters in length, possibly seven. But none of the letters projected below the line, so that cut out all words with p's and g's and j's and so forth.

What cities or towns in Europe did I know beginning with the letters TO and six or seven letters in length? Not so very many, I realized, at least not of any size, and the WHO didn't hold its meetings in villages. Torquay—no good, letters projecting below. Totnes—too small. In Europe? Tornio in Sweden, Tönder in Denmark—again both relatively insignificant. Toledo, now—no one could call that a village; but MacDonald had never been to Spain. The best bets were probably either Tournai in Belgium or Toulon in France. Tournai? Toulon? For a moment or two I mulled the names over in my mind. If that was a clue, I didn't have a clue as to what it meant. I put the album to one side and picked up the bundle of letters.

There must have been thirty or forty letters in the bundle, faintly scented and tied, of all things, with a blue ribbon. Of all the things I would have expected to find in Dr. MacDonald's possession, this was the last. And, I would have bet a month's salary, the most useless. They looked like love letters and I didn't particularly relish the prospect of making myself conversant with the good doctor's youthful indiscretions, but just at that moment I would have read Homer in the original if I thought it would be any good to me. I untied the bow on the ribbon.

Exactly five minutes later I was speaking on the phone to the General.

"I want to interview a certain Madame Yvette Peugeot who was working in the Pasteur Institute in Paris, in nineteen forty-five and nineteen forty-six. Not next week, not tomorrow, but now. This afternoon. Can you fix it, sir?"

"I can fix anything, Cavell," the General said simply. "Less than two hours ago the Premier, a badly frightened man, put the entire resources of all the services at our disposal. He's as windy as hell. How urgent is this?"

"Maybe life-or-death urgent, sir. That's what I've got to find out. This woman appears to have been on very intimate terms with MacDonald for about nine months around the end of the war. It's the one period of his life about which information is lacking. If she's still alive and traceable she may be able to fill in this period."

"Is that all?" The voice was flat, disappointment barely concealed. "What of the letters themselves?"

"Only read a couple so far, sir. Seem perfectly innocuous, though not the sort of stuff I'd care to have read out in court if I had written it."

"It seems very little to go on, Cavell."

"A hunch, sir. More than that. It is possible that a page has been abstracted from the security dossier on MacDonald. The dates on those letters correspond to this missing page—if it is missing. And if it is, I want to find out why."

"Missing?" His voice crackled sharply over the wire. "How could a page from a security dossier possibly be missing? Who would have—or have had—access to those dossiers?"

"Easton, Clandon, myself—and Cliveden and Weybridge."

"Precisely. General Cliveden." A significant pause. "This recent threat to Mary to let her have your head on a charger: General Cliveden is the only man in Mordon who knows both who I am and the relationship between myself and Mary. One of the only two men with access to security dossiers. Don't you think you should be concentrating on Cliveden?"

"I think Hardanger should be concentrating on Cliveden. I want to see Madame Peugeot."

"Very well. Hold on." I held on, and after some minutes his voice came again. "Drive to Mordon. Helicopter there will fly you to Stanton airfield where they're testing the Diamante—the new vertical take-off supersonic night-fighter. Forty minutes from Stanton to Paris. That suit you?"

"I don't fancy it at all. But thanks very much. I'm afraid I've no passport with me, sir."

"You won't require it. If Madame Peugeot is still alive and still in Paris, she'll be waiting for you in Orly airport. That I promise. I'll see you when I return—I'm leaving for Alfringham in thirty minutes."

He hung up and I turned away, the bundle of letters in my hand. I caught sight of Mrs. Turpin by the open door, her face expressionless. Her eyes moved from mine down to the packet of letters in my hand, then met mine again. After a moment she turned and disappeared. I wondered how long she had been there, looking and listening.

The General was as good as his word all the way through. The helicopter was waiting for me at Mordon. The jet at Stanton took exactly thirty-five hair-raising minutes to reach Orly airport. And Madame Peugeot, accompanied by a Parisian police inspector, was waiting for me in a private room there. Somebody, I thought, had moved very fast indeed.

As it turned out, it hadn't been so difficult to locate Madame Peugeot—now Madame Halle. She still worked in the same place as in the later months of her acquaintanceship with MacDonald—the Pasteur Institute—and had readily agreed to come to the airport when the police had made plain the urgency. She was a dark, plump, attractive forty and had readily smiling eyes. At that moment she was hesitant, unsure and slightly apprehensive, the normal reaction when police start taking an interest in you.

The French police officer, an Inspector Jourdan whom I knew well and who had evinced typically Gallic lack of surprise at my changed face, made the introductions. I said, wasting no time: "We would be most grateful if you could give us some information about an Englishman whose acquaintance you made in the middle forties—forty-five and forty-six, to be precise. A Dr. Alexander MacDonald."

"Dr. MacDonald? Alex?" She laughed. "He'd be furious to hear himself described as an Englishman. At least, he would have been. In the days when I knew him he was the most ardent Scottish—what do you call it?"

"Nationalist?"

"Of course. A Scottish Nationalist. Fervent, I remember. Forever saying, 'Down with the old enemy'—England—and 'Up with the old Franco-Scottish alliance.' But I do know he fought most gallantly for the old enemy in the last war, so perhaps he was not so terribly sincere." She broke off and looked at me with an odd mixture of shrewdness and apprehension. "He—he's not dead, is he?"

"No, Madame, he is not."

"But he is in trouble? Police trouble?" She was quick and clever, had seized at once on the almost imperceptible inflection in my voice.

"I'm afraid he may be. How and when did you first meet him, Madame Halle?"

"Two or three months before the war ended—the European war, I mean. Colonel MacDonald, as he was then, was sent to examine a munitions and chemical factory that had been run by the Germans for years at St. Denis. I was working in the research division of the same factory—not from choice, I assure you. I did not know then that Colonel MacDonald was himself a brilliant chemist. I took it upon myself to explain to him the various chemical processes and production lines, and it wasn't until I'd finished the tour of the factory that I found out that he knew far more about it than I did." She smiled. "I think the gallant colonel had taken rather a fancy to me. And I to him."

I nodded. Judging from the highly combustible tone of her letters, she was considerably understating the case.

"He remained for several months in the Paris area," she continued. "I don't quite know what his duties were, but they were mostly of a technical nature. Every free moment we had we spent together." She shrugged. "It's all so long ago, it seems another world. He returned to England for demobilization and was back inside a week. He tried to find employment in Paris, but it was impossible. I think he eventually got some sort of research job with the British Government."

"Did you ever know or hear or suspect anything shady or reprehensible about Colonel MacDonald?" I asked bluntly.

"Never. If I had I would not have associated with him." The conviction of the words, the dignity of manner, made it impossible not to believe her. I had the sudden hollow feeling that perhaps the General had been right, after all, and that I was just wasting valuable time—if, on bitter reflection, my time could be called valuable—on a wild-goose chase. Cavell returning home with his tail between his legs.

"Nothing?" I persisted. "Not the slightest thing you can think of?"

"You wish to insult me, perhaps?" Her voice was quiet.

"I'm sorry." I changed my approach. "May I ask if you were in love with him?"

"I take it Dr. MacDonald didn't send you here," she said calmly. "You must have learnt of me through my letters. You know the answer to your question."

"Was he in love with you?"

"I know he was. At least he asked me to marry him. Ten times at least. That should show, no?"

"But you didn't marry," I said. "You lost touch with him. And if you were both in love and he asked you to marry him, may I ask why you refused? For you must have refused."

"I refused for the same reason that our friendship ended. Partly, I'm afraid, because in spite of his protestations of love, he was an incurable philanderer, but mainly because there were profound differences between us and we were neither of us old enough or experienced enough to let our hearts rule our heads."

"Differences? May I ask what differences, Madame Halle?"

"You are persistent, aren't you? Does it matter?" She sighed. "I suppose it does to you. You'll just keep on until you get the answer. There's no secret about it and it's all very unimportant and rather silly."

"I'd still like to hear it."

"No doubt. France, you will remember, was in a most confused state politically after the war. We had parties whose views could not have been more divergent, from the extreme right to the very furthest left. I am a good Catholic and I was of the Catholic party of the Right." She smiled deprecatingly. "What you would call a true-blue Tory. Well, I'm afraid that Dr. MacDonald disagreed so violently with my political opinions that our friendship eventually became quite impossible. Those things happen, you know. When one is young, politics become so terribly important."

"Dr. MacDonald didn't share your conservative viewpoint?"

"Conservative!" She laughed in genuine amusement. "Conservative, you say! Whether or not Alex was a genuine Scottish Nationalist I cannot say, but this much I can say with complete certainty: outside the walls of the Kremlin there never existed a more implacable and dedicated Communist. He was *formidable*."

One hour and ten minutes later I walked into the lounge of the Waggoner's Rest in Alfringham.

CHAPTER 10

I'd had a phone call put through from Stanton airfield, and both the General and Superintendent Hardanger were in the lounge waiting for me. Although it was still early evening, the General had on the table before him the remains of what appeared to have been a pretty considerable whisky. I'd never before known him to have his first drink of the day before nine o'clock at night. His face was pale, set and strained, and for the first time ever he was beginning to look his age—nothing I could put my finger on, just the slight sag of the shoulders, the indefinable air of weariness. There was something curiously pathetic about him, the pathos of a man with a broad and upright back who has suddenly, finally felt the burden of the weight he is carrying to be too much.

Hardanger didn't look a great deal better either.

I greeted them both, collected a whisky from old shirtsleeves, who was safely out of hearing range, and gladly took the weight off my feet. I said: 'Where's Mary?'

"Out visiting Stella Chessingham and her mother," Hardanger said. More broken wings for her to mend. "She wanted to give them what sympathy and encouragement she could. I agreed with her that they must both be feeling pretty grim after young Chessingham's arrest, but said I didn't think it either necessary or wise. This was before the General came down. She wouldn't listen to me. You know what your wife is like, Cavell. And your daughter, sir."

"She's wasting her time," I said. "On this occasion. Young Chessingham is as innocent as the day he was born. I told his mother so at eight o'clock this morning—I had to, she's a sick woman and the shock might have killed her—and she'd have told her daughter as soon as the van called for Chessingham. They don't need either sympathy or consolation."

"What!" Hardanger leaned far forward in his seat, face dark with rising anger, his big hand threatening to crush the glass clasped inside it. "What the devil are you saying, Cavell? Innocent? Damn it all, there's enough circumstantial evidence—"

"The only evidence against him is the fact that he very understandably told a lie about his driving, and that the *real* murderer has been sending him money under a false name. To throw suspicion on him. To buy time. Always to buy time. I don't know why it is, but it is essential for this murderer to buy time. He buys time every time he throws suspicion on someone else, and he's so outstandingly clever that he's managed to throw suspicion on practically everyone; he tried to buy time when he kidnapped me this morning. The thing is, he knew *months* before the crime—money was first paid into Chessingham's account at the beginning of July—that it was going to be necessary to buy time. Why? Why buy time?"

"You fooled me, damn you," Hardanger said harshly. "You trumped up this story—"

"I told you the facts as I had them." I was in no mood to placate Hardanger. "If I'd said he was innocent, would you have arrested him? You know perfectly well you wouldn't. But you did, and that has bought *us* time, because the murderer, or murderers, will read their evening papers and be convinced that we're on the wrong track."

"You'll be saying next that Hartnell and his wife are being framed, too," he said gratingly.

"As regards the hammer, pliers and mud on the scooter, of course they are. You know that. For the rest, Hartnell and wife are guilty as charged. But no court's ever going to convict. A man's blackmailed into having his wife shout and wave at a truck. Damned little criminal about that. All he'll get is a couple of years, on the entirely unrelated charge of embezzlement—if the Army chooses to press the charge, which I doubt. But again his arrest is buying us time; the murderer's planting of hammer and pliers was another method of buying *them* time. They don't know we haven't bought that one. Another point in our favor."

Hardanger turned to the General. "Were you aware that Cavell was working behind my back, sir?"

The General frowned. "That's pitching it a bit strongly, isn't it, Superintendent? As for my being aware—damn it all, man, it was *you* who talked me into bringing Cavell into this." Very adroit indeed. "I must admit he works in a highly unorthodox fashion. Which reminds me, Cavell. Dig up anything interesting about MacDonald in Paris?"

I didn't answer for a moment. There was something offhand, strangely indifferent in his manner, as if his mind was on other and more important things. I answered in kind.

"All depends what you call interesting, sir. I can give you with certainty the name of one of the men behind it all. Dr. Alexander MacDonald. And beyond all doubt he's been a top-flight Communist espionage agent for the past fifteen years. If not more."

That got them. They were the last two men on earth ever to go in for goggling, but they went in for it all the same. Just for a second. Then they stared at each other, then back at me. I told them in a minute flat what had happened. Hardanger said: "Oh, dear God!" very quietly and left to call a police car.

The General said: "You saw the police radio van outside?"

I nodded.

"We're in constant touch with the Government and Scotland Yard." He fished in an inside pocket and brought out two typewritten notes. "The first of those came in about two hours ago, the second only ten minutes ago." I looked at them quickly and for the first time in my life realized that the phrase about blood running cold might have some basis in physical experience. I felt unaccountably cold, icy even, and was glad to see Hardanger, back from ordering his car, bring three more whiskies from the bar. I knew now why both the General and Hardanger had looked so ill, so close to desperation, when I'd come in. I knew now and could understand why my trip to Paris had been a matter of relative indifference to them.

The first message had been delivered at almost the same time to Reuter's and A.P., and was very brief. The florid style was unmistakable. It read: "The walls of the home of the antichrist still stand. My orders have been ignored. The responsibility is yours. I have taped a virus ampoule to a simple explosive device which will be detonated at three-forty-five this afternoon in Lower Hampton, Norfolk. The wind is W.S.W. If the demolition of Mordon has not commenced by midnight tonight I shall be compelled to break another ampoule tomorrow. In the heart of the City of London. The carnage will be such as the world has never seen. Yours is the choice."

"Lower Hampton is a hamlet of about one hundred fifty people four miles from the sea," the General said. "The reference to the wind means that the virus would cover, only four miles of land and then be blown out over the sea. Unless the wind changed. The message was received at two-forty-five this afternoon. Nearest police cars were rushed to the area and all people in the village and as many as could be reached in the area between the village and the sea were evacuated to the West." He broke off and stared at the table. "But that's rich farming land. There are many farms and few cars. It was not possible to reach them all in time, I'm afraid. A hurried search was made in Lower Hampton for the bomb, but it was worse than the needle in the haystack. At three-forty-five precisely, a sergeant and two constables heard a small explosion and saw fire and smoke coming from the thatch of a disused cottage. They ran for their car and you can just imagine how they took off."

My mouth felt as dry as last year's ashes. I washed some of the ashes away by draining half a large whisky in one gulp.

The General went on: "At four-twenty an R.A.F. bomber, a photo-reconnaissance plane, took off from a base in East Anglia and flew over the area. The pilot was warned not to fly below ten thousand feet, but it's a clear evening up there, and with the kind of cameras they have in the Air Force today there was no trouble in making a close reconnaissance. The entire area was photographed—from two miles up it doesn't take long to photograph a few square miles of territory—and the bomber landed half an hour after takeoff. The pictures were developed within minutes and examined by an expert. That second paper shows his findings."

It was even briefer than the first. It read: "Over a wedge-shaped area, with its point at the village of Little Hampton and its base two and a half miles of seacoast, there are no discoverable signs of life, either around houses and farm buildings, or in the fields. Dead cattle in fields estimated between three and four hundred. Three flocks of sheep, also apparently lifeless. At least seven human bodies identified.

Characteristic postures of both men and cattle suggest death in contorted agony. Detailed analysis following."

I finished the second half of my whisky in a second gulp. I might as well have been drinking soda pop for all the taste or effect it had. I said: "What's the Government going to do?"

"I don't know," the General said tonelessly. "Neither do they. They will make a decision by ten o'clock tonight—and now they'll decide even faster when they hear your news. It completely alters everything. We thought we were dealing with some raving crackpot, however brilliant that crackpot; it seems instead that we're dealing with a Communist plot to destroy the most powerful weapon that Britain—or any other country, for that matter—has ever had. Maybe it's the beginnings of a plot to destroy Britain itself, I don't know; damn it all, I've just come to the thought and I haven't had time to think about it. Could it be that the Communist world is planning a showdown with the West, that they're convinced that they can strike so hard and so savagely that there'll be no possibility of retaliation? Not, that is, once Mordon and its viruses are out of the way. God only knows. I think I'd rather be dealing with a crackpot any day. Besides, Cavell, we don't know that your information is correct."

"There's only one way to find out, sir." I rose to my feet. "I see the police driver is there. Shall we have a chat with MacDonald?"

We reached Mordon in eight minutes flat, only to be told at the gate that MacDonald had checked out over two hours previously. Eight minutes later we pulled up at the front door of his home.

Dr. MacDonald's house was dark and deserted. Mrs. Turpin, the housekeeper, should not have been gone for the night. But she was. MacDonald had also gone, not for the night, but forever. Our bird had flown.

MacDonald hadn't even bothered to lock the door when leaving. He'd have been in too much of a hurry for that. We made our way into the hallway, switched on lights and looked quickly over the ground floor. No fires, no still-warm radiators, no smell of cooking, no cigarette smoke still hanging in the air. Whoever had left hadn't left by a back window as we had come in by the front door. He'd left a long time ago. I felt old and sick and tired. And foolish. Because I knew now why he'd left in such a hurry.

We went over the house, not wasting time, starting from the attic darkroom. The battery of expensive photographic

149

equipment was as I had seen it before, but this time I was seeing it in a new light. Given sufficient facts and sufficient time, even Cavell could arrive at a conclusion. We went over his bedroom, but there were no signs of hasty packing or hasty departure. That was strange. People going on a journey from which they have no intention of returning usually take a bare minimum of supplies to tide them over, no matter what their hurry. An inspection of the bathroom was equally puzzling. Razor, brush, shaving cream, toothbrush—they were all still there. MacDonald's old colonel, I thought inconsequentially, wasn't going to be any too happy when he arrived to identify MacDonald and found no one left to identify.

Even more baffling was the kitchen. Mrs. Turpin, I knew, used to leave every night at six-thirty when MacDonald arrived home, leaving his dinner prepared. MacDonald had been in the habit of helping himself and leaving the dishes for his housekeeper the following morning. But there were no signs whatsoever of any food preparations. No roasts in the oven, no pots of still-warm food, an electric stove so cold that it couldn't have been used for hours.

I said: "The last of the plain-clothes men on the search job would have been gone by half-past three at the latest. No reason why Mrs. Turpin shouldn't have got on with the cooking of dinner for Dr. MacDonald—and MacDonald strikes me as a character who would be very huffed indeed if he didn't find his chow ready. But she prepared none. Why?"

"She knew he wouldn't be wanting any," Hardanger said heavily. "From something she heard or saw this afternoon she knew our worthy doctor wouldn't be wanting to linger too much around these parts after she'd told him what she'd heard or seen. Which argues connivance, or at least knowledge of MacDonald's activities."

"It's my fault," I said savagely. "That damned woman! She must have heard me telephoning the General about going to Paris. God only knows how long she was standing there in the doorway, watching me, seeing the letter in my hand. But I didn't see her because she was on my blind side. She must have noticed that and the limp and told MacDonald by phone. And what I was talking about. He'd have known straight away that it must have been me, limp or no limp. It's all my bloody fault," I repeated. "It never crossed my mind to suspect her. I think we should have a talk with Mrs. Turpin. If she's at home, that is."

Hardanger moved off to a phone while the General accompanied me into MacDonald's study. I moved over to the big old-fashioned knee-hole desk where MacDonald's correspondence and photographic albums had been discovered. It was locked—where possible, police search details always left things as they found them. Unfortunately, police search details carried around with them a large variety of instruments for picking almost any type of lock. I didn't. I gave the drawer a hefty tug, but all I did was move the whole desk. I said to the General, "Back in a minute, sir," and went outside.

I borrowed a torch from the police driver and went to the garage. There I didn't need the torch—electric power was laid on. I turned the switch and went inside. Most of the space was taken up by MacDonald's sand-and-beige Bentley. At the moment, I wasn't particularly interested in the Bentley. When a wanted man takes it on the lam he doesn't, unless he's blown a mental gasket, clutter himself up with sand-and-beige Bentleys. There are easier ways for a wanted criminal to call attention to himself, such as dragging a murdered victim along the Strand in the evening rush hour, but not many. On the other hand, he could have driven it to some spot to pick up his getaway car, if car it was. At the moment it didn't seem worth worrying about.

There was nothing in the garage that would be of any use to me. Backing on the garage was a large tool shed. No light here. I switched on the torch and looked round. Garden implements, a small pile of gray breeze blocks, a pile of empty cement sacks, a work-bench and bicycle. No claw-hammer, which was what I was looking for, but I found the next best thing, a fairly heavy hatchet.

I went back to the study with this and crossed to the desk just as Hardanger came into the room.

"You going to smash that desk open?" he demanded.

"Let MacDonald object if he feels like it." I swung the hatchet twice and the drawer splintered. The albums and the doctor's correspondence with the World Health Organization were still there. I opened the album at the page with the missing photograph and showed it to the General.

"A photograph our good friend didn't seem to care to have around," I said. "I have more than a vague, obscure feeling that it may be important. See that scratched-out caption, something about six letters, some town certainly, starting with TO. I can't get it. With any kind of paper or with two different kinds of ink, it would have been easy for the lab boys. But white ink on this porous blotting paper stuff? No good."

"Not a chance." Hardanger gave me a suspicious look. "Why is it important?"

"If I knew that, I wouldn't worry about what the caption was. Did you find our dear Mrs. Turpin at home?"

"No reply. She lives alone, a widow, as I found out from the local station after I'd called her number. An officer has gone to check, but he'll find nothing. I've put out an all-stations call for her."

"That'll help," I said sourly. I went quickly through Mac-Donald's correspondence, picking out replies from his WHO correspondents in Europe. I knew what I was looking for, and it took me only two minutes to isolate half a dozen letters, from a Dr. John Weissmann in Vienna. I handed them across to the General and Hardanger. "Exhibit A for the Old Bailey when MacDonald's en route to the gallows."

The General looked at me, his face old and tired and expressionless. Hardanger said bluntly: "What are you talking about, Cavell?"

I hesitated and looked at the General. He said quietly: "It'll be all right now, my boy. Hardanger will understand. And it'll never go any further."

Hardanger looked from me to the papers and then back to me again. "What will I understand? It's time I understood. I knew from the beginning that there was something I couldn't touch in this damned business. You accepted this job with too much alacrity in the first place."

"I'm sorry," I said. "It had to be this way. You know I've been in and out of a few jobs since the war—Army, police, Special Branch, Narcotics, Special Branch again, security chief in Mordon, and then private detective. None of it really meant anything. I've been working for the General here non-stop for the past sixteen years. Every time I was heaved out of a job—well, the General arranged it."

"I'm not all that surprised," Hardanger said heavily. I was glad to see he was more intrigued than angry. "I've had my suspicions."

"That's why you're a Superintendent," the General murmured.

"Anyway, about a year ago, my predecessor in security in Mordon, Easton Derry, began having *his* suspicions. I won't go into the where and the when of it, but he came to the conclusion that certain highly secret items in the bacteriological and virus line were being smuggled out of Mordon. His suspicions became certainties when Dr. Baxter approached him privately and said *he* was convinced that certain stuff was going astray."

"Dr. Baxter!" Hardanger looked slightly stunned.

"Yes, Baxter. Sorry about that, too—but I *told* you, plain as I could, not to waste time on him. He said to Derry that although it wasn't the top-secret stuff that was going—that was impossible to get out of 'A' laboratory—it was nevertheless pretty important stuff. Very important stuff, indeed. Britain leads the world in the production of microbiological diseases for wartime use against men, animals and plants. You'll never hear of this when the Parliamentary Estimates for Mordon Health Center are being passed, but our scientists in Mordon have either discovered or refined to their purest and most deadly forms, the germs for causing plague, typhus, smallpox, rabbit and undulant fever in man; hog choleras, fowl pest, Newcastle disease, rinderpest, foot-and-mouth, glanders and anthrax in livestock; and blights like the Japanese beetle, European corn borer, Mediterranean fruit fly, boll weevil, citrus cancer, wheat rust, and heaven knows what else in plants. All very useful in either limited or all-out warfare."

"What's all this got to do with Dr. MacDonald?" Hardanger demanded.

"I'm coming to it. Over two years ago our agents in Poland began taking an interest in the newly built Lenin Museum on the outskirts of Warsaw. So far, this museum has never been opened to the public. It never will be—it's the equivalent of Mordon, a purely microbiological research station. One of our agents—he's a card-carrying member of the party—managed to get himself employed there and made the interesting discovery that the Poles were discovering and refining the various bugs I just mentioned a few weeks, or at most months, after they had been perfected in Mordon. The inference was too obvious to miss.

"Easton Derry started investigating. He made two mistakes: he played it too close to the cuff, without letting us know what was going on, and he unwittingly gave himself away. How, we've no idea. He may even have taken into his confidence, quite unknowingly, the man who was responsible for smuggling the stuff out of Mordon. MacDonald, for a certainty—it would be too much to expect two espionage agents operating at the same time. Anyway, someone became aware that Easton Derry was in danger of finding out too much. So Derry disappeared.

"The General here then made arrangements to have me removed from the Special Branch and introduced into Mordon as security officer. The first thing I did was to stake out a decoy duck. I had a steel flask of botulinus toxin, strength one—it was so labeled—introduced into a cupboard in number one lab annex. The same day, the flask disappeared. We had a VHF receiver installed at the gates, for that flask contained not toxin but a microwave, battery-powered transistor sender. Anyone carrying that and coming within two hundred yards of the gate would have been picked up at once. You will understand," I said dryly, "that anyone picking up a flask of botulinus toxin is unlikely to open it up to see if it really does contain toxin.

"We picked up no one. It wasn't hard to guess what had happened. After dark someone had strolled across to a deserted part of the boundary fence and chucked the flask into an adjacent field—it's only a ten-yard throw to clear all the fences. Not because they had any suspicions of the contents, but because this was the way it would usually be done—you know how often spot checks and searches are made of people leaving Mordon. By eight o'clock that evening we had microwave receivers installed at London airport, Southend and Lydd airfields, the Channel ports and—"

"Wouldn't the shock of having been flung over the fences have smashed the transmitter?" Hardanger objected.

"The American watch company that makes those transmitters would be most displeased if one did break," I said. "They can be fired from a high-velocity naval gun without being affected in the slightest. Anyway, late that night, we picked up a signal in London airport. Almost inevitably if was from a man boarding a BEA flight to Warsaw. We took him and he told us he was just a courier, picking up stuff about once a fortnight from an address in south London. He'd never actually seen his contact."

"He told you that?" Hardanger said sourly. "I can imagine how you made him volunteer that information."

"You'd be wrong. We told him—he was a naturalized British subject, ex-Czech—that espionage was a capital offense, and he thought he was turning Queen's evidence. He turned it pretty fast, too. It was his supplier from Mordon we wanted to nail, so I was duly thrown out of there and have been haunting this damn address and neighborhood for the past three weeks. We couldn't get anyone else to do the job because I was the only one who knew and who could identify all the scientists and technicians in Mordon. But no luck—

except that Dr. Baxter reported that the disappearances had stopped. So we seemed to have stopped that leak—temporarily, anyway.

"But, according to Baxter and our Polish informant, that wasn't the only leak. We had learnt that the Lenin Museum had developed viruses that had *not* been stolen from Mordon—but which had been *produced* in Mordon. Someone, obviously, was sending them information on the breeding and development of those strains. And now we've found that out, too." I tapped the papers, MacDonald's correspondence with his WHO contact in Vienna. "Not a new system, but almost impossible to detect. Microphotography."

"All that expensive photographic equipment upstairs?" the General murmured.

"Exactly. There's a camera expert due from London to look at his stuff, but his journey's hardly necessary now. Look at those letters from Dr. Weissmann. In every one you will note that a dot from an 'i' or a full stop is missing in the first paragraph. Weissmann typed a message, reduced it to the size of a dot by micro-miniature photography and stuck it on the letter in place of some other dot. All MacDonald had to do was to pry it loose and enlarge it. And he, of course, did the same in his correspondence with Weissmann. And he didn't do it for pennies, either." I glanced around the richly furnished room. "He's earned a fortune over the years—and not a penny tax, either."

There was a minute's silence, then the General nodded. "That must be the right of it. At least MacDonald won't be troubling us any more." He looked up at me and smiled without humor. "When it comes to locking stable doors after the horse has taken off, we have few equals. There's also another door I can lock for you, supposing it's any use to you. The caption that's been scratched out in this album."

"Toulon? Tournai?"

"Neither." He turned to the backboard of the album. "This has been prepared for certain members of the WHO by a firm called Gucci Zanoletti, Via XX Settembre, Genoa. The word that has been scratched out is Torino—the Italian, of course, for Turin."

Turin. Only a word, but he might as well have hit me with a sledge hammer. It had about the same effect. Turin. I sat in a chair because all of a sudden I felt I had to sit, and after the first dazed shock started to wear off, I managed to whip a few of the less lethargic brain cells out of their coma and started thinking again. It wasn't much in the way of thinking, not as thinking went, for with the beating and the soaking I had received, the lack of sleep and food, I was a fair way below my best insofar as anything resembling active cerebration was concerned. Slowly, laboriously, I assembled a few facts in the befogged recesses of my mind, and no matter how I reassembled them, those facts formed the same mosaic every time. Two and two always came out to four.

I rose heavily to my feet and said to the General: "It's like the man says, sir. You speak more truly than you know."

"Are you all right, Cavell?" There was sharp anxiety in the voice.

"I'm falling to pieces. My mind, such as it is, is still on its hinges. Or I think so. We'll soon find out."

Torch in hand, I turned and left the room. The General and Hardanger hesitated, then followed. I suppose they were exchanging all sorts of apprehensive glances, but I was past caring.

I'd already been in the garage and shed, so those weren't the places to look. Somewhere in the shrubbery, I thought drearily—and it was still raining. In the hall I turned off into the kitchen and was about to make for the back door when I saw the flight of steps leading down to the cellar. I remembered vaguely that Sergeant Carlisle had made mention of this when he and his men had been searching the house that afternoon. I went down the flight of steps, opened the cellar door and switched on the overhead light. I stood aside to let the General and Hardanger into the cellar.

"It's as you said, sir," I murmured to the General. "MacDonald won't be troubling us any more."

Which was not quite accurate. MacDonald was going to give some trouble yet. To the police doctor, the undertaker, and the man who would have to cut the rope by which he was suspended by the neck from the heavy iron ring in the overhead loading hatch. As he dangled there, feet just clear of the floor and brushing the legs of an overturned chair, he was the stuff that screaming nightmares are made of: eyes staring wide in the frenzied agony of death, bluish-purple face, swollen tongue protruding between blackened lips drawn far back in the snarling rictus of dissolution. No, not the stuff that dreams are made of.

"My good God!" The General's voice was a hushed whisper. "MacDonald." He gazed at the dangling figure, then said slowly: "He must have known his time was running out."

I shook my head. "Someone else decided for him that his time had run out."

156

"Someone else—" Hardanger examined the dead man closely, his face giving nothing away. "His hands are free. His feet are free. He was conscious when he started to strangle. That chair was brought down from the kitchen. And yet you say—"

"He was murdered. Look at the streaks and marks in that coal dust a few feet from the chair, and that disturbed pile of coal with lumps kicked all over the cellar floor. Look at the weals and the blood on the inside of the thumbs."

"He could have changed his mind at the last minute," Hardanger rumbled. "Lots of them do. As soon as he started choking he probably grabbed the rope above his head and took the weight until he couldn't hang on any more. That would account for the marks on his thumbs."

"The marks on his thumbs were caused by twine or wire binding them together," I said. "He was marched down here, almost certainly at gun-point, and made to lie on the floor. He may have been blindfolded—I don't know. Probably. Whoever killed him passed a rope through the ring and had the loop around MacDonald's neck and had started hauling before MacDonald could do anything about it. That's what caused all that mess in the coal and dust—MacDonald trying to scrabble madly to his feet as the pressure tightened round his neck. With his thumbs bound behind his back he made it with the assistance of his executioner, but it wouldn't have been easy. It only postponed death by seconds, the man on the end of the rope just kept on hauling. Can't you see MacDonald almost tearing his thumbs off in an effort to free them? By and by he would be on tiptoe—but a man can't stand on tiptoe forever. When he was dead our pal on the heaving end got a chair and used it to help him lift MacDonald clear off the floor—MacDonald was a big, heavy man. When he'd secured him there, he cut the twine on MacDonald's thumbs and kicked over the chair—to make it look like suicide. It's our old buy-time-at-any-price friend. If he could make us think that MacDonald did himself in because he thought the net was closing round him, then he hoped that we would believe that MacDonald was the king-pin in this business. But he wasn't sure."

"You're guessing," Hardanger said.

"No. Can you see a never-say-die character like MacDonald, not only a highly decorated officer who fought in a tank regiment for six years but also a nerveless espionage agent for many years after that, committing suicide when things started closing in on him? MacDonald thinking of giving up

157

or giving in? He wouldn't have known how to go about it, most probably. MacDonald was well and truly murdered—which he no doubt richly deserved to be, anyway. But the real point is that he wasn't murdered *only* so that our friend could cast more red herrings around and so buy more time; he *had* to die, and our friend thought he might as well make it look like suicide while he was about it in the hope of stalling us further. I *was* guessing, Hardanger, but not any more."

"MacDonald had to die?" Hardanger studied me through a long considering silence, then said abruptly: "You seem fairly sure about all this."

"I'm certain. I know." I picked up the coal shovel and started heaving away some of the coal that was piled up against the back wall of the cellar. There must have been close on a couple of tons of the stuff reaching almost as high as the ceiling, and I was in no condition for anything much more strenuous than brushing my teeth, but I had to shift only a fraction of it; for every shovelful I scooped away from the base almost a hundredweight of lumps came clattering down onto the floor.

"What do you expect to find under that lot?" Hardanger said with heavy sarcasm. "Another body?"

"Another body is exactly what I do expect to find. I expect to find the late Mrs. Turpin. The fact that she tipped off MacDonald about me and didn't bother preparing dinner, because she knew MacDonald wouldn't be staying for dinner owing to the fact that he would be taking off for the high timber, shows beyond all doubt that she was in cahoots with our pal here. What MacDonald knew, she knew. It would have been pointless to silence MacDonald if Mrs. Turpin had been left alive to squawk. So she was attended to."

But wherever she had been attended to, it hadn't been in the cellar. We went upstairs, and while the General went to talk for quite a long time on the scrambler radio-phone in the police van that had followed us from Alfringham, Hardanger and I, with the assistance of two police drivers and a couple of torches, started to scour the grounds. It was no easy job, for the good doctor, who had done so well for himself in the way of furnishing his house, had also done himself pretty well in the way of buying himself privacy, for his policies, half-garden, half-parkland, extended to over four acres, the whole of it surrounded by an enormous beech hedge that would have stopped a tank.

It was dark and very cold with no wind, the heavy rain

falling vertically through the thinning leaves of the dripping trees to the sodden earth beneath. The appropriate setting, I thought grimly, for a search for a murdered body—and there's an awful lot of searching in four acres on a black and miserable night.

The beech hedge had been trimmed some time during the past month and the clippings piled up in a distant corner of the garden. We found Mrs. Turpin under this pile, not very deep down, just enough branches and twigs over her to hide her from sight. Lying beside her was the hammer I had failed to find in the tool shed, and it required only a glance at the back of her head to know the reason why the hammer was there. At a guess I would have said that the person who had tried to stave in my ribs had also wielded the hammer on Mrs. Turpin; my ribs, like the dead woman's head, bore witness to the insensate and unreasoning feral ferocity of a broken and vicious mind. In the light of my torch I could see one of the police drivers, a youngster barely in his twenties, turn a greenish sallow color and walk away quickly into the darkness.

We found a tarpaulin lying beside the cement sacks in the tool shed and covered the body with it, I don't know why—it was a senseless thing to do, but whether she had deserved to die or not, it seemed wrong to leave her lying there in the rain.

Back in the house I broached MacDonald's whisky supply. He wouldn't be wanting it any more, and as he'd carefully pointed out to me that he had no relations and therefore no one to leave it to, it seemed a pity to waste it. We needed it, badly. I poured out hefty tots, one apiece for Hardanger and myself, the other two for the police drivers, and if Hardanger took a dim view of this theft of property and contravention of standing orders by offering intoxicating liquor to policemen on duty, he kept it to himself. He finished his whisky before any of us. The two policemen left just as the General returned from the radio van. He seemed to have aged a year for every minute since last I'd seen him, the lines about the nose and mouth more deeply trenched than ever.

"You found her?" He took the offered glass.

"We found her," Hardanger acknowledged. "Dead, as Cavell said she would be. Murdered."

"It hardly matters." The General shivered suddenly and took a deep gulp of his whisky. "She's only one. This time tomorrow—how many thousands? God knows how many thousands. This madman has sent another message. Usual biblical language, walls of Mordon still standing, no signs of demolition, so has advanced his timetable. If demolition doesn't start on Mordon by midnight, he's going to break a botulinus toxin ampoule in the heart of London, at four o'clock this morning, within a quarter of a mile of New Oxford Street."

This seemed to call for some more whisky. Hardanger said: "He's no madman, sir."

"No." The General rubbed his forehead wearily. "I told them what Cavell found out, what we think. They're in a complete panic now. Do you know that some of the national dailies are already on the streets—just before six o'clock? Unprecedented, but so is the situation. The papers seem to be very accurately reflecting the terror of the people and are begging—or demanding—that the Government yield to this madman—for at the time of printing everyone thought it was just a crazed crackpot. Word of the wiping out of this segment of East Anglia is just beginning to come through on constant radio and TV news broadcasts, and everyone is terrified out of his wits. Whoever is behind all this is a brilliant devil; a few hours and he has the nation on its knees. It's the man's frightening speed of operation, the lack of time-lag between threat and carrying out of threat that's so terrifying. Especially with every paper and news broadcast plugging the theme that this madman doesn't know the difference between the botulinus toxin and the Satan Bug, and that it may very well be the Satan Bug he uses next time."

"In fact," I said, "all those who have been moaning and complaining so bitterly that life is hardly worth the living in the shadow of a nuclear holocaust have suddenly discovered that it might very well be worth living after all. You think the Government will give in?"

"I can't say," the General admitted. "I'm afraid I rather misjudged the Premier. I thought he was as windy as they come. I don't know, now. He's toughened his attitude amazingly. Maybe he's ashamed of his earlier panic-stricken reaction. Maybe he sees the chance to make his imperishable mark on history."

"Maybe he's like us," I said. "Maybe he's been drinking whisky, too."

"Maybe. He's at present consulting with the Cabinet. He says that if this is a Communist scheme, he'll be damned if he gives in. If the Communists *are* behind it, he says the last thing in the world we can afford to do is to give in, for though not yielding to their demands that Mordon be demolished may bring death to many, yielding to their demands will bring eventual death to all. Myself, I think that attitude is the only one, and I agree with him when he says he's ready to evacuate the city of London before he gives in."

"Evacuate London?" Hardanger said in disbelief. "Ten million people in ten hours? Fantastic. The man's mad. Impossible."

"It's not quite as drastic as all that, thank heaven. It's a windless evening, the Met office forecasts a windless night, and it's raining heavily. It seems that an airborne virus is carried down to earth by heavy rain, having a much greater affinity for water than for air. The experts doubt whether in windless rainy conditions the virus will get more than a few hundred yards from its point of release. If the need arises, they propose to evacuate the area between Euston Road and the Thames, from Portland Street and Regent Street in the West to Gray's Inn Road in the East."

"That's feasible enough," Hardanger admitted. "Place is practically deserted by night anyway—mainly a business, office and shop area. But this virus. It'll be carried away by the rain. It'll pollute the Thames. It may get into the drinking water. What's to happen—are people to be told to refrain from washing or drinking until the twelve-hour oxidization period is up?"

"That's what they say. Unless the water has been stored and covered beforehand, that is. My God, what's going to come of it all? I've never felt so damned helpless in my life. We don't seem to have a single solitary lead into this business. If only we had a suspicion, the slightest pointing finger as to who is behind all this—well, by heaven, if we could get to him I'd turn my back and let Cavell here get to work on him."

I drained my glass and put it down. "You mean that, sir?"

"What do you think?" He glanced up from his glass, then stared at me with his tired gray eyes. "What do *you* mean? Cavell? Can *you* point a finger?"

"I can do better than that, sir. I know. I know who it is."

The General was a great disappointment as far as reaction went. He always was. No gasps, no wide-eyed stares, no emotional pyrotechnics. He murmured: "Half of my kingdom, Pierre. Who?"

"The last proof," I said. "The last proof and then I can say. We missed it and it was staring us in the face. At least, it was staring me in the face. And Hardanger. To think the country depends upon people like us to safeguard them.

Policemen, detectives. We couldn't detect the holes in Gruyère cheese." I turned to Hardanger. "We've just made a pretty thorough search of the garden. Agreed?"

"Agreed. So?"

"Hardly missed a square foot?" I persisted.

"Go on," he rumbled impatiently.

"Did you see any signs of freshly built masonry? Huts? Sheds? Walls? Fishponds? Decorative stonework? Anything?"

He shook his head, his eyes wary. I was going off my rocker. "Nothing. There was nothing of the kind."

"Then what happened to all the cement in the empty cement bags in the tool shed? The ones we saw when we found the tarpaulin there? It didn't just vanish. And the few breeze blocks we saw? Probably only the remainder of a fair stack of them. If outdoor masonry work wasn't a hobby of MacDonald's, then what would be the most likely place to find such masonry work? In a dining-room? In a bedroom?"

"Suppose you tell me, Cavell?"

"I'll do better than that. I'll show you." I left them, went out to the tool shed and hunted around for a crowbar or pick. I could find neither. The nearest was a small sledge. It would have to do. I picked it up, along with a bucket, went into the kitchen where the General and Hardanger were waiting for me, filled the bucket at the kitchen sink and led the way down the stairs to the cellar. Hardanger, apparently oblivious of the presence of the dead man dangling from the ceiling, said heavily: "What do you propose to demonstrate, Cavell? How to make coal briquettes?"

The telephone bell rang in the hallway upstairs. Automatically, we all looked at each other. Dr. MacDonald's incoming calls might be very interesting. Hardanger said: "I'll answer it," and left.

We heard his voice on the phone, and then my name being called. I started up the stairs, conscious of the General following me.

Hardanger handed me the phone. "For you. Won't give his name. Wants to speak to you personally."

I took the receiver. "Cavell speaking."

"So you are on the loose and the little lady wasn't lying." The words came over the wire like a deep, dark and throaty whisper. "Lay off, Cavell. Tell the General to lay off, Cavell. If you want to see the little lady alive again."

These new synthetic resins are pretty tough, so the receiver didn't crush in my palm. It must have been pretty close, though. My heart did a long, slow somersault and landed on its back with a thud. I kept my voice steady and said: "What the hell are you talking about?"

"The beautiful Mrs. Cavell. I have her. She would like to speak to you."

A moment's silence, then her voice came. "Pierre? Oh, my dear, I'm so sorry—" Her voice broke off abruptly in a gasp, followed by a scream of agony. Silence. Again the dark whisper: "Lay off, Cavell," and then the click of a replaced receiver. I replaced mine, the receiver making a sharp staccato rattle against the rest. My hand was the hand of a man with the ague.

Shock or fear or both may have frozen my face into an expression of normalcy, or maybe the make-up on my face didn't transmit expression too well. Whichever it was, they didn't notice anything amiss, for the General said: "Who was it?" in a normal, curious tone.

"I don't know." I paused and went on mechanically: "They've got Mary."

The General had had his hand on the door. Now he dropped it to his side in a ridiculously slow-motion gesture that took almost ten seconds while something in his face died. Hardanger whispered something, something unprintable; his face was like a stone. Neither of them asked me to repeat what I had said, neither was in the slightest doubt as to what I had meant.

"They told us to lay off," I went on in the same wooden voice. "Or they'd kill her. They have her, all right. She spoke a few words and then screamed. They must have hurt her, badly."

We stood there, a frozen tableau from an old morality play. I knew what was in the thoughts of the other two men, the same glacial thought as was in my own. A man who had murdered twice to get the viruses, a man who had killed hundreds of animals and heaven yet only knew how many people to demonstrate the deadly seriousness of his threats and his intentions—such a man would snuff out Mary's life like a candle, and with as little thought and compunction.

Hardanger said, almost desperately: "How could he have known that you had escaped? Or even suspected? How—"

"Dr. MacDonald is how," I said. "He knew—Mrs. Turpin told him—and the killer learnt from MacDonald." I stared almost unseeingly at the General's face, a face still impassive, but with all the life and animation gone from it. I went on: "I'm sorry. If anything happens to Mary it will be my fault. My own criminal folly and negligence."

The General said: "What are we going to do, my boy?" The voice was tired and listless to match the dullness that had replaced the soldierly fire in his eye. "You know they are going to kill your wife. People like that always kill."

"Your wife," he had said. "My daughter," he had meant. One day, perhaps, I, too, would be such a man.

"You know there is no choice, sir. Impossible to call off the hunt now. Hers is only one life. God knows how many thousands of others lie in the balance with this crazed killer at large. He *must* be stopped. So many lives at stake."

"And you'd gladly trade them all for Mary's," the General said, "I'm terribly sorry, my boy."

"We're wasting time," Hardanger said harshly.

"Two minutes," I said. "That's all I need. To make sure."

I ran down to the cellar, picked up the bucket and tossed half its contents against the opposite wall. The water spread and ran down quickly to the floor. As a cleaning agent it was a dead failure, making hardly any impression whatsoever on the ingrained coal dust of a score or more of years. With the General and Hardanger still watching uncomprehendingly, I threw the remainder of the bucket's contents against the rear wall, where the coal had been piled so high before my recent excavation. The water splashed off and ran down into the coal, leaving the wall almost as clear and clean and fresh as if it had been built only a few weeks previously. Hardanger glared at it, then at me, then back at the wall again.

"My apologies, Cavell," he said. "That would be why the coal was piled so high against the wall—to conceal the traces of recent work."

I didn't waste time speaking, time was now the one commodity we'd run clear out of; instead, I picked up the sledge hammer and swung at the upper line of breeze work—the lower portion was solid concrete. One swing only. I felt as if someone had slid a six-inch stiletto in between my right ribs. Maybe the doctor had been right, maybe my ribs weren't as securely anchored as nature had intended. Without a word I handed the sledge to Hardanger and sat down wearily on the upturned bucket.

Hardanger weighed sixteen stone, and in spite of the calm impassivity of his features, he was just clear mad all the way through. He removed his coat, handed it ceremoniously to the General, and with all the power and vicious determination that was in him, attacked that wall of breeze as if it were the archtype of all things evil on earth. The wall hadn't a chance. On the third stroke the first block of breeze was splintered and dislodged, and within thirty seconds he had hammered in a hole about two feet square. He stopped, looked at me, and I rose to my feet like the old, old man I felt I was and switched on my torch. Together, we peered into the hole.

Between the false wall and the real cellar wall behind, there was a gap of under two feet, and jammed at the bottom of this narrow space and half-covered with broken masonry, chips, and dust from the fractured breeze blocks lay the remains of what had once been a man. Broken, twisted, savagely mutilated, but still undoubtedly the remains of a man.

Hardanger said in a voice ominously clean and steady: "Do you know who this is, Cavell?"

"I know him. Easton Derry. My predecessor as security chief in Mordon."

"Easton Derry." The General was as unnaturally controlled as Hardanger. "How can you tell? His face is unrecognizable."

"Yes. That ring on his left hand has a blue Cairngorm stone. Easton Derry always wore a ring with a blue Cairngorm. That's Easton Derry."

"What—what did this to him?" The General stared down at the half-naked body. "A road crash? Some—some wild animal?" For a long minute he stared down in silence at the dead man, then straightened and turned to me, the age and weariness in his face more accentuated than ever, but the old eyes bleak and icy and still. "A man did this to him. He was tortured to death."

"He was tortured to death," I said.

"And you know who did it?" Hardanger reminded me.

"I know who did it."

Hardanger pulled a warrant form and pen from an inside pocket and stood waiting. I said: "You won't need that, Superintendent. Not if I get to him first. In case I don't, make it out in the name of Dr. Giovanni Gregori. The man calling himself Dr. Giovanni Gregori. The real Dr. Gregori is dead."

CHAPTER 11

Eight minutes later the big police Jaguar braked hard to a stop outside Chessingham's house, and for the third time in just under twenty-four hours I climbed the worn steps over the dried-out moat and pressed the bell. The General was close behind me; Hardanger was in the radio van, alerting the police of a dozen counties to be on the lookout for Gregori, to identify, follow, but not, for the present, apprehend: Gregori, we felt, wouldn't kill until desperate, and we owed her at least that slender hope of life.

"Mr. Cavell!" The welcome Stella Chessingham gave me bore no resemblance to the one I had received from her at dawn that morning. The light was back in her eyes, the anxiety vanished from her face. "How nice! I—I'm so sorry about this morning, Mr. Cavell. I mean—it is true what my mother told me after they'd taken him away?"

"It's perfectly true, Miss Chessingham." I tried to smile, but with the way I felt and with my face still aching from the hasty scrubbing away of the now-useless disguise before leaving MacDonald's house, I was glad I couldn't see what sort of attempt I'd made at it. As far as our respective positions were concerned, compared to twelve hours ago, the boot was on the other foot now, and with a vengeance. "I am sincerely sorry, but it was at the time necessary. Your brother will be released tonight. You saw my wife this afternoon?"

"Of course. It was so sweet of her to come to see us. Won't you and your—um—friend come in to see Mother? She'd be delighted, I'm sure."

I shook my head. "What time did my wife leave here?"

"About five-thirty, I should say. It was beginning to get dark and—has something happened to her?" she ended in a whisper.

"She's been kidnapped by the murderer and held as hostage."

"Oh, no! Oh, no, Mr. Cavell, no." Her hand clutched her throat. "It—it's not possible."

"How did she leave here?"

"Kidnapped? Your wife kidnapped?" She stared at me, round-eyed in fear. "Why should anyone want—"

"For God's sake, answer my question," I said savagely. "Had she a hired car, taxi, bus service—what was it?"

"Bus," she whispered. "There's a twenty-minute bus service to Alfringham. She—yes, she would have caught the twenty-to-six bus. At least—"

"Where's the nearest bus stop?"

"Down the road. About three hundred yards."

I wheeled and left her without a word, went down those steps three at a time—in a way that would have done credit to an Olympic steeplechaser far less a man with two sound legs and his full complement of uncracked ribs—and ran down the drive into the road. It was a deserted, dripping, ill-lit lane, pavement on one side only and a thin scattering of houses on both sides. I chose the side with the pavement, ran up the drive of the first house and leaned on the door bell until the door opened and a beefy, collarless character with braces, evening paper, and an annoyed expression appeared.

"Where's the fire, mate, eh?" he demanded angrily. "Just tell me that? Where's—"

"Police." I flashed my bogus credentials. "Did you see a fair-haired girl walking down towards the bus stop between five-thirty and five-forty tonight?"

"Police, eh?" He peered at me without interest and leaned a shoulder against the lintel. "Fair-haired girl, you said?"

"Yes." I wondered whether you could actually hear a blood vessel bursting, or whether it was just a sensation.

"Well, now." He settled himself more comfortably—give him time and he'd be drawing out his damned pipe and asking me for a match. "Live and let live, I say. I mind my own business, let others mind theirs. Besides—"

"Did you see her, you bloody idiot?" I yelled.

His jaw dropped and he shook his head slowly. I left him there like a stranded fish, ran down the driveway and along the lane to the next house. Out of the corner of my eye I caught a glimpse of the police car, followed by the radio van, cruising slowly down the road, and of Hardanger disappearing into the first driveway on the righthand side and the General hurrying along the pavement after me.

At the second house a rather scared-looking housewife answered my ring. No luck. At the third, both husband and wife appeared at the door and assured me that they had seen nothing because they had been watching television, and the man asked me what I thought of the latest rock-and-roll sensation whom they'd just been watching, and because his wife was a fairly respectable looking woman I didn't tell him what he could do with his television and sensation. At the fourth house I struck oil.

I asked the question of a young woman who came to the door, and an eager voice behind her piped up: "I did. I saw her, mister."

"You saw her?" I peered doubtfully at the young tow-head, peering half-shyly, half-excitedly from behind his mother's skirt. "You were out in this pouring rain, sonny?"

"There's a larch tree down by the gate that keeps him dry

in any weather," his mother explained. "Danny spends most of the day down there, watching people and cars go by."

"He's not at school, Madam?" The General had come up behind me, puffing slightly.

"Come here, Danny," his mother said. She brought him round into the light, a thin little boy of five or six with a gleaming chrome crutch under his right arm and a chrome brace supporting a pitifully wasted right leg. "I'm afraid Danny won't be going to school for some little time yet."

"She gave me a shilling, mister," Danny declared happily. He dug into his trouser pocket and showed me a gleaming coin. "She said it was for being a brave boy and that I'd soon grow up to be big and strong and playing football with the other boys. She did, didn't she, Mummy?" I'd no doubt left. Mary, all right, with her magnetic affinity for broken wings.

"Can you see the bus stop from here?" I asked.

Danny nodded solemnly.

"Did the lady walk on to the bus stop?"

"She didn't have to," Danny said matter-of-factly. "A gennelman stopped his car and gave her a lift. She gave me the shilling and then he gave her the lift."

"You're sure of that, Danny?" the General asked.

"Sure I'm sure," he said sturdily. "The car stopped at our gate. The man opened the door with one hand and he took his hat off with the other and he asked her to come in. He was her friend."

"Her friend?" I asked. "How do you know that, Danny?"

"Because the lady smiled and said 'Hullo.' And the man in the car knew her name. I heard him say it."

"What name, Danny?"

"I forgot. You see," he explained simply, "it was a long time ago."

I looked at my watch. Six-thirty. An hour would be a long time to Danny. I said: "Was it Mrs. Cavell?"

He brightened. "Yes. Yes, I think so."

"Did you see the gentleman in the car?" I asked.

His mother glanced at Danny and said in almost a whisper: "Is it—is it one of those horrible pick-up cases?"

"I'm afraid so, ma'am." I saw no point in elaborating further. "Well, Danny?"

"It was too dark. He was sitting inside the car. He was a big man."

"What color was the car? Blue?"

"Blue, mister. That's right."

"Like your Mummy's skirt here?" the General asked. The skirt was navy-blue, the same color as Gregori's Fiat.

"No, no," Danny said impatiently. "Mummy's skirt is the same color as the lady's umbrella. The car was the same color as the lady's suit. It was just the same. Just. I saw it. It was—it was a greeny-blue."

"She has a turquoise suit," I said to the General. "Hardanger saw her leaving the Waggoner's Rest. He can confirm. Our friend's ditched his Fiat and picked up another machine. What kind of car, Danny? Big? Small? Low? Or—"

"It was a Vanden Plas Princess," he said precisely, then added, "three-litre."

"What?" I looked incredulously at him, but his mother said, smiling: "Danny spends his life by that gate. He knows the name of every car on the road. If Danny says it was a Vanden Plas whatever it was, then that's what it was."

"You didn't happen to see the number on the car, Danny," the General asked.

"Don't be silly, mister," Danny said indignantly. "I can't read."

I fumbled in my wallet and brought out the first note that came to hand. A nice new crisp Bank of England fiver, but it couldn't have mattered less to me if it had been the Kohinoor diamond. I thrust it into Danny's hand and ran for the police car. I saw Hardanger emerging from a driveway and shouted: "Come on. We have a lead." He came puffing up to the car and I said quickly: "Was Mary wearing her turquoise suit when she left Alfringham this afternoon?"

He nodded. "Why?"

"Because that's the color of the car that picked her up. Gregori's got rid of the Fiat." The three of us piled into the back seat and I said to the driver: "Alfringham. Then the London road. Sergeant, cancel the call for the Fiat. It's now a turquoise Vanden Plas Princess, three-litre. All stations. Locate, follow, but don't close in."

"Blue-green," the General murmured. "Blue-green, not turquoise. It's policemen you're talking to, not their wives. Half of them would think you were talking about their Christmas dinner."

"It all started with MacDonald," I said. The big police car was hissing along the wet tarmac, the pine trees lining the road cart wheeling back into the pitch darkness behind, and it seemed easier to talk than to sit there going quietly crazy with worry. Besides, the General and Hardanger had been patient long enough. "We all know what MacDonald wanted, and it wasn't just to serve the cause of the Communist world. Dr. MacDonald had only one deeply felt and abiding interest in life—Dr. MacDonald. No question but that he was a genuine, dyed-in-the-wool fellow-traveler at one time—Madame Halle did not strike me as a person who would make a mistake over anything—and I don't see how he could otherwise have formed his contacts with the Communist world. He must have earned a great deal of money over the years—you'd only to look at the contents of his house—but he spent it fairly judiciously and wisely, not splashing it around too much at a time."

"The Bentley Continental he had," Hardanger said. "Wouldn't you call that splashing it around a bit?"

"He'd that expense well covered, with a water-tight explanation. But," I acknowledged, "he got greedy. He was getting in so much money during the past few months that it was burning a hole in his pocket."

"Working overtime sending samples to Warsaw and information to Vienna?" the General asked.

"No," I said. "Blackmailing Gregori."

"Sorry." The General stirred wearily in his corner seat. "I'm not with you."

"It's not difficult," I said. "Gregori—the man we know as Gregori—had two things: a beautiful plan and a stroke of very bad luck. You will remember that there was nothing *sub rosa* about Gregori's arrival in this country—it sparked off a minor international crisis, the Italians being hopping mad that one of their very top-notch biochemists should turn his back on his own country and go to work for Britain. Somebody—somebody with more than a smattering of chemistry and a fairly close resemblance to Gregori—read all about it and saw in Gregori's impending departure for Britain the opportunity of a lifetime, and made his preparation accordingly."

"The real Gregori was murdered?" Hardanger asked.

"No question of that. The Gregori who set off from Turin with all his worldly wealth stacked in the back of his Fiat was not the Gregori who arrived in Britain. The original Gregori met with a very permanent accident en route and the imposter, no doubt with a few judicious alterations to his features to make his resemblance to the now-dead man even closer, arrived in Britain in Gregori's car, complete with clothes, passport, photographs—the lot. So far, so very good.

"Now the bad luck. Apart from the reports of his work,

the original Gregori was completely unknown in Britain—as a person, that is. There was probably only one man in Britain who knew him well—and by a one-in-a-million chance, Gregori found himself working in the very same laboratory as this man. MacDonald. Gregori didn't know that. But MacDonald did—and knew that Gregori was a fake. Don't forget that MacDonald had for many years been a delegate to the WHO, and I'll wager anything you like that the original Gregori held a similar position for Italy."

"Which accounts for the missing photograph in the album," the General said slowly.

"The two of them—MacDonald and the original Gregori—standing arm in arm, no doubt. In Turin. Anyway, probably after weighing up the situation for a day or two, MacDonald told the spurious Gregori that he was on to him. We can guess what happened. Gregori would have produced a gun and said that it was just too bad but he would have to silence him, and MacDonald, nobody's fool, would have produced a piece of paper and said that *that* would be just too bad because if he died suddenly, his bank—or the police—had orders to open immediately a sealed envelope containing a copy of that paper, which would contain a few interesting facts about Gregori. Gregori would then have put his gun away and they would have made a deal. A one-way deal. Gregori to pay MacDonald so much per month. Or else. Don't forget, MacDonald was now in a position to pin a murder rap on Gregori."

"I don't get it," Hardanger said flatly. "It doesn't make sense. Can you imagine the General here having two men working for him on the same project in, say, Warsaw, men who were not only unknown to each other but completely at cross purposes and potentially at each other's throats? I'm afraid, Cavell, that I have a higher opinion of Communist intelligence than you seem to have."

"I agree with Hardanger," the General said.

"So do I," I agreed. "All I said was that MacDonald was working for the Communists. I never once said that Gregori was, or that this Satan Bug has anything to do with Communism. It was you and Hardanger who made that assumption."

Hardanger bent forward to see me better. "You mean—you mean that Gregori is just a raving crackpot after all?"

"If you still believe that," I said nastily, "it's time you had a long holiday. There was a very powerful and pressing reason why Gregori wanted the viruses, and I'll stake my life that he told MacDonald what it was. He would have had to, to ensure his co-operation. If he'd told MacDonald that he just wanted to take off with the botulinus, I doubt if MacDonald would have touched the business. But if he'd offered him, say, ten thousand pounds, MacDonald would have changed his mind pretty fast, that being the kind of man MacDonald was."

We were fairly into Alfringham now, the big police Jaguar with its siren switched on, doing twice the legal speed limit, dodging in and out among the thinning evening traffic. The driver was an expert, the pick of Hardanger's own London men, and he knew exactly how much he and the car could do without killing the lot of us in the process.

"Stop the car!" Hardanger interrupted me suddenly. "That traffic policeman." We were closing rapidly on Alfringham's one and only set of traffic lights, apparently hand-controlled at what passed for Alfringham's rush hour. White cape glistening in the lamp-lit rain, he was still standing by a control box attached to a lamp-post. The car stopped and Hardanger, window wound down, beckoned the man across.

"Superintendent Hardanger, London," he said abruptly. "Did you see a bluish-green Vanden Plas Princess pass this way this evening? An hour ago, slightly less?"

"As a matter of fact I did, sir. He was coming at a fair lick on the amber and I saw he would be on the intersection when it was red. I blew my whistle and he stopped just after he'd passed the second light. I asked the driver what he thought he was up to, and he said his back wheels had locked on the wet road when he tried to brake, and when he took his foot off he was frightened to brake again, or brake hard, because his daughter was asleep in the back seat and she might have been injured if he'd stopped too suddenly and she'd been flung forward. I looked in the back seat and she *was* asleep. Sound asleep, even our voices didn't waken her. There was another man beside her. So—so I gave him a warning and waved him on . . ." His voice trailed away uncertainly.

"Exactly," Hardanger roared. "Now you're realizing. Can't you tell the difference between someone sleeping and someone being forced to fake sleep with a gun in her side. She slept on, forsooth," he said fiercely. "You miserable nincompoop, I'll have you drummed out of the Force!"

"Yes, sir." The policeman, eyes staring unseeingly over the roof of the Jaguar, stood at rigid attention, a dead ringer for a guardsman on parade about to collapse with the thumbs still at the seams of the trousers. "I'm sorry, sir."

"Which way did he go?" Hardanger demanded.

London, sir," the policeman said woodenly.

"It would be too much to expect you to have taken his number, I suppose," Hardanger said with heavy sarcasm.

"XOW nine seventy-three, sir."

"What!"

"XOW nine seventy-three."

"Consider yourself reinstated," Hardanger growled. He wound up the window and we were off again, the sergeant talking softly into the hand microphone. Hardanger said: "Bit rough on him, I suppose. If he *had* been smart enough to notice anything he'd have been twanging his harp by now instead of playing about with his traffic-light buttons. Sorry for the interruption, Cavell."

"It doesn't matter," I said. I was glad of the interruption, glad of anything that would take my mind off Mary, Mary with a killer's gun in her side. "MacDonald—I was speaking of MacDonald. Money mad—but also a pretty shrewd character. Very shrewd—he must be to have survived so long in the espionage racket. He knew the theft of the botulinus—I'm certain Gregori never mentioned his intention of taking the Satan Bug as well—would start off an intensive probing into the past life of all the suspects—those working in number one lab. He may also have suspected that his own espionage activities were liable to start a re-check on all scientists. He knew that all the known details of his life were down on his security record card, and he was pretty certain that one or more of those details, the ones referring to his immediate post-war activities, wouldn't stand up to rigorous investigation. He knew the security chief, Derry, held those records. He told Gregori that there would be no dice, no co-operation, unless he saw that record first. MacDonald had no intention of being the fall guy in subsequent police investigations."

"So Easton Derry—or what's left of him—lies down in that cellar now," the General said quietly.

"Yes. I'm only guessing now, but they're pretty safe guesses. Apart from the records MacDonald wanted, Gregori also wanted something—the combination of number one lab door, which was known only to Derry and Dr. Baxter. I think they arranged for MacDonald to ask Derry to call at his house, saying that he had something of importance to tell him. Derry came, and when he passed through MacDonald's door he was already as good as dead. Gregori, who would have been waiting hidden, gun in hand, saw to it that he did die. First of all they took the keys from him, the keys to the safes in Derry's house where the records were kept: the security chief had always to carry those keys on his person. Then they tried to make him tell the combination of number one lab door. At least, Gregori tried—I don't see MacDonald having any part in this, although he must have known—or seen—what was going on. While Gregori may not be a crackpot, I think he must be some sort of psychopath—a man with a streak of sadistic blood-lust a yard wide. Look what he did to Derry, to the back of Mrs. Turpin's head, not to mention my ribs and hanging MacDonald alive."

"And defeated his own ends," Hardanger said heavily. "He tortured and mutilated Derry so savagely that Derry died before he could talk. It shouldn't be too difficult to find out who this fake Gregori is. A man with his records and techniques is bound to have a record. Given his prints and cephalic index, Interpol in Paris will identify him within the hour." He leaned forward, gave instructions to the sergeant.

"Yes," I said. "It won't be hard. But it's not important now. Having killed Derry before he could talk, Gregori had to find another way into number one lab. First of all they searched his house—and I would bet, incidentally, that they searched his private effects also and came across a photograph showing Derry as the best man at a wedding. My wedding. The General is in the photograph too, of course. That's why they kidnapped me, then Mary. They knew. Anyway, they unlocked the safe, abstracted the dicey page from MacDonald's dossier—and had a damned good look at the other dossiers while they were there. They found out about Dr. Hartnell's financial troubles and decided he could be blackmailed into helping them by acting as decoy for the break-out from Mordon. For, having failed to get the lab combination from Derry, Gregori had to devise a new plan to get the viruses."

"Break-out?" Hardanger frowned. "Break-in, you mean."

"Sorry, break-out." While Hardanger sat there in the semi-darkness in the back of the car looking at me with an expression I didn't much care for, I told him the theory I'd expounded to the General in the early hours of that morning, about how two men had been smuggled into number one lab in crates, one disguised as the criminal X, the other as Baxter, both leaving at the normal time and handing in their security tags, while the real X stayed there till eleven o'clock, first killing Baxter with the botulinus toxin, then Clandon with the cyanide butterscotch, before breaking out, complete with viruses, through the wire fence.

"Very, very interesting," Hardanger said at the end. Professional interest and pique were in voice and face. He said: "My God, and you spoke of Easton Derry playing it too close to the cuff. I suppose you got a kick out of leading me up the garden path, damn you."

"I didn't lead you," I said. "You went by yourself. We were on parallel paths, anyway." I tried to think how, but I couldn't. "The break-through came from you, not me. It was *you* who had the suspicions about the completeness of MacDonald's dossier."

The car radio crackled suddenly. The owner of the Vanden Plas, a doctor making a call, had reported the theft of the machine. He'd also added the interesting fact that his tank had been almost empty. Hardanger curtly ordered sergeant and driver to keep their eyes open for the nearest garage, then turned to me. "Well, go on." He was only half-mollified by my last remark, and I didn't blame him any for his annoyance.

"There's not much. Gregori not only found out about Hartnell's entanglements with Tuffnell, the moneylender, but he also made the discovery that Hartnell, as mess secretary, was embezzling mess funds. Don't ask me how. After that—"

"I can tell you," Hardanger broke in. "Too damn late as usual," he added disgustedly. "MacDonald was mess president in Mordon, and finding out the financial trouble Hartnell was in would have made him suspicious. As president, of course, he would have access to the books—and he checked."

"Of course, of course." I was as disgusted as Hardanger. "I knew he was president. Just too damn obvious, I suppose. Good old Cavell. Anyway, after that Hartnell was at his mercy—and knowing from Hartnell's dossier that Hartnell was bound to come under the microscope, he confused things still further by dumping the hammer and pliers used in the break-out in Hartnell's place, smearing some red loam on his scooter for good measure. If not Gregori, one of his assistants. Red herring number one. Red herring number two—posing as a mysterious Uncle George, he made payments into Chessingham's account weeks in advance of the crime. He knew, of course, that bank accounts would be one of the first subjects of police scrutiny."

"Red herrings," Hardanger said in bitter complaint. "Always those accursed red herrings. Why?"

175

"To buy time. I'm coming to that."

"And then the two killings in Mordon and the theft of the viruses, just as you suggested?" the General said.

"No." I shook my head. "I was wrong on that."

The General looked at me, his face not saying very much but saying a great deal all the same, and I continued: "My idea was that one of the number one lab scientists killed both Dr. Baxter and Clandon. Every single thing pointed unmistakably to that. I was wrong. I had to be wrong. We've checked and re-checked, and every single scientist and technician in that lab had an unbreakable alibi for the night of the murder—unbreakable because they were true. Two men were smuggled in, all right—maybe even three. I don't know. We do know Gregori must have quite an organization working for him. Three is possible. Say three. Only *one* of those men left at the usual knocking-off time—the one disguised as Baxter. The other two remained, but X didn't—he also took off at the normal time and arrived home to establish a nice cosy little alibi for himself. X, of course, was almost certainly Gregori—MacDonald was a sleeping partner in this business. Gregori may or may not have taken the viruses with him—probably not, in case he was caught in one of the occasional spot-checks. Anyway, he certainly left behind him one botulinus ampoule—and one cyanide-coated butterscotch. You will remember that none of us has been happy at the idea of Clandon meekly accepting a butterscotch from a potential suspect in the middle of the night."

"But the botulinus, the cyanide. Why?" the General demanded. "They were completely unnecessary."

"Not the way Gregori saw it. He ordered them to tap Baxter on the head and break open the virus ampoule as they left. Once outside the lab, one of them probably acted as decoy while Clandon, who had been watching the corridor from the house, came haring across, gun in hand. While he pointed his gun at one of the men the other appeared from behind and took his gun off him. They then forced the cyanide butterscotch into his mouth. God alone knows what Clandon thought it was; he was dead before he could find out."

"The fiends," the General murmured. "The ruthless fiends."

"All done to give the impression that the killer was known to both Baxter and Clandon. And it certainly worked. The third major red herring, and it put us completely on the wrong track. Buying time, always buying time. Gregori has a

176

genius for deception. He fooled me, too, about that first phone call that was made to London at ten o'clock last night. He made it himself. Red herring number heaven-knows-what."

"Gregori phoned?" Hardanger looked at me, hard. "He had an alibi for the time the call was made. You checked personally. Typing a book, or something.".

"You can't beat Cavell when it comes to insight," I said sourly. "The sound of a man typing undoubtedly came from his room. He'd pre-recorded it on tape and switched on the record before he left via his ground-floor window. There was a peculiar smell in his room and a pile of white ashes in the fireplace when I visited him in the early hours of this morning. The remains of the tape."

"But *why* all the red herring—" Hardanger began, when the voice of the sergeant in the front seat cut in.

"Here's a garage now."

"Pull in," Hardanger ordered. "Make inquiries."

We pulled off the highway, the driver switched on his police siren. A noise to waken the dead, but it didn't waken up the filling-station attendant on duty. The sergeant up front didn't hesitate. He was outside and into the brightly-lit office within five seconds of our skidding to a halt. He came out almost immediately afterwards and disappeared round the back of the filling-station, and that was enough for me. I piled out of the back seat, Hardanger at my heels.

We found the attendant in a garage at the back of the station. He had been expertly bound and gagged by someone who had not stopped to consider the price of scotch tape. The same someone, for good measure, had also cracked him over the back of the head with something heavy, but the attendant had recovered from that—more accurately, he had regained consciousness—by the time we got to him. He was a burly, middle-aged character, and what was probably a normally red face anyway was crimson from rage and his struggles to free himself.

We cut the tape round wrists and ankles, pulled it none too gently off his face, and helped him to a sitting position. He had some highly homicidal observations to make and even in our desperate urgency we had to allow him that, but after a few seconds Hardanger cut in sharply.

"Right. That'll be enough. The man who did this is a murderer on the run and we're police officers. Every second you sit and curse increases his chances of escaping. Tell us about it, quick and sharp."

The attendant shook his head. I didn't have to be a doctor to tell that he was still pretty groggy. He said: "A man, middle-aged, swarthy-looking character, came in here for petrol. Half-past six, it was. He asked—"

"Half-past six," I interrupted. "Only twenty minutes ago. Are you sure?"

"I'm certain," he said flatly. "He'd run out of petrol for his car, a mile, maybe two back, and he must have been hurrying some, for he was pretty much out of breath. He asked me for a gallon in a can and when I turned to find one, he let me have it over the head. When I came to I was in the garage in the back and tied as you saw me. I didn't let on I was conscious. The first thing I saw was another man with a gun pointing at a girl—a blonde. The other guy, the bloke who had crowned me, was just backing the boss's car out of the door and—"

"Make, color and license number of the car?" Hardanger snapped. He got them, and went on: "Stay here. Don't move around. That's a nasty crack. I'll radio the Alfringham police and there'll be a car out here pretty soon." Ten seconds later we were on our way, leaving the attendant holding his head and staring after us.

"Twenty minutes," I said, half-listening to the sergeant speak rapidly and urgently into the telephone. "They'd have lost time pushing the car off the road to fox us, then they had a long walk to the garage. Twenty minutes."

"They've had it," Hardanger said confidently. "There's a half a dozen police cars patrolling in the next thirty miles or so, and they know those roads as only local county policemen do. And once one of those cars gets on Gregori's tail—well, he'll never shake them off."

"Tell them to set up roadblocks," I said. "Tell them to stop him at all costs."

"Are you mad?" Hardanger said shortly. "Are you out of your mind, Cavell? Do you *want* your wife to be killed? Damn you, you know he'll use her as a living shield. As it is, she's safe. Gregori hasn't seen a policeman—except that fellow on traffic duty—since he left MacDonald's house. He'll be half-believing now that we *have* called off the search. Can't you see that, man?"

"Roadblocks," I repeated. "Set up roadblocks. Where are the cars going to tail him to—the heart of London? Where he's going to release his damn botulinus? Once in London they'll lose him, they're bound to lose him. Don't you see, he *has* to be stopped somewhere? If he's not, if he's let loose in London—"

"But you yourself agreed—"

"That was before I knew for sure that he was headed for London."

"General," Hardanger appealed. "Can't you make Cavell—"

"She's my only child, Hardanger, and an old man shouldn't be asked to decide life or death for his only child," the General said tonelessly. "You know as well as any man what I think of Mary." He paused, then went on in the same level voice: "I agree with Cavell. Please do as he suggests."

Hardanger swore bitterly under his breath and leaned forward to speak to the sergeant. When he had finished, the General said calmly: "While we're waiting, my boy, you might fill in the few remaining pieces in the jig-saw. I'm in no condition to fill them in for myself. The question the Superintendent is always coming up with. The red herrings. All those red herrings. Why?"

"To buy time." I was in no condition to fill in jig-saws myself, but what was left of my mind was still working just well enough to appreciate the reason behind the request—to try to take our minds off the car in front, the trapped and terrified girl at the mercy of ruthless and sadistic killers, to reduce the tearing anxiety, to ease the destructive tension that was slowly pulling tired minds and bodies to pieces. I went on, fumbling along mentally: "Our friend in the car up front had to buy time. The more false leads we followed and the more blind alleys we blundered into—and there were plenty—the more time it would take us to get around to inquiring in the really dangerous places. He overestimated us, but for all that we moved faster than he had expected—don't forget that it's only forty hours since the crime was discovered. But he knew that sooner or later we would get around to make inquiries in the one place he feared—MacDonald's. He knew he might have to dispose of MacDonald sooner or later. And the later, the better—for within a few hours of MacDonald's death, a sealed envelope in a bank or police station would be opened and then we'd be on to him like an express train. Whatever Gregori's ultimate intentions are, he would obviously have preferred to carry them out while still a respectable member of the Alfringham community instead of a wanted murderer on the run from half the police in Britain."

"It's difficult to threaten the Government—and the nation—

with the law breathing down the back of your neck," the General conceded. The old man's detachment, his iron control, was almost more than human. "But *why* did MacDonald have to die?"

"Because of two things. Because he *knew* what Gregori's ultimate end was, and if MacDonald had lived to tell it, all his, Gregori's, plans would be ruined. And because of Mrs. Turpin. MacDonald was a pretty tough character and he might not have talked even when the police got on to him—after all, although he almost certainly had no hand in any killing, he was pretty deep in the mire himself. But Mrs. Turpin would have made him talk—if not, she'd have talked herself. Madame Halle gave me to understand in Paris that MacDonald was pretty much of a philanderer—and philanderers don't change their ways easily. Not before eighty, anyway. Mrs. Turpin was a good-looking woman—and her fiercely protective attitude towards MacDonald was a dead give-away. She was in love with him—whether he was with her I couldn't guess, and it doesn't matter. If things had gone wrong she'd have had MacDonald turn Queen's evidence and lower the boom on Gregori by betraying his plans. I think his evidence might have been so important, so vastly important, that either she or MacDonald or both would be convinced that at the most MacDonald would have received no more than a light sentence. With all hopes of his money from Gregori gone, I don't think MacDonald would have hesitated between turning Queen's evidence—if it was important enough he might even have received a free pardon—and being held as an accessory to murder for gain, which still calls for a walk to the gallows in this country. And if he had hesitated, Mrs. Turpin would have made up his mind for him.

"My guess—it's only a guess, but we can check at Mordon —is that Mrs. Turpin phoned MacDonald at the lab immediately after I had left, and that Gregori either overheard or was told what had happened. He probably accompanied MacDonald home to see how the land lay—and it didn't take him a couple of minutes to find out. The heat was on MacDonald, and that could have been fatal for Gregori. To prevent this, Gregori had to make it fatal for MacDonald and Mrs. Turpin."

"All neatly buttoned up, eh?" Hardanger said. His face was dead-pan; he was still a fair way from forgiving me.

"Net tightened and completely closed," I agreed. "The only trouble is that the big fish has already escaped and what's left is useless. But one thing we know. We can forget all this rubbish about demolishing Mordon. If that was Gregori's plan, it wouldn't have helped or hindered him in the execution of it if MacDonald had talked, for the whole country knew of it already. Whatever it is is something on a much bigger, much more important scale, something that *might* have been foiled, probably *would* have been foiled, had we known of it in advance."

"Such as what?" Hardanger demanded.

"You tell me. I'm done with guessing for the day." And I was through with guessing and talking for the day, except where necessity absolutely demanded it. Slumped back in the warmth and comfort of the deeply cushioned seats, reaction was beginning to set in. The anaesthetizing effect of the need for non-stop action and urgent thinking was beginning to wear off, and the more it wore off the older and more worn I felt. And the more pain. I thought of the widely held belief that you can't feel more than one pain at one time and wondered what misinformed idiot had started that one. I wondered what part of me was causing me the most pain, my foot, my ribs, or my head, and came to the conclusion that my ribs won, by a short head. Was that a pun? The driver was reaching over ninety on the longer stretches of wet road, but he drove so smoothly and skillfully that even with my fear and anxiety for Mary, I think I was beginning to doze off when the loudspeaker up front began to crackle.

First came the identification sign, then the message: "Gray Humber saloon, answering description of wanted car, number not identified, has just turned left from London road to 'B' road to avoid block at Flemington crossroad, two and a half miles east of Crutchley. Am following."

"Flemington crossroads." The voice of the sergeant in the front seat, an Alfringham man, held a rising note of excitement. "He's on a blind road. It doesn't lead anywhere except to Flemington and then back onto the main London road about three miles further on again."

"How far are we from what's the name of this place—Crutchley?" Hardanger demanded.

"Near enough four miles, sir."

"So that would make it between nine and ten miles to the junction where Gregori must rejoin the main London road. This side road through Flemington, the one he's on. How long is it, how long would it take him?"

"Five or six miles, sir. It's pretty twisty. Maybe ten minutes if he kept his foot down and took chances all the way. The road is full of blind corners."

"Do you think you could get there in ten minutes?" Hardanger asked the driver.

"I don't know, sir." He hesitated. "I don't know the road."

"I do," the sergeant said confidently. "He'll make it."

He made it. The rain was sluicing vertically down, the roads were slippery, straight stretches were at a premium, and I think we all added a few more gray hairs to our quota that night, but he made it. He made it with time to spare. From the constant stream of reports pouring in from the police car pursuing Gregori, it was quite evident that the man at the wheel was anything but a skillful driver.

Our car braked to a halt and parked broadside across the Flemington road, completely blocking the exit onto the main London road. We all climbed quickly out of the car while the sergeant trained the powerful roof spotlight up the side road in the direction from which Gregori's stolen Humber would appear. We took up positions in the pouring rain behind the Jaguar and, as a precaution, about ten feet back from it. In that blinding rain a misted windscreen or ineffective wipers could prevent the driver of a car traveling at high speed from seeing the Jaguar until it was too late. Especially if the driver was as incompetent as claimed.

I took a good look around me. Dick Turpin couldn't have chosen a better spot for an ambush. The top and one side of the right-angle T junction were completely covered in dense beech woods. The third side of the T, illuminated by the still-blazing headlights of the Jaguar, was open pastureland with a tree-lined farmhouse about two hundred yards away, and at less than half that distance, a barn and scattered farm buildings. I could just make out a light from one of the windows in the farmhouse, blurred and misty through the heavy rain.

There was a deep ditch on one side of the Flemington road, and I considered hiding myself there about the point where Gregori's car would be forced to pull up, then rising and heaving a heavy rock through the driver's window, thereby eliminating fifty percent of the opposition before they could even start anything. The only trouble was that I might eliminate Mary—the fact that she hadn't been in the front seat when Gregori had passed through Alfringham was no guarantee that she wasn't there now. I decided to stay where I was.

Over the sound of the rain hissing whitely on the tarmac

and drumming heavily on the roof of the car, we could suddenly hear the steadily rising note of an engine being revved up furiously, and far from skillfully, through the gears. Seconds later we caught sight of the first white wash of its headlights, the barred beams shining eerily through the boles of the beeches and the pale rods of rain. We dropped to our knees behind the shelter of the police Jaguar, and I eased out the Hanyatti, slipping the safety catch.

Then all at once, to the accompaniment of a high-pitched grating of gears and mad revving of the engine that wouldn't have got its driver very far at Le Mans, the car was round the last corner and heading straight for us. We could hear it accelerating as it came out of the corner, just over a hundred and fifty yards away; then came the abrupt cessation of engine noise, succeeded almost immediately by the unmistakable tearing, hissing sound of locked wheels sliding on a wet road. I could see the headlight beams of the approaching car swing wildly from one side to the other as the driver fought to retain control, and I instinctively tensed, waiting for the crash and the shock as the car ploughed into the side of the Jaguar blocking its path.

But the crash and the shock did not come. Owing everything to good luck and nothing whatsoever to good management, the driver managed to pull up less than five feet from the Jaguar, in the middle of the road and slewed only very slightly to the left. I straightened and walked up to the side of the police Jaguar, my eye screwed almost shut against the glare of the Humber's headlights. Sharply outlined though I was in that blinding wash of light, I doubted whether the occupants of the car could see me—the spotlight on the roof of the Jaguar was a powerful one and shining directly into Gregori's windscreen.

I'm no Annie Oakley with a gun, but at a distance of ten feet and with a target the size of a soup plate, I can hold my own with the best. Two quick shots and the headlights of the Humber shattered and died. I walked round the front of the Jaguar, the others following, as a second car—the pursuing police car—pulled up behind Gregori's. I was still rounding the nose of the Jaguar when the two right-hand doors of the stolen car were flung wide and two men scrambled quickly out. For one second and one second only I had the game in my hands, I could have gunned them both down where they stood, and the fact that I would have had to shoot one of them through the back wouldn't have worried me at all, but like a fool I hesitated and was slow in bringing up my gun, and then the second was gone and so was my last chance, for Mary was out of the car now, jerked out with a brutal violence that made her gasp in pain, and was held in front of Gregori while his gun pointed at me directly over her right shoulder. The other man was a squat, broad-shouldered and very tough-looking Latin type with a pistol the size of a sawed-off cannon held in his hairy left hand. His left hand, I noticed. It had been a left-handed man who had used the wire-cutters to break out of Mordon. Here, probably, was the killer of both Baxter and Clandon. Nor had I any doubt but that he was a killer; when you've seen enough of them you recognize one instantly. They might look as normal, as happily innocuous, as the next man, but always, far back in the eyes, lies the glint of empty madness. It's not something they have, it's something they don't have. This was such a man. And Gregori? Another? He was the same Gregori as I'd ever known, tall, swarthy, with grizzled hair and a quizzical expression on his face, but at the same time a completely different man. He no longer wore his glasses.

"Cavell." His voice was soft, colorless, conversational almost. "I had the chance to kill you weeks ago. I should have taken it. Negligence. I have known of you for a long time. I was warned of you. I didn't listen."

"The boy friend," I said. My own gun was hanging by my side. I stared at the barrel in that hairy left hand: it pointed straight at my right eye. "Left-handed. The killer of Baxter and Clandon."

"Indeed." Gregori tightened his grip round Mary. Her fair hair was wildly dishevelled, her face streaked with mud, and there was the beginning of an unpleasant bruise above her right eye—she must have tried a breakaway on the walk between abandoned car and garage—but she wasn't scared much, or if she was, she was hiding it. "I was rightly warned. Henriques, my—ah—lieutenant. He is also responsible for some other slight accidents, aren't you, Henriques? Including the slight damage to yourself, Cavell."

I nodded. It made sense. Henriques the hatchet-man. I looked at the hard, bitter face and the empty eyes and I knew Gregori was telling the truth. Not that that made Gregori any less innocent. It just made him more understandable; master criminals of Gregori's class almost never touched the physical side of their business.

Gregori glanced quickly at the two policemen who had come out of the pursuing car and gave Henriques a quick jerk of the head. Henriques swung his gun and lined it up on the two policemen. They stopped. I lifted my own gun and took a pace nearer Gregori.

"Don't do it, Cavell," Gregori said evenly. He pressed the muzzle of his gun into Mary's side with such violence that she moaned with the pain of it. "I won't hesitate to kill."

I took another step forward. Four feet separated us. I said: "You won't harm her. If you do, I'll kill you. You know that. God only knows what it is that you have at stake, but it's something almighty big to justify all the work and planning you've put in, the killing you've done. Whatever that is, you haven't achieved it yet. You wouldn't throw it all away just by shooting my wife, would you, Gregori?"

"Take me away from this horrible man, Pierre," Mary murmured. Her voice was low and not steady. "I—I don't care what he does."

"He won't do anything, my dear," I said quietly. "He doesn't dare to. And he knows it."

"Quite the little psychologist, aren't you?" Gregori said in the same conversational tone. Suddenly, completely unexpectedly, his back braced against the side of the car, he sent Mary catapulting towards me with a vicious thrust of both arms. I broke ground to lessen the impact, staggered back two steps before steadying us both, and by the time I'd put her to one side and was bringing my gun up again, Gregori was holding something in his outstretched hand. A glass ampoule with a blue sealed top. In the other hand he held the steel flask from which he's just abstracted it. I looked at Gregori's impassive face, then back at the ampoule in his hand, and I could feel the sudden moisture between my palm and the butt of the Hanyatti.

I turned my head and looked at the General, Hardanger, and the two policemen behind me—both the General and Hardanger, I saw, with heavy pistols in their hands—faced front again and looked at the other two policemen under Henriques' gun. I said slowly and distinctly: "Don't do anything, anybody. That ampoule in Gregori's hand contains the Satan Bug. You've all read the papers today. You all know what will happen if that glass breaks."

They all knew, all right. We'd have made the figures in any waxworks look like characters with the St. Vitus's dance doing the Twist. How long would it be, Gregori had said yesterday, before all life in Britain would become extinct if that refined polio virus escaped? I couldn't remember. But not long. It didn't matter much, anyway.

"Correct," Gregori said calmly. "The crimson top for the

185

botulinus virus, the blue top for the Satan Bug. When Cavell was gambling with his wife's life just now there was an element of bluff involved. I would beg you to believe that I am not bluffing. Tonight I hope to achieve something that I have set my heart on." He paused and looked at us all individually, his eyes glittering emptily in the glare of the police searchlight. "If I am not permitted to go unmolested, then I cannot achieve this object and have little wish to prolong this life of mine. I shall then smash this ampoule. I would beseech you all to believe that I am in the most complete and deadly earnest."

I believed him implicitly. He was as mad as a hatter. I said: "Your lieutenant. Henriques. How does he feel about your casual attitude towards his life?"

"I have once saved Henriques from drowning and twice from the electric chair. His life is mine to dispose of as I see fit. He understands that. Besides, Henriques is a deaf-mute."

"You're insane," I said harshly. "You told us yesterday that neither fire nor ice, seas nor mountains, can stop the spread of the Satan Bug."

"I believe that to be essentially correct. If I have to go, it matters nothing to me if the rest of mankind accompanies me."

"But—" I paused. "Good God, Gregori, no sane man, not even the most monstrous criminal in history, would ever dream of such, of such—in the name of heaven, man, you can't mean it!"

"It may be that I am not sane," he said.

I didn't doubt it. Not then. Gripped with fear and fascination such as I had never known, I watched him as he handled the ampoule carelessly, then stopped swiftly and laid it on the wet road, under the sole of his left shoe. The left heel was still on the ground. I wondered briefly if a couple of heavy slugs from the Hanyatti would drive him over backwards, jerking his foot off the ampoule, but the thought died as it came. A madman could juggle carelessly with the lives of his fellow men, but I had no justification of madness. Even had there been only one chance in ten million of being executioner instead of keeper, I could never have taken it.

"I have tested these ampoules in the elaboratory—empty ones, I need hardly say," Gregori went on conversationally, "and have discovered that a pressure of seven and a half pounds is sufficient to shatter them. Incidentally, I have taken the precaution of providing concentrated cyanide tablets for Henriques and myself; death from the Satan Bug, as we have observed from experiments on animals, is rather more prolonged than death from botulinus, and most distressing. You will each come forward at a time and hand me your guns, butt foremost, at arm's length. You will take the greatest care to do nothing that might upset my balance, so transferring my weight to my left foot. You first, Cavell."

I reversed the gun and handed it to him, slowly and deliberately at the full extent of my arm, taking excruciating care indeed not to upset his balance. Our complete defeat, the fact that this madman and murderer would now escape and almost certainly achieve what evil and desperate ends he had in mind, just didn't matter a single solitary damn then. The only thing that mattered was that Gregori's balance should not be in the slightest upset.

One by one we all handed our guns over to him. After that he ordered us all to line up while Henriques, the deaf-mute, passed along behind us searching swiftly and skillfully for further weapons. He found none. Then, and not until then, did Gregori carefully remove his foot from the ampoule, stoop, pick it up and slide it back inside its steel jacket.

"I think conventional weapons will serve us now," he said pleasantly. "One is so much less liable to make mistakes of a—well—permanent nature." He picked up two of the guns that Henriques had piled on the bonnet of the Humber, checked that the safety catches of both were off. He beckoned to Henriques and spoke rapidly to him. It was a weird sight—because there was no sound—Gregori doing his speaking with exaggerated lip movements in complete silence. I know a little of lip-reading, but could make out nothing; possibly he talked in a foreign language, not French or Italian. He stopped speaking and Henriques nodded comprehension, looking at us with a queer anticipation in his eyes. I didn't like the look one bit: Henriques struck me as altogether a very nasty piece of work. Gregori pointed one of his guns at the two policemen who had been in the pursuing car.

"Off with your uniforms," he said curtly. "Now!"

The policemen looked at each other, and one said through clenched teeth, "I'll be damned if I will!"

"You'll be dead if you don't, you fool," I said sharply. "Don't you know what kind of men you are dealing with? Take it off."

"I won't take my clothes off for any man." He swore bitterly.

"It's an order!" Hardanger barked savagely, urgently. "It won't give him much more trouble to remove your uniforms when there is a bullet between your eyes. Take it off," he finished with slow and heavy emphasis.

Reluctantly, sullenly, the two officers did as they were told and stood there shivering in the cold, heavy rain. Henriques collected the uniforms and threw them into the police Jaguar.

"Who operates the short-wave radio in this Jaguar?" Gregori said next. I felt as if somebody had run a skewer through my middle and given it a twist, but I had been expecting it all the same.

"I do," the sergeant admitted.

"Good. Get through to headquarters. Tell them that you have taken us and are proceeding to London. Tell them to call all police cars in the area back to their stations—except, of course, those on routine patrol duties."

"Do as he says," Hardanger said wearily. "I think you're too intelligent to try any fancy stuff, Sergeant. Exactly as he says."

So the sergeant did exactly as he was told. He didn't have much option, not with the muzzle of one of Gregori's pistols grinding into his left ear. When he had finished, Gregori nodded his satisfaction.

"That will do very well." He watched Henriques climb into the stolen Humber. "Our car and the one belonging to our two shivering friends here will be driven into the woods and their distributors smashed for good measure. They won't be found before dawn. With the search called off, the other police car and those two uniforms, we should have little trouble in clearing this area. Then we switch cars." He looked regretfully at the Jaguar. "When your H.Q. catch onto the fact that you are missing, this car is going to become very hot property indeed. That leaves only the problem of what to do with you."

He waited until Henriques had disposed of both cars, gazing out with empty disinterest under the dripping brim of fedora, then said: "Is there a portable searchlight in this Jaguar? I believe such equipment is standard. Sergeant?"

"We have a battery-powered light in the boot," the sergeant said stolidly.

"Get it." Gregori's eyes and mouth crinkled into a smile, the kind of smile a tiger trapped in the bottom of a pit shows when the man who dug the hole trips and falls in beside him. "I can't shoot you, though I wouldn't hesitate if that house were not so near. I won't try tapping you all on the head because I doubt if you would submit quietly to that. I can't tie you up for I'm not in the habit of carrying on me sufficient ropes and gags to immobilize and silence eight people. But I suspect that one of those farm buildings there will offer all I require in the way of a temporary prison. Sergeant, switch off the car headlamps and then lead the way with your light to those buildings. The rest will follow in double file. Mrs. Cavell and I will bring up the rear. The gun in my hand will be pressed against her back and should any of you try to run for it or otherwise cause trouble, I shall merely pull the trigger."

I didn't doubt him. None of us doubted him.

The farm buildings were deserted—of human life, that was. From the byre I could hear the moving and slow champing of the cows, but the evening milking was over. Gregori passed up the byre. He passed up the dairy, a stable now converted to a tractor shed, a large concreted pig-sty and a turnip shed. He hesitated over the barn and then found exactly what he wanted. I had to admit that it certainly suited his purpose.

A long, narrow stone building, with head-high embrasured windows that made one instinctively look for the crenelated battlements above, it looked more like an old-time private chapel than anything else; its true function couldn't have been more different. It was a cider house, with a heavy, old-fashioned oaken press at the far end, one long wall lined with duck-board shelving for apples, the other with bunged casks and covered vats of freshly made cider. The door, like the press, was made of solid oak, and once the drop-bar on the outside was in position it would have taken a battering-ram to break it down.

We'd no battering ram, but we'd even better, we had desperation, resource and, between us all, a fair amount of intelligence. Surely Gregori wasn't so crazy as to think that that cider house could hold us indefinitely? Surely he wasn't so crazy as to think that our shouts wouldn't be heard eventually, either by passers-by on the road or the occupants of the farm itself, not much more than a hundred yards away? With a sudden dread conviction and heart-chilling finality that momentarily paralyzed all reasoning, I knew that Gregori was indeed not that crazy. He *knew* we would be making no assaults on the door, he *knew* we wouldn't be shouting out for help, because he knew beyond all question that none of us would ever be leaving that cider house again except on a bier and covered by a blanket. Somebody with super-chilled icicles in lieu of fingers started playing Rachmaninoff up and down my spinal column.

"Get to the far end and stay there while I lock the door from the outside," Gregori ordered. "Time does not permit elaborate farewell speeches. Twelve hours from now when I've shaken the dust of this accursed country from my feet for the last time, I shall think of you all. Good-by."

I said steadily: "No magnanimous gestures towards a defeated enemy?"

"You beg, Cavell. I have time for one little thing more, time for the man who cost me so much, so nearly ruined all my plans." He stepped forward, jammed the automatic he held in his left hand into my stomach, and with the sights of the pistol he held in his right, deliberately and viciously raked both sides of my face. I felt the skin tearing in thin lines of white-hot pain and the warm blood trickling down cold cheeks. Mary said something unintelligible in a high voice and tried to run to me, but Hardanger caught her in powerful arms and held her till her futile struggles ceased. Gregori stepped back and said: "*That* is for beggars, Cavell."

I nodded. I didn't even raise my hands to my face, anyway he couldn't have disfigured it much more than it had been before. I said: "You might take Mrs. Cavell with you."

"Pierre!" Mary's voice was a sob, anguish in it, a cruelly hurt and stricken despair. "What are you saying!" Hardanger swore, softly and viciously, and the General looked at me in dumb incomprehension.

Gregori stood very still, dark expressionless eyes looking emptily into mine. Then he gave a queer little duck of the head and said: "It is my turn to beg. Forgive me. I did not know that you knew. I hope when my turn comes—" He broke off and turned to Mary. "It would be wrong. A beautiful child. I am not, Cavell, devoid of all human sentiment, at least not where women and children are concerned. For instance, the two children I was forced to abduct from Alfringham Farm have already been released and will be with their parents within the hour. Yes, yes, it would be wrong. Come, Mrs. Cavell."

She came instead to me and touched my face lightly. "What is it, Pierre?" she whispered. No reproach in her voice, only love and wonder and compassion. "What is so wrong?"

"Good-by, Mary," I said. "Dr. Gregori doesn't like to be kept waiting. I'll see you soon." She made to speak again, but Gregori had her by the arm, already leading her towards the door while the deaf-mute, Henriques, watched us with mad eyes and a pistol in either hand, and then the door closed, the heavy bar dropped solidly into place and we were left there staring at each other by the light of the spot-lamp which still burned whitely on the floor.

"You lousy, filthy swine," Hardanger ground out savagely. "Why—"

"Shut up, Hardanger!" My voice was low, urgent, desperate. "Spread out. Watch those embrasures, the windows. Quickly! For God's sake, *hurry!*"

I think there was something in my voice that would have moved an Egyptian mummy. Quickly, silently, the seven of us started to space out. I whispered: "He's going to throw in something through a window. He's going to throw in an ampoule of the botulinus toxin. Any second." I knew it would take moments only for him to unscrew the top of the steel flask that held the ampoule. "Catch it. You can catch it. If that ampoule hits the floor or the wall we're all dead men."

Even as I finished, we heard a sudden movement outside, the shadow of an arm fell across the side of an embrasure and something came spinning into the room. Something glittered and flashed in the light from the lamp on the floor. Something made of glass, with a red seal on top. A botulinus ampoule.

It came so swiftly, so unexpectedly and thrown at such a deliberately downward angle that no one had a chance. It spun across the room, struck at the precise junction of stone wall and stone floor, and shattered into a thousand tinkling fragments.

CHAPTER 12

I'll never know what made me do it. I'll never know why I reacted with what I can only regard now, looking back on it, as incredible swiftness. The split second that elapses between the downward sweep of the enemy club and the reflex upflinging of your arm in defense—that was all the time it took me to react. It was automatic, instinctive, without any thought in the world—but there must have been thought behind it, an instantaneous form of reasoning below the level of awareness that didn't have time to be transmitted to the surface mind in the form of conscious thought, for I did the one thing in the world that offered the only, the slenderest, the most desperate hope of survival.

Even as that ampoule came spinning through the air and I could see there was no chance on earth of its being intercepted, my hands were reaching out for the barrel of cider on the trestle by my side, and the tinkling of the smashed ampoule was still echoing in the shocked silence in that tiny little room when I smashed down the barrel with all the strength of my arms and body exactly on the spot where the glass had made contact. The staves split and shattered as if they had been made of the thinnest ply, and ten gallons of cider gurgled and flooded out over the wall and floor.

"More cider," I shouted. "More cider. Pour it on the floor, down the side of the wall, spray it through the air above where that damned ampoule landed. For God's sake, don't splash any cider on yourselves. Hurry! Hurry!"

"What the hell is all this for?" Hardanger demanded. His normally ruddy face was pale and set and uncomprehending, but for all that he was already carefully tipping a small vat of cider on the floor. "What will this do?"

"It's hygroscopic," I said quickly. "The botulinus, I mean. Seeks out water in preference to air every time, it has a hundred times the affinity for hydrogen that it has for nitrogen. You heard the General speak of it this evening."

"This isn't water," Hardanger objected almost wildly. "This is cider."

"God help us!" I said savagely. "Of course it's cider. We haven't got anything else here. I don't know what the effect, the affinity will be. For the first time in your life, Hardanger, you'd better start praying that an alcohol has a high water content." I tried to lift another, smaller cask but gasped and dropped it as a sharp spear of agony struck at the right side of my chest. For one terrible second I thought the virus had struck, the next I realized I must have displaced my strapped broken ribs when I hurled that barrel through the air. I wondered vaguely whether a broken rib had pierced the pleura or even a lung, and then forgot about it; in the circumstances, it hardly mattered any more.

How long to live? If some of the botulinus virus had escaped into the atmosphere, how long before the first convulsions? What had Gregori said about the hamster when we'd been talking outside number one lab yesterday? Fifteen seconds, yes, that was it, fifteen seconds for the Satan Bug and about the same for botulinus. For a hamster, fifteen seconds. For a human being? Heaven alone knew, probably thirty seconds at the most. At the very most. I stooped and lifted the portable lamp from the floor.

"Stop pouring," I said urgently. "Stop it. That's enough. Stand high; if you want to live, stand high. Don't let any of that cider touch your shoes, touch any part of you, or you're dead men." I swung the lamp round as they scrambled high to avoid the amber tide of cider already flooding rapidly across the stone floor, and as I did I could hear the police engine of the Jaguar starting up. Gregori taking off with Henriques and Mary towards the realization of his megalomaniac's dream, secure in the knowledge that he was leaving a charnel house behind.

Thirty seconds were up. At least thirty seconds were up. No one twitching yet, far less in convulsions. More slowly this time, I played the lamp beam over each and every one of us, starting at strained, staring faces, and moving slowly down to the feet. The beam steadied on one of the two constables whose clothes had been taken.

"Take off your right shoe," I said sharply. "It's been splashed. *Not* with your hand, you bloody idiot! Ease it off with the toe of the other shoe. Superintendent, the left arm of your jacket is wet." Hardanger stood very still, not even looking at me as I eased the jacket at the collar and slid it down carefully over arms and hands before dropping it to the floor.

"Are we—are we safe now, sir?" the sergeant asked nervously.

"Safe? I'd rather this damned place were alive with cobras and black widow spiders. No, we're not safe. Some of this hellish toxin will escape to the atmosphere as soon as the first of those splashes on the wall or floor has dried up—there's water vapor in the air, too, you know. My guess is that as soon as any of those splashes dry up we'll all have had it inside a minute."

"So we get out," the General said calmly. "Fast. Is that the idea, my boy?"

"Yes, sir." I glanced quickly round. "Two barrels on either side of the door. Two more in line with them and a bit back. Four men standing on those and swinging that cider-press between them. I can't do it, something's wrong with my ribs. That press must weigh three hundred pounds if it weighs an ounce. Think four of you could do it, Superintendent?"

"Think we can do it?" Hardanger growled. "I could do it myself, with one hand, if it meant getting out of this place. Come on, for God's sake, let's hurry."

And hurry they did. Maneuvering casks into position while having to stand on others was no easy trick, more especially as all the casks were full, but desperation and the fear that borders on overmastering panic gives men ability to perform feats of strength that they can never afterwards understand. In less than twenty seconds all four barrels were in position, and in another twenty, Hardanger, the sergeant and two constables, a pair on each side of the heavy, ponderous cider-press, were starting on their back swing.

The door was made of solid oak, with heavy hinges to match and a draw-bar on the outside, but against that solid battering ram, propelled by four powerful men with their lives at stake, it might as well have been made of plywood; the shattered door was smashed completely off its hinges and the cider-press, released at the last moment, went cart-wheeling through the doorway into the darkness beyond. Five seconds later the last of us had followed the cider-press.

"That farmhouse," Hardanger said urgently. "Come on. They've probably got a telephone."

"Wait!" There was twice the urgency in my voice. "We can't do that. We don't know that we're not carrying the toxin on us. We may be bringing death to all that family. Let's give this rain time to wash off any virus that may be sticking to the outside."

"Damn it, we can't afford to wait," Hardanger said fiercely. "Besides, if the toxin didn't get us in there, it's a certainty it won't get us now. General?"

"I'm not sure," the General said hesitantly. "I rather think you're right. We've no time—"

He broke off in horror as one of the uniformless constables, the one whose shoe had been splashed by the cider, screamed aloud in agony, the scream deepening to a tearing rasping coughing moan; his clutching hands clawed in a maniac frenzy at a suddenly stiffened, straightened neck where the tendons stood out whitely like quivering wires; then he toppled and fell heavily to the muddy ground, silent now, the nails of his fingers trying to tear his throat open. His crewmate, the other uniform-less constable, made some sort of unintelligible sound, moved forward and down to help his friend, then grunted in pain as my arm hooked around his neck.

"Don't touch him!" I shouted hoarsely. "Touch him and you'll die too. He must have picked up the toxin when he brushed his shoe with his hand, and then touched his mouth.

Nothing on earth can save him now. Stand back. Keep well clear of him."

He took twenty seconds to die, the kind of twenty seconds that will stay with a man in his nightmares till he draws his last breath on earth. I had seen many men die, but even those who had died in bullet- and shrapnel-torn agony had done so peacefully and quietly, compared to this man whose body, in the incredibly convulsive violence of its death throes, twisted and flung itself into the most fantastic and impossible contortions. Twice in the last shocking seconds before death he threw his racked and tortured body clear off the ground and so high in the air that I could have passed a table beneath him. And then, as abruptly and unexpectedly as it had begun, it was all over and he was no more than a strangely small and shapeless bundle of clothes lying face downwards in the muddy earth. My mouth was kiln-dry and full of the taste of salt, the ugly taste of fear.

I can't say how long we stood there in the heavy cold rain, staring at the dead man. A long time, I think. And then we looked at each other, and each one of us knew what the others were thinking, because each one of us knew that the others were capable of thinking only one thing. Who was next? In the pale wash of light from the lamp I still held in one hand, we all stared at each other, one half of our senses and minds outgoing and screwed up to the highest pitch of intensity and perception to detect the first signs of death in another, the other half turned inwards to detect the first signs in ourselves. Then, all at once, I cursed savagely, perhaps at myself, or my cowardice, or at Gregori, or at the botulinus toxin, I don't know, turned abruptly and headed for the byre, taking the lamp with me, leaving the others standing there round the dead man in the rain-filled, pitchy darkness like darkly-petrified mourners at some age-old heathen midnight rites.

I was looking for a hose, and I found one almost immediately. I carried it outside, screwed it onto a standing plug and turned the tap on full: the results in the volume and pressure would have done justice to any city hydrant. I clambered awkwardly onto a hay wagon that was standing nearby and said to the General: "Come on, sir, you first."

He came directly under the earthward-pointed nozzle, and the jet of water on head and shoulders from a distance of only a few inches made him stumble and all but fall. But he stuck it gamely for all of the half-minute that I insisted he remain under the hose, and by the time I was finished, he was as sodden as if he'd spent the night in the river and shivering so violently that I could hear his teeth chatter above the hiss of the water; but by the time he was finished I knew that any toxin which might have been clinging to face or body would have been completely washed away. The other four all submitted to it in their turn and then Hardanger did the same for me. The force of the water was such that it was like being belabored by a non-stop series of far from light-weight clubs, and the water itself was ice-cold; but when I thought of the man who had died and how he had died, a few bruises and the risk of pneumonia didn't even begin to be worth considering.

When he had finished with me, Hardanger switched off the water and said quietly: "Sorry, Cavell. You had the right of it."

"It was my fault," I said. I didn't mean my voice to sound dull and lifeless, but that was the way it came out, to my ears anyway. "I should have told him not to touch his mouth or nose with his hand."

"He should have thought of that himself," Hardanger said, his voice abnormally matter-of-fact. "He knew the dangers as well as you—they've been published in every paper in the land today. Let's go and see if the farmer has a phone. Not that it'll make much difference now. Gregori knows that police Jaguar is too hot to hang on to for a second longer than is necessary. He's won all along the line, damn his black soul, and nothing is going to stop him now. Twelve hours he said. Twelve hours and then he would be gone."

"Twelve hours from now Gregori would be dead," I said.

"What?" I could sense him staring at me. "What did you say?"

"He'll be dead," I repeated. "Before dawn."

"It's all right," Hardanger said. Cavell's mind had cracked at last, but let's play it casual, let's not any of us make a song and dance about it. He took my arm and started out for the lamp-lit rectangles which showed where the house stood. "The sooner this is over, the sooner we'll all get the rest and food and sleep we need."

"I'll rest and sleep when I've killed Gregori," I said. "I'm going to kill him tonight. First I get Mary back. Then I'll kill him."

"Mary will be all right, Cavell." Mary in that madman's hands, that was what had sent Cavell's last few remaining gray cells tottering over the brink, he thought. "He'll let her go, he'll have no reason to do anything to her. And you *had* to do what you did. You thought that if she stayed there with us in the cider house she would die. Isn't that it, Cavell?"

"I'm sure the Superintendent is right, my boy." The General was walking on my other side now, and his voice was quiet because loud voices excite the unhinged. "She won't be harmed." It was damned decent of the old boy, lying like fury and trying to console me when he himself must have been racked by anxiety over his own daughter, but all the same I wished they'd stop behaving like a board of alienists turning the old thumbs down, in the nicest possible way, on the last inmate seeking discharge.

I said rudely, to both: "If I'm round the bend, what the hell does that make you two?"

Hardanger stopped, tightened his grip on my arm and peered at me. He knew that those whose minds have gone off the rails never talk about it, for the simple reason that they are unshakably convinced that their minds are still on the track. He said carefully: "I don't think I understand."

"You don't. But you will." I said to the General: "You must persuade the Cabinet to go on with this evacuation of the Central London area. Continuous radio and TV broadcasts. They'll have no difficulty in persuading the people to leave, you can believe that. It shouldn't cause much trouble—that area's pretty well unlived in, by night anyway." I turned again to Hardanger. "Have two hundred of your best men armed. A gun for me, too—and a knife. I know exactly what Gregori intends to do tonight. I know exactly what he hopes to achieve. I know exactly how he intends to leave the country—and exactly where he will be leaving from."

"How do you know, my boy?" The General's voice was so quiet that I could hardly hear it above the drumming of the rain.

"Because Gregori talked too much. Sooner or later they all talk too much. Gregori was cagier than most; even when he was convinced that we would all be dead in a minute, he still said very little. But that little was too much. And I think I've really known ever since we found MacDonald's body."

"You must have heard things that I didn't hear," Hardanger said sourly.

"You heard it all. You heard him say he was going to London. If he really wanted the bug set loose in London to have Mordon destroyed, he's have stayed in Mordon to see what happened and have some stooge do the job in London. But he has no interest in seeing Mordon destroyed, he never had. There's something he has to do in London. Another of

197

his never-ending red-herrings—the Communist red herring, of course, was purely fortuitous, he'd no hand in that at all. That's the first thing. The second—that he was going to achieve some great ambition *tonight*. The third—that he had twice saved Henriques from the electric chair. That shows what kind of a man he is—and I don't mean a criminal defense lawyer of the American Bar Association—and what kind of ambition he has in mind; I'll take long odds not only that he's on the Interpol files but also that he's an ex-big-time American racketeer who has been deported to Italy—and the line of business in which he used to specialize would make very interesting reading, because the criminal leopards, even the biggest cats in the jungle, never change their spots. The fourth thing is that he expects to be clear of this country in twelve hours' time. And the fifth thing is that this is Saturday night. Put all those things together and see what you get."

"Suppose you tell us," Hardanger said impatiently.

So I told them.

The rain still fell as vertically, as heavily as ever, just as heavily as when we had left that farmhouse some hours previously, where the torrential rain in conjunction with the quick evacuation of the area had robbed the botulinus toxin of all victims other than the unfortunate policeman who had died so terribly before our eyes. Now, at twenty minutes past three in the morning, the rain was ice-cold, but I didn't really feel it. All I could feel was my exhaustion, the harsh stabbing pain in my right ribs that came with every breath I took, and the continuous rending worry that, in spite of the confidence I'd shown to the General and Hardanger, I might be hopelessly wrong, after all, and Mary lost to me forever. And even if I were right, she might still as easily be lost to me. With a conscious and almost desperate effort of will, I turned my mind to other things.

The high-walled courtyard where I'd been standing for the past three hours was dark and deserted, as deserted as the heart of London itself. Evacuation of the center of the city—the temporarily homeless going to prepared halls, ballrooms and theaters—had begun shortly after six o'clock, just after the last of the offices, businesses and shops had closed; it had been hastened by radio broadcasts at nine o'clock, saying that according to the latest message received, the time for the release of the botulinus toxin had been advanced from four a.m. to half-past two. There had been no hurry, no panic, no despair; in fact there would have been no sense of anything unusual happening had it not been for the unusual number of people carrying suitcases: the phlegmatic Londoners who had seen the City set on fire and suffered a hundred nights of mass area-bombing during the war weren't to be stampeded into anything for anybody.

Between half-past nine and ten o'clock, over a thousand troops had combed their methodical way through the heart of the city, checking that every last man, woman and child had been moved to safety, that no one had been inadvertently overlooked. At half past eleven, a darkened drifting police launch had nosed silently into the north bank of the river and put me ashore on the embankment, just below Hungerford Bridge. At midnight, troops and police, all of them armed, had completely sealed off the entire area, including the bridges across the Thames. At one o'clock a power failure on a large scale had blacked out the better part of a square mile of the city—the square mile cordoned off by troops and police.

Twenty past three. Fifty minutes after the timed release of the botulinus toxin. It was time to go. I eased the borrowed Webley in its ill-fitting holster, checked the knife that was strapped, handle downwards, to my left forearm, and moved out into the darkness.

I'd never seen a picture of—far less visited—the new helicopter port on the north bank, but an Inspector of the Metropolitan police had briefed me so exhaustively that by the time he had finished, I could have found my way up there blindfolded. And that, to all intents and purposes, was exactly what I was. Blindfolded. Blind. In that blacked-out city and on that weeping overcast night, the darkness was just one degree short of absolute.

I had been told that there were three different ways up to the heliport, perched on the roof of the station, a hundred feet above the streets of London. There were two lifts, but with the power failure those would be out of operation. Between those lifts was a glassed-in, circular staircase without a shred of cover from top to bottom; using it would be as neat a way as any of committing suicide if there was a reception committee waiting, and I could not see Gregori as a man who would leave his main line of approach unguarded. And then there was the third way, the fire escape on the other side of the station. That was the only way in for me.

I walked two hundred yards from the courtyard, along a narrow cobbled lane. In spite of the darkness I stayed close to the high wall on my left, soundless on rubber-soled shoes.

When the wall gave way to an equally high wooden fence, I reached for the top and pulled myself up. For a moment or two I perched there, swaying dizzily and trying to dispel the brightly colored lights that coruscated before my eyes. My ribs were in no condition for mountaineering, I couldn't have brushed my teeth without injuring myself. When the world steadied down a bit I slipped quietly down on the other side and set off across the railway tracks. It would have been easier, of course, to go round by the front of the station, but I wasn't going to be of much use to anyone with a lot of holes blown through my middle. Armed guards would be patrolling there. If I was right about Gregori, that was.

The reference book compilers who assert that Clapham Junction has more sets of parallel tracks that any place in Britain wouldn't go around making silly statements like that if they'd tried this lot on a pitch-black October night with the sleety rain falling about their ears. There wasn't a single piece of ironware in the whole interminable width of those tracks that I didn't find that night, usually with my ankles and shins. Railway lines, wires, signaling gear, switch gear, hydrants, platforms where there shouldn't have been platforms—I found them all. To add to my discomfort, the burnt cork that had been so heavily rubbed into my face and hands was beginning to run, and burnt cork tastes exactly as you would expect it to taste; and when it gets in your eyes it hurts. The only hazard I didn't have to contend with was live rails—the power had been switched off.

I found the fence on the other side of the track easily enough, just by walking into it. Once down in the lane on the other side, I turned left and made my way towards the fire escape which came down, I had been told, into a small recessed court. I found the court, crossed the entrance and flattened myself against the far wall. The fire escape was there all right, just barely discernible twenty feet away against the fractionally lighter darkness of the sky, gaunt and stark and angular, and zig-zagging upwards out of sight. The first two or three flights of the fire escape were invisible, lost against the darkness of high walls beyond.

For three minutes I stood there, showing as many signs of life as a wooden Indian. Then I heard it—even above the drumming of the sleet on my sodden shoulders and sound of water running in the gutters, I heard it: the slight shuffle of a shoe on pavement as someone changed his cramped position. The sound didn't come again, but then I didn't need to hear it again. Once was enough. Someone was standing directly under the lowermost platform of the fire escape, and if he turned out to be the soul of innocence doing it for his health's sake, it would be surprising, to say the least. It was also going to be unfortunate for him, but he wouldn't be caring much when he was dead.

Finding this man here didn't give me any feeling of dismay and frustration because of the possible threat and setback he offered; all it afforded me was the sense of profound satisfaction and a relief that could not be described. I had gambled, but I had won. Dr. Gregori was doing exactly what I'd told the General and Hardanger he would be doing.

The knife came free of its sheath and I brushed the blade with the ball of my thumb. It had a point like a lancet and an edge like a scalpel. It was only a very little knife, but three-and-a-half inches of steel can kill you just as dead as the longest stiletto or the heaviest broadsword. If you know where to hit, that is. I had a fair idea where to hit, and how. And at anything up to ten paces I was twice as accurate with a knife as with a gun.

I covered sixteen of the intervening twenty feet in just over ten seconds, making no more sound than the moonlight shadow of a drifting snowflake. And now I could see him quite clearly. He was directly under the first platform of the fire escape, to get what shelter he could from the rain. His back was to the wall. His head was bowed, as if his chin were resting on his chest, as if he were half-asleep on his feet. He'd only to glance sideways under raised eyelids and he'd have had me.

He wasn't going to remain so obligingly unseeing for an indefinite period. I twisted the knife until the blade pointed upwards, then found myself hesitating. Even with Mary's life in the balance I found myself hesitating. Whoever this character was, I'd little doubt but that he deserved to die anyway. But to knife an unsuspecting and half-asleep man, however much he deserved it? This wasn't the war any more. I slid out the Webley, quiet as a mouse tiptoeing past a sleeping cat, caught the barrel and swung for a spot just below the dripping brim of his hat, just behind the left ear, and because I was feeling illogically angry about my queasiness in knifing him I struck him very hard indeed. The sound was the sound of an axe sinking deep into the bole of a pine. I caught and lowered him gently to the ground. He wouldn't wake up before dawn. Maybe he'd never waken again. It didn't seem to matter. I started up the fire escape.

There was no hurry, no haste, in my going. Haste could be

the end of it all. I went up the steps slowly, one at a time, always staring upward. I was too near the end of the road now to let rashness be the ruin of everything.

After the sixth or seventh flight of steps I slowed down even more, not because my leg and a queer shortness of breath were troubling me, which they were, but because I had become suddenly aware of an area of diffuse light in the darkness of the wall above me, where a light had no right to be. There shouldn't have been a light anywhere, for all the lights of Central London were out.

If ghosts are allowed to have black faces—though I suspected mine was getting pretty streaky by this time—then I went up the next flight of steps like a ghost. As I approached the light, I could see that it came not from a window but from a grill-work door set in the wall. Cautiously, I raised my head to the level of this door and peered inside.

It was on a level with the massive iron girders that spanned and supported the roof of the station. At least a dozen lights were burning inside the station, small, weak, isolated sources of illumination that served only to emphasize the depth of the gloom that lay over most of that huge and cavernous building. Six of the lights were directly above sets of hydraulic buffers at the end of tracks, and I suddenly realized why they were burning there: some lights are essential to the safe operation of a railway station, and those must have been battery-powered lamps designed to come on in the event of a power failure. A prosaic enough explanation and, I was sure, the correct one.

I looked for some moments at the geometric tracery of soot-blackened girders that dwindled and vanished into impenetrable darkness at the furthest reaches of the station, then put a slight experimental pressure on the door. It gave under my hand. And the damned thing squeaked, like a gibbet creaking in the night wind. A gibbet with a corpse on it. I put the thought of corpses out of my mind and withdrew my hand from the door. Enough was enough.

But the door was sufficiently open to let me see a couple of vertical iron ladders leading away from the steel platform just inside. One led upwards to a long gangway immediately below the vast skylights, the other down to another gangway about the level of the highest of the lights inside the station: the former would be for the window-cleaners, the latter for the electricians. It was a great help to me to know that. I straightened. At least six flights of stairs to go yet before I started getting really interested.

The arm that locked round my throat and started throttling the life out of me belonged to a gorilla, a gorilla with a shirt and jacket on, but a gorilla for all that. In those first two hellish seconds of immobilized shock and pain I thought my neck was going to snap, and before I could even begin to react something hard and metallic smacked down on my right wrist and sent the Webley flying from my grasp. It struck the iron platform and then spun off into space.

I never heard it land on the roadway beneath. I was too busy fighting for my life. With my left hand—my right hand was momentarily paralyzed and quite useless—I reached up, caught his wrist and tried to tear his arm away. I might as well have tried to tear a four-inch bough from an oak tree. He was phenomenally strong and he was squeezing the life out of me. And not slowly.

Something ground savagely into my back, just above the kidney. The unspoken order was clear as day, but for all that I didn't stop struggling, a few more seconds of that pressure and I knew my neck would go. I smashed my right foot against the grill door and sent us both staggering back against the outside platform rail. I felt his feet leave the platform as the rail struck him about hip-level, and for a moment we both teetered there on the point of imbalance, his arm still locked around my neck; then the pressures on neck and back were simultaneously released as he grabbed desperately for the rail to save himself.

I staggered away from him, whooping painfully for breath, and fell heavily against the next flight of steps leading upwards. I landed on my right side, just where the ribs were gone, and the world darkened and dimmed in a haze of pain. If I'd let myself go then, relaxed even for the briefest moment and yielded to the body's clamorous demands for rest, I should have passed out. But passing out was the one luxury I couldn't afford. Not with this character, anyway. I knew who I had now. If he'd wanted merely to knock me out, he could have tapped me over the head with his gun; if he'd wanted to kill me, he could have shot me in the back, or if he'd no silencer and didn't want noise, a tap on the head and a heave over the rail to the roadway sixty feet below would have served his purpose equally well. But this lad didn't want anything so quiet and simple and painless. If I was to die, he wanted me to know I was dying; for me he wanted the tearing agony of death by violence, for himself the delight of savoring my agony. A vicious and evil sadist with a dark mind crimsoned by the lust for blood. Gregori's hatchet-man. Henriques. The deaf-mute with the crazy eyes.

Half-lying, half-standing against the steps, I twisted to face him as he came at me again. He was crouched low and he had his gun in front of him. But he didn't want to use his gun. Not if he could help it. From a bullet you died too quickly, unless, of course, you were very careful with the placing of the bullet. Suddenly I knew this was just what he had in mind, the muzzle was ranging down my body as he searched for the spot where a bullet would mean that I would take quite some time dying, unpleasantly. I straightened my arms on the steps behind me and if the scything upward sweep of my right foot had caught him where I had intended, Henriques wouldn't have worried me any more. But my vision was fuzzy and my co-ordination poor. My foot glanced off his right thigh, swept on and struck his forearm, jarring the gun from his hand; the gun carried over the edge of the platform and clattered down a couple of steps on the flight below.

He turned like a cat to retrieve it, and I was hardly any slower myself. As he leaned over the top step, scrabbled for and found his gun, I jumped and caught him with both feet. He grunted, an ugly, hoarse sound, then crashed and cartwheeled down the steps to the platform below. But he landed on his feet, and he still had the gun.

I didn't hesitate. If I'd tried running up the remaining flights to the heliport on top of the station roof, he'd have caught me in seconds or picked me off at his leisure; even had I managed to reach the top, assuming that the days of miracles were not yet over, secrecy and silence would have vanished and Gregori would be waiting for me, I'd be trapped between two fires and everything would be over for Mary. It would have been just as suicidal to go down and meet him, or wait for him where I was; I'd only the knife strapped to my left forearm, and my numbed right hand was not yet sufficiently recovered to ease it out from its sheath, far less use it—and even had we both been weaponless, even had I been at my fittest and best, I doubt whether I could have coped with the dark violence of that phenomenally powerful deaf-mute. And I was a very long way from my fittest and best. I went through that grill door like a rabbit bolting from its hole with a ferret only half a length behind.

Desperately I glanced round the tiny platform. Up the vertical ladder to the window cleaners' catwalk or down to the electricians'? It took me all of half a second to realize I couldn't do either. Not with one hand still out of commission and hope to get to either the top or the bottom of the ladder before Henriques came through that door and picked me off in his own sweet time.

Six feet away from the platform was one of the giant girders that spanned the entire width of the station roof. I didn't stop to think of it; subconsciously I must have known that if I had stopped to think, even for a second, I'd have chosen to remain there and have it out with Henriques on that platform, gun or no gun. But I didn't stop. I ducked under the waist-high chain surrounding the platform and launched myself across that sixty-foot drop.

My good foot landed fair and square on the girder, the other came just short and slipped off the thickly treacherous coating of soot deposited there by generations of steam locomotives. As my shin cracked painfully against the edge of the metal, I grabbed the beam with my left hand and for two or three dreadful seconds I just teetered there while the great empty station swam dizzily around me. Then I steadied and was safe. For the moment. I rose shakily to my feet.

I didn't crawl along that girder. I didn't pussyfoot along with arms outstretched to aid my balance. I just put down my head and ran. The beam was only eight or nine inches wide, it was covered with the dangerous layer of soot, and the two rows of smooth rivet-heads running along its entire length would have been my death had I stepped on their slippery convexities. But I ran. It took me seconds only to cover the seventy feet to the great central vertical girder that disappeared into the darkness above. I grabbed it, edged recklessly round, and stared back in the direction from which I had come.

Henriques was on the platform by the grill door. His gun was extended at the full stretch of his right arm, pointing directly at me, but he was lowering it even as I looked; he'd seen me, all right, but too late to draw a bead before I'd vanished behind the shelter of that vertical girder.

He looked around him, seemed to hesitate. I stood where I was, clinging to the girder while some of the numbness drained from my right hand; and while Henriques was making up his mind I cursed myself for my folly. All the way up that fire escape from street level I'd never once thought to look behind. The deaf-mute must have been making a round of the posted guards, found the unconscious man at the foot of the fire escape and drawn the inevitable conclusions.

Henriques had made up his mind. The idea of the leap from the platform across to the girder obviously didn't ap-

peal to him, and I couldn't blame him. He swarmed up the
iron ladder to the window cleaners' catwalk above, moved
over to a position directly above the girder I was standing
on, crossed the catwalk rail and lowered himself until his feet
were only inches above the girder. He dropped, steadying
himself with his hands on the wall, turned carefully and
started coming towards me, his hands outstretched like a
tightrope walker's. I didn't wait for him. I turned and started
walking also.

I didn't walk far, for there wasn't far to walk. The beam I
was on stretched to the other side of the main hall of the
station and there it ended, vanishing into the grimy brickwork. There was no convenient platform here. No catwalk
above or below. Just the beam vanishing into the wall. And
sixty feet below, the dull gleam of rails and hydraulic buffers.
Just myself and the girder and that blank wall. The end of
the road and no way out. I turned and made ready to die.

Henriques had reached the vertical girder in the center,
had safely negotiated his way past it and was advancing on
me. Fifty feet away he stopped, and even in the gloom I
could see the white glimmer of his teeth as he smiled. He had
seen how it was with me, that I was trapped and quite at his
mercy. It must have been one of the highlights in the life of
that crazy man.

He started moving again, slowly closing the distance between us. Twenty feet away he stopped, stooped, lowered his
hands to the girder and sat down, locking his legs securely
under the beam. He was wearing a very smooth line in
Italian sacking and all that soot wouldn't be doing it any
good at all, but he didn't seem to care. He raised his pistol,
holding it with both hands, and pointed it at the middle of
my body.

There was nothing I could do. With my hands at my back,
bracing myself against the wall, I stiffened in futile preparation for the slamming, rending impact of the shock. I stared
at his hands and imagined I could see the fingers whiten. In
spite of myself I winced and closed my eyes. Only for a
second or two. When I opened them again he'd lowered the
gun until his hand was resting on the beam, and he was
grinning at me.

For sheer, calculated sadism and feline cruelty, I'd never
met its equal. But I should have known it, I should have
expected it. The monstrous madman who had forced a cyanide sweet down Clandon's throat, who had strangled Mac-
Donald alive at the end of a rope, who had pulped in the back

of Mrs. Turpin's head, who had tortured Easton Derry to death—and for good measure, had stove in my ribs—such a man wasn't going to pass up the exquisite pleasure of watching me die by inches, even although, for once, the dying was to be by terror of the mind instead of agony of the body. I could visualize those empty eyes now, hot and greedy for the suffering of others, I could almost visualize the wolf-like slavering of that twisted grinning mouth. He was the cat, I was the mouse, and he was going to play with me until he had extracted every last ounce of pleasure from his macabre game. And then, regretfully, he would shoot me, although he would still have that one last joy of seeing me fall and being smashed and mangled on the steel and concrete far below.

I had been very afraid. I'm no hero when I see that death is certain, when my murder is certain, nor do I believe anyone else is. I had been close to physical paralysis with that fear, and that numbness had extended to the mind, but now the petrifaction of body and mind vanished in a suddenly overwhelming warm flood of pure anger, anger that my life and the fate of Mary should be at the mercy of the whims of a sub-human creature like this.

I remembered my knife.

Slowing I brought together the hands behind my back until they were touching. The fingers of my right hand, painful still but no longer numb, reached up under my left sleeve and closed on the haft of the knife. Henriques lifted his gun again, pointing it at my head this time, his lips lifted back in a snarling smile, but I just kept on working away slowly till the knife was clear of the sheath. It was too soon for the deaf-mute to kill me yet; there was still a great deal more innocent pleasure to be extracted from this harmless game before he grew bored and blew the last whistle on me by leaning on the trigger.

Henriques lowered the gun a second time, shifted slightly to lock his ankles even more securely under the girder, and dug into his jacket pocket with his left hand. He brought out a packet of cigarettes and a book of matches. He was smiling like a crazy man, because this was the zenith, the towering pinnacle of refinement of torture: the killer taking his luxuriantly insolent ease while the trembling and terror-stricken victim waits, not knowing when the last moment will come, but knowing it must inevitably come—and he'd thought it all up by himself.

He got a cigarette into his mouth, bent over a match to

strike it. The gun was still in his right hand. The match flared and for half a second of time he was blind.

Steel flickered and gleamed briefly in the weak backwash of light and Henriques coughed. The knife buried itself to the hilt in the base of his throat. He jerked violently, arching over backwards, as if a heavy electric shock had passed through the steel girder. The gun flew from his hand and curved earthward in a long, lazy curve. It seemed to take an age to fall and I couldn't look away from it. I didn't see it land, but I saw sparks on the line below as steel struck steel.

I looked back at Henriques. He'd straightened and bent slightly forward and was staring at me in perplexity. His right hand reached up and pulled the knife clear, and in a moment his shirt front was saturated in the pumping blood. His face twisted in a snarl, a snarl already tinged with approaching dissolution, and he raised his right hand up and back over his shoulder. The blade no longer gleamed in the lamplight. He leaned back to give impetus to his throw, and then tiredness came into the dark and evil face and the knife slipped from his dying hand and clattered to the concrete below. The eyes closed and he slipped to one side, slipped right over until he was beneath the girder and held only by his locked ankles. How long he hung like that, I couldn't later say. It seemed a very long time. And then, at last, in a weird, slow-motion sequence, the ankles slowly unlocked and he fell from sight. I didn't see him fall, I couldn't see him fall. But when at last I did look, I saw him far below, his broken body hanging limply over the gleaming ram of a gigantic hydraulic buffer. For Henriques' sake, wherever he was now, I hoped the shades of his victims weren't waiting for him. I became vaguely aware that my cheek muscles were aching. I had been smiling down at the dead man. I had never felt less like smiling.

Sick and dizzy, and trembling like an old man with the ague, I made my way back across the girder by crawling on my hands and knees. It took me a long time, I think, and I'll never be clear how I managed the six-foot jump from girder to platform, even although it was easier this time, for the chain was there for my hands to catch. I staggered through the grill door to the fire escape and half lowered myself, half collapsed onto the platform. The night air of London had never smelled so sweet.

How long I lay there I don't know, I can't remember whether I was conscious or not most of the time. But it couldn't have been long, for when I looked at my watch it was still only ten minutes to four.

I pushed myself to my feet and made my way wearily down the fire escape. When I reached street level I didn't even bother looking for my Webley; it might have taken me long enough to find it, and the chances were that some part of its mechanism had been damaged in its long fall. I would have been very surprised if the guard I'd disposed of hadn't been carrying a gun. I wasn't suprised. I didn't know what make of automatic it was, but it had the trigger and safety catch in the usual positions and that was all I wanted. I started to climb the fire escape again.

I made the last two flights to the roof of the station on my hands and knees. Not from the need of stealth or secrecy, I just coudln't make it any other way. I was as far through as that. I rested for a bit with my back to the wall of the passenger lounge, then walked slowly across the concrete to the hangar in the far corner.

A faint wash of light shone weakly through the open doors; it would be invisible from below, for the hanger doors opened onto the center of the heliport. The light came not from the hangar itself but from what was inside it—the big twenty-four-seater Voland Helicopter that the Inter-City Flights were now operating on their new routes.

I could see the control cabin thrust away over the nose of the helicopter, and it was from there that the light was coming. I could see the head and shoulders of the pilot, hatless and in a gray uniform jacket, in the left-hand seat. In the right-hand seat sat Dr. Gregori.

Circling the hangar I came to the side door and pushed it back slowly on its oiled tracks. It made no sound. The base of the short flight of portable steps leading up to the open passenger door in the center of the helicopter's fuselage was less than twenty feet away. I pulled the automatic, safety off, from my coat pocket and crossed to the steps. If you could have heard a blade of grass growing, then you could have heard me going up those steps.

The passenger cabin was also lit, but the illumination was poor—one single overhead lamp in line with the door. I poked my head cautiously through the doorway—and there, not three feet away, sitting with wrists bound to the arm-rests of the first of the backward facing seats, was Mary. The bruise above her eye had swollen to duck-egg proportions, her face was scratched and deathly pale, but she was wide awake and staring directly at me. And she recognized me.

With my soot-blackened and battered face I must have looked like a man from Mars, one, moreover, who'd just managed to walk away from the smashed-up remains of his flying saucer. But she recognized me immediately. Her lips parted, her eyes stared wide, and I at once raised finger to mouth in the age-old gesture for silence. But I was too late, I was a lifetime too late. She had been sitting there in the black thrall of a hopeless and defeated misery and grief, with the bottom dropped from her life and nothing to live for, and now her husband, whom she surely knew to be dead, had returned from the land of the dead, and the world was going to be all right again and if she had not reacted, immediately and instinctively, then she would not have been human.

"Pierre!" Her voice was part shock, part hope, all wonder and joy. "Oh, Pierre!"

I wasn't looking at her. My eyes were on one place only—the entrance to the pilot's cabin. So was my gun. From up front came the sound of a dull blow, then Dr. Gregori appeared, one hand clutching a gun, the other above his head to steady himself as he peered through the low archway. The eyes were narrowed, but the rest of the face still and cold. The gun, curiously, was hanging by his side. I shifted mine slightly till it centered on his forehead and increased the tension on the trigger.

"The end of the road, Scarlatti," I said. "And the end of my long wait for you. There'll be nobody coming here tonight. Only me, Scarlatti. Only me."

CHAPTER 13

"Cavell!" Gregori hadn't realized who I was until I had spoken, and now the swarthy face paled and he stared at me like a man seeing a ghost, which for Gregori was exactly what I was. "Cavell! It is impossible!"

"Don't you wish it were, Scarlatti? Into the cabin and don't try lifting that gun."

"Scarlatti?" He didn't seem to have heard my order; the second shock had staggered his mind, already reeling from the first. He whispered: "How do you know?"

"Five hours now since Interpol and the F.B.I. gave us your life history. And quite a history it is. Enzo Scarlatti, one-time graduate research chemist who became the big-time czar of American crime in the Midwest. Extortion, robberies, killings, machines, drugs, the lot—the great king-pin and they could never lay a finger on you. But they got you in the end, didn't they, Scarlatti? The usual, income-tax evasion. And then they deported you." I advanced two paces towards him, I didn't want Mary in the line of fire when the war started. "Right into the cabin, Scarlatti."

He was still staring at me, but his face underwent a subtle change. The man's resilience, his powers of mental recuperation, were fantastic. He said slowly: "We must talk about this."

"Later. Inside. Or I'll drop you where you stand."

"No. You won't. You'd like to, but not yet. I know when I look at death, Cavell. I'm looking at death now. You wish me to come in and sit down in a chair and then you will kill me. But not until I am in that chair will you kill me."

I took another step towards him and his left hand came into view. "This is what you are frightened of, isn't it, Cavell? You were afraid that I might have one of those in my hand or on my person, that it would smash when I fell. Isn't that it, Cavell?"

That was it indeed. I stared down at the ampoule in his hand, that little glass vial with the sealed blue plastic top. He went on, his face strained and tight: "I think you had better put that gun down, Cavell."

"Not this time. As long as I have this gun pointing between your eyes, you won't try anything. The moment I put it down you'd let me have it with your own gun. And I know now what I didn't know before. You won't use that ampoule. I thought you were insane, Scarlatti, but I know now you were only using the threat of insanity to terrify us into doing what you wanted. But I know you now and I know your record. You may be crazy, but you're crazy like a fox. You're as sane as I am. You won't use that thing. You value your own life, the success of your plans, too much."

"Wrong, Cavell. I'll use it. And I do value my life." He glanced quickly over his shoulder and then turned back to me. "Eight months now since I entered Mordon. I could have had that vaccine out any time I liked. But I waited. Why? I waited till Baxter and MacDonald had successfully developed an attenuated strain of the Satan Bug, a strain still deadlier that the botulinus toxin, but with an oxidization life of only twenty-four hours. I waited till they had come across the precise combinations of heat, phenol, formalin and ultra-violet to produce a killer vaccine for this weakened strain." He held the vial between finger and thumb. "In this glass, the attenuated Satan Bug; in my blood-stream, the inactivated micro-organisms we have produced against it. The cyanide was bluff—I don't need cyanide. You will understand why Baxter had to die—he *knew* about the new virus and vaccine."

I understood.

"You will understand, also, that I am not afraid to use it. I will—"

He broke off, the swarthy face suddenly cold and grim. "What was that?" I'd heard it too, two short bursts of harshly metallic sound, like a riveter's gun, only five times as fast.

"Why, don't you know? That was the Merlin Mark Two, Scarlatti. The new type of rapid-fire machine carbine issued to NATO forces." I looked at him consideringly. "Didn't you hear what I said? There's no one else coming tonight. Only me."

"What are you saying?" he whispered. I could see his knuckles whiten as his left hand clenched involuntarily over the glass vial. "What are you talking about?"

"About all your friends who won't be seeing their homes again for many years to come. About all the scum—the top scum, admittedly—of the criminal world, who have vanished so mysteriously in recent weeks from their haunts in London, America, France and Italy. All the top specialists in oxyacetylene work, nitroglycerin, combination-twiddling and what have you. The world's best at blowing and opening vaults and safes. We knew weeks ago, from Interpol, that those men had disappeared. We did not know that they had all been assembled together in the same place—here, in London."

The dark glowing eyes stared into mine. The breath whistled thinly between his teeth. His face was like a wolf's.

"The F.B.I. regard you as the best planner and organizer they've been up against since the war, Scarlatti. It's quite a compliment, isn't it? But deserved. You had us all fooled. This insistence on knocking down Mordon, this demonstration of the botulinus drug in East Anglia, this pretense that you were unaware that three of the vials you had stolen were of the Satan Bug strain, this apparent ignorance of the effects of the Satan Bug—you had us all convinced that we were dealing with a madman. We were sure that this threat against the square mile of London was to achieve the destruction of Mordon to satisfy the whims of a lunatic. Then we thought it was part of a Communist plot to destroy our last but most powerful line of defense. It was only a few hours ago that we realized that this threat against the heart of London had one

212

purpose and one purpose only—to empty the heart of London, to evacuate it so that not one person remained.

"In this small area of London are a score of the greatest banks in the world, banks bulging with the negotiable currencies of fifty nations, banks with fortunes in bullion, banks with safe-deposits containing jewels that would ransom a dozen millionaires. And you were going to take the lot, weren't you, Scarlatti? Your men and equipment have been hidden in empty buildings or innocent-seeming vans since last evening. All they had to do was to walk into the banks during the hours of darkness after the last man had vanished. There would be no trouble. Every one of those banks has a double security system—guards and automatic alarms that ring in any of the local police stations. But the guards had to leave, hadn't they—they didn't want to die from the botulinus toxin? As for the burglar alarms, some of your men with access to the electricity board's wiring diagrams—that would cause no trouble—pulled the switches, blew the fuses, tripped the overload coils, or cut the cables supplying electric power to this area. Which is why the city is in darkness. Which is why no alarm bells would ring in the police station. You're with me, Scarlatti?"

He was with me, all right. His face was masked in hatred.

"After that it was easy," I went on. "I suppose you kidnapped that poor devil of a pilot earlier in the day. You bring the stuff here, load it aboard the helicopter and make a fast take-off for the continent; it was the only way; you knew the entire area would be cordoned off and that there would be no other way to get the stuff out. Your men would just stay put until the scare was over, mingle with the returning crowds and disappear. As for the banks, no one would find out anything till at least three o'clock this coming afternoon, which will be the earliest that people would be allowed to return to the area. And as this is now Sunday, it would probably have been Monday morning before the discovery of the looted banks was made. By which time you would have been a couple of continents away. But not now. It's as I told you, Scarlatti: this is the end of the road."

"You mean—you mean it's all over?" Mary whispered behind me.

"It's all over. By ten o'clock tonight, long before the troops had finished clearing the area, there were two hundred detectives scattered at strategic points all over the city—in banks or close to banks. Hidden. With instructions not to move before three-forty-five this morning. It's after four now. It's all over. Every single one of those men was armed with the latest Merlin sub-machine gun loaned from the Army, with specific instructions to shoot to kill if anyone batted an eyelid. That noise we heard a couple of minutes ago—someone must have batted an eyelid."

"You're lying." Scarlatti's face was twisted and vicious, and his lips were working even when he wasn't speaking. He went on in a hoarse whisper: "You're making all this up."

"You know better than that, Scarlatti. You know that I know too much that is true for the rest not to be true."

He looked at me with murder in his eyes, then said softly and savagely: "Close the cabin door. Close it I say, or by God, I'll end it all now." He took two steps down the aisle, the vial of the Satan Bug virus lifted high above his head.

I watched him for a moment, then nodded. He'd nothing to lose now and I wasn't going to throw away Mary's life and my own—not to mention the pilot's—over a thing like that. I moved back and closed the sliding passenger door. My eyes, my gun never left him.

He took another two steps forward, his left hand still high above his head. "And now your gun, Cavell. Now your gun."

"Not my gun, Scarlatti." I shook my head and wondered whether he wasn't after all mad, or whether he was just a magnificent actor. "Not my gun. You know that. Then you'd kill us all, while you escaped. As long as I have this gun you won't escape. You smash that vial, but I'll get you before the Satan Bug gets me. Not my gun."

He advanced again, his eyes wide and gleaming, the left hand moving back as if ready to throw. Maybe I was wrong, maybe he was crazy. "Your gun," he screamed. "Now!"

I shook my head again, he said something in a high, wild voice and his left hand came arching over his shoulder, the back of his hand facing me instead of the front as I would have expected. Darkness flooded the cabin as his bunched fist smashed the single overhead light, a darkness momentarily illuminated by two stabs of orange flame as I squeezed the trigger twice, an illumination and reverberating roar followed by darkness again and sudden silence, and in the sudden silence, a gasp of pain from Mary and Scarlatti saying: "My gun is at your wife's throat, Cavell. She is about to die."

He hadn't been crazy after all.

I dropped my gun on the composition floor. It clattered loudly. I said: "You win, Scarlatti."

"The main cabin switch," he said. "By the left-hand side of the door."

I groped, found it and pulled it down. The entire cabin flooded with light from a dozen lamps. Scarlatti pulled himself up from the seat beside Mary where he'd flung himself as soon as he'd smashed the light, lifted the gun from her neck and pointed it at me. I lifted my bent arms and looked at his left hand. The vial was still intact; he'd taken a hellish risk, but it had been the only risk left to him. I noticed where the upper sleeve of his left arm was torn: I'd come pretty close to getting him. And pretty close to ending it all for us, too. If I'd hit him, the vial would have been smashed. But then, I thought, it had been about to be smashed anyway.

"Move back," Scarlatti said quietly. His voice was controlled, conversational; he'd won his Oscar for the night and packed in the acting. "Right to the back of the cabin."

I moved. He came forward, picked up my gun, stuck the vial in his pocket and gestured with both guns. "The pilot's cabin. Into it." I went forward. As I passed Mary's seat she looked up at me and smiled through the tangle of blonde hair that had fallen forward over her face. Her green eyes were masked in tears. I smiled back. As actors, not even Scarlatti could show us anything.

The pilot was slumped forward over the controls. That explained the sound I'd heard just after Mary had exclaimed at the sight of me. Before coming to investigate, Scarlatti had made sure that the pilot wouldn't be giving him any trouble. The pilot was a big man, with black hair, and the part of his face I could see was tanned and sun-lined. At the back of his head a little blood oozed through the dark hair.

"Into the co-pilot's seat," Scarlatti ordered. "Wake that man up."

"How the hell can I?" Under the unwavering eyes of the two pistol barrels I eased myself into the seat. "You coshed the poor devil."

"Not hard," he said. "Hurry up."

I did what I could. I'd no option. I shook the pilot, slapped his face gently and spoke to him, but Scarlatti must have hit him harder than he thought. In the circumstances, I thought grimly, he hadn't had much time for finesse. Scarlatti was becoming impatient and as nervous as a cat, staring out through the windscreen towards the hangar doors. For all he knew there was a regiment of soldiers or police out there in the darkness; he wasn't to know that I'd begged and pleaded with the General and Hardanger to be allowed to go alone, secrecy and stealth not only offering the only chance of saving Mary's life but also being far less liable to panic

Scarlatti into an indiscriminate use of the Satan Bug. I'd certainly done a great job.

After five minutes, the pilot stirred and woke. He was as tough as he looked, for he came out of his unconsciousness fighting mad and it was all I could do to hold him off until the ungentle nudging on the back of his neck from Scarlatti's pistol let him know he was picking the wrong man. He twisted round in his seat, recognized Scarlatti and said a few words to him that left no doubt but that he came from the other side of the Irish Sea. What he had to say was interesting, but irrelevant and unprintable. He broke off when Scarlatti stuck the barrel of a pistol into his face. Scarlatti had an unpleasant habit of sticking pistol barrels into people's faces but he was too old to be cured of it by now.

"Get this helicopter airborne," Scarlatti ordered. "Now."

"Airborne!" I protested. "He's not fit to walk, far less fly." Scarlatti prodded him again. "You heard me. Hurry."

"I can't." The pilot was sullen and savage at the same moment. "It has to be towed out. Can't start the engines in here. Exhaust fumes and fire regulations—"

"The hell with your regulations," Scarlatti said. "She can roll under her own power. Don't you think I checked, you fool? Get moving."

The pilot had no option and he knew it. He started his engines and I winced at the deafening clamor echoed back at us from the narrow metallic confines of the hangar walls. The pilot couldn't have liked it any more than I did: either that or he knew it was dangerous to linger. Whatever the reason, he lost no time. He engaged the two giant rotors, moved the cyclic pitch to tilt the blades forwards and downwards, and released the brakes. The helicopter began to roll.

Thirty seconds later we were airborne. Scarlatti, more relaxed now, reached for a rack above his head and handed me a square metal box. He reached again and this time brought down an ordinary close-mesh string bag.

"Open that box and transfer the contents into this bag," he said curtly. "I advise you to be careful. You will see why."

I saw why and I was very careful. I opened the box, and there, packed in straw, lay five chromed steel flasks. Under his direction I opened each in turn and with infinite gentleness laid five glass ampoules inside the net bag. Two with blue tops—two vials of the Satan Bug. Three with red tops—three vials of the botulinus toxin. Scarlatti handed me another blue-topped vial from his pocket. That made six altogether. I placed that in also, gingerly gathered up the string bag and handed it back to Scarlatti. It was cold inside that cabin, but I was sweating as if I were in a steam bath, and it took an effort of will to keep my hands steady. I caught a glimpse of the pilot looking at the bag and I can't say he looked any happier than I felt. He knew all right.

"Excellent." Scarlatti took the bag from me, reached back into the passenger aisle and placed the bag on the nearest seat. "You will be able to convince our friends that I am not only willing but ready to carry out my threat."

"I don't know what you are talking about."

"You will. I want you to make a radio call and get in touch with your father-in-law and then give him a message." He turned to the pilot. "You will keep circling above the heliport. We will be returning there shortly."

I said: "I don't know how to operate the damned radio."

"You've just forgotten," he said soothingly. He was getting too confident of himself for my liking. "You will remember. A man who has spent his life in his country's intelligence service and cannot operate a transmitter? If I take a walk back into the passenger cabin and you hear your wife scream, do you think you will remember then?"

"What do you want me to do?" I asked savagely.

"Get on the police wave length. I don't know what it is, but you're bound to. Tell them that unless they immediately release all my captured men—and the money they have—I shall be compelled to drop botulinus and Satan Bug toxins over London. I have no idea where they will fall, nor do I greatly care. Further, if any attempt is made to follow, trace or capture me or my men, I shall use toxin regardless of the consequences. Do you see a flaw, Cavell?"

I said nothing at once. I stared ahead through the high-speed windscreen wipers into the rain and the darkness. Finally I said: "I see no flaw."

"I am a desperate man, Cavell," he said with quiet intensity. "When they deported me from America they thought I was completely finished. Completely. A has-been. I was laughed out of America. I was—and am—determined to show them all how wrong they were, to bring off the biggest criminal coup of all time. When you intercepted us in that police car this evening, much that I said was false. But this one thing was true: I shall achieve this ambition regardless of cost, or I shall die trying. I am not acting now. Nothing is going to stop me, nothing on this earth is going to thwart me at this very last moment. They should not have laughed at Enzo Scarlatti. I am in the most deadly earnest, Cavell. You believe me?"

"I believe you."

"I shall not hesitate to do exactly as I threaten. You must convince them of that."

"You've convinced me," I said. "I can't speak for the others. I'll try."

"You had better succeed," he said evenly.

I succeeded. After a few minutes' twiddling and dial-twisting, I managed to get through on the police wave length. There was a further delay while the call was relayed and re-routed by phone, and then I heard Superintendent Hardanger's voice.

"Cavell here," I said. "I'm in a helicopter with—"

"Helicopter!" He swore. "I can hear the damn thing. Almost directly above. What in God's name—"

"Listen! I'm here with Mary and a pilot of the Inter-City Lines, a Lieutenant—" I glanced at the man beside me.

"Buckley," he said harshly.

"Lieutenant Buckley. Scarlatti has the drop on us all. He's got a message for you, for the General."

"So you fouled things up, Cavell," Hardanger said savagely. "God above, I warned you—"

"Shut up," I said wearily. "This is his message. You'd better listen." I told them what I'd been told to say, and after a pause the General's voice came through on the earphones. No reproaches, no time-wasting.

He said: "What chance that he's bluffing?"

"Not one in the world. He's in deadly earnest. He'll wipe out half the city sooner than fail. What's all the banknotes and bullion in the world compared to a million lives?"

"You sound as though you were afraid," the General's voice came softly.

"I'm afraid, sir. Not just for myself."

"I understand. I'll call back in a few minutes."

I removed the earphones. I said: "A few minutes. He has to consult."

"That is understandable." He was leaning back negligently now, one shoulder against the doorway, but the guns as steady as ever. He hadn't the shadow of a doubt about the outcome now. "I hold all the cards, Cavell."

He wasn't exaggerating any. He held all the cards all right; they couldn't afford not to let him win. But far back in my

218

mind were the first stirrings of a hope that he might yet lose the last trick of all. A despairing one-in-a-million hope, but then I was a man in the extremes of despair and willing to gamble on a one-in-a-million chance. And it would all depend upon so many imponderable factors. Scarlatti's state of mind, the confidence and fractional lowering to relaxation that might—just might—come with the knowledge that the day was finally his, Lieutenant Buckley's acuteness, intelligence and co-operation; and my speed of reaction. The last was the biggest 'if' of all: the way I felt, if Scarlatti could cope with an ailing nonagenarian, then he shouldn't have much trouble with me.

The earphones crackled. I slipped them on and the General's voice came through. He said without preamble: "Tell Scarlatti we agree."

"Yes, sir. I'm most desperately sorry about it all."

"You did what you could. That's over. Our first concern now must be to save the innocent, not to punish the guilty."

One of the earphones was knocked forward, none too gently, and Scarlatti said: "Well? Well?"

"He agrees," I said wearily.

"Good. I'd expected nothing else. Find out how long the release of my men and money will take, when the police would expect to be clear of the area."

I asked, and told him the answer. "Half an hour."

"Again excellent. Switch off that radio. We shall cruise around for that length of time and then descend." He leaned back comfortably against the doorway and for the first time permitted himself a smile. "A small hold-up in the execution of my plans, Cavell, but the ultimate results will be the same. I cannot tell you how much I look forward to seeing tomorrow's headlines in all the American newspapers which so contemptuously wrote me off as a nonentity and washed-up has-been when I was deported two years ago. It will be interesting to see how they set about eating their words."

I swore at him, without enthusiasm, and he smiled again. The more he smiled, the better for me. I hoped. I slumped down in my seat, huddled in bitter dejection, and said sullenly: "Any objection if I smoke?"

"None at all." He put one pistol in his pocket and handed me cigarettes and matches. "With my compliments, Cavell."

"I don't carry exploding cigars around with me," I growled.

"I don't suppose you do." He smiled again, he was really

going to town tonight. "You know, Cavell, bringing this off gives me an immense satisfaction. Almost as much as I get from outwitting an opponent like yourself. You have given me more trouble and more nearly caused my downfall than any man I have ever met."

"Except the Internal Revenue agents of America," I said. "Go to hell, Scarlatti."

He laughed. I drew heavily on my cigarette, and at that moment the helicopter shuddered slightly as it lifted over some rising current of warmer air. This was my opening. I twisted in my seat and said to Scarlatti, half peevishly, half nervously: "I wish to God you'd sit down or hang on to something. If this chopper hits an air pocket you might be thrown back on top of those damn toxins."

"Relax, friend," he said comfortably. He leaned his back against the doorway and crossed his legs. "You don't get air pockets in weather like this."

But I wasn't really listening to him. And I certainly wasn't looking at him. I was looking at Buckley—and then I saw Buckley looking at me. Not a movement of the head, just a sideways shift of the eyes that Scarlatti, behind him, couldn't see. He lowered one eyelid in a slow wink—no question, the big Irishman caught on fast. He dropped one hand negligently from the controls and laid it on his leg. He rubbed his hand down his thigh till the fingers stretched out horizontally over his kneecap. And then his fingers dipped sharply into a vertical position . . .

I nodded twice, slowly, staring out the windscreen so as not to give any significance to the action. It wouldn't have meant anything to even the most suspicious, and by now Scarlatti was too confident and content to go looking for signs of trouble where none existed. He wouldn't be the first man who relaxed too much when the game seemed overwhelmingly as good as won—and finished up at the losing end when the final whistle blew. I glanced at Buckley and saw his lips frame the word 'Now.' I nodded a third time and braced myself.

Out of the corner of my eye I saw Scarlatti shift his position slightly as Buckley eased the helicopter a fraction upwards. His legs were still crossed. Suddenly Buckley thrust the cyclic pitch right forward, at the same time banking heavily, and Scarlatti, completely off balance, pitched head-long forwards almost directly on top of me.

I'd twisted and half risen to my feet as he came lurching

towards me. My roundhouse right caught him a fraction too high, just on the breastbone, and his guns went flying wildly to clatter against instrument panel and windscreen.

Scarlatti went berserk. Not viciously fighting mad, but completely berserk. Knees, feet, teeth, fists, head, elbows—he used the lot on me, smashing me back in my seat and utterly ignoring the blows I rained on him in return. He growled and screamed alternately like some wounded animal, battering at me with frightening power and speed and with everything he could bring to bear. I was twenty years younger and twenty pounds heavier, but I couldn't even begin to hold him. I felt the blood begin to hiss dangerously in my ears, my chest felt as if a giant vise were crushing it in half, and then, seconds before I knew I was going to pass out, the insensate battering suddenly stopped and he was gone.

Dazed, bleeding, half-crazed with pain, I tore myself out of the seat and went after him. The helicopter was still in its dive and Scarlatti was scrambling desperately up the aisle pulling at the seats to give him purchase against the force of gravity. And he could use only one hand: the other held the bag with the botulinus and Satan Bug viruses. Momentarily crazed Scarlatti might have been—almost certainly was—but there was still one corner of his mind working: he could no longer threaten us directly with the Satan Bug, for seconds after the release of the viruses the helicopter, with a dead pilot at the controls, would have crashed into the streets of London with Scarlatti, the only person left alive aboard it, hopelessly trapped.

He reached the door before I was halfway up the aisle. He grabbed the handle and tried to slide it open, but found it impossible against the pull of the plummeting plane. He braced his feet against the seat next to Mary's and hauled with all the power he had, his swarthy face crimsoning with the effort. Slowly, inexorably, the door began to slide open, and I was still six feet away. Then, abruptly, the floor leveled as Buckley brought the craft back on even keel, the door flew open and Scarlatti staggered and fell. A second later I was on him.

I wasn't worried about Scarlatti. I was worried about what he held in his hand. I tore it from him, viciously, hearing one of his fingers break as it was caught in the mesh; then he'd leapt to his feet and I was fighting for my life—and fighting for it with one hand.

He was silent now, his face the face of a madman, and he

221

was going to kill me. He caught me by the throat, shoved me violently backwards. I thrust my left foot behind to gain enough purchase on the side of the cabin to thrust him off and Mary screamed. My foot met no resistance, there was nothing behind me, only the open door. Instantly I flung wide both arms and stiffened my back and shoulders. Both forearms smashed with cruel force against the raised metal edge of the doorway and the upper edge was like a guillotine against the back of my neck. Momentarily the world was a red haze shot through with blinding flashes of light and then it cleared. Mary, sitting in the doorway seat just beside us, was staring at me with terror-stricken eyes, green and enormous in the dead-white face. And Scarlatti still had me by the throat. His face was inches from mine.

"I warned you, Cavell," he shouted hoarsely. "I warned you. There'll be a million dead tomorrow, Cavell. A million dead, and *you* killed them. You, not me." He sobbed, sunk his hooked fingers deeper into my throat and started to thrust me out into the sky and the darkness.

There was nothing I could do. I couldn't even use one of my hands to fight him off: take away any one point of my supports and I'd be through that doorway. In front of me was Scarlatti's face and whatever he had been in the past, I knew he was insane now. My rigidly outthrust arms were beginning to bend inwards at the shoulder, rubbing along the raised metal edges of the door, and my shoulders were afire with agony as Scarlatti thrust me further and further out into the darkness. I could feel the cold wind rushing by, the rain drumming against my back and side with the force of a howling storm. This was the way some people die. I tried to open my left hand so as at least not to take the Satan Bug down with me when I fell, but I couldn't even do that: my fingers were caught in the meshes and jammed against the metal.

It was then that Mary broke through her terror-ridden thrall. She was tied to the arms of her seat, but her feet were free and suddenly she jack-knifed herself and kicked up with both legs with all the strength that was in her. She was wearing Italian shoes and for the first time in my life I put a prayer of thanksgiving for those sharply pointed monstrosities. Scarlatti cried out with pain as they caught him just behind the right knee, his leg sagged and for the one moment that would be the only moment I would ever have, his grip on my throat slackened. With a convulsive jerk of arms and neck I braced myself forward, my left leg swinging high, and he staggered backward. And then I was clear of the door, chopping aside his snarling crouched figure as I passed him and ran up the aisle.

I didn't run far. Buckley was coming through the doorway at the other end, a gun in his hands. I wondered dimly what in the name of God had kept him until now—it shouldn't have taken more than ten seconds to set the helicopter on automatic pilot and scrabble around for a gun after he'd straightened out—and then I realized that no more time than that *had* passed since he had straightened out the helicopter. It had only seemed like an eternity, that was all.

He saw me coming, threw the gun at me. I caught it, taking care even at that moment not to let it strike anywhere near the viruses. I whirled, gun in hand, but Scarlatti wasn't coming for me any more.

He was standing quietly by the doorway, still doubled over with pain. His eyes were on me, but they didn't seem crazed any more. He straightened slowly and said: "Don't bother to fire, Cavell."

"I won't fire," I said.

"End of a dream," he said conversationally. He was standing close to the doorway, the wind and the rain were driving in hard against him, but he didn't even seem to notice it. "Maybe this is the way the dreams of people like myself always end." He paused, then looked at me almost quizzically. "You never really expected to see me in the Old Bailey?"

"No," I said. "I never expected it."

"Can you see a man like me on trial for my life?" he persisted.

"I can't see it," I said.

He nodded, as if in satisfaction. He took a step nearer the open doorway, then turned again. "But it would have been nice," he said, "to see what they would have said in the *New York Times*." His voice was almost sad. Then he turned away and stepped out into the darkness.

I cut Mary loose and chafed the blood back into her hands while Buckley went forward to contact the police and call off their Flying Squad cars. After a few minutes we both went forward, as Buckley drifted down towards the heliport, and I picked up the phones.

The General said: "So she is safe."

"Yes, sir. She's safe."

"And Scarlatti is gone?"

"That's it, sir. Scarlatti is gone. He just stepped out of the plane."

Hardanger's voice broke in, harsh and gravelly as ever. "Did he fall or was he pushed?"

"He fell." I hung up the phones. I knew they would never believe me.